Praise for M. Jol

"Mike Harrison is the only writer on Earth equally attuned to the essential strangeness both of quantum physics and the attritional banalities of modern urban life."
　　—Iain M. Banks, author of *The Algebraist* and *Use of Weapons*

"Taut as Hemingway, viscerally intelligent, startlingly uplifting, Harrison's ideas have a beauty that unpacks to infinity."
　　—Stephen Baxter, award-winning author of *Transcendent*

"M. John Harrison is a writer whose work detonates in the mind after putting the book down. His prose runs like silk but his ideas work like some principle of atomic fission. I'm in awe of his writing powers."
　　—Graham Joyce, author of *The Silent Land* and *Some Kind of Fairy Tale*

"The Persian poet Rumi wrote, 'Open your hands if you wish to be held.' Almost the same could be said about M. John Harrison... Open your mind if you wish to be enthralled."
　　—Jonathan Carroll, author of *Glass Soup* and *White Apples*

"M. John Harrison is a blazing original. His books are fictions of elegant delirium, dark and transcendent by turns... a great imaginer, and an extraordinary writer."
　　—Clive Barker, author of *Abarat* and *Coldheart Canyon*

"Stylish, accomplished, evocative... exemplary fictions of unease shot through with poetic insight and most beautifully written."
　　—Angela Carter

"Harrison writes with fearsome, dexterous, certainty about pretty much everything."
　　—*The Times Literary Supplement*

"For more than twenty years, Harrison's work has anticipated the amphetamine buzz and bleak ardor of the early 21st century: it's just taken the world that long to catch up with him."
　　—*The Magazine of Fantasy & Science Fiction*

"Harrison displays a masterful control of character, language, and landscape and an ability to expose the unnerving sense of the inexplicable that runs beneath the surfaces of life."
—*The Review of Contemporary Fiction*

"M. John Harrison uses the conceits of science fiction, fantasy and horror fiction to expose the follies and sorrows of the human condition... Harrison is always worth reading"
—*The New York Times*

In direct line from Cordwainer Smith and Keith Laumer, Michael Moorcock and Norman Spinrad, Harrison has adapted the conceits of space opera until the form is big enough to hold all the marvels he jams within."
—*SciFi.com*

"Harrison.... has turned descriptions of quantum mechanics and astrophysics into a poetry of longing and awe, with an almost Sylvia Plath-like sense of dread."
—*Boston Globe*

"An extraordinary precise writer who deals in suggestion rather than statement.... Harrison keeps you constantly at the corners of what you know."
—*Telegraph*

"The painter's precision with which Harrison works and the aversion to cliche and generic detail make his prose style hyper-real... and compare favorably with the work of any fiction writer in the world, whether genre or mainstream. Wise, unflinching, precise..."
—*Publishers Weekly*

"Harrison displays a masterful control of character, language, and landscape and an ability to expose the unnerving sense of the inexplicable that runs beneath the surfaces of life."
—*The Review of Contemporary Fiction*

EMPTY SPACE:
A Haunting

Other Books by M. John Harrison

EMPTY SPACE:
A Haunting

M. JOHN HARRISON

NIGHT SHADE BOOKS
SAN FRANCISCO

Cover art by Bruce Jensen
Cover design by Martha Wade
Interior layout and design by Amy Popovich

First Edition

ISBN: 978-1-59780-461-5

Night Shade Books
www.nightshadebooks.com

To Forced Ent

"No point is more central than this, that empty space is not empty. It is the seat of the most violent physics."
—*John A Wheeler*

"Our instruments have limits. Since knowledge of physical reality depends on what we can measure, we will never know all there is to know...Much better to accept that our knowledge of physical reality is necessarily incomplete..."
—*Marcelo Gleister*

"In a certain sense, everything is everywhere at all times."
—*A E van Vogt*

Contents

1: Organs

Anna Waterman heard two cats fighting all evening.

At ten o'clock she went out into the garden and called in the family tom. A decade or so ago, her daughter Marnie, age thirteen and already unfathomable, had named this animal "James."

Late summer displayed a greenish afterglow at the bottom of a sky full of stars. Anna's was a long garden, perhaps fifty yards by twenty, with lichenous apple trees in unmown grass and a leaning summerhouse which looked like something from a 1970s Russian film—falling apart, surrounded by overgrown flowerbeds, filled with those things you discard but don't throw away. The flowerbeds had an unhealthy vitality. Every year, tended or not, they produced dense mixtures of indigenous weeds, wild flowers and—since the warming of the mid-2000s—exotics with large petals and fleshy leaves, blown in as seeds from who knew where.

"James!" Anna called.

James didn't respond, but neither were there sounds of him killing or being killed. Anna was encouraged.

She found him in the base of the hedge at the end of the garden, where he had something cornered among the roots and dry earth. He was nosing it about, tapping at it with a front paw, purring to himself. She stroked him and he ignored her.

"You old fool," she said. "What have you found now?"

Some gelid bits and pieces loosely scattered with soil. Except for the size and colour, they looked like internal organs. They had the swelling curve of pig's kidney. There was a faint glow to them. Anna picked one up and dropped it immediately—it was warm to the touch. The cat, delighted, sprang upon it and knocked it about.

"How disgusting you are, James," Anna told him.

Later she put on Marigold gloves, slid two or three of the objects into a plastic bag and carried them back to the house. There, she emptied them into a glass dish. Slumped on the worktop they looked like any offal, unused to supporting themselves in the world. Their colours resembled the flasks of liquid you could still see in the windows of pharmacies when Anna was young—blues, greens and a rich permanganate—now faded and a touch acidic under the halogen lights. Anna removed her best Wusthof knife from the block and then, nerve failing her, put it back again. She stared at the contents of the dish from different angles, then went to telephone Marnie.

"Why are you calling?" Marnie said, after five minutes.

"I suppose I just wanted to tell you how lucky I'd been. In all sorts of things."

At a glance, Anna knew, this seemed absurd. She had been anorexic throughout her twenties; twice a failed suicide. Her first husband, Michael, who wasn't much better, had walked into the sea one night off Mann Hill Beach south of Boston. They never found his body. He had been a brilliant man but unbalanced. "He was a brilliant man," she would tell people, "who took things too much to heart." But since then she had remarried, borne Marnie, lived a life. She had made quite a nice life with Marnie's father, first in London and then in this quiet, expensive house near the river. It wouldn't have suited Michael. Living had to be an effort for him; a kind of punishment.

"Neither of us knew how to live," she said now.

"Anna—"

"He had some difficulties."

Marnie received this in silence.

"You know," Anna said. "Sex difficulties. Your father was much better at that side of things."

"Anna, that's more information than I need."

Marnie had been conceived out of both guilt and relief at losing Michael—literally, misplacing him—that night on Mann Hill Beach. Confused, Anna had flown home to London and fucked the first kind person she found. That was the only way to put it, especially from this distance. She had no regrets, although at times the memory made her feel she ought to be especially nice to Marnie. Now she had a sudden surprised recollection of Michael leaning over her in the dark, and one of them saying something like, "Sparks! Sparks in everything!"

"Anna? Anna, I have to go now. It's late. It's midnight."

"Is it, dear?"

"You've got Dr Alpert tomorrow," Marnie reminded her.

"I'm afraid I've lost the details of that appointment," said Anna in a vague but mutinous way.

"Good job I kept a note of them, then."

Anna, suddenly overwhelmed with anxiety and love, said, "Oh, Marnie, I do hope you enjoy sex. I'd hate to think of you missing out on something so lovely."

"I'll drive you to the station in the morning. Goodnight, Anna."

Why *was* I phoning? Anna asked herself. When no answer came, she went to the kitchen door and looked out. Mist had pooled two or three feet deep in the rough pasture between the garden and the river. Above it, she could just make out a line of willows. She called the cat; offered him rabbit-flavoured food; took herself to bed, where her dream woke her as usual at ten past four in the morning, soaked to the skin and with a kind of leaden buzzing in her ears. It was less a sound, as she often tried to explain to Dr Alpert, than a feeling. "It's a feeling from the dream," she would say. It was a physical sensation. "I'm not even sure it's me who's feeling it." She struggled out of bed, weary and ill, and went downstairs to get water. Grey light was creeping in round the edges of the kitchen blinds. She thought she might have another look at the organs—or whatever they were—in the dish, but they'd gone. James could easily have jumped up on the counter and eaten them, but Anna felt they'd simply melted away. There was a drop of liquid left. It looked enough like ordinary water to be tipped down the sink. She decided not to use the dish for food again.

Every night since Michael walked into the sea, Anna had gone out to call in a cat, fetch a chair from the lawn to save it from the damp, look up at the stars. Wherever she lived it was the same. Each night it had been the same dream.

She thought: I was phoning for someone to talk to.

Next morning she truanted on Dr Alpert, changed trains at London Victoria and made her way down through the postal codes until, the other side of Balham, she thought she recognised the way the streets curled and dovetailed across the swell of a hill. "Orchid Nails," read the signs outside the station: "Minty Pearls Dental Clinic." Anna descended from the train and wandered thoughtfully along, staring into the windows of empty houses.

She had no plan. She favoured quiet residential avenues and a particular kind of four-bedroom mock-Tudor, with laurels and a slip of driveway to one side of its front garden. The shabbier a place looked, the more likely it was to hold her attention. By mid-afternoon she thought she might be in Sydenham Hill. She had covered miles under the enamel light, trespassed on the hard standings of a dozen middle-class homes. She was exhausted. Her ankles hurt. She was lost. It wasn't the first time she had done this.

Sydenham Hill turned out, in point of fact, to be Norbiton, a place named after the suburb in an Edwardian novel. Anna sat down with a cup of tea in the station café and emptied her bag on to the table. It was full of the usual silt—ends of make-up, a single glove, an address book bloated with the names of people she never saw anymore, her phone with its flat battery. There were receipts folded into very small squares, foreign coins and coins no longer in circulation. There was an old outboard computer drive: this, she took up.

It was perhaps two inches by three, with curved, organic-looking edges, its smooth dull surface interrupted at one end by a line of firewire ports—one of those objects which, new and exciting in its day, now looked as dated as a cigarette case. Michael had left it with her, along with some instructions, putting his warm hand over Anna's—they were in a railway café just like this one—and urging her:

"You will remember, won't you?"

All she could remember now was being afraid. When you're afraid of everything, especially each other, you have to walk away; consign each other to the world.

Anna had arrived in Norbiton between trains. She drank a second cup of tea and stared out with vague good will at the empty platform, where everything had a thick fresh coat of paint. After about twenty minutes an old man was helped into the café by some railway staff. He had outlived himself. His bald brown head seemed too big for his neck; his underlip, the colour of uncooked liver, drooped in exhausted surprise at finding himself still there. They sat him at Anna's table, where he banged her feet and legs about with his stick, shoved the contents of her bag carelessly across the table towards her, and, as soon as he was settled, began eating salmon sandwiches directly from a paper bag. His hands were ropy with veins, the skin over them shiny and slack. He ate greedily but at the same time with a curious lack of interest, as if his body remembered food but he didn't. As he ate he whispered to himself. After some minutes he put the bag down, leaned across the table and tapped Anna's hand sharply.

"Ow," said Anna.

"Nothing is real," he said.

"I'm sorry?"

"Nothing is real. Do you understand? There are only contexts. And what do they context?" He gave Anna an intent look; breathed heavily a few times through his mouth. "More contexts, of course!" Anna, who had no idea how to respond, stared angrily out of the window. After a moment he said, as if he hadn't already spoken to her, "I have to get on the next train. I wonder if you would be kind enough to help me?"

"I wouldn't, no," Anna said, collecting up her things.

It was almost dark when she arrived home. Marnie had left irritable messages on the answerphone. "Pick up, Anna. I'm really very cross with you. It's not the first time you've done this." Anna made herself an omelette and ate it in the kitchen standing up, while she rehearsed what she would say to Marnie. The last of the daylight was fading out of the sky. James the cat jumped up on to the kitchen top and begged. Absent-minded with guilt, Anna gave him more of the omelette than she had intended to.

"I forgot to go," she repeated stubbornly to herself. "Marnie, I simply forgot."

Later, she thought she saw a glimmer of light in the summerhouse. Thin river mist had lapped up past the garden hedge and now hung between the apple trees. The grass was damp. Everything smelled sharply of itself, including the cat who—his faith in the generosity of the world confirmed—ran ahead of Anna with his tail up until he found something to interest him in the hedge. Anna pulled at the summerhouse door. Junk lay about in the dark: two leather chairs, Marnie's old Cambridge bicycle, a carpet someone had brought back from India. Rooting about under the window, she burst a cardboard box, from which spilled a quantity of ornaments, photograph frames, bits of china and silk, shellac records—family stuff of Tim's going all the way back to the 1920s, stuff she had been meaning to clear out since he died. Each generation, she thought, leaves itself scattered in a kind of alluvial fan across postcodes and sideboards, inside wardrobes, jukeboxes, second-hand shops and places like this.

"Titanium," Michael had said as he closed her hands round the computer drive: "Today's popular metal."

All those years ago she had promised to return it to a colleague of his in South London. She remembered the man's name: Brian Tate; but though she remembered what his house looked like, she couldn't really remember where it was. If she saw it she would recognise it. Something awful had happened, or was about to happen, the last time she was there. We never went back, she told herself. I know that. We were too afraid.

2: Hard Goods

One piss-wet night in Saudade City a broker called Toni Reno made his way down Tupolev Avenue to the noncorporate spaceport, out of which he ran his small but successful operation.

Toni didn't mind walking in the rain. He could always turn up the collar of his Sadie Barnham work jacket, or, if that sensation got old, flag down a rickshaw. When he looked up between the buildings there were already gaps in the cloud cover, revealing part of the Kefahuchi Tract opened like a map of the city across clear wet sky. The rain would stop in half an hour, the streets would dry out fast in an offshore wind. Meanwhile Toni could enjoy the feeling of weather. He could enjoy the way the monas laughed past him on Tupolev, on their way to the bar they called the Tango du Chat, huddled up in their short fur coats, stepping out bravely in those inappropriate shoes they loved. Nothing new, nothing old, people believed in Toni's time of the world: everything in that thin yet endless tranche of sensation between the past and the future.

Waiting for traffic at Tupolev and 9, he got a dial-up from his loader, a woman called Enka Mercury who'd been on the Beach longer than Toni was alive. The pipe was poor and Enka sounded as if she was calling from outer space.

"Your goods you wanted are in the yard," she said.

"That's good, Enka."

"Is it?" she said. "The fucker spoke to me, Toni."

Toni laughed. "What did it say?"

"Mind your own business. I hope you know what you're doing here."

"Hey kid," Toni said: "You tell me."

You knew Toni Reno without ever having seen him before: the usual thirty-year-old hipster with a girlfriend in middle management, he was unconnected, young to be in business on his own. Five per cent earned him a refurb townhouse in the Magellan Ladder and quality off-the-shelf tailoring from a contact he had at Preter Coeur. At that time, which turned out to be his life's high point, he was brokering cargo from all across the Beach, taking a significant tranche of his profit off interplanetary tax gradients, which—steep, complex and subject to sudden variation—caused him inevitable sleepless nights. For the times he wasn't working, he and his girlfriend maintained a rewarding but controllable tank habit, an experience called *Brass Arm* they shared with their cohort all across Saudade.

"Fucked if I ever saw anything like this," Enka said. "You'd think it was—"

At that point the pipe went down.

"Call me if you need to," Toni Reno said into the air, in case his loader could still hear him. "I'll be with you in ten."

Toni rarely looked at a shipment. Live produce from Perkins Rent or Peterburg, alien cultural items from Port Ferry, cold-stored indentured cultivars from Silicon New Turk, they were all the same to him. But he was interested to know what would unnerve Enka Mercury, a woman who had seen it all, so he hailed a rickshaw. The rickshaw rattled off down Cobain with Toni in it, then hung a fast right, trailing ambient music and ads that resembled soft-focus moths in shades both pastel and neon. The rain had stopped but to Toni there still seemed to be plenty of water on the road.

He found the cargo where he expected it, in a long, otherwise empty shed down by the port's south fence.

It was perhaps twelve feet by three, a sealed tube not quite circular in section, with a porthole at one end over which someone had recently welded a thick plug of different material; and a panel of lights, broken. Left to itself, it tended to float waist-height above the dusty concrete floor, the air immediately around it flickering in a way that made Toni nauseous but which didn't impede him from touching it. He walked around it. Its surface was dull and ablated as if it had spent time in empty space. It struck him as old, rotten, guilty. In the bills of lading—downloaded from an FTL router thirty-five lights along the Beach—it was logged as "hard goods"; but the object itself, though unlabelled, had illegal artefact written all over it.

No point of origin was on record.

"Enka!" he called. "Where the fuck are you?"

He thought he heard a shout from somewhere out on the windy hard standings in the dark, too far away to be an answer, or to be anything to do with him.

Toni Reno's percentage always generated itself in a financial space far removed from the physical transaction itself. It was a given for everyone in this kind of arrangement that they never knew how their part of it related to any other. In this case, the paperwork advised him, his responsibility ended when the goods were stowed in the hold of a freighter named the *Nova Swing*. So when he discovered he could move the object just by pushing it, he decided to load it himself.

It was hard work, like manhandling something in water. Once he manoeuvred it out of the shed, there were six or seven hundred yards to cover. The arcs were off in the whole south sector of the port, the rain coming on again. One moment clouds filled the sky, the next they had passed over and the Tract cast down a bluish light. Reno would push a while; stop and call out, "Enka!" or try to dial her up; then bend down to get his hands and forearms underneath one end of the tube, almost embracing it. That was the position to push from, the embrace. Each time he pushed, the tube dipped and rocked a little on its long axis before moving forward in a slow, oily way. One moment it had more inertia than you expected, the next a breath of wind was enough to send it off course.

The boat they called the *Nova Swing* stood up against the night sky among all the other shorthaulers—tubby, three-finned, brass-looking. Her cargo cradle was out. A man known around the port as Fat Antoyne sat on the cradle rail drinking from a pint of Black Heart, his unzipped leather pilot jacket and oiled pompadour flapping in the wind up there. When he saw Reno he waved. The lift descended its eighty feet slowly, with whining servo noises, and jolted to a halt; at which Reno put in one last embrace and shoved the goods aboard.

"Hey, Fat Antoyne," he said.

Fat Antoyne said hey. He said, "What's this?"

Reno brushed down his Sadie Barnham coat. "I don't know," he admitted.

He felt rain cooling the back of his neck and his scalp. It darkened the surface of the tube, the way rain soaks a little into any porous surface; which he somehow didn't expect. You didn't think about this object—which he now saw had faint remains of moulded features, worn down to bulges and vague crockets long ago—as being subject to weather. The two of them contemplated it for a moment, then compared paperwork in case that helped. Fat Antoyne had "mortsafe." "You know what a 'mortsafe' is?" he asked Toni Reno.

Reno admitted he had never heard that word. His lading bills had "hard goods," that was all.

Antoyne chuckled. "Hard goods is right," he said. "I'll sign off on that." Close up, you saw his chinos, tailored for comfort in some kind of twill, had grease stains down the front. He was on his own tonight, he said. His crew were getting rest and relaxation in a bar they liked, he wasn't so keen himself. He offered Reno a drink, but Reno regretfully declined.

"You take care," Reno told him.

When Reno had gone, Fat Antoyne put the cap back on the bottle and put the bottle in his jacket.

"Asshole," he said.

He hoisted the tube up into his number one hold. "Mortsafe," he said, and chuckled. That was a word he could get used to. When he touched the tube, it was cold. He knelt down and carefully passed his hands underneath, feeling the faint resistance you feel when you try to press two magnets together. He studied its surface with the help of a loupe designed to operate in three different regimes, making a clicking noise with his tongue as if he was thinking. Then he shrugged—because what did he know?—secured it, and left. After the arcs went off in the hold, and Fat Antoyne had closed the hatch, and his footsteps had gone away inside the ship, the tube seemed to settle a little in its restraints. A few minutes went by, then a few more. A couple of lights flickered suddenly on the panel up by the porthole.

When Reno got back to the warehouse to have one more look for his loader, he found her hanging some feet in the air above the place where the artefact had been. She was turned towards him as he entered, her face presenting upside down, her back arched as if he had caught her in the middle of a suspended moment of jouissance, a sort of unpremeditated back-flip. She was naked.

"Christ, Enka," Reno said. He wondered if she had been there all along.

The patch of air around her was dark and bluish, despite the lights being on, and in it the shadows fell at wrong angles both to one another and to the shadows in the rest of the shed. This gave Enka an effect of being snatched from the world inhabited by people like Reno to another, colder, more complex regime, as if in seeking release she had exchanged one set of predictabilities for another. Her arms and legs were still moving slowly. Although that action caused her to rotate a little, it seemed to make no difference to her position in the air; or to her essential plight. Her expression was one of understanding, the slow understanding that will lead to panic in another moment. At an undetermined point before this understanding set in, something had inserted itself powerfully at a diagonal from her left armpit to the lower part of her ribcage on the opposite side. A long triangular flap of tissue was hanging down, but it was a white and fishy colour unsuited to a human being. If he stood on his toes and extended his reach, Toni could catch the end of it, but it had a rubbery touch made it hard to hold, and when he got sufficient grip to pull on it nothing seemed to happen. If her new state shared enough of the boundary conditions of the normal to anchor her there, it was also different enough for Enka to be unreachable by Toni Reno.

Toni couldn't think how it happened.

"Fuck you, Enka," he said aloud. "For getting yourself into this."

As if in answer a voice said: "My name is Pearlent and I come from the future."

The shed was empty under the arcs. Enka swam backwards towards him through her new reality, like someone suspended in a low-grade hologram.

Toni ran out the shed, past the *Nova Swing*—now closed and dark—and across the noncorporate port in the wind. He would have run all the way home to his refurb in the Magellan Ladder if a woman—or what he thought of as a woman—hadn't come at him in a side street off Tupolev. She came at him very fast and at an odd angle out of the shadows—as if before Toni arrived she had been lying down in the shadows at the base of a building—and took hold of him round the upper body. Toni's tailoring was state of the art, but a millisecond or two after it cut in, her tailoring somehow switched it off again. Toni was ramped—nerve propagation speeds were up all over his body, his haemoglobin structures were retuning themselves in the picosecond range—but he never landed a punch. He felt as if he had run into a brick wall. He was behind the action. He was still seeing her come up from the pavement when she wrapped her left arm almost lovingly round his head and pushed the barrel of a weapon up into his armpit.

"So what do you want to do next?" she asked him, in a voice which seemed really interested to know.

When Toni moved his head fractionally to be able to speak, she pressed the trigger and that was that. A couple of b-girls on their way back from a night at the Ivory Coast found him very early the next morning. Apparently he was surrounded by black and white cats. "We're knee deep in them," one of the b-girls explained to the police detectives. "So cute. But then we find this guy." When Toni's girlfriend heard later how suddenly he died, she said it was the way Toni would have liked it. He dug his existence in this world but he didn't cling to it. Toni's belief, she said, was that if you could get your life down to a nanometre thick it would stretch out forever.

She added: "As far as you were concerned, obviously."

3: Swimming with Eels

Saudade, Friday, 4 am: Two agents and a wire jockey were in a holding cell in the basement of the old SiteCrime building at the corner of Uniment & Poe, servicing a client.

It was a small cold room, with a retro-medical decor of cracked white tiles and large, complex overhead lighting. Straps confined the client to a stainless steel table; there were tubes in many of his orifices. They had run the wire up into his brain, and by moving it about drew from him a few warm, puppylike yips and yaps, also some twitching of the limbs. No one expected much. It was a calibration period. Every so often the wire jockey leaned back from the green felt eyepieces of his equipment and massaged the small of his back. He was tired, and he wasn't even sure what he was looking for. Meanwhile the client, a New Man with the characteristic shock of bright red hair, tried out fresh expressions each time the wire moved.

He was naked, had suffered a brief convulsion and was secreting a wide range of pheromones. He seemed eager to please. He would laugh vaguely, then wince. Or his eyes would turn up as if he was trying to look into his own head and he would say, in a tired voice he had copied from some old film: "My face is a mess tonight."

"We should call an operator," the wire jockey suggested. "Then whatever this alien knows we know it too."

The agents looked at one another.

"So you organise that," one of them said.

No one wanted an operator. It would be an admission of failure. While they were talking, they cast nervous glances at the fourth person in the room.

12

This woman had a fuck-off way of moving achievable only by the heavily tailored. Her white-blond hair was cropped to nothing much. She was statuesque and a frank air of sexual boredom surrounded her, as if she had come down here because there was nothing else to do in the dog hours of a Friday night. Her career had begun a year or two before, under the auspices of Lens Aschemann, SiteCrime's late, legendary investigator. Though she had never been more than his assistant, she remained in the building even after his death in the Saudade event site. Rumour had it she was connected, but no one knew who to; and on the present occasion none of the agents understood why she was in the basement with them. They were happy enough to defer to her; but they didn't like the amused way she stared into the bright light and polluted air above the client's head, so they were relieved when after an hour she got a dial-up.

"Send my car to the front," she said. Then, to the agents: "Boys, we must do this again. No, I mean it."

She was halfway out of the building when the client broke his straps and sat up. At the same time everyone heard a soft voice in the holding cell say:

"My name is Pearlant and I come from the future."

At that the situation changed rapidly. The assistant's tailoring came up and took control of the space, carefully inhibiting any electromagnetic activity except its own. The lights went out. The wire jockey's signal went bottom-up. The agents found that their tailoring had quit. Six and a half thousand resident nanocameras, drifting in the air like fish semen, all burned out at once. What would they have recorded? Some silvery, mucoid blurs connecting different parts of the room, which, upon analysis, would turn out to be the signature of a single woman moving at abnormal speeds. Each contact she made slowed her down for a fraction of a second, partly resolving this image, freezing her in a curious half-turn; or looking over her shoulder into the upper corner of the room; or with her head at an inhuman angle, face transfigured by a radiant smile.

Fifteen seconds after it had initiated the engagement, her tailoring stood down. The agents lay in opposite corners. The wire jockey sat puffing and blowing on the floor, his back against the wall, his legs stuck out stiffly in front of him. One eyepiece hung on its flex, the other seemed to have been driven into his skull. The body of the New Man rolled slowly off the table and on to the floor at the assistant's feet. She stared down at it as if waiting for something else to happen, then left. The nanocameras came back on. The holding cell was silent for a while, then you got a small sigh as of final bowel sounds, which was the wire jockey giving up.

Heavy rain fell vertically into the alley off Tupolev, where a man named Toni Reno could be found performing slow fishlike movements eight feet above the pavement in a dark blue Sadie Barnham work jacket. Toni was dead. The uniform branch was already on scene, under the supervision of a thin cop called Epstein. Toni faced away from them, up into the weather, his back arched, his arms and legs dangling bonelessly. Water poured off each limb; shaking it off their faces like a cluster of big shapeless animals, the cops in their slickers peered up.

"This is how you found him," the assistant suggested.

"He started lower down."

"You couldn't start much lower than Toni."

Epstein ignored this. "When I get here," he explained, "the guy is on the floor like any other dead guy. Then he floats up. Not so quick that you can see it: but when you turn away, next time you look he's a little higher. It takes maybe twenty minutes." The assistant regarded him with not much expression on her face.

He shrugged. "Thirty at the outside."

She said, "Get me into one of these houses."

"Dead guys don't float," Epstein said.

The uniforms banged on a door until someone let them in. It was a four-floor walk-up designed to have an ambience of shiny brown paintwork and roach smells in passageways. West of Tupolev, over as far as Radia Marelli, all the buildings were like this: warrens falling into the ramified tunnels and flooded cellars underneath, patrolled by crime tourists enjoying an economy of low-rent donkey parlours, futurology joints and tank farms where you could get the bootlegged experience of being a plant from a distant world. The assistant went up to the second floor and opened a window so she could look down on the corpse.

"What do you notice?" she said.

There was a flicker in the air immediately above Toni Reno, a very pale blue illumination like neon seen at night from the next street along. The Sadie Barnham jacket had fallen away to reveal his ribcage, emphasising its curve up out of the diaphragm. Say what you like, Toni kept himself in shape. His face was waxy, his expression one of surprise. There was no clue to how he was hanging there like that.

"I notice the rain falling off him," Epstein said, "but not on to him."

The assistant smiled briefly. "That was Toni's ambition all his short life," she said. "Perhaps it gives us a clue to the type of crime we have here." As if thinking about this, she stared down at the corpse a minute or two more. Eventually she said:

"Pull him down if you can. If you can't, leave someone to watch what happens. I'll send a SiteCrime team over. Maybe an operator."

The thought of working with an operator dampened Epstein's spirits. The uniforms nodded to one another, they had guessed all along it would play this way. Halfway down the street stairs the assistant stopped as if she had forgotten something. "You go on," she told Epstein. She waited until the uniforms were out of the building, then entered the first room she found, where an alien of some kind, bipedal, its strigiform skull drilled for electrical access, lay on a pallet surrounded by drifts of its own feathers. Several small objects—including a pair of Entreflex dice turned up to display the "Tower of Cloud" face; a cheap hologram of the Kefahuchi Tract; and a handful of intricately etched wide-bore titanium needles— were arranged on the nightstand. Two or three weeks ago, the assistant estimated, someone had begun recording these things through the alien's sensorium, then lost interest. There was a mouldy smell in the room, like pigeons under a bridge. The assistant made two or three dial-up calls, spoke briefly to her office, then stood the way people do when they are waiting for someone to talk to them by holographic fetch. Nothing happened, although for a moment a half-formed shape seemed to flicker in an upper corner of the room.

"Are you there?" she said encouragingly.

"Yes," whispered the alien on the pallet. It thrashed about briefly, sending up a cloud of feathers. "I am. I am here."

The assistant maintained an office on the fifth floor of the building at Uniment & Poe. She had staff, she had a budget, she had a '52 mint-blue Cadillac roadster in the parking garage: no one knew how she achieved this kind of success. You saw the Cadillac outside the bar they called the Tango du Chat where she often spent an evening; two or three times a week she would leave it at the kerb on C-Street and enter Cedar Mountain, an upscale tank farm where they kept several personalised immersive art experiences on file for her, based on the life of a fictitious Twentieth Century housewife called Joan. As Joan, the assistant cooked meals, used "cleaning products" and serviced her man 1956-style, which generally meant he grunted a lot and came on her leg (despite its exoticism, she found this aspect of the experience profoundly calming). Today, though, she chose another Cedar Mountain favourite: the five-star *Room 121*, based on a tableau of the same name by Sandra Shen, in which she could be a woman—unnamed but still perhaps Twentieth Century— "alone" in a hotel.

It was night. She was lounging in the tropical heat of a single room. She was at the window, a tall woman whose eyes were blue, whose age was hard to tell, whose clothes—a black two-piece with lightly padded shoulders, a striped grey and black blouse of some glazed material—scarcely hid an untidy sexuality. She never did much in the room. She drank rum; she stared out the window, thinking that wherever you are at night in the city you can always see, beyond the roof of the next building, the faint glow of floodlights. The radio played a musing version of a popular tune, "Rhapsody in Blue." It was all as it should be. It was leading to the moment when her hands went impersonally into her underwear, when it would seem to the assistant that she was not so much having sex with herself as with the room, the song, the hotel: with every object in that instance of the liquid world.

This time, though, Room 121 went dark and dropped sideways. A million silver eels flickered past the windows. Whispers filled each dusty corner. She felt the tank world come apart around her, into dark and streaming pixels: next thing, she was hanging in the parking orbit above a rusty alien artefact the size of a brown dwarf. Things were such an effort. She was swimming with eels, down to the pocked and gouged surface. Somewhere in the fractal labyrinth beneath, a woman like herself lay on the allotropic carbon deck, a white paste oozing from the corner of her mouth. This woman was barely human. She was neither conscious nor unconscious, dead nor alive. There was something wrong with her cheekbones. She was waiting. She came from the past, she came from the future; she was about to speak.

The assistant thrashed about. Lost in space, trying to place herself equidistant from everything else in the universe, she heard her own faint cry in the dark and moved towards it. Yellowish oily liquid filled her mouth. Later she listened tiredly while the twink-tank patched her up. In her anxiety, it told her, she had choked on the tank fluid or "proteome." She had ripped out the main cable. She was losing cerebro-spinal fluid and later today she might experience a little light bleeding from neurotypical energy sites; it wasn't so bad.

"Something happened in there," she said.

"Once immersed," the tank reminded her, in the voice of a real mother, "you should never move or try to shout."

"I don't expect to feel like that."

Over on the other side of town, Epstein and his soldiers were still trying to bring Toni Reno back to earth. Toni's reaction seemed coy, especially for a dead man. Every time one of them touched him he bounced gently away, making curious swimmy elastic movements in the air, curving his back in a clean arc, circling some invisible central point as the uniforms jumped and waved their arms twelve feet below him. It was puzzling. It was even elegant. The rain had stopped. Morning traffic clogged Tupolev; downtown was solid.

4: Givenchy

Left to herself, Anna Waterman tended to medicate with reasonably priced red wine, a bottle of which, taken before bed, only made things worse next day, when—full of guilts like a ball of living eels she couldn't disentangle without each one slipping away quietly into the dark—she would ring the consulting rooms to see if Dr Alpert had a cancellation. This she did at half past eight one morning a week or two after missing her last appointment.

Her first husband had spent much of the previous night running away from her, until she cornered him in King's Cross at a cheap hotel. In the dream Michael hadn't looked much like himself. Neither of them had looked much like themselves, in fact. But Anna had felt exactly as she felt then, when she was young and he was still alive: exhausted and angry. "You're always afraid!" she tried to convince him. "You're always hiding from me!" Once in the hotel room together they fucked again and again in a blind panic, as if both of them were trying to avoid thinking about something else. After that, events moved themselves on with the usual kind of dreary predictability. Her husband became agitated and ran away again while she was asleep, leaving a note in which he talked of his "great discovery." In the final lobe of the dream, Anna found herself lying alone on a cold, black, reflective surface—this time she described it to Dr Alpert as resembling a hotel bathroom floor—in an echoing space the nature of which she couldn't describe at all. It was very tall; it was "dark and light at the same time." She had a sense of dread. She couldn't see much; she could see everything, but she didn't know what any of it was. She felt as if she was changing into something.

"And is that what you remember most clearly from the dream?"

"Oh no. I remember the frock I was wearing. Is that absurd?"

"Not entirely," said Dr Alpert, although she thought it was.

"It was beautiful." Anna frowned intently for a moment, as though, if she focused, she could have the frock in front of her. "Givenchy, from the early 1960s. The most marvellous grey, in some shiny fabric like satin. I can't say more than that." She blinked at Dr Alpert. "Did Givenchy ever make anything like that? Does that sound like him?"

"Just to pick up on an earlier point," the doctor said, "I wonder what you mean when you say that your guilt is 'like a ball of eels'?"

"You see, I'm not really talking about guilt. Not at the moment."

"Perhaps not."

Recognising this as a difference of opinion, the two women stared at one another thoughtfully. For now there didn't seem to be a way around it. Anna fiddled with the clasp of her bag. After a minute or two she offered:

"I'm afraid I forgot to bring the test results you asked for."

Helen Alpert smiled.

"Please don't worry," she said. "Your daughter had the hospital copy them to me. She was worried you might lose them on the train."

And she slid the documents, three or four sheets of printout in a plastic sleeve, across her desk. Anna, whose history of lost documents was extensive, pushed them back without looking at them.

"It was wrong of Marnie to do this," she said. "It was controlling." Then, feeling she had been disloyal, tried to explain: "I don't want tests. I don't want to know these things about myself. I want just to live my life until it's over. Marnie is the wrong generation to understand that."

"Neurologically, Anna, you're very sound. You should be relieved. There are signs of a couple of tiny strokes. Otherwise you're fine."

But Anna—who had feared all along things would go in this direction once Marnie lost her patience—remembered Michael Kearney, trembling in her arms in his paralysis of anxiety, and could only repeat, "I don't want to know things like that about myself." Helen Alpert identified this, perhaps correctly, as a defensive stubbornness; baffled, they stared at one another in silence again until Anna shrugged, looked at her watch, and said: "I think my time's up."

"Is there anything else?" the doctor said.

"My cat is bringing home the internal organs of exotic animals."

"I meant, really, if there was anything else you remembered about the dream."

After Anna had gone, the doctor leaned back in her chair and rubbed her eyes tiredly.

Helen Alpert was a tall woman, given to skinny jeans and soft leather coats, whose career had begun in the psychology of chronic pain; veered during her troubled second marriage into PTSD and trauma management; and finally come to rest in private consulting rooms by the Thames in Chiswick, where she facilitated the inner lives of mid-range production executives from the surrounding BBC enclaves. Perhaps ten years younger than Anna, she had made her home on the opposite side of the river in one of the quiet streets around Kew Green. Mornings, she jogged by the river. At weekends she wandered the Gardens or drove her temperamental first-generation Citroen XM to a cottage in East Anglia, where she trudged up and down the shingle beaches in the rain and ate pea mousse with Parma ham & shallot dressing, followed by roast breast & confit leg of squab on puy lentils with parmentier potatoes and jus, at the local Michelin-starred pub conversion. Despite or perhaps because of this regime, she remained single. She had been treating Anna Waterman for three years. It was slow going. They had layered up this peculiar dream of Anna's until it was a rich and satisfying fiction, but not one that offered an easy reading of itself; and they had never seemed quite suited to one another. Now, knowing Anna to be too young to have worn 1960s Givenchy, the doctor assumed the garment to be a symbol of the parent, entering the words, "The unthought known?" into Anna's case file and emphasising them heavily.

Then she leafed back through the file, parts of which were easier to understand than others.

Born Anne-Marie Selve in 1976, to a provincial couple already in middle age, Anna had formed herself early. Academically focused at eight, she had been obsessive by fourteen. It was a familiar story. Arriving at Girton a year ahead of her cohort she allowed a further year to pass before succumbing to anorexia. Self-harm and her first suicide attempt followed. By then, the parents—never much more than pleasantly surprised to find themselves parents in the first place—were too old to offer emotional help; in addition there remained, according to psychiatric reports, some unidentified tension between father and daughter. Girton patched Anna together. For a time she was, as she put it, everyone's favourite suicide.

"They knocked on my door if they thought things were too quiet." But soon the Selve's place in her life was taken by a visiting professor of mathematical physics. This man, Michael Kearney, uncommunicative, narcissistic and easily depressed, turned out to have his own problems. They were married fast and divorced even faster; yet, sustained perhaps by its fiercely mutual structures of manipulation, the relationship proved more durable than either of them believed, lurching along in its disordered way until Kearney ended it on the eve of the Millennium by walking into the Atlantic just north of Scituate, Massachusetts.

At this remove, the mathematician became unidentifiable. He had no family Helen Alpert could trace; while Anna claimed to have "forgotten everything," and wouldn't be certain about his age or even the colour of his eyes. When she could be persuaded to speak about Kearney, he was transformed into careful fiction. Vague one day, meaninglessly particular the next, Anna's revision of Kearney presented him as a gap in her life even as he had filled it.

Publicly there was a little more. He had written, probably as a joke, a pamphlet on randomness and the Tarot. Some topological speculations— stimulated by exchanges with the reclusive mathematician Grigori Perelman—had been published a year or two before his death, to cautious peer approval. Otherwise Michael Kearney's contribution to science lay in an unfinished quantum computing project, most of the work on which had been done by an unassuming experimental physicist called Brian Tate. Tate—newly divorced, unequal even to the brief publicity surrounding Kearney's suicide, and wrong-footed by a minor funding scandal involving the venture capital firm MVC-Kaplan—went down with the ship. His results proved unrepeatable. With his collaborator dead, and his claim to have coaxed massive parallel processing from a train of cheaply modified desktop PCs dismissed as junk science, he faded from view in a month. All this was a matter of record.

By that time, Anna's parents were plaques on a chapel wall somewhere in East Cheshire. She had no friends. The Millennium was over, the fireworks had gone out. Everyone else seemed to know what they wanted. Back in London, she bought a self-help manual and taught herself to eat again. She entrapped Tim Waterman and, still confused but with a growing sense of self-preservation, set about reducing the chaos in her life. Waterman was a kind and successful man whose work often took him abroad. The first time he went away, Anna found she could cook. She put on weight, toyed with the Women's Institute and, discovering a gift for flowers, the Prettiest

Village competition. Tim, who had known her briefly during the Michael Kearney era, seemed calmly amused by it all. She brought up their daughter with care, the best humour she could manage, and a real sense of the worth of that.

But everything, Helen Alpert reminded herself as she put away the file and locked the consulting room door behind her for the day, is language.

Pushing her old car west along the Thames through heavy evening traffic, she recalled Anna's description of "fucking in a blind panic" with her first husband. "In fact I always quite liked sex to be that way," Anna had added. "It made it seem more central somehow, a means of saying something urgent about yourself. The problem was always what could happen next." Then, when Helen Alpert raised her eyebrows at this, Anna laughed suddenly and advised: "Never do anything unless you're lost or on fire, Doctor. Otherwise how will you remember it?" Balked by the Mortlake roundabout, gazing vaguely at a thick red sunset behind layered fringes of trees, Dr Alpert wondered how she could make sense of this except as bravado. Anna Waterman had reinvented herself with the century: now she was discovering that Anna Selve remained the disordered substrate beneath it all. Whatever had drawn her to Michael Kearney underlay everything else she had made.

In her repeating dream, in her fear of neurological disease, in her increasing sense of the instability of her life—in her denial of all of that—her original disorder had found its voice again.

Anna, unaware of these judgements, took home two bottles of Fleurie and a tub of pistachio ice cream, then telephoned Marnie and conducted a short but satisfying row; after which they agreed to more broadly respect one another's feelings and Anna listened to news of Marnie's ex-boyfriend's new job. Her plan for the rest of the evening had been to turn on her fifty-inch Sony and eat all the ice cream while watching an ageing wildlife presenter gambol in the brackish waters of the North Sea with the half-dozen mouldy-looking grey seals left in the Shetland Islands; but, four of the animals having the previous week contracted human norovirus, the spectacle was cancelled. Anna wandered about. After her exchange with Marnie the house seemed hot and airless. She took a shower. She stood looking out of the kitchen doorway with a glass of Fleurie in her hand. Called the cat. He didn't come.

"James, you depressing animal," she said.

At nine, the telephone rang. She picked it up expecting Marnie again, but there was no one at the other end. Just as she put the receiver down, she heard an electronic scraping noise, like starlings in a gutter; a distant voice which shouted, as if to a third person even further away than Anna:

"Don't go in there!"

When the cat hadn't come in by ten o'clock, she went out to look for it.

The air outside seemed even warmer. There was no moon. Instead the summer constellations wheeled above the water meadow. Anna made her way slowly down the lawn, and imagined she saw the cat's eyes glittering ironically at her from the base of the hedge. "James?" Nothing, only the grey earth still disturbed and scattered about. A strip of orchard ran down one side of the garden, old apple varieties left to themselves to split and fall apart from the centre outward so that their moss-covered boughs curved back down to the ground. The cat would often crouch among them at night; listen for bank voles; chase a moth. He wasn't there now. Anna balanced her wine glass in the crook of a branch, let herself out through the side gate. "James? James!" she called, all the way across the pasture to where the river, glimmering in the starlight, wound between crack-willow and beds of nettle in soft black earth. Anna, ambushed and thoughtful, stood gazing into the water. Where in daylight it would be solid and brown, with a glassy turbulence at the surface, now it seemed fine-grained, weightless. She trailed her hand. She forgot the cat. She laughed. Suddenly she sat down on the bank and took off her shoes, and was about to take off her clothes, when something—she wasn't sure what, it might have been the slightest shift of light on the willow leaves—caused her to turn and look back the way she had come.

Her summerhouse was on fire.

Huge red and gold flames rose at an angle from its conical roof. There was no smoke; and though they cast a great light, and threw long oblique shadows across the pasture, the flames looked stiff, idealised, as though painted for a Tarot card. For a moment she saw herself on the card too, in the foreground but well to one side so that the focus remained firmly on the burning building (which could now be seen to be isolated in the field, with a suggestion of a hedge, or perhaps some kind of earthwork, at its base): a woman hard to age, wearing a 1930s-looking floral print dress, running with her mouth open and a paradoxical expression, a mask of dissociated consternation, on her face. No shoes. Her hair, flying back in the wind, painted as a single mass. Her lips were moving. "Go away. Go away from here!" The flames roared silently up, amid showers of gold sparks. Anna could feel the heat of them, stretching the skin across her cheekbones. Yet by the time she reached the garden gate everything was dark again; and, despite the heat, nothing had been burned. There wasn't even a smell of smoke—although through the summerhouse windows she glimpsed what looked like embers, still whirling about inside, just above the floor.

The door had dropped on its hinges a decade before. Anna dragged it open. Two or three houses' worth of garden furniture and tools met her gaze. Tim had liked to garden. From an early age, Marnie had liked to help. They had liked to be in the garden together, around the flowerbeds or the kidney-shaped pond, while Anna watched with a drink. Deckchairs, sunshades, long-handled pruners. Marnie's quite expensive ping-pong table. Then, in the shadows, shelves full of half-used garden chemicals. The chemical smells of dusts and powders, spilled across the floor or gone solid in their tins and packets. Then the smell of cardboard boxes, lax with damp, bulging with everything from photograph albums to ornaments. Something was spilling off the shelves, in a shower of fantastic sparks! They were just like the sparks from a firework! They paled slowly but didn't fade. Anna approached. She let them fall through her upturned hands. She sat on the floor and sifted through them like a child. Light dripped off her fingers, soft-feeling embers, objects like cool sachets of gel, the neon colours of the organs the cat brought in. After a time these colours leached away, just exactly like heat from embers, to leave a drift of small objects she could barely make out in the dark. Anna sorted through them. She turned them over uncomprehendingly. She found a shoebox, green, a trusted brand, and shovelled them into it. Opening the summerhouse door she had thought she heard sounds: laughter, music, the smells of fried food, alcohol and human excitement in a seaside at night. She rubbed the palm of her left hand with the thumb of her right. Presently, she went outside and looked across the river pasture, where her own running footprints made an erratic track through the thick dew.

"Michael?" she called softly. "Michael?" She called, "Is this you? Are you doing this? Michael, this is you, isn't it?"

She slept heavily and did not dream. The next morning, she drank a cup of weak green tea; ate a dessert spoon of honey stirred into Greek yoghurt; upended the shoebox across the kitchen counter and watched its contents bounce and roll. They were just small things—ordinarily tawdry but in resonant colours—which she thought must once have belonged to Marnie. She stared at them, strewn across the counter like coloured buttons. Some of them *were* buttons, in different shapes and sizes. Some of them were more like old-fashioned enamel badges—emblems of someone's military career, or a life in nursing or conducting buses, brought up short by pancreatitis or stroke in the early 1970s. There were things that resembled Lego bricks, made of a translucent material too substantial to be plastic; two or three pinchbeck rings with interesting symbols; a cluster of tiny porcelain rosebuds you could pin to a frock; beads, charms, iron-on tattoos, yellowing dice and a pair of moulded plastic lips at the very beginnings of a kiss. Miniature playing cards slipped from a pasteboard box. There was a plastic mug with a mirrored bottom, so that when you drank from it your own face was revealed. A little red Valentine's heart with diodes inside that even now lit up when Anna pressed the tiny button on the back—although God knew how old it must be. They were the kinds of things that turn up in trays at flea markets. Costume jewellery fallen out of a Christmas cracker thirty years before. Anna was compelled. She phoned Marnie and they had another disagreement.

"But do try and remember," Anna urged. "Little 3D pictures! And enamel badges like the ones you wore when you were at Cambridge."

"Anna," Marnie said, "It is five o'clock in the morning."

"Is it, darling?" Anna said. "I thought they were just the type of thing a child might collect," she tried to explain. "I thought you'd be interested."

"Do you know something?" she said. "Some of them are *warm*!"

"Hang up, Anna," Marnie advised. "I am."

Anna stared at the items for some minutes, as if they had given her a new lease of life. Then she fetched her handbag from the hall and out of it, after some rummaging, took Michael Kearney's pocket drive. This she put down among all the other stuff, where the light could shine off its slippery titanium surface. While she was staring at it, James the cat came in and began butting and fussing around her calves, his purr thick and close, breathy and mechanical at the same time. Suddenly he went to his bowl and began to eat tuna as if his life depended on it. The milkman left the milk. A train went past on the valley line. The phone rang again. She wondered what had really happened to the summerhouse in the night: everything had remained perfectly silent throughout, she thought, like a fire in a difficult film. She wondered what had happened to her. Eventually, she swept everything back into the shoebox, put the pocket drive in her bag, and caught the next train to London, where she expected to spend the afternoon nosying into other people's houses. For once she rather looked forward to it.

5: Archive Style

In his glory days Fat Antoyne Messner had run a number of petty mules like the *Nova Swing*. All featured illegal propulsion systems, capacious holds and occult service histories: they were registered out of planets with made-up names. He had operated them, so he claimed, on behalf of numerous Halo celebrities: Emmie-Lou Parang, Impasse van Sant, Margot Furstenburg, Ed Chianese. Why rocket-sport stars and entradistas like that would need the services of a rusty cargo vessel, when they were up to their eyes in smart carbon and BMG-composite hulls with salvaged alien machinery bolted the other side of the pilot bulkhead, he never made clear. Maybe it was to haul spare parts. Maybe it made them feel good to have a fat man around.

Whether you believed these claims or not, one thing was certain: Antoyne was no longer the loser you used to see beached-up in Saudade City, narratising his bad luck, drinking Black Heart rum, reduced to making small points at the very edge of the game as errand boy for cheap crooks like Vic Serotonin or Pauli DeRaad. He owned his own ship. He had an eye for a transaction. He wasn't even fat anymore.

At 4 am the morning after he met with Toni Reno, Antoyne made some FTL calls, as a result of which he found himself down in the *Nova Swing* number one hold, re-examining the payload Toni left behind. On the bills of lading it was described, "Delivery, insurance, freight, documents on sight," which is not to say much. Because of his previous career, Antoyne experienced a natural anxiety when it came to Port Authority paper. About the payload itself, technology had told him all it could. He concentrated

26

instead on its viewport, situated at the front end and constructed of three-inch quartz glass, opal in colour, elliptical in shape. To obviate reflections, Antoyne had switched off the halogen lights. Every so often he was forced to wipe condensation from the glass with a piece of rag.

If he cupped his hands round his face, he could make out a greenish object, like something alive viewed under low-power photomultiplication. This object moved about, or maybe not. Antoyne didn't like what he saw. He didn't like being in the dark with it, or the way the *Nova Swing* main hold seemed warmer than usual, or the carmine LEDs that occasionally flickered into life up and down the mortsafe's lateral line.

Two years before, Antoyne's company—Bulk Haulage, aka Dynadrive-DF—had won a six-month contract to tow hulks in the Vera Rubin's World quarantine orbit. Antoyne left the *Nova Swing* at home, hired an 18/42 series Weber tug—the *Pocket Rocket*, old but serviceable—and ran the job out of a landing-field bar known to its habitués as "The East Ural Nature Reserve." He took a room for the duration, not far down Gravuley Street from the field, and ate with all the other quarantine dogs at the Faint Dime diner, where he liked the way the light reflected off the chromed faux-Deco panels behind the counter. Early evening would find him at the window of his room, eyeballing the Neapolitan layers of a late sunset while he waited for the neon to come on. It was a two-storey town on a one-issue planet. Their idea of style was yellow Argylls and black loafers. Gravuley Street seemed to go on forever, especially at night.

A week after he arrived, Antoyne watched something strange emerge from a boarded-up building not far from the Faint Dime: the naked body of a baby, magnified to adult size and the same olive-drab colour as the frontage. At first, looking up from the sidewalk to the second floor, he had it as some kind of novelty sign. What would you advertise with a giant baby? He didn't know. Any kind of baby was a mystery to Antoyne. He didn't like them much. This one, which appeared perhaps three months old, protruded at an odd angle, so that its pudgy legs lolled apart. It was a girl. Antoyne averted his gaze, as if he had seen some kind of porn not to his taste. He thought he heard a faint, squeezing rustle: when he made himself look again the baby had forced itself out a millimetre or two more. It was working its way into Antoyne's world. A voice from beside him said without preamble:

"Have you ever been inside a quarantine hulk?"

This voice belonged to MP Renoko, a man you often met at The East Ural

Nature Reserve, where he would begin a conversation by saying: "You agree there's no necessity to confuse a practical tool with a theory of the world?" Renoko came and went, but always bought rounds of drinks.

"I'm relieved to see you," Antoyne said. "Considering this."

"Considering what?"

"That," Antoyne said, pointing above his head; but the baby was gone. He looked up, around, behind him: nothing.

Gravuley Street offered no aid. To the left lay darkness and the empty planet; to the right, the savagely lighted window of the Faint Dime. He could see every item of interior decoration, pressed-out and perfect in candy colours. Someone was drinking Ovaltine with rum. Someone else was getting a big-size ham on rye sandwich with fries. Antoyne wiped his mouth. The hair went up on his neck. One o'clock in the morning, and a light wind blew dust in ribbons down the middle of the street.

"Something was here," he asserted. "Why don't we get a drink?"

"I'm buying," said MP Renoko. "It seems to me you've had some sort of shock."

Renoko looked like a photograph of Anton Chekhov, if Chekhov had aged more and come to favour a little white chin-beard. Otherwise his look successfully teamed used raincoats with grey worsted trousers five inches too short. His hair—white, swept back to a grubby collar—always seemed full of light. He was small-boned, and intense in manner. His clothes came spattered with outmoded foods such as tapioca and "soup." On his feet he wore cracked tan wingtips without socks, and it was a feature of this careful image that his ankles went unwashed. As soon as he and Fat Antoyne had settled themselves in the comparative safety of The East Ural Nature Reserve, he returned to his original subject as if he had never left it:

"'Everyone their own evolutionary project,'" we tell each other here in the Halo. Excuse me, this can only be an element of cultural self-dramatisation, even in times like ours." His smile meant he was prepared to forgive that. "But if there *is* a new species," he said, "perhaps it's up there in those quarantine hulks."

Fat Antoyne said he didn't get it.

Renoko smiled. "You get it," he said.

Leaked navigational nanoware or eleven-dimensional imaging code slips up someone's anus at night and discovers it can run on a protein substrate. In a similar way, ads, memes, diseases and algorithms escape into the wild. They can run on your neurones, they can run inside your cells. They perform a default conversion. Suddenly the cops are out with the loudhailers,

"Stay inside! Stay Indoors!" but it's too late: on your street, in your house, everything collapses suddenly into an unplanned slurry of nanotech, half-tailored viruses and human fats—your husband, your two little girls in their identical dresses, you. "Entire planetary populations," Renoko said, "are converting to this stuff. Is it an end-state?" He threw up his little hands. "No one knows! Is it a new medium? No one is willing to say! It's as beautiful as water in strong sunlight, yet it stinks like rendered fat, and can absorb an adult human being in forty seconds. The hulks are full of it, the quarantine orbit is full of hulks. Men like you keep it safe." Obsolete pipeliners that worked the Carling Line, decommissioned Alcubierre warps the size of planetesimals, anything with a thick hull, especially if it's easy to reinforce further: Fat Antoyne had a sudden clear image of those pocked relics in the interplanetary darkness—used-up ships mysterious with the dim crawling lights of beacons and particle dogs, pinwheeling around on near-chaotic operator-controlled trajectories.

He shook his drink and watched it settle. "Not me," he said. "I got a six month contract to move some of it around, that's all."

"And how are you enjoying that?"

Antoyne made the universal gesture for money. "This way," he boasted. "Mostly though my pilot does the work, you've seen her in here. She goes by Ruby Dip." Suddenly it occurred to him to ask: "Why are we talking about this?"

"Because once all the other questions are asked, the last one left is: what does this new species *want*?"

Renoko leaned forward intently. He looked in Fat Antoyne's eyes.

"Would your pilot ever take a passenger up to the orbit? Would that seem possible?" Immediately he suggested it, he began to laugh. They both knew he'd gone too far. Up there, the Quarantine Bureau was all over you with every kind of licence and paperwork. In addition they had oversight by EMC assets, the fragmentary orbits of which looped round Vera Rubin's World as tight as the lines of a paranoid magnetic field. "Before you answer that," said Renoko, to release the tension, "let me get you another of those weird drinks you like."

But Antoyne now shook his head no thanks and got to his feet. Some said MP Renoko was a twink addict and orbital miner, real name "Remy Kandahar," wanted for crimes on all those worn-out planets of the Core. Others believed him to be all that remained of the notorious Circus of Pathet Lao—aka Sandra Shen's Observatorium & Native Karma Plant—the assets of which he had been in the process of stripping since Sandra Shen's disappearance fifty years before. Fat Antoyne, who subscribed to neither of these options, took out a hologram business card for Dynadrive-DF. This he placed on the table next to Renoko's empty glass, saying: "'We haul anything,' is our pledge. Find us at Carver Field, Saudade, if you ever want to do business of that kind. Just get in touch.

"Thanks for the drink, I needed that after what I saw."

Later that night, having found his way without further incident down the unreliable perspectives of Gravuley Street to Ruby Dip's room, he said:

"It makes you think."

"I know what it makes me think," said Ruby.

Ruby Dip was a short, broad, muscular woman fifty years old, whose skin not only told the whole story of life in the Halo through tattoos reading "Tienes mi corazon" and "They Came from Planet E!", but also featured treasure maps; fragments of secret code which, interpreted freely, could show any man the way home; and smart red worms of light that propagated across her substantial tits and into her armpits like the embers at the edge of a piece of burnt paper. Though she had her passions, Ruby liked the continual entertainment that was the rocket jockey's life, and saw no reason to want much else. Her hair was cadmium yellow stubble. She favoured cropped and faded denim, smelled of the *Pocket Rocket*, and collected antique Spanish tambourines stuck all over with deep red roses and bits of sheet music and lighted from the inside, several examples of which now lay scattered across the cheap furniture or hung from the walls.

"But have you ever seen inside a hulk?" said Fat Antoyne, who if nothing else knew how to persist at the wrong moment.

Ruby confessed herself puzzled.

"Honey," she said. "I just push them around." She looked up at him. "Now come on and push me around, Fat Antoyne, don't wait!" Besides which, she said, after they finished gasping and grunting at one another and Ruby rolled away to look at the ceiling, where did he get these ideas? She climbed up on the sink in the corner, sat there for a while, then got off again impatiently. She wouldn't piss now for half an hour, she said, as if that was Antoyne's fault.

"Ruby, at least run the water."

"I never saw anyone less like a human being than MP Renoko."

If you wanted Ruby's opinion, he was a Shadow Boy. He was one of those mysterious, almost metaphysical entities whose reign in the Halo predated that of the Earth people, and whose motives remained, even now, opaque.

"If indeed they have motives the way we do."

"Or if they even existed," Antoyne reminded her.

Ruby Dip waved this away.

"Wait 'til you owe those boys money," she said, "you'll find they exist! You'll owe them half your brain as well! One day they pull you in and collect," she promised him. "They're the gangsters, they're the cops: fact is, you don't know who they are. Don't you get it? They look just like you and me!"

Antoyne shrugged. "Hey, no problems."

If that was the way Ruby Dip wanted it, he said, that was OK with him. By then they were back on the bed again.

"No, this is the way I want it," Ruby Dip said.

Ruby's unreasonable anger at Renoko, it turned out, stemmed from an argument she had with him one lunchtime in the Faint Dime diner. It concerned the nature of kitsch. Renoko felt that kitsch was a product of an event he named "the postmodern ironisation," prior to which it could not exist: before that, the objects you could now describe as kitsch were actually trash objects. "Without the operation of irony on trash," he maintained, "there would be no kitsch." To him, the postmodern ironisation was like the Death of History or the coming Singularity. "Everything was changed by it. Nothing could be the same again. It had the irreversibly transformational qualities of a Rapture." He believed it had those qualities even now.

Ruby's commitment to body-art and collectible tambourines couldn't let this go unchallenged. Prior to the age of irony, she thought, kitsch was already established. "It was low art's idea of high art," she said—the aesthetic of people with no taste. Its keynote was sentimentality, not simply in conception but in use. Trash, for her, was another thing altogether, and it was with trash she found herself at home. A true low art, trash was the aesthetic of people who had no aesthetic, and in use it could almost be described as utilitarian. "In all its forms," she insisted to MP Renoko, "and across every media platform, trash is the art of demonstrating, celebrating—and above all getting—sex. It is a Saturday night art."

Antoyne scratched his head. "What happened when you said that?"

"What happened then was that a fist fight followed, which it soon drew in the entire lunchtime clientele of the Faint Dime, becoming a legend in its own time."

"It doesn't seem enough," he said.

"That, Fat Antoyne, is the big difference between us."

Because of the weird grimness of the work they do, Ruby believed, quarantine dogs live their opinions hard and proud: so it was predictable Antoyne wouldn't see such things as intensely as she did. Perhaps because of that it was good that their liaison retained its temporary nature.

They were standing outside the Faint Dime, 9:15 am. There was a smell of cinnamon coffee—a Dime speciality—and eggs. Morning light came down between buildings onto cracked tarmac. On Gravuley Street, everything else lay in grainy shade. It was like a black and white photograph, except for the triumphant pressed-steel values of the diner itself, caught in a ray of light and shining, as Ruby put it, "like this real future we are in, rendered with such impossible 3D fidelity as it is, in the language of algorithmic texture and image map!" A few weeks later, the job was over. Antoyne never saw Vera Rubin's World or The West Ural Nature Reserve or Ruby Dip again.

He never saw the huge baby either, though the memory of it gave rise to dreams in which he became certain it had found its way through the walls of Gravuley Street to him at last. And in the end, he wished he hadn't given his business card to MP Renoko. That gesture returned to haunt him too, because Renoko kept the card and later got in touch through Toni Reno, that well-known cunt; and that was how Fat Antoyne came by the mortsafe.

Five am, Saudade: not late enough to be morning, too late to be night. Fat Antoyne stood out on the loading platform and stared across the noncorporate port at the dawn, just then arriving in streaks of pale green and salmon over the distinctive silhouette of the Rock Church. He wiped his hands. The rag, which had originally been a white cotton singlet of Irene's, cropped short and bearing the slogan **HIGGS**, made him feel both horny and full of an almost nostalgic guilt. A little later, as if to further demonstrate his condition, Irene herself appeared, walking brassily across the windswept cement arm in arm with Liv Hula. They leaned into one another for balance—also a little forward as if compensating for a strong headwind—and sang. Irene was wearing a Vinci Nintendino bolero jacket featuring footlong alien pinfeathers dyed pink. In one hand she clutched her signature see-thru cosmetics bag; in the other a pair of five-inch heels, red patent leather and with an otherworld glow all their own.

"Hey," called Fat Antoyne.

They waved and called, "Hey! Fat Antoyne! Fat Antoyne!" as if it were a big surprise to see him there, 5 am, on the rocket ship they all three owned. Back on board the women tuned to Radio Retro and filled the air with old time hits, including "Ya Skaju Tebe" and Frenchie Haye's understated but durable version of "Lizard Men from Deep Time." They were sleepy, though prone to sudden inexplicable bursts of energy, during which they had brand new ideas about things in general. Soon, owlish yet prone to giggle, they too were examining the payload.

"Fat Antoyne, it's big," was Irene's conclusion.

"Do you think?" said Liv Hula. "It's not as big as I expected."

Fat Antoyne stared at them. "I could make you eggs," he said. It was a puzzle, the women often thought, how Antoyne maintained his new thin looks, when all he ever did was eat. "We could get eggs in the control room. Coffee and raisin bread too."

Irene hung from her arms around his neck.

She said, "Or—Fat Antoyne, listen! Listen, Liv!—we could take a rickshaw to Retiro Street and dance! Eat cake!"

Liv, meanwhile, bent down and peered into the porthole.

"Don't encourage him," she said.

"My turn," said Irene, pushing her away. "What's a mortsafe anyway?"

"I don't see anything much in there," Liv Hula said. "Can we have the lights on?" She sought out the bills of lading. "'MP Renoko,'" she read. "'Hard goods. D.i.f. Documents on site.' Where are we taking this?"

"Da Luz Field," Antoyne said. "Somewhere called World X. It's fifty lights down."

"Everywhere's fifty lights down, Fat Antoyne."

6: Skull Radio

The assistant rented her room from someone she knew, a woman called Bonaventure who ran a bar on Straint Street near the event site. At night the rocket launches lit the room's warm air like a bad tank experience, psychic blowback from the engines reinscribing the thoughts and feelings of the people who had lived there before her. They sweated out on to the walls in layers of swirled colours like graffiti written on top of one another. Maps, artefacts, butterflies from another world, all of that kind of thing. For some reason, the assistant didn't mind. She was used to it. She enjoyed it—although "enjoyment" was a word she had never used much about her own experiences. Sometimes she wondered whose dreams she was having.

The evening after she first heard the word "Pearlant," a man called Gaines walked in through the wall of the room. She understood instantly he was not one of the past's stories. His appearance made her afraid. In response, her tailoring switched itself on; but something he could do—or didn't even need to do—switched it off again, so that she came up off the bed hard and fast, then had to stand there in the middle of her own room, feeling naked and displaced, like a child who has made a bad judgement and sees it too late, while he walked around her to the window as if she was a fixed object, something almost interesting in a shop, something that wasn't in his way.

"This is a quaint place to live," he said, looking down into the street, which had once been gentrified but which was going downhill again. It was late. The bars and nuevo tango joints were opening slowly, their neon-cluttered facades pulsing and sucking. Ads patrolled the pavement with

34

the soft voices of children. Rocket dub basslines thumped in the walls. The street was opening like a glass anemone against the steepening food gradient of the night. "But all this cultural babble out here, don't you sometimes want a rest from it?"

"It's only what people want," the assistant said. She wasn't sure what people wanted.

"They mistake it for substance."

"I don't know what that means."

It meant that there was something down underneath all this, Gaines informed her. "It means that the world isn't all signs and surfaces."

She indicated the walls of the room, still imbricated and flickering with hallucinations, hard sweats, failed or partial communications from other planets. "How could there be?" she said. "Anything fixed? In this physics universe?"

He came away from the window then and stood close in to her, calculating and looking her up and down with a new interest. "Hey," he said, "I know there is because I've seen it."

He laughed. "And now it wants to see you," he said.

He was one of those men you don't know if they're older than they look or younger than they look. He had good skin and a smile which seemed satisfied with all the deficiencies of the world as they had revealed themselves to him. He possessed a deep, withering bitterness he thought he was hiding. Longish grey hair curling into the nape of his neck, maybe a little gelled to stay in place. Chinos and a polo shirt, light canvas shoes whitened with pipeclay—an outfit that meant something, she could see; an outfit that made references the assistant couldn't follow. He had a carefully trimmed grey beard which thrust the lower part of his face forward into the room. He had a good nose, too. But in the gloom and fading inflorescence of the launch, that was the important part of him, his jaw and his quiet blue eyes.

"You're from EMC," she guessed.

"Think that if you like."

"I wonder if you're here at all."

At that, he smiled again. "I'll be in touch," his voice said, from the empty air.

After he'd gone, she went to the window and looked into the street and tried to see what he had seen. Earlier that day there had been an escape of mathematics from the ram-head control loops of one of the visiting cruise ships, a big Creda Starliner. Daughter code, running on a substrate of nanotech and human proteins, had swum into some unlucky rocket jockey's vestibular lymph during the night. He had made it through port gate security before it began to change him, then he rolled around Saudade sneezing and buying drinks in bars. There would be outbreaks of new behaviour by dawn. The port was shut, and the uniform branch was touring its northern peripheries with sound equipment, advising people to stay in the house.

"You are all right if you have only touched yourself. You are OK if you have only touched yourself."

They were giving out a help centre number to call if you thought you were infected: no one would dream of going there, because in the middle term it meant only the quarantine orbit.

Meanwhile, Gaines was reporting to his colleagues at the Aleph Project. As an EMC fixer with a satisfyingly broad remit, Gaines occupied various different kinds of space, most of them electronic; although, as he said, some things he did went a little too fast for normal channels. There were actions he could do, assets he had access to, which didn't seem very physics. But when he reported to the project, it was in the ordinary way, as a holographic fetch, via a system of private FTL routers.

"She's not in touch with it," he concluded his report. "And if it's in touch with her, it's using some part of its personality we haven't explored yet."

He listened for a moment, staring into the air, then laughed. "She lives in this room," he said. "You should see it. No, she has no idea what she is—come to think of it, nor do I. She has ten-year-old datableed technology running probability estimates down the inside of her arm. What? Yes, some kind of cheap local police thing. What do you say? Welcome to the Halo, man." He laughed again and then his voice went flat.

"No," he said. "It's too early to bring them together."

But the next morning he appeared in the assistant's room again, carrying two plastic cups of coffee—one mocha, one Americano—and some pastries. This time he was wearing a light shortie raincoat, spotted with rain, over twill cargo pants. His bare chest was grizzled, and the skin had slackened around the nipples, over stringy but powerful-looking pectoral muscles. If he was younger than he appeared, some odd things had happened to him.

"So," he said. "Why don't we sit on the bed here?"

That was hard for her to understand. She slept on the bed, she sat in the chair. She didn't sit on the bed.

When he had got her to understand, he gave her some quite complicated co-ordinates, which even to the assistant implied an object travelling towards the Kefahuchi Tract. "If anything strange happens to you," he said, while they were eating the pastries. "If anything at all odd happens, why don't you dial me up? Better still," he said, "why not use this?" From his raincoat pocket he took out a thing like a cheap pressed-tin box with a skull in it. The box had a glass front. The skull was small, like a child's. Sometimes it seemed to have a body, like a baby's, a partial homunculus hanging part way through the back wall of the box; sometimes it didn't. "Skull radio," he said to the assistant. "It brings down most of the major vibes. Like sucking on the universe through a wide-bore straw. If anything at all odd happens, you give me a call on this."

"What for?" she asked.

Gaines smiled at her. "Because you don't understand yourself," he said. "Because you're bored. I'm leaving you the mocha, OK?" When he was happy, he had a passive, easy look.

The assistant watched him fade back into the walls. The raindrops never dried on his coat, she thought. They stayed fresh. How did a holographic fetch bring coffee? When he had quite vanished, she pushed the tin box as far away from her as she could, until it fell off the end of the bed and on to the floor. She didn't like it. To be sure Gaines had gone, she waited until she could feel her tailoring come back to normal; then she drank the mocha. She opened a secure pipe to SiteCrime and instructed one of her shadow operators to search the name Gaines. "And send me the car," she said. She took calls, and as a result of one of them, drove the Cadillac across town to the noncorporate rocket port, locally dubbed Carver Field. She manoeuvred between the tubby little tramp ships until she arrived at the bonded warehousing facility, where, forty hours after the crime occurred, she found herself staring up at the corpse of Toni Reno's loader.

Enka Mercury had risen five or six feet higher in the air since Toni Reno found her; but Epstein the thin cop, who had brought in a cherrypicker to get a closer look, thought her rate of ascent was slowing down. Like Toni, she was still joyfully circling some invisible point. Unlike him she had begun to fade somewhat. The colour leached out of her almost as you watched, Epstein said; at the same time she was becoming transparent. In a day or two she might disappear. He had been no more successful with Enka than with Toni. She wouldn't be caught. Whatever you did, she was out of reach. He stood shrugging apologetically in the chilly space of the warehouse and, indicating the flap of skin dangling from the vic's armpit, said:

"At least it looks like she was shot."

The assistant stepped into the cage of the cherrypicker and manoeuvred it all around Enka Mercury's corpse. Puffs of gas were emitted irregularly from its valves. After five minutes she set herself down again.

"What did you get from the operator I sent?" she asked Epstein.

Epstein shrugged. Like everyone else, he had been frightened the whole period the shadow operator was in the alley off Tupolev. Even the experienced uniforms had backed off to let it do its work. They'd rather stand in the rain all day at a traffic intersection than get near an operator. Dazzling light poured out of its mouth when it saw the corpse. "This is really *interesting*," it said, watching Toni Reno through a couple of revolutions as if he were an expert performer of some kind. It vomited some more light, then approached Epstein. It had to stand on its toes to speak to him. Despite himself, Epstein bent down so he could hear. "I've got a little secret," it whispered in his ear. Nothing else. "I've got a little secret," and off along the alley, turning back once to wave shyly—more at Toni Reno, perhaps, than the cops—before it disappeared into one of the buildings, the vaporous air opalescing briefly around it as if responding to some phase transition. That morning it was running itself on a seven-year-old girl—a local mite dressed in the customary white floor-length frock of white satin sprigged with muslin bows and draped with cream lace; also what looked like her mother's shiny high-heeled pumps—but its voice had three or four separate components, mostly male.

"What does anyone get from an operator?" Epstein said to the assistant.

"They live by their own rules," the assistant agreed. "Was it the one that calls itself The Sea?"

"I don't know which one it was," Epstein said, meaning he didn't care to know.

The assistant gave him an oblique smile. "It had on red fuck-me pumps," she predicted. "A seven-year-old kiddie in a wedding dress and red patent leather fuck-me pumps with five-inch heels, what do you say to that, you big hero?"

She dialled up her office and had them pipe over a holographic fetch of Toni Reno's corpse, so that she could compare Tony and his loader side by side. In those circumstances neither of them appeared exactly real. Enka Mercury was colourless except for the faint bluish tinge to her face and hands. Toni presented as if he had been imperfectly modelled in a mixture of brown, red and yellow tones. While she came across as coy as ever, he only looked preserved and shiny and as if he was made of wood. One of his Fantin & Moretti handcrafted moccasins had fallen off. The bodies circled at different rates until space seemed to adjust itself to accommodate them and they fell into a synchrony never experienced in life.

"You see that?" Epstein said. "It's like they're aware of one another."

"You're uncomfortable with that."

He shrugged again. "How does it happen?"

"Perhaps it's love," the assistant said.

Then she said: "Ninety per cent of what we see every day is an artefact of some other process. Of the things that are really going on." Epstein didn't know how to reply to that. "Don't you think?" she said. Then: "The investigator must always take account of that."

She stood companionably next to him for a moment, hands on hips, looking around the mostly empty space as if oil-stained floors and fluorescent warning stripes held an innate interest for her. Epstein didn't like the way she relaxed. He found her as disturbing at close quarters as the operator had been. She was too hard to avoid. Her tailoring occupied the warehouse like another personality: everything interested it, from a momentary change in Epstein's breathing to the sound of footsteps half a mile away. Every time its attention shifted, he caught the rank, exciting smell of hormonal gradients. She would smile at you behind that as if remembering something sexual you had enjoyed together, while pictographs ran chaos patterns down the inside of her forearm, from elbow to wrist like print from the historical times. She was some cheap cutter's idea of the future.

"I want to know when Enka disappears," she told him.

For the same reason, she explained, she would recommend they keep an eye on Toni Reno. In her judgement, she said, they were at a weird place with this. "But we won't know how weird until the next thing happens." There wasn't much else they could do unless The Sea had discovered something. She enquired of her office if Reno had any kind of Port Authority paperwork in process at the time of his death, and, learning that he did, went off to investigate. Epstein watched her leave, asking himself all the same questions her colleagues asked about her in the building at Uniment & Poe. The difference? Epstein's perspective on it was not SiteCrime perspective. It was cop perspective, and to him she resembled nothing more than some toxic one-shot personality the kids downloaded in Carmody on a Saturday night.

Unaware of these harsh judgements, the assistant made her way across the rainy cement of the noncorporate port.

Toni Reno's paper trail—chiefly bills of lading, along with some transcripts of FTL uplinker calls—led to a ship called the *Nova Swing*, a crew-owned HS-SE shorthauler well known to the Port Authority as what they called in those days a "petty mule." Like all those mules, *Nova Swing* was seen in every port on the Beach; today, the assistant found her parked on the southern edge of Carver Field waiting on freight from some point of origin two or three lights along. The crew of this brassy old three-finner were familiar to her from the Straint Street bars. More significantly perhaps, as far as the assistant went, they were the small change of Lens Aschemann's last case: a port whore named Irene, who had adopted the mona package early and done well on it; an ex-smuggler everyone still called Fat Antoyne, though he was slim and fit-looking now, tan from all those distant suns he visited; and Liv Hula, a retired rocket jockey. It was this third crew-member the assistant met with, up in the control room alone and just that moment plugging into the ship's mathematics.

A thin, grey-haired woman about fifty years old, she lay in the pilot couch stripped to a white cotton singlet and simple boy-leg underpants slightly too large for her, while a two-inch bundle of colour-coded wires forced its way into her mouth. Her head was turned to one side as if to facilitate this. Her eyes looked passively away. The wires pulsed and wriggled, inserting themselves deftly through the soft palate and into the lower architecture of the brain. As they connected, a cascade of busy, shivery movements went up and down her body like the beginning of an orgasm. In response there was a chaotic run of lights across the bakelite and grey-paint control consoles; a smell of hot insulation filled the room. Then, in a startlingly accurate imitation of Liv Hula's voice, the ship's speakers said:

"Really, everyone should try this. The sex never fails."

"You could not pay me enough money," the assistant said. "First it violates your mouth, then it crawls in your ear at night? And you die?"

The pilot laughed. In some phenomenological sense she was now the self of the *Nova Swing*, its identity. She was housekeeping its motors and systems, watching distant events with its senses. Being the boat, she sometimes said, relieved her of the burden of having a self of her own. To the assistant she boasted, "These are the pussiest mathematics. You should see what the grown-up stuff does." As she spoke, ki-gas primers fired off in one of the outboard fusion pods; servos ran up to a clingy high-pitch whine, then shut down abruptly. "Fuck it," Liv Hula complained. "Boundary layer turbulence. Antoyne?" she called. "Are you down there? Your fucking old machinery is on the fritz again." When no answer came she asked the assistant, "I wonder if you met Antoyne anywhere on your way up through the ship? Because as you see I am busy, and he could help you better than I can at this time." When she talked, a clotted buzz emerged from around the pilot wires, as if she was still trying to form the words with her mouth like an ordinary human being; her hands made small unrelated movements. Her body looked tired, fallen in on itself. "Could you find something to put over me? I'm cold."

The assistant smiled and nodded. It was forty degrees in the control room; humid. She said:

"I'm interested in your relationship of commerce with Toni Reno."

Liv Hula claimed she did not deal with that side of things. She added, in an aside, that Toni Reno was a well-known cunt, and a bad dresser besides. "You would have to ask Fat Antoyne about him. If you didn't see Antoyne on your way up here, he is probably having sex with Irene in their cabin. It's their habit this time of day."

"Captain, I'm interested to know if you loaded anything of Toni's recently." The ki-gas primers fired again. This time the fusion engine came to life, its deep groans of self-pity resonating in the vessel's gamma-ablated hull. Liv Hula laughed. "I'm not the captain!" She cut the engine and when it was quiet again, added: "My father gave me the soundest advice, 'Neither a follower nor a leader be.' For the *Nova Swing* we decided not to have a captain that way. It was a decision we all made."

"This is the paper on Toni Reno's cargo. Maybe you recognise it."

"Could you find something to cover me?" Liv Hula asked again.

The assistant went to the control room door, looked up and down the passageway outside, as if she might find what was needed out there. When you touched things in a rocket like this, your fingers came away slick with the generic talc of other worlds. "I see the three of you in the Straint Street bars," she called over her shoulder. "You get on so well together. Two or three nights a week you'll find me down there. Since Aschemann vanished, those bars are my responsibility." She had depended on Aschemann. His ghost, which lived among the shadow operators clustered in the ceiling corners of her office, was less use. Most of the time it was just a face. It often seemed to be warning her against something. "He taught me to look inward, at places like the Tango du Chat; then, in places like this, outward at the stars. I can never make my mind up what it is I see." In the end she found a pink cellular blanket at the foot of the command couch. It smelled as if someone had wrapped an animal in it. "Be sure and ask Fat Antoyne to dial me up over this Toni Reno problem. I'm always available, always interested in the things you do."

She drew the blanket tenderly up over Liv Hula's body. "Warmer now?" she said; and, pausing at the door before she left, "A space captain like you can afford nicer pants than those, honey."

The assistant thought of herself as someone unafraid to meet her own eyes. She looked into them every day but did not necessarily see anything there. She had her predictable circuit, at work or leisure. Mid-day, she could be found walking between the booths at Preter Coeur, where she knew by heart the fighters, the cutters, the chops; they were like an old-time collection of "stamps" or "cigarette cards" to her. Early mornings she parked her big pink repro car on the Saudade Lots, where the event site bled into its own aureole and something large but not quite visible could often be sensed repositioning itself in the rags of mist. In the evening it was the bars on Straint or the tank farm on C-Street—or she sat in her GlobeTown room, looking in the mirror, watching rocket-port physics crawl over the walls and trying out names for herself.

She tried "Sekhet," she tried "Sweet Thing." She tried "Roses," "Radtke," "Emily-Misere." She tried "Girl Heartbreak!" and "Imogen."

She tried "L1 Dominette."

She looked in the mirror and said: "She is too pretty not to get married."

7: England Calling

I n London, the weather had turned. Anna Waterman changed trains at Clapham Junction, and, taking the twelve-ten to Epsom, alighted at Carshalton Beeches. From there she walked east, then south under a sky that looked like both sunshine and rain, through long suburban perspectives off which the dense ranks of detached and semi-detached suburban homes—each with its hundred-metre garden and mossy old wooden garage—stretched towards Banstead. Not far from HM Prison Downview she wandered into a street she thought she might remember, entering the garden of the first house she came to. It was three storeys, detached, with gable-front dormers, walls done out in whited pebbledash, and clean bay windows on the ground floor. Clean windows were a counter-indication: the house she was looking for, Anna felt certain, would have dirty, unused-looking windows, as if the person who lived there did not place a great premium on seeing out. It would be a house turned in on itself.

Nevertheless she took the pocket drive from her bag just in case, and held it in one hand. If she was stopped, she planned to offer it as proof of her good intentions. She could say, "I came to return this," and it would be the truth. She was used to trespassing in people's gardens by now. She had never been caught anyway.

A short, weedy drive gave on to the garage, and a front garden where ilex and old roses greened in a fitful light. Standing up at the bay window, squinting between her cupped hands to eliminate reflections, she found herself looking into a room full of partly unpacked boxes and crusty dust-covers, as if someone had started to move in years ago and never finished.

Items of furniture, including mismatched dining chairs and a hospital bed, were shoved up against the walls, off which hung narrow triangular strips of wallpaper stiff with old paint. Unplugged electrical leads curled and trailed about the floor. The upper surfaces of everything, from the treads of the stepladders to the shoulders of the unshaded light bulb hanging from the ceiling rose, were laminated with the gritty dust that collects in unused London houses, baking on year by year like a specialised industrial coating. The effect was of a room abandoned but not yet used. At the rear, a door lay open—wide enough to admit some light, not wide enough to see if a similar dereliction prevailed the other side of it.

Anna was shrugging and moving away when she heard footsteps on concrete, and a boy of about sixteen came round the corner of the house, glancing back over his shoulder as if he had been up to something inside. He was dressed in tight jeans rolled at the ankle, a T-shirt too small for him, lace-up boots covered in drips of black and pink enamel paint. Such disorder had been gelled into his short yellow hair that it resembled an old scrubbing brush. When he saw Anna, he jumped in surprise and said hastily:

"I don't know what you think, but I've come to read to a woman who lives here. Sometimes I bring her a film, but mostly I read."

Anna, not knowing how to answer this, said nothing. The boy stared expectantly. He was shorter than Anna, and his face had a raw appearance, as if he lived in a blustery wind no one else could feel. Perhaps in an attempt to convince her, he held up a paperback book, thick, warped, browned at the edges of the pages. "She's an old woman," he said. "She's lived here years. Some people like her, some don't. She does her shopping down in Carshalton. She enjoys a film but it's always something old-fashioned, that old-fashioned kind of film she likes." He shrugged. "You want something more modern than that, don't you. My eyes get tired though, with all this reading. It's the dust. It makes your face feel tight."

"I came to return something," Anna offered.

The boy didn't seem to hear. He wiped his left forearm across his face and said, "I could read to you, too, if you like. That's an idea! I could come to your house and read this book." He held the book up again, and Anna, filled with fear and disgust, saw that it was a very old copy of *Lost Horizon*. Its pages were bunched and rippled where it had been dropped long ago into someone's bathwater; the back cover was missing. It might easily have come from the room she had been looking into.

"I don't think I want that," she said. "Goodbye."

"I never use the toilet here," the boy called after her, "even if I need to go. She's too dirty, the old woman." Anna lurched into a flowerbed, then away across the lawn. He thumped along behind her, without, she thought, making any real effort to catch up; then, as soon as they reached the road, jogged away towards the Royal Marsden hospital. "It's a good book," she heard him say. "I've read it more than once."

She hurried in the opposite direction until, out of breath, she reached Carshalton Ponds. The ponds lay under a leaden sky, two strange, shallow, purposeless, industrial-looking sheets of water separated from the road only by a railing, home to fractious ducks and gulls. Anna walked around them twice. I'm calming down now, she thought, surprised by her own resilience. He was only a boy. He was as guilty as me. To demonstrate calm to herself—to act it out—she bought a tuna wrap and an apple from the supermarket on the High Street. These she ate sitting on a bench by the water, while the young mothers more or less patiently urged their toddlers to and fro in front of her to feed the ducks. Sunshine came and went, but then it began to rain. To Anna, something smelled stale, perhaps the water itself, which had a light, cobwebby film, a skin of dust supported by surface tension; perhaps the birds pottering about in front of her. She hoped it wasn't the children.

Carshalton is served by two stations; to reduce her chances of meeting the boy again, she decided against Carshalton Beeches and made her way up North Street to the other one. It was closer anyway.

Arriving home an hour or two later, she discovered Marnie in the garden, frowning puzzledly over the contents of the flower-border at the base of the summerhouse.

"I don't know where all these have come from. Did you plant them?"

Anna, who had anticipated having her house to herself and felt put out, first claimed to have no idea; then, feeling that she ought to show some kind of authority, though she hadn't gardened for years, amended: "They're exotics, darling. I think they're doing rather well. Don't you?"

They were. Though none of them were tall, they occupied the little border with a kind of dense self-confidence. Slack, poppyish blooms predominated, but there was a form of lunaria too, and something that promised to uncurl into an oversized altar lily. The poppies had a curious brown metallic colour to their petals, which drooped from pale green fleshy stems, curved towards the top like the stems of anemones, as if they weren't made to support weight. Between them, lower down, as thick as a lawn, you could see the pubic tangle of a single dark feathery growth—similar to yarrow leaves but finer in construction—which seemed to repeat itself at every scale; you soon lost your place in it. There was no point in admitting that the border had fostered no poppies before today. "They look as if they're made of paper," Marnie said, separating the flowerheads with her fingers, bending the stems this way and that so that she could peer down between them—as if she had been thinking of buying them but was changing her mind. "Do you think they smell of anything? They're very artificial colours." She stood back, stared up at the summerhouse, and seemed about to speak further.

"Before you start," Anna warned her, "I'm not having it renovated, pulled down or redeveloped as a granny annexe."

Marnie looked disappointed but gave the most uncombative of shrugs. They stood there a moment or two more, listening to the liquid early evening notes of a blackbird in the orchard; then made the mutual if unspoken decision to go back into the house. On the way, Marnie said: "I thought we'd do omelettes."

"I hope you brought wine, Marnie, or you can bugger off."

While her daughter cooked the omelettes Anna made salad.

"That box of old things you found?" Marnie said. "I put them back in the summerhouse. They were just some old pin-badges and things from college." She laughed. "God knows what I was like," she said. "Early 1980s social science postgrad, fifty years too late. You'd have thought the world would change more in all that time." Her career in contemporary economic history prompted her to add, "But the money went, I suppose." There was, she believed, no money without change; no change without money. She poked about in the back of the fridge where Anna stored, for periods of fourteen days to three weeks, very small portions of leftovers: half a boiled Maris Bard potato, two dessert spoons of frozen peas dried up in a saucer. "What's in this awful bit of paper?"

"It's cheese, darling. Please don't make faces like that. I bought it because of the name. But then I forgot the name. It was something like '100 yards,'" she decided. "It's cheese. I bought it at the cheese shop in the village."

After they had eaten, they finished the bottle of wine. Marnie switched on the TV and surfed desultorily, sampling a reality show in which people were invited to queue for items they couldn't afford to buy; then *Ice Melt!* now in its fifteenth season; before fixing with an impatient sigh on the second half of a documentary which traced the slow demise of the great Chinese manufacturing cities of the 2010s. Anna was reminded of the images of Detroit and Pripiat popular in the early days of the century, when decline and reversal—quick or slow, economic or catastrophic—had seemed like temporary conditions, anomalous and even a little exciting. Long bars of light falling obliquely into the vast rubble-filled interiors of factories already stripped of everything from doors to heating ducts; smoky pastel dawns in abandoned flagship housing projects where drug addicts queued patiently for an early fix; vegetation pushing up through orbital roads closed to traffic less than ten years before; faded, uninterpretable graffiti: lulled by these dreamy images of dereliction, she felt herself falling asleep.

"While I was in the summerhouse," Marnie said suddenly, "I thought I heard something moving about."

"That James!" Anna complained.

"I don't think it was him. I haven't seen him since I arrived. If this is boring you, Anna, we could always watch one of those old films you like."

Anna shuddered. "I don't think so, dear," she said.

She thought she would call in the cat, then go to bed. She felt as if today had been too much for her. She couldn't forget the boy with the book, that was one thing—it was as if she had found him creeping around outside her own house: but there was more—

Huddled on the platform that afternoon, waiting for the service from Carshalton back into central London, she had watched rain spill out of a clear sky while a train from Waterloo pulled in on the other side and the station announcer warned everyone on board, "This is Carshalton. This is Carshalton." And when the train pulled away again, it had deposited half a dozen commuters, among whom she made out the old man she had encountered some days before in the café at Norbiton station.

He seemed disoriented. Long after the other passengers had gone, he stood trembling on the platform, looking bemusedly about, his underlip hanging loosely. The afternoon light slicked off his bald skull. His raincoat was undone. In one ropy-veined hand he clutched his walking sticks; in the other, a damp-looking brown paper bag, which, every so often, he seemed to offer vaguely to the empty air, as if expecting someone to take it from him. Eventually, two men did come and try to help him. He began to argue with them immediately, though he seemed to know them. While they were persuading him to leave the platform, Anna went out through the ticket hall and stood on the pavement outside. She couldn't have explained why. A single minicab waited in the parking area: after perhaps five minutes, the old man, now minus his paper bag, was ushered out by the railway staff, who manhandled him gently but firmly into the back of it. For a minute or two nothing happened except that he wound his window down and stared out into the rain.

"Found anything real yet?" Anna was prompted to call.

He gave her a cold, alert look and wound the window up again. The driver turned round to speak to him, but he didn't seem to answer. Taking a right into North Street, the cab was balked by traffic; as soon as things started moving, it vanished towards Grove Park. Anna imagined the old man sitting in the back alone, looking from side to side as the vehicle slipped between Carshalton ponds, listening for the faint action of his own blood. She wondered where he was going. She imagined him being driven back to a house like the one she had seen that afternoon. She imagined him meeting the boy with the bad hair there and though the picture was incongruous found that it had lodged itself as solidly in her world-view as Carshalton itself.

After a few minutes, the voice of the station announcer drifted out on to the forecourt again—"This is Carshalton. This is Carshalton."—its bland yet rawly self-conscious accents clearly recognisable as those of a fictional 1940s radio-operator, pumped up with the importance and strangeness of a brand new official medium. It had sounded, Anna now tried to explain to Marnie, as if he was auditioning for a part in an as-yet unmade Powell and Pressburger film. But Marnie, who had never been convinced by Powell and Pressburger, didn't seem interested.

"Can we turn this off, darling?" Anna said, piqued. "Because I find it rather depressing."

"England calling," she had expected to hear the announcer say. England calling, into night, bad weather and bad reception. England begging, with that desperate but almost imperceptible interrogative lift of the last two syllables, "Is anyone out there?"

8: Rocket Jockeys

The *Nova Swing* had history. Inside, she preserved the sort of worn out light that reminded visitors of a photograph from Old Earth. Her architecture smelled of metal, electricity, animals. There was a lot of time in her for a ship only a hundred years old, the residual time, you felt, of some improbable, uncompleted journey. Even when the Dynaflow drivers weren't running, the plates of her hull reported nauseous low-frequency vibrations, as if the ship were constantly making its way back from somewhere in order that its crew be able to occupy it. Liv Hula felt the same about her life. Early lessons were still working their way through: in consequence, even while she was completing it, an action often felt both tardy and experimental. And then, when you are a pilot, so much of you is externally invested anyway—in the ship, in the dyne fields—and may be increasingly unable to find its way home. "Home" being understood as some secure location of personality in space and time. This sense of displacement, perhaps, is what sensitised her.

Initially it was visible only as disorder in the schematics. At warm-up time, still aware of the thick, used taste of the pilot connexion in her mouth, she received fail reports from minor systems checks. There were fluctuations in power, barely detectible. "If we had wires," she told Fat Antoyne, "there'd be mice in them." Later, as she jockeyed the ship out of its parking orbit, she thought she saw someone enter the room behind her—a dark figure, oily and flowing in the way it moved, in and out before she could see who it was, quick but not somehow giving that impression.

"For fuck's sake, Antoyne," she said absently.

"What?" said Antoyne, who was a hundred feet lower down the ship, staring out a porthole at the Kefahuchi Tract, listening to Irene whisper:

"I will never get tired of these things we see!"

During the journey it stayed down by the holds. The onboard cameras disclosed a passing shadow in 4 or 6, but Liv was always too late to catch what cast it. There was movement at the top of a companionway, or in the central ventilation shaft. Later, she tracked it to the living quarters, but only as a discoloration of the air or a rubbed-out graffiti left by some bored supercargo forty years ago. These were isolated incidents. Saudade to World X proved to be the usual disorienting trudge. Irene fucked Antoyne. Antoyne fucked Irene. Out beyond the hull, mucoid strings of non-baryonic matter streamed past like Christ's blood in the firmament. Liv Hula tuned to the Halo media, where the breaking news was never good. Two days out she tipped the ship on its base, put them down neatly less than a hundred yards from the Port Authority building at da Luz Field, and lay there in the pilot couch too tired to disconnect, listening to the fusion engines tick and flex as they cooled.

Half an hour later, she woke up to find herself alone. She gagged ejecting the pilot connexion, threw up a handful of bile, sat disconsolately on the edge of the couch with her arms folded across her stomach. Monitors came to life. The nanocams had caught something in motion in the dark in the junction between two corridors: its appearance was half-finished, as if someone had begun painting a man on the air of the corridor then lost interest. The head, torso and arms were present though in need of work; from there it became notional until, around the navel, only a few shreds and rags of colour remained. It was the right height from the floor to have legs, but they weren't visible. Not to Liv Hula, anyway. As it began to turn towards her, she saw that the rags and shreds weren't paint after all but dark hanging strips of flesh. It was real. It was hollow. It was ripped and charred. She ran out of the control room, her arms outstretched in front of her, palms forward, calling, "Irene! Antoyne!" at the top of her voice.

No one heard her, and that gave her time to feel a fool. She stood on the loading platform in the glaring light.

That night she dreamed of her old friend Ed Chianese, incontrovertibly the great rocket jockey of his day. In the dream, it was the morning after Liv's big dive. Ed lay next to her. They were at the Hotel Venice, home to rocket sport bums of every description, but especially hyperdip jockeys between attempts on the photosphere of France Chance IV. Thick sprays of photons, most of them originating in that same photosphere, poured into the room, over-egging the yellow walls and prompting Liv to wonder out loud what the weather was like in the Bénard cells today. She was so happy. Ed was thinking about breakfast. At the same time the dream had him falling—the way Liv herself had fallen, with only the paper-thin hull of the *Saucy Sal* between her and it—into France Chance IV. "Ed!" she called, in case he didn't know. "Ed, you're falling!" Hot gas raged all about him, putting stark shadows under his handsome cheekbones. Caught in descending plasma at four and half thousand Kelvin, his hyperdip had lost confidence in itself and was breaking up. Those things were a neurosis with an engine.

Ed turned his head slowly and smiled at her. "I'll never stop," he said. "I'll always fall."

Liv woke up wet.

They spent some days waiting for Antoyne's contact.

Abandoned fifteen years earlier, after inexplicable climate shifts and abrupt changes in range and distribution of native species, World X's single continent was now a commercial limbo, its pastel spintronics factories and EMC-funded radio frequency observatories mothballed, its lower management dormitories and holiday resorts closed down. Da Luz Field continued to operate, but at reduced traffic volumes. The Port Authority maintained an oversight staff. The single small bar and pâtisserie, L'ange du Foyer, was little more than a handful of stamped aluminium tables set out in the blazing sun, at one or another of which Irene the mona could be found every morning after breakfast, wearing huge black sunglasses and drinking chilled marzipan-flavour lattes. Toni Reno's paperwork, weighted down by an empty cup, fluttered in the warm wind. By the third day it was grubby from being handled, covered with brown rings; by the fourth it seemed like an obsolete connection to another world.

Irene drank. Antoyne fixed the fusion engines. Everyone was bored. Liv Hula walked restlessly around the da Luz hinterland, a few acres of heat-bleached scrub and building projects fallen into disuse before completion. Thin black and white cats hunted across it, concentrating minutely among the rubbish and broken glass. Liv felt unusually centred, unusually herself; yet at the same time unable to shake her sense of being haunted. North, in the port suburbs, a few New Men still lived, treating the single storey white houses like nodes in a warren. They bred happily, but—quiet and subdued, uncertain what to do next—kept to the old suburban boundaries. The population remained at replacement rate. The males lay on the patios all day, masturbating in the unrelenting sunlight, and at night scoured the well-planned streets, ranging ten or fifteen miles at a time at a steady loping pace. What they were looking for they were unsure. On *Nova Swing*'s fifth day in da Luz, a group of women appeared at the port itself, to stand patiently outside the terminal buildings as if waiting, Liv thought, for tourists who no longer came.

When she said this aloud, Irene smiled. "We're the tourists, hon," she said. She removed her sunglasses, looked around in satisfaction, then slid them back on to her nose again.

The women brought with them a boy, Liv thought six or seven years old, thin and white, with a large round head on which the features seemed too small and delicate. He had wide eyes and an expression somehow both inturned and outgoing. He pottered about in the landing field dust, then, picking up what seemed to be a dead bird, came and stood as close as he dared to L'ange du Foyer.

"Hello," Liv said. "What's your name?"

"Careful, hon," said Irene.

The boy sat down in front of them and played with the bird, looking up occasionally as if for approval. The bird was grey and desiccated, its beak fixed open in a pained little gape. Its head lolled eyeless. Extended, its wings revealed iridescent bars of colour, green and dark blue, over which could be seen crawling hundreds of minute parasites. "Jesus," said Irene. The women stood twenty yards from L'ange du Foyer, listlessly watching this performance through the heat of the afternoon; then one of them came over suddenly, picked up the boy by his armpits and swung him away, saying something Liv didn't understand. She seemed to be trying to take the bird from him. The boy struggled grimly to keep it and, being set down, ran off.

Later, they all left. "It's cooler now," said Irene. "Why don't we have an ice cream?"

Later still, with the sunset lodged in the sky above the central massif, the boy slipped out from where he had been hiding. Before Liv could say anything, he had dropped the bird at her feet and run off. Without quite understanding herself, she followed. Irene the mona stared after them, shaking her head.

The boy made his way quickly through the suburbs. Every so often he stopped and beckoned. His feet were bare. A mile or two south of da Luz lay a line of steep undercut cliffs, the buff-coloured guardians of some ancient fossil beach. He ran to and fro along the base for a minute looking for the way up; finding it, he turned and waved his arms. "Not so quickly!" Liv called. He vanished. The cliffs swallowed the last of the light. The boy stared down at her as she climbed steps in a gully. All she could see was his head against the sky. "Infierno," he said quietly at one point. "Infierno." Above the cliffs long ridges of yellow earth rose to the dry central massif, where at noon the heat would ring in the dusty aromatic gullies and across the rocky pavements. Now it was faint night winds in the lava tunnels that threaded the country like collapsed veins. She stood at the lip of a *jameo*, listened to water thirty feet down, threading its way through the tumble of fallen rocks. Paths glowed in the starlight, so clever in their use of the contours that after a while she seemed to be finding her way without the boy. He was leading her, but he was less obviously there. She came upon him from time to time, squatting on a rock, or made him out half a mile away, a pale flicker against a hillside. If the route became difficult, he fell back; otherwise, she was on her own under the blaze of stars. In this way he brought her to a plateau strewn with rocks, the only feature of which was a low, ramshackle structure—bits of bleached, unshaped wood, stones piled on one another, a door banging in the wind—built over a *jameo*.

"I'm not going in there," Liv Hula said.

The boy smiled at her then, turning away and pulling down his pants, pissed loudly against the stones, sighing every so often, straddling his legs and tightening his buttocks, staring over his shoulder at her with a grin. It seemed to take a long time. When he turned back he had left his little white penis hanging out.

"Put that away," Liv said.

He laughed. "Here," he said, beckoning and holding open the door.

"I'm not going in there," she repeated. Then—as if she had arrived on World X for this purpose alone; as if the logic of every journey she'd made, including the brief pointless dive into the photosphere of France Chance IV, led here—she pushed past him. Inside, steps led down from the lip of the *jameo* to the floor of a lava tube perhaps twenty feet in diameter. Looking up at her with his arms stretched wide was a New Man, tall and thin, with a shock of red hair standing up from a wedge-shaped head. His limbs had the characteristic articulation, wooden in one joint, pliable in another. He looked anxious, like someone trying to act, in all good faith, an emotion they have experienced only as a set of instructions.

"Hello?" she said.

"Come down!" the New Man said. "Come in!" The wind closed the door behind her, opened it again. "If you have come for cock," he said, "you have come to the right place!"

He had it there, in his hand. Liv stared at it, then back up at his face, then around his house, the uneven walls of which, niched, limewashed and in places caulked with bundles of vegetable fibre, seemed clean and dry. He had used the old flow-ledges as shelves. There was a bare table with a white bowl and a ewer; some items of the sort the New Men collected, believing them to be from their lost home planet—perhaps art, perhaps just toys or ornaments. At one end a curtain, at the other a mattress, next to which he had laid out clean towels, candles, aromatic oils in handmade pots.

"You're the last of tourist trade," she said.

"Yes," he said. "They come for our cock. Look, look. Our cocks are a little different than yours."

"They are," Liv Hula said.

"But they work nicely. They work well for you."

"I'm sure."

"We can fuck you," he said, as if quoting from an advert.

He had the resinous, warm New Man smell, a little like creosote, but not entirely unpleasant. His cock was, after you had got used to it, just a cock. What Liv enjoyed was the surprising calm he made her feel despite his own anxieties, a kind of temporary erasing of her own life that had nothing to do with sex. It was an easing of the memory of herself. In the end, she thought, perhaps I came here for that. When she woke in the morning, the lava tube was empty. There was a trickle of water behind the curtain, which she used to wash in. She wandered along the flow shelves as if she was in a shop, picking up his things and putting them down. She left money on the table. The child reappeared and led her back down to the rocket port at da Luz, which she saw with proprietary amazement a long way off through cool air and soft, floury light. There was the *Nova Swing*, standing up on its fins like the flying buttresses of a brassy little cathedral! Under daylight the landscape wasn't so barren as she had imagined. The gullies and lava tunnels were often full of cool green vegetation: shafts of sunlight fell on constant little rills and trickles of water. She soon outdistanced the boy, who seemed preoccupied.

Just before noon, crossing the cement field through the heat ripples, she saw Fat Antoyne and Irene outside L'ange du Foyer, talking to a small, old-looking man she took to be MP Renoko. No one was sitting down. There was a lot of gesticulating and raised voices. Antoyne waved Toni Reno's paperwork about and said something; the small man shook his head no. He wore a shortie single-breasted raincoat over a yellowed woollen singlet and tapering red trousers which ended halfway down his calves; black loafers.

His agreement with Toni Reno, he said, was that no one got paid until all the items were delivered to an as-yet-undetermined location. He had the second one here now. That was the way it was. Irene snatched the paper off Antoyne, made eye contact with MP Renoko and tore it in half. He smiled and shrugged. She put the pieces down on one of the aluminium tables with exaggerated care before walking off.

Liv Hula, unwilling to become involved, avoided everyone's eyes and went into L'ange, where she ordered frozen yoghurt.

Irene came in behind her and said, "I'll have one of those too, but I'm getting vodka in mine." They sat down and watched Fat Antoyne and MP Renoko walk off towards the edge of the landing field, still arguing.

"Who does that little shit think he is?" Irene asked.

Liv said she didn't know. "Well I do," the mona said, as if she had won an argument. "I do."

"I don't like the beard he has."

"Who does?" said Irene. "I suppose you had a good time last night?"

When Liv smiled and looked down at her yoghurt it was already full of flies. Later, the three of them stood in the *Nova Swing* main hold examining what Renoko had left them: another mortsafe, a metre or two longer than the first and floating a few inches higher off the floor, tapered to both ends and much more knocked about.

"There should be a viewing plate," Antoyne said, "but I don't find it."

You saw these things in all the old travelling shows, MP Renoko had explained. They were pressure vessels. The carnie narrative was they contained an alien being: people paid to stare in, maybe their kids would bang on the tank with a stick, everyone went away happy. This one, riveted like an old zinc bucket, had streaks of corrosion, sublimated sulphur and char along its sides, as if it had been through a recent low temperature fire or failed industrial process: some event, Fat Antoyne said, with barely enough energy to boil a kettle. After that it had been stored in damp conditions. It was more work to move about than the first one. And if you put your hand underneath it—which he didn't recommend anyone did that—it would be microwaved.

Liv Hula shivered.

"Sometimes I hate it in here," she said.

Irene laughed darkly. "'As-yet-undetermined,'" she said. "That cunt Toni Reno has let us in for it again."

9: Emotional Signals Are Chemically Encoded in Tears

Last practitioner of a vanishing technique, with specialisms in diplomacy, military archeology and project development, R. I. Gaines—known to younger colleagues as Rig—had made his name as a partly affiliated information professional during one of EMC's many small wars. He believed that while the organisation was fuelled by science, its motor ran in the regime of the imagination. "Wrapped up in that metaphor," he often told his team—a consciously mongrelised group of policy interns, ex-entradistas and science academics comfortable along a broad spectrum of disciplines— "you'll always find politics. Action is political, whether it intends to be or not."

Some projects require only an electronic presence. Others plead for some more passionate input. Today Gaines was in-country on Panamax IV, where the local rep Alyssia Fignall had uncovered dozens of what at first sight seemed like abandoned cities. Microchemical analysis of selected hotspots, however, had convinced her they were less conurbations than what she loosely termed "spiritual engines": factories of sacrifice which, a hundred thousand years before the arrival of the boys from Earth, had hummed and roared day and night for a millennium or more, to bring about change or, more likely, hold it off.

"Close to the Tract," she said, "you find sites like these on every tenth planet. You can map the trauma front direct on to the astrophysics."

They stood on a low hill, planed to an eerily flat surface about five and a

56

half acres in extent, thick with dust despite the scouring summer winds, and covered with the rounded-off remains of architecture. There were pockets of vegetation here and there in the avenues between the ziggurats—clumps of small red flowers, groups of shade trees under which Alyssia's people gathered each mealtime to rehearse their sense of excitement and optimism. They were discovering new things every day. A white tower of cloud built itself up in the blue sky above the mountains to the south; smoke rose from an adjacent hilltop which seemed to be part of some other excavation. In the end, Gaines thought, anything you can say about ritual sacrifice is just another act of appropriation. It reveals more about you than about history.

"So what's different here?" he said.

Alyssia Fignall glanced away, smiling to herself. Then she said: "It worked. They moved the planet."

Suddenly she was looking direct into Gaines' eyes, deliberately seeking out his soul, making contact, her own eyes wide with awe. "Rig, everyone has been so wrong about this place. That's why I called you! A hundred thousand years ago, using only sacrifice—mass strangulation, we think, of perhaps half the population—these people moved their planet *twenty light minutes* out of orbit. We think they were trying to keep it in the Goldilocks zone. There's evidence of increased stellar output," here she shrugged, "though to be realistic, it's not high enough to explain much. In the texts we found, they don't seem to be able to describe exactly what they're afraid of. Soon after that they give up—vanish from the historical record."

"Possibly they had some regrets," Gaines suggested.

"Not in the way I think you mean."

They stared silently across the hilltop, then she added, "They were some sort of diapsid."

"Alyssia, this is a result."

"Thank you."

"What do you need?"

She laughed. "Funding."

"I can get you more people," he offered.

He received a dial-up from the Aleph project. Alyssia moved away a little out of politeness, her feet kicking up taupe dust with a high content of wood-ash and wind-ground bone. Her people were finding thick bands of the same substance in polar ice cores; there, it was glued together by fats.

She was still excited. That morning, aware she would be seeing Rig again after so many years, she had picked out a short sleeve knit sweater in red botany wool, fastened with a line of tiny faux-nacre buttons along one shoulder; pairing it with a flared calf-length skirt of faded green cotton twill. Her thin tan feet said she was in her forties, but the sunshine and the clothes celebrated only enthusiasm and youth. Gaines stared at her with a kind of absent pleasure, while spooky action at a distance filled the FTL pipe and a voice he recognised said:

"About an hour ago we got uncontrolled period doubling, then some kind of convulsion in the major lattices. It's jumped to another stable state."

"Is it still asking for the policewoman?"

"Like never before."

"Anything else?"

An embarrassed pause, then: "It wants to know everything about domestic cats. Should we help it with that?"

Gaines laughed out loud. "Tell it what you like." So many years in, and they didn't even know what the Aleph was. They could be programming a computer, they could be talking to a god. They weren't even sure who they were working for at EMC. But Gaines had the complex professional philosophy of any good fixer. "Keep going," he ordered. "In a situation like this all the benefits are at the front end. Later we find a way out of the consequences." Most projects seem minor, irrelevant: big or small, cheap-and-cheerful or funded at the planetary level, they always remain oblique to the real world. Others flower when you least expect it. They become your own. They lodge right in your heart.

"Get me a K-ship," he said.

SiteCrime, fifth floor, Uniment & Poe: a slow morning. Bars of light from the slatted window blinds fell like weight across the policewoman's shoulders. Shadow operators clustered viscously in the ceiling corners. (Once or twice a week, the ghost of her old employer could also be seen there. This apparition had been less use to her than she hoped. It consisted only of a face—the face of the older Albert Einstein like a photograph under water, its eyes distended, its mouth opening and closing senselessly—which seemed to be warning her against something.) Her desk was heavy with reports. In Saudade City, topology itself is the crime. While the rest of the planet can offer nothing more bizarre than rape or murder, Site-Crime—the frail human attempt to bring order to a zone which cannot be understood—must deal with boundary-shifts, abrupt fogs of hallucination, a daily illegal traffic in and out of the event site—people, memes and artefacts no one can quite describe. The assistant busied herself with these puzzles. Bells rang faintly in the distance. At approximately eleven forty, shouting could be heard in the corridor outside and she was called to one of the basement interrogation rooms. Two or three days ago, atrocities had occurred down there under cover of a nanocamera outage only now repaired. The fifth floor was alive with accounts, substantiated and otherwise. "It smells like fresh meat," someone reported; someone else said it was like war had broken out in their building. Everyone, anyway, wanted a piece of it. Alarms were going off. In-house fire teams, weighed down with hand-held thermobarics and bandoliers of Chambers ammunition, grinned out of every lift. The assistant took the stairs. Halfway down, something so strange happened she never reached the basement. An emergency door opened on to the echoing stairwell in front of her and the figure of a woman emerged on to the landing. She was tall, built, shaven-headed, looking back over her shoulder, finishing a sentence with a word that sounded like "Pearlent." At that, the assistant raised her hand. "Stop!" she called. Her tailoring launched but would not come up to operating speed: instead, she saw the world at a subtle wrong angle, as if she was someone else, with annunciative light pouring in a dazzle down the stairwell. The figure turned towards her, mouth open in a laugh she couldn't interpret, and whispered, "Don't jump, babe!" Half blind and full of inexplicable dread, she watched it vanish round the next turn in the stairs. Footsteps hurried away. Lower down, a door boomed closed. Nothing else. The assistant sat down, breathing heavily, nauseous with waste chemicals from her own overdriven systems. They had not been interdicted from outside; they had simply become emotional and confused. They were all right now.

She left the building, and later turned up at Sharp Cuts, a downscale tailor parlour on Straint, where the owner, who had made his way to Saudade City after an accident in an Uncle Zip franchise nearer the Galactic core, took one look at her and said:

"I can't do anything for someone like you." At the same time, his clients that morning—half a dozen gun-kiddies from the beach enclaves of Suicide Point, in for a midprice growth blocker called *7-4eva*—were leaving by the back door. Five feet from the assistant you could smell the heavy metals in her blood, the hiked ATP transport protocols, the immune system add-ons: they would be enough to drive anyone away. Among other gifts, she could hear naturally to 50 kHz, then process up to 1000 kHz by frequency-division, heterodyne and expansion systems, the product of which was delivered as one of a hundred realtime visual overlays. Her skin, infrared sensitive, reported to biological chips laid in subdermally on a metamaterial mesh. These kinds of cuts weren't police, or even SportCrime. She had Preter Coeur written on her at every biological scale. You could smell the animal smell of the fights, the chemicals in her tears. She encouraged the tailor to come out from behind his counter and stepped in close to him.

"Try," she said.

He would look at anything but her—out the window, all around his storefront. His own hormones had come up in some half-forgotten response. He was trying not to feel helpless. "I've seen you up and down the street," he said. "This stuff of yours, it isn't just some franchise job." She smiled and asked him his name, which he gave as George. She said he shouldn't talk himself down. He was just the expert she needed. She said she thought she might have an ion channel problem. "You should go to Preter Coeur," he tried to persuade her. "Here we just do the cheap bolt-ons." She made him meet her eyes. He went and found a six-regime loupe, which looked like a child's stereopsis toy from the deep historical times, and she jumped up on one of his cutting tables where he could insert probes.

"I don't get most of this," he said after a minute or two. "I'd be scared and confused, I met you on the street."

"George, you're scared and confused in here."

"Keep still," he cautioned her. "Jesus," he said, after a minute more. "They wired everything through the amygdala. You ever act without knowing why? Cry a lot? Use metaphors? Who did this to you?" He poked around in her ion channels. "Forget I asked that," he said. He said she could get up, she might feel as if she had low blood sugar for a time. It wouldn't be much. "You got Kv12.2 expression issues. When they tuned the neuronal gates for spatial perception, they put Kv12.2 on a hair trigger. Every so often that's going to fall over, you'll see damping of the potassium channel. What happens then, the nerve cells fire excessively."

The assistant stared at him.

"It's nice when you talk like that," she said.

"They put a control loop in but someone like me can't unpick it. You hear any voices when this fault happens? Speak in tongues? See anything odd?"

"Everything I see is odd."

"Kv12.2," the cutter said, "is a very old gene."

He washed his hands under a tap he had at the back of the store. "Even a fish has it. Are you going to kill me?"

"Not today, hon."

She left, but almost immediately came back.

"Hey, look, Tango du Chat is just over the road!" she said, as if she had only just discovered that fact about the world.

The parlour filled up with her rank smell again. Outside, the sun warmed each shabby frontage, picking out the unlit bar sign across the street—a black and white cat dancing on its hind legs—while two monas in pencil skirts and seamed nylon stockings gossiped at the intersection of Straint and dos Santos; inside, it was matt-black walls, dust. There was a smell of stale lipids in the air around the proteome tanks, with their rows of LEDs and torn posters for year-old fights, long-dead fighters. The tailor, rigid with disquiet, looked away from her as hard as he could. His anxiety flipped suddenly into depression. "You got Preter Coeur written all through you," he said, "but no one signed the work. This isn't something they would do for a sport fighter. There's military stuff in there too."

"So do you want to get a drink sometime, George?"

"No thanks."

"Yes you do," the assistant said.

Later, as puzzled by her own motives as anyone else's, she left him in the bar listening to Edith Bonaventure play the sentimental accordion solo from "Ya Skaju Tebe"—2450's favourite song—and drove herself up Straint Street, through acre after acre of industrial dereliction and out on to the Lots, where she slipped her '52 Cadillac quietly into the row of cars already parked there, on the cracked expanse of weed-grown cement in a long curve facing the Event site.

The cloudbase was down since lunch, Saudade City afternoon rain coming on. Fifty yards into the gloom, she saw rubble and sagging razor wire. Beyond that the landscape crawled constantly, as if uncomfortable with itself, or as if you were viewing it through water flowing on glass. Further away, you could make out unfamiliar objects being tossed up into the air by a silent but convulsive force. This force, though it had been given many names, was as impossible to understand as the objects themselves, which, scaled in incongruous ways—giant crockery, huge shoes, ornaments and jewellery, bluebirds and rainbows, tiny bridges, tiny ships and tiny public buildings—were so unconstrained by context that they seemed less objects than images, collaged on to a further image of bad weather and ruined landscape. They rose, floated, toppled, thrown up as if by the hands of a gigantic, bad-tempered, invisible child. The assistant shook her head over all this. Cars came and went around her; something big broke the cloud cover and settled near her briefly. (It brought an extra pressure to the air, along with heat, feelings of invasion, the stink of metamaterials and intelligent nanoresins. Then it was gone.) Finally, she started up the car and drove off at walking pace across the cement. Every afternoon was the same: rickshaws and sedans arrived from all over the city to take part in this drive-in of the Saudade soul. By 3 pm the Lots were rammed. A fluttering, soft-focus carnival of mothy adverts filled the air above each car. In the darkened rear seats, someone always had their floral print up round their waist, laughing and grunting at the same time as their friend drove them into a corner in the luxury smell of leather. No one was afraid of the site any more. They came openly, just to enjoy a fuck in its aureole of weirdness. It was quantum sex, the news media said, and could even be good for you. Some of them were going as far as to leave their vehicles and wander the empty streets and piles of rubble in the mist beyond the wire, picking up objects they thought might make souvenirs.

These were not precisely crimes. What was she to do?

Still later, R. I. Gaines banged on the door of her room.

When she opened the door, he was laughing and running his hands over his scalp. The shoulders of his coat were wet—this time it looked real. "Hey!" he said. "I hate the rain, and I bet you do too." Behind him, the port was full of activity. The shadows and lights of alien, fiercely contradictory theories-of-everything poured across the field: three ships landing at once, one of them the General Systems "New World" starliner *Pantopon Rose*, in from a four-week tour of Boudeuse, O'dowd and Feduccia XV. Gaines, too, gave the impression of having just arrived back from somewhere. His skin was a little more tan. He wore a bit of bright red cotton as a neckscarf and carried, in a loose bunch, some dusty-looking flowers the same colour. A small cheap suitcase rested on the floor by his leg, as if he had just set it down. The assistant, who felt nothing at all about the rain, stood in the doorway and stared at him.

"First you open the door," Gaines coaxed her, "then you let me in."

"Why?"

He held out the flowers.

"Because I brought something for you."

Eventually she took the flowers and turned them over in her hands. She had never seen a red quite like it; but the stems were flimsy and brittle, already dry. One or two fell on the floor.

"I'll sit on the bed," she said. "You can sit in the chair."

Gaines gave her an alert look. "Have you invented irony?" he wondered aloud. In her room, by contrast with the mayhem over at the port, some fleeting piece of physics had washed and softened the light. He placed the suitcase carefully on the bed: its clasps being snapped, complex fields sprang to life, radar green on a velvety black backdrop, unwinding in endless strings around a strange attractor. Additionally, the case contained generous lengths of scabby rubberised flex and a pair of bakelite headphones clearly included for show. "Look inside," Gaines said. "See this?"

"Are you really here this time?"

"First look in the suitcase," Gaines said, "then we can discuss that."

She looked.

Immediately she felt herself transported a thousand light years from Saudade City, out somewhere in Radio Bay, inside an EMC outpost so secret even R. I. Gaines had difficulty finding it. Her viewpoint toppled about at high speed. It was jerky and full of interference; once stabilised, it had a curiously assembled feel, as if it had been built up from three-dimensional layers. What the assistant saw was this: a trembling grey space with echoes and a sense of walls far back, and somehow suspended inside it a single perfect teardrop of light so bright she had to look away. It was the tiniest instant. Even her tailoring couldn't slow it down. A tear, immobile but constantly falling, so bright you couldn't really see it. Then darkness came down, the viewpoint gave the impression of tilting violently, and the image of the tear repeated again. By the third or fourth repetition, "tear" had somehow translated in her mind to "rip": at that everything stopped, as if such understanding could be, in itself, a switch.

She felt elated. "I don't know what that was!" she said. "Do you?"

"It's a thing no one should admit to knowing about. Not you," here, Gaines gave a wry smile, "not even me.

"We call it the Aleph. We believe it's very old. When we found it, no one had been near it for a million years—perhaps more. When we ask it about itself, it asks for you." It was an artefact at least a million years old, he said, the deepest problem anyone had encountered to date in Radio Bay: a built object as far as could be understood, a machine constructed at the nanometre length, the purpose of which was *to contain a piece of the Kefahuchi Tract itself*. "You see it like that, as a series of repetitions," he said, "because we're catching it in the Planck time. You can't see it for longer because it's already in its own future, already something different. The pause between images is lag, as the instrument tracks it quantum to quantum."

The Aleph, he said, was buried inside an abandoned research tool the size of a small star: and recently the thing it most asked for was her. The assistant stared at him, then down at the suitcase.

"Is it in there?"

Gaines shook his head. "It thought for a week, then it asked for a police detective on a planet no one had ever heard of."

"I don't understand what I was looking at."

"For now," Gaines said, "we think it's wise to keep the two of you apart." He closed the suitcase. "Given the weirdness of this." He added, in a kind of aside: "When we use the word 'constructed,' we don't rule out the idea of self-construction." Then he said:

"We had some trouble finding you from the description it gave."

10: Down to the River

Anna Waterman got up early and walked through Wyndlesham village to the downs. She preferred the village empty. Just after dawn at that time of year a soft, grainy light warmed its pantile roofs, flint facings and herringbone brick garden paths; the only thing moving was a cat.

From behind Wyndlesham church she took a muddy lane, then steepening chalk paths up through hawthorns to where the remains of a second village, long abandoned, lay like a geographical feature, a series of intimate sunken bays floored with sheep-cropped turf. Stands of elder had overgrown the old walls. What presented itself at first as a chalk bank, cut deeply by the footpath, suddenly revealed ends of Georgian brick. Anna loved that sense of enclosure, and then, as you walked further up the hillside, the way everything opened again suddenly to wide grassy re-entrants, long ridges dotted with isolated hawthorns and patches of burnet rose. She loved the way the wind opened everything out and moved it along.

By the time she reached Western Brow, the sun had come out. Skylarks went up and down like elevators in the clear air; though the curve of the downs obscured it, she could smell the sea; northwards the Low Weald stretched away towards London, scattered with villages in the morning haze—Streat, Westmeston, St Johns Without, then Wyndlesham itself, built around a bend on the B2112 not far from the Lewes Road. The village would be awake by now. Sought after because it was close to the Downs but out of their shadow, Wyndlesham was the sort of place where, even in these harsh economic times, everyone kept a pedigree Australian cattle dog.

On the walls of The Jolly Tinker you could examine tinted reprographs of Victorian farm labourers, their impressive facial hair and rural machinery; but at Sunday lunchtime, only brand managers, retired CEOs and bankers of every stripe, especially investment bankers who had made their money before 2008, could afford to drink there. Their SUVs saw only trophy mud; their wives, though they rode well, in tight little jodhpurs and shiny boots, did not come from riding families.

Light struck off an opened bedroom window; the man who owned Dainty Dot's Café & Bookshop came to his door and shook out a mat. Two or three ponies, suddenly delighted by life, ran about in a paddock. Looking down on the cat-slide roofs and higgledy-piggledy main street at 8 am on such a perfect morning, it was hard to find anything to dislike. Then a van drew up to deliver the impressive range of French fermiers—air-freighted in with the dew still on them twice a week—for which the cheese shop was justly renowned, and you saw that while it yearned for vanished values, Wyndlesham had long ago priced out any representative of them. Anna set her back to Ditchling Beacon and the upland wind and walked east, where, beside the broad, flinty, footworn reach of the South Downs Way between Western Brow and Plumpton Plain, she came upon a clump of the brown poppies that had colonised her garden.

Up here, they grew taller and more vigorous: rather than being defeated by the wind, they seemed to thrive on it. The stems rattled together. The flowers yearned upward into the streaming light. Anna got out her phone to take a picture of them for Marnie, but, becoming nervous, put it away again. She touched the coppery, foil-like petals in wonder and astonishment. Thinking that she could hear something, she knelt down and listened to them. Nothing; or nothing she could be sure of. Nevertheless she shivered. Then she let the wind and the glory of the skylarks usher her into the downlands—out of which, an hour later, still feeling blessed and strange, she emerged at an unexpected angle, having lost her way. She found herself descending steep chalky ground into sweeps of water meadow and low-lying pasture dotted here and there with thistles, dog rose and spreading bramble, where willows lined a small river winding through. This composition was spoiled only by the house that stood to one side of the pasture.

A four-bedroom new build in the 1990s, assembled from unremitting pale brick and still looking like an architectural drawing, it hadn't weathered. Its profile was low, yet it was clearly not a bungalow. There was a patio like a hard standing for machinery. The white lattices of security grilles, which from a distance looked as if they had been taped on, divided every window. Sunshine glittered off the clutter of photovoltaic and hot water panels set into the shallowly sloping roof. The only character it possessed lay at the end of its long asymmetric garden: a few trees inherited from some previous, more authentic dwelling on the site. Something resembling life would be lent it each spring by the energetic scraping conversations of the starlings that nested in its gutters. Otherwise, it reminded Anna of a cheap toy abandoned on a carpet; something unable to age because of the sheer purposive artificiality of the materials used to construct it. If it was familiar, she realised, that was because it was her own house.

"I'm not sure I like it any more," she told Dr Alpert that afternoon. "I can't explain why."

But she could. Too many rooms like plaster boxes. Too much furniture that had aged but somehow never gained character. Clothes she no longer wore. A car she never drove. It was less a house than a place to store things.

"Every room is a box-room," she complained.

"Are you sure it's your house we're talking about?"

Anna laughed. "I have three toilets," she said. "One in the en suite, one in the house bathroom and one downstairs. Who needs three toilets? I wake up at night wondering which one to use and wishing I lived in a single room again. I know exactly what I'd want. I often imagine it."

Dr Alpert was interested in that.

"Tell me about the room you imagine," she said.

"Why?"

Because it's been a slow session, the doctor thought, and we might as well have met for tea somewhere instead. Because a wet afternoon had followed the promise of the morning. Because, she thought—glancing out of the consulting-room window at Chiswick Eyot, then down at her desk where the open case file, a vase of pale yellow narcissi and a box of Kleenex lay like something more than themselves in a clear puddle of watery light—the Thames is up as high as the road and nothing is drearier than rain on the tideway. Because today you seem like such a nice ordinary woman.

"Because it's interesting," she said. "Oh come on, Anna, what fun!"

"Well, I'd like it to be wooden," Anna said. "But less like a garden shed than a beach hut. Or if it was brick I would want it wainscoted." White wainscoting to shoulder height, then dove grey paint above. Bare floor-boards painted the same grey. One good-size window behind curtains of heavy, off-white linen featuring thin vertical stripes in ice-cream colours; a similar curtain across the door to keep out the draught. No pictures on the walls. That's all she saw, really. Her imagination ended there. Obviously there'd be a bed, a chair; they wouldn't take up a lot of space. Nothing that forced itself on you, she thought, although perhaps a bedspread or a rug, something bright that captured the eye. "I'd like a shelf or two of books, but no more." A lot of books would pass through her room but not many would stay. "If I couldn't have a view of the sea from the window, then I'd want a quiet garden which perhaps belonged to someone else but they never used it. I would know them but I wouldn't be involved with them. When I think," she said, "I see it mainly as autumn or spring. In winter I would hope to be somewhere else. Somewhere warm."

She was describing the summer house, she realised, or an idealised version of it. She was imagining how she might end her days there. She began to cry. She couldn't stop. "I feel such a fool!" she said.

Helen Alpert watched her for some moments, a satisfied expression on her sharp features. Then she pushed the box of tissues across her desk.

"Take as many as you need, Anna," she recommended.

The rest of the day Anna was prone to weep suddenly for no reason; on the platform at Clapham Junction, at home in front of the TV news. Exhausted by the effort of it, she went to bed early, and dreamed she could feel a needle penetrating the inside of her gum. It was a sensation difficult to interpret: not painful so much as certain and invasive. She knew that if she thought about the needle, it would go in elsewhere too. Wherever her concentration was, there it would go. She would feel it slipping into her chest, high up; feel it touch the collarbone—not prick, but just touch it—on the way out, just momentarily rest against the bone as it was drawn past. She had no idea why this was being done to her, although she believed it to be her own fault. Saliva filled her mouth as if she could taste the needle—as if the taste of it was a branch or possibility or consequence of the feel of it. That thought made even more saliva come. She woke up to moonlight—tireder than ever and convinced that someone had just spoken—and went down to the kitchen.

"I'd give anything," she told James the cat, "for a night of beautiful dreams in which someone really wanted me."

James, padding disdainfully about around her legs, indicated that he would like to go out. Anna opened the back door and watched him run off towards the orchard with his tail up.

A minute later, for no reason she understood, she slipped into her shoes and followed him. He soon vanished beneath the apple boughs. "James?" She left him there, listening at the small tunnels in the grass, and went to the back fence to gaze across the water meadow.

All evening a benign weather system, stalled over Europe, had been pulling warm air out of Morocco to drape across the southern counties like a shawl: it was a night that smelt faintly of cinnamon, prone to faint mists. The light of half a moon lay across the field like the light in some wood-cut—forgotten before Anna was young—in which the shadows of figures fell a little too strongly across the ground. Everything was roughened by that raw moonlight, especially the grass. Anna, who thought she saw a small oblique shadow make its way in quick, low dashes and pounces from thistle to clump of thistle, let herself out of the garden and went down to the river, to which everything stretched away.

The water lay in short serpentine reaches, black and shiny between willow and elder. The soft earth bank, stamped down by generations of ducks, was churned anew each morning by excitable Labrador dogs. Anna stood for what seemed a long time, like someone listening. She took off her shoes, tugged her white nightdress over her head, and, having bundled them together out of sight, waded into the river until she felt it push insistently at her upper thighs. Oh dear, she thought. Who swims alone at night? Dr Alpert would find it interesting; Marnie—who, seven years old, some scraps of sinewy brown nothing in a red swimsuit, had loved to be towed around in the river by her father, coming in late to meals all summer—would judge it irresponsible. Anna took one lurching step back towards the bank, then, changing her mind again, knelt down and launched forward, careful to keep the water out of her mouth. The river accepted her. It was warmer than she expected, the current amiable and slow. Midstream, a faint narrow track reflected the sky; but the shadows were bulky and like objects in themselves. She swam fifty yards slowly; after a further thirty turned on her back; then—arms out, feet together—allowed the stream to take her and float her along, past a line of poplars, between some darkened houses, through the village and out again. Wyndlesham appeared drenched in starlight but condemned by its own pleasures: litter and dog-droppings, discarded paper tissue, the bleak poached turf of the sports field with its goalposts as luminous as bone, a concrete culvert, a used condom hanging from a branch over the water, long gardens from which Anna heard quiet voices or loud bursts of music. Beyond that used space, out along reaches fringed with reeds and rushes, between long fields sloping shallowly up to woods, it was no longer the river she knew. The current strengthened. The water, its motives discernibly its own, moved darker and heavier between the banks. Anna wasn't being swept away but she was certainly picking up speed, while the Moroccan air grew warmer still; and the night, clear and white to begin with, tinted itself a sourceless neon pink. Pink then blue, then both, then neither, a colour as faint and sourceless as neon seen a street or two away, as if the fields themselves were gently broadcasting it. Copper poppies nodded and swayed over the water in a warm dry wind. Bit by bit she began to see things. Long shadows from short objects, falling across the landscape like pointing fingers—stones, simple, slate, shattered, still upright, tumbled about at all angles. Then large isolated figures with a look of two dimensions, very still, placed at curiously precise distances from the river bank like some exercise in perspective. Complex in silhouette, uninterpretable except as Seventeenth Century illustrations of satyrs, they were men with the rear legs of horses. They had the cocks of horses too. Really, they were quite big. Their heads were turned away in three-quarter profile, frozen in stylised attitudes of listening. They meant her no harm: it wasn't certain they knew she was there. And beyond them so much was going on—bustling city streets, noises like a building site, powerful beams sweeping a horizon which had withdrawn and was withdrawing still, to a considerable distance. That was the place, Anna suspected, where things would change completely and suddenly; if you left the water and walked up there, you might begin to learn things you didn't want to know. Up above, subtly pulsing stars: a great ragged arc of them pulled and pushed into chaos by the black radio winds Michael Kearney had spoken of so eloquently before he walked into the sea. Michael Kearney, afraid of everything, yet rendered almost like an ordinary person by sex, for a brief time able to have feelings. Past every surface, he had taught her, at every level, things were so wrong and inhuman: get below any surface and instantly you saw how wrong things were for us. "Forget all the anthropic crap," he used to insist. "None of this made itself for us." His own advice would frighten him and he would be ready to fuck again. Anna had always felt like the calm one in those situations. "I was the least damaged one," she told herself now, looking up at the stars and then down at the satyrs in their inexplicable landscape, each one looking out of the corner of its eye at her, a faint sidelong glitter of intelligence, self-awareness, self-regard. She was leaving them behind now. They looked quite small again.

Five minutes later, the night cooled and darkened. The fields were fields again, washed clean of mystery. The river widened and slowed, pooling into the shape of a long glass, a champagne flute perhaps. A fierce steady rushing sound filled the night. Anna pulled herself into the bank and listened: water plunging over the old four-foot broadcrest weir at Brownlow, perhaps a mile outside the village; beyond which the river, bending east to look for a way through the downs to the sea, would lose confidence and, a few miles further on, somewhere above Barcombe Mills, submerge its identity in the Ouse. Part-beached, Anna sat contentedly in the warm shallows, letting the water support her legs so that they bobbed and glimmered out in front of her, just beneath the surface. A small grey moth flickered about. She could smell guelder rose, night-scented stocks from some distant garden; and above that the replete, weighted, yeasty scent of tonne after tonne of water pouring over the weir. I don't feel in the least tired, she thought. Seeing herself with a sort of loving amusement from the outside, she wondered what she might do next. A minute or two later she was crossing the pool step by difficult step, hugging the upstream side of the weir itself, pummelled and deafened by the roar, struggling to move her legs against the vast, steady sideways pressure of the water. Halfway over, something made her stop. She dipped one hand into the shining flow across the crest—it was like pushing at the shoulder of some big, steady animal and feeling it push back. What else was there to do? she would ask herself later. Once you saw a thing could be done, what else could you do but try to do it? Shiver with excitement, laugh aloud as the water shoved your hand about, stumble out on the other side and walk the mile home along the river bank in your sodden knickers. She had a powerful urge to pee. It was dark, and who, after all, would see? She felt very calm and satisfied, even when, trudging back across the pasture with her wet shoes in her hand, she saw that her summerhouse was on fire again. Great silent orange and yellow flames went up from the roof at the same odd angle as before. There was no smoke. There was no smell of smoke. The summerhouse seemed taller, and as if it was leaning away from her. Heat shimmer gave it a squat conical shape like a windmill. Glorious showers of sparks, blown in a strong wind despite the dead calm below, lit up the crowns of the orchard trees beneath. Beneath the sound of the flames, she thought she heard a voice calling her.

"Michael?" she whispered. "Is this you? Are you here?"

There was no answer, but Anna smiled as if there had been. She dropped her shoes and opened her arms.

"Michael," she begged him, "it's safe to come back."

But if it was him, he was as afraid as ever, and as Anna let herself in through the gate, her face turned up and tightening in the heat, the fire went out. She stood there in the dark, caught between one movement and the next, between one feeling and the next—until, just before dawn, she heard the birds waking up and let herself back into the house.

11: Empty Space

Nova Swing, out from Saudade—via da Luz Field, World X—to an unnamed destination. She chewed and foraged her way along. Her hull shook with dyne fever. Down in the main hold, the mortsafes lay, old, alien, not good to be around. They had fallen into a sort of synchrony: every time Liv Hula made a course change, they turned slowly to regain their original orientation. They seemed aware of one another, Liv said, though no one else believed that; they seemed inert until they thought you weren't looking at them. She wouldn't go in the hold alone. She spent her free time plugged into the ship, reviewing the internal surveillance data. Meanwhile, Irene the mona stared out the portholes and marvelled at all the wonders of space, and you could hear her say:

"Don't you know, Fat Antoyne, that three old men in white caps throw dice for the fate of the universe?"

No, Fat Antoyne said, he had never heard that.

"Their names are Kokey Food, Mr Freedom and The Saint. Another thing: these three play not just for the universe's fate, but the individual fates of every person in it." They threw the dice, of which, she said, there were a different number according to the day they played on, and at every throw they would say something in a ritual way, such as "Heads over ends!" or "Trent douce" or "Down your side, baby!" sometimes speaking singly and sometimes all together. One or all of them would clap their hands sarcastically, or blow on their fingers to indicate scorching. Or two of them would smirk at the third and say, "You fucked now, sonny," which at least could be understood by a normal person.

"So you've seen these dice guys?" Antoyne enquired.

"In dreams I have, Fat Antoyne, yes. And when I say that, you need to stop looking at me, in your precise way you're about to laugh at me. Because a dream is a kind of truth too." Antoyne laughed at that, and she pushed him off the bed. "They pay and they play, Fat Antoyne. And if they ever stop? Why, their faces slacken and crumple. And those old men weep."

Why was that, Antoyne wanted to know.

"Because," she said, "they look out into the same unmeaninged blackness as you and me."

Fat Antoyne looked at Irene and thought that he loved her. He wished he could be truer to her, and so did she. She said: "What they see, it's beautiful but it's dark. And there's no way to know what it is, not even for them."

Just then, alerts rang softly through the ship, and Liv Hula's voice came out of the speakers.

"We're here," she said.

Although, she added, she didn't know where here was.

MP Renoko's co-ordinates, a skein of figures and symbols compressing eleven dimensions to a single point in the dark interstellar medium, at first revealed nothing: then an orphaned asteroid drifting towards the Tract, into which it would be absorbed after an uneventful journey of less than half a million years. "We've got a structure of some sort in orbit around it," Liv Hula was able to confirm. And then: "It's a wreck." Later, as she steered an eva suit into the dark, a single riding light glimmered to no purpose against the dim yellow rim of the asteroid. Data flickered in her helmet head-ups. "No activity," she said. It was as she expected. A very old nuclear powerplant could be detected inside, towards the prow of the wreck. It was lightly shielded, and had been designed with no controls or moving parts, as a single mass, like an Oklo reactor. At the stern end, chemical engines and a Dynaflow driver: first-class equipment bolted on less than fifty years before. It looked as if someone had made an attempt to salvage the wreck, machining new parts at a base on the asteroid, then giving up when test-accelerations broke it in two. "I don't know how they found it in the first place. Modern cosmology tells us that if there's an arse-end of the universe it's probably here." There was a click. "I'm approaching the fracture now." After that, communications would remain poor for the duration. Back on the *Nova Swing*, displays showed the feed from her headpiece cameras failing briefly before offering a series of uninterpretable still pictures of hull plates, detached structural members, and sudden voids which seemed to imply a completely different spatial relationship with the asteroid. Miles of cable had unreeled into the void. "Sorry," she said. "There's interference in the pipe." Then: "I'm in now." A cross section of the wreck would have revealed brittle, organic-looking structures of tubules and fibres in faded blues, purples, pinks and browns. Inside, however, it was dark. Curiously leaning speleothems divided the passageways, which eventually gave way to more recognisable architecture. "Whatever this started out as, it wasn't a ship. I think it might have been an animal. The ductwork and cabling was laid in by hand. Even the hull is a retrofit. It's an afterthought. I'm getting near the reactor now." There was a long pause, then: "Jesus. Holes." Fifty million candlepower jittered around an undefinable space, throwing the shadows of pillars at odd angles on to the walls. "Are you getting this?" She was in some sort of chamber. Wherever she looked, perfectly straight, perfectly circular tunnels, half a metre in diameter, had been bored through the ancient organic mass. They displayed the surface glaze of high-temperature events. "This is new. About the time of the salvage attempt, or perhaps just before. Fuck. What's that? *What's that?*"

The light flew about the walls, then went out.

A further silence.

"Antoyne? Antoyne? Are you getting this? Antoyne, something's in here with me."

Up in the pilot room of the *Nova Swing*, shadow operators whirled around, their hands to their faces, whispering:

"What has she done now? Oh, what has she done now?"

Fat Antoyne got out of the crew quarters and into the pilot chair without thinking. "Accept," he told the systems, and then, as the connexion burrowed its way up through his soft palate, causing him to sneeze, then vomit without warning, remembered he was a man who had sworn never to fly again. The systems were all over him as soon as they sensed that. For a moment, struggling to shut down the navigational software, he felt as if he was seeing in too many directions at once. His identity was gone. He seemed to be throwing up endlessly. Everything stank of rubber, then—as the ship tried to calm him down—of gag-reflex dampers and some kind of low-grade norepinephrine reuptake inhibitor it was pumping into him.

"For fuck's sake," he told it thickly. "Just get me alongside."

pSi engines fired in the dark. At the same time, the vacuum took on an ionised look. Phase-changes rippled through a smart gas of nanodevices, billions of tiny cameras poured between the two vessels like milt. Despite that, Fat

Antoyne, his connexion still partial and unstabilised, remained blind.

"Hey, Liv," he said. "Liv?"

Nothing. Then static in the pipe, and a distant noise like gak gak gak, the sound of the galaxy talking to itself in FTL bursts.

"Hello? Antoyne?"

"For fuck's sake."

"Antoyne, I'm sorry. There's nothing here. I got disoriented."

Wearily, Antoyne began to close down the pilot connexion. "Welcome to the club," he told Liv Hula.

"Antoyne! Bodies! Bodies!"

According to the names stencilled above their faceplates, she had found one third of the original salvage crew. Arranged as an element in a tableau installation or primitive waxwork, the title of which might be *Death Site XIV* or *The Final Exploration*, MENGER sat, legs splayed wide and shoulders slumped, at the base of the wall, the headpiece of her eva suit nodding forward, hands resting lightly between her thighs. SIERPINSKI, posed awkwardly on one knee as if proposing, proved in fact to be writing on his suit forearm the word "curvature." Was it less an observation, Liv Hula wondered, than a warning? "There isn't a mark on either of them," she informed the *Nova Swing*. Which of them had died first? The woman, certainly, seemed caught in the very act of giving up. Was there an element of solicitude, even tenderness, in the way SIERPINSKI leaned towards her? The tunnel, narrowing here and split into three by curiously marbled and streamlined pillars, curled over their heads like a frozen wave. Unwilling to look into the dulled faceplates, an act which would turn discovery into voyeurism, and frightened less that she would see MENGER & SIERPINSKI than that she wouldn't, that the suits would prove to be abandoned and empty, Liv skirted them and went on. The dial-up remained open but silent, until she remarked suddenly, "The whole wreck's been penetrated again and again from the outside. Hard to guess when." The closer she approached the reactor, the more openings she found. Here and there, yellow Tract light fell from one of them in a slanting beam on to ductwork or a sheaf of cable; low level ionising radiation lent everything else a bluish glow. She heard her own breath: behind that, Fat Antoyne coughing and choking into the dial-up pipe as he tried to extricate himself from the ship's systems. Behind Antoyne, the familiar FTL interference everyone describes differently, but which Liv always heard as distant shouts of alarm. "I've got the reactor in front of me." It was in a containment vessel the size of a house, around which the original material of the wreck had tried to grow. Pipes led in and out of this fibrous crystalline mass. "They pumped water into a slurry of 235U, it vented itself as superheated steam on a five-hour cycle." She consulted her head-ups. "Decay levels indicate it was last operating in the Devonian period of Old Earth. It's not attached to an output device. God knows what it was for. All it ever did was raise its own temperature a couple of hundred degrees. I think it might have been an environment for whatever lived here originally." On the *Nova Swing* they experienced a long pause. Then: "Antoyne, I heard the same noise as before." A dull buzz, at sufficiently low frequencies to feel as if it had not so much invaded her nervous system as *replaced* it, this was accompanied by sensations of vertigo and a metallic taste in the mouth. Later, the chaotic pans recorded by her helmet cameras would reveal only a bluish, mucoid blur. "I'm heading back." As she turned to leave, it was obvious that something was in there with her after all. "Antoyne? Are you getting any of this?" Her visual feed went down, and for a minute or two only broken phrases could be heard from her, "shiny lacquerwork," "domed head" and repeatedly—"Antoyne?" Liv dragged herself and her equipment through the fibrous corridors. It was like being lost inside a major organ. Behind her, she could sense the artefact tunneling its way impassively towards her across the pumice-like structural grain of the wreck, bursting out of one wall only to disappear instantly through another. She imagined it waiting there for four hundred million years. Had it hunted the salvage crew the way it was hunting her?

Irene the mona, though she loved space, would often wonder what caused people to want to be out in it. If you asked her, it was almost entirely a visual experience anyway. Sometimes those billowing towers of gas, infused with hyacinthine light, ripped by shockfronts from, whatever, exploding quasars and like that, were beautiful; sometimes they only seemed monstrous. Irene preferred warm, solid-earth cities, where on a rainy day the windows of each retro-shop and tailor parlour glowed with personal options. She preferred the lights, the saxophone music, the pink and purple ads like moths, the souls which sprang so readily to meet your own. All phony, all gorgeous. But it was also a fact that she could not be entirely a stay-home girl. Because someone had to handle the fiscal and aspirational sides of the enterprise that was Saudade Bulk Haulage, not to mention human resources!

"So here I am," she told herself aloud, "out among the stars and galaxies, which I have to say look almost as remarkable as a new pair of Minnie Sittelman fuck-me pumps." Around that time her name was called on the ship speakers: "Irene, Irene," followed by a noise of gak gak gak.

She found Antoyne lying on the control room couch in a puddle of sick, both hands clutching the bundle of coloured pilot wires as if he had been trying to rip a snake out of his mouth. His knees were drawn up to his chest and he was shaking. If Antoyne had a secret, Irene believed, it was that he didn't do well alone; but there were days, too, when he didn't seem to do well even when he had people to look after him. "Honey," she said, lifting his head and tenderly detaching the wires, on the gold tips of which she was able to discern tiny specks of brain matter, "this is not your job, and you really need a shave too." Antoyne threw up again and rolled off the acceleration couch.

"Am I here?" he said.

"Yes, Antoyne, you are here all right."

The control-room displays came to life suddenly. In them Irene could see: jerky fragments of light bobbing along ribbed slick-looking tunnels; shadows caught by a panicky glimpse behind; misleading images from the gas of nanocameras now investing the wreck. Everything was processed to look "real," arriving pre-assembled as a narrative from selected points of view, a software psychodrama in which Liv Hula dragged herself along, surrounded by a slow explosion of cable ripped off the walls during the salvage attempt. Through the eva faceplate her lips could be seen opening and closing, though nothing came out. Behind her, clearly imaged and yet difficult to understand, something was emerging from the tunnel wall.

Irene, who had no intention of allowing the ship any time inside *her*, took a moment to study the manual filter options. Then she shook Fat Antoyne awake. "Honey, I need you."

Antoyne crawled back on the couch. He cleared his throat loudly. "Fuck," he said.

"I wish there was time for that, I really do."

Antoyne adjusted the displays but soon gave up the attempt to interpret what he was seeing. "Why is it drilling holes everywhere?" he said.

"We can none of us know that, Fat Antoyne."

Liv Hula found herself at a junction she recognised. The tunnel split into three. MENGER knelt solicitously over SIERPINSKI but wrote "curvature," as if he was thinking of something else. For her part, SIERPINSKI stared down at the floor as if it had betrayed her. They had died the way every entradista expected, doing what they wanted to do, and now cast three or four shadows each in this tableau of escalating bad luck. It was, in short, the classic entradista soul-fuck, which Liv recalled with great contempt. "Come *on*," she was heard to urge them, looking back over her shoulder: "Everyone is culpable here, guys." Then, exactly four minutes and thirty-two seconds later: "For fuck's sake, Antoyne, I'm back at the reactor housing." She was tired. Her senses were dull. She was running out of air. If she didn't do something soon, the eva suit would perform an emergency spinal puncture, reduce her metabolic rate by twenty or thirty per cent, set its FTL beacon and await extraction. They would find her sitting on the floor, head slumped, legs splayed, HULA stencilled above her faceplate, another identical fuck-up in the house of fun. Behind the reactor she discovered the rest of the salvage team, tumbled together in a heap. Unlike MENGER & SIERPINSKI, her head-ups told her, these bodies had high residual radiation counts. They were armed with hand-held thermobarics, but seemed to have made no attempt to use them. Backed against the reactor housing, too tired to take any further action, watching a low-grade dosimeter alarm blink on and off in the side of her eye, she tried once more to raise the *Nova Swing*. "Hello? Are you getting this?" A two-minute gap, during which she seemed to whisper fractiously to herself before calling out, "Christ! The reactor's heating up again!" For Liv, yellow light fell through blue. There was a dull buzz, less a sound than a vibration in her central nervous system: a moment of vertigo. Then an object half a metre in diameter and two metres long emerged stealthily from the tunnel wall beside her. It was made of some slick black ceramic. Along its sides, bizarre reflections from the context could be discerned as a calligraphy of dim blue splatters. It slipped out of the wall, two or three feet up, blind-looking but with an air of intelligence. It knew she was there. It was at her elbow. When she looked away, it bumped and pushed at her thigh. Her whole body filled with the taste of metal. She turned her head and tried to puke clear of her faceplate. Nothing else happened, except that when she left, the artefact followed her attentively out into empty space, its blunt nose never more than ten inches away from her left hip. Comms sorted themselves as soon as she cleared the wreck. The first thing she heard was Antoyne's voice.

"Jesus, Liv, where have you been? Liv, if you can hear me, we believe the thing you saw is the item we were sent to collect."

"Fuck you, Fat Antoyne."

After they attempted to store it separately, the new cargo drilled its way through the bulkheads until it could float between the other items in the main hold, its surface spattered with reflections which didn't quite match the lighting pattern. It seemed newer than the others. It was certainly less knocked around.

"You could shop for it," was Irene the mona's conclusion.

She licked her finger and touched. Tiny electric feelings! She liked it for its shiny values and—now that it could be examined more closely—those faint, smooth, organic deviations from the cylindrical that made its front end such a lighthearted phallic parallel. Fat Antoyne approached with more caution, and though the object allowed itself to be examined with a basic six-regime loupe, learned little. He couldn't date it, he said. It was alien. It was ceramic all through, although deep inside he found minutely structured variations in density which he took to be high-temperature superconducting devices.

"We'll never know," he said, implying that someone else might.

Still shaken and sweating, with her electrolyte levels shot to hell, Liv Hula refused to enter the hold, confining herself instead to the pilot cabin and a determined program of rehydration coupled with shots of Black Heart no ice. These puzzles had such nightmare significance for her, she said, she was reluctant even to join the discussion: but she had revised her estimate of the object's age.

"I think the salvage team brought it with them."

Although what they had intended to do with it, she had no idea. If, as rumour had it, MP Renoko had begun stripping the assets of Sandra Shen's Observatorium & Native Karma Plant at around that time, perhaps they had acquired it from him, sight unseen as illegal items often were. Maybe it was some kind of mining machine. "As for *this*," she said, bringing up a blurred image of the Oklo reactor down in the wreck, "what to make of it?" After four hundred million years of downtime this crude artefact was back on its five-hour cycle, venting hot steam into empty space for no purpose known to man. "I don't think they were connected with one another at all."

MENGER & SIERPINSKI haunted Liv's dreams from then on, seen waving to her through a radioactive glow, their headpieces enigmatically empty.

12: I Am Not Renoko!

Gaines took his suitcase and left.

In the following days, the assistant tried to forget what she had seen. Routine being as important to her as ever, she sat in her car, she sat in her office, she sat upright in the immersion tank on C-Street watching herself come. Everywhere the job took her, she thought up names for herself. She tried Ysabeau, Mirabelle, she tried Rosy Glo. She tried Sweet Thing and Pak 43. She was a police detective, in the street and in her car, looking in the wing mirror, signalling left or right. Day and night the town surrounded her with all the elements of her profession: gun kiddies cruising the shadows, cutters up to their elbows in the black heart of humanity, trade goods smuggled down from the stars; soft intuitions, sneaking suspicions. She was taking notes, making reports. She was sitting at her desk while shadow operators crawled about among the papers like old cobwebs and dusty, unfinished hands. She tried Shacklette, Puxie, Temeraire; Stormo! and Te Faaturuma. She dialled up the uniform branch and asked for Epstein.

"That hauler you boarded," he informed her: "It's long gone from Carver Field."

She opened the *Nova Swing* paperwork across one wall. A picture of Epstein's face appeared on another. "What's a 'mortsafe'? It says here they took on a 'mortsafe.'"

"You're the educated one," Epstein's face said.

He'd been at the Port Authority all morning, drinking java from a paper cup; then in the port itself. "Enka Mercury's still here," he said. She was

80

high in the warehouse ceiling now, the colour of oily smoke and tars, as transparent as soap. She was still hanging open under one arm. Still dead. From a distance the flap of skin resembled torn cloth. "Get alongside Enka in the cherrypicker, you'll detect what I'd call a faint but definite smell."

"She's still rotating?"

"Toni Reno too," the cop confirmed. "Although Toni seems a little slower today. I can provide footage of that."

The assistant advised him not to bother, and had him wait while she examined the transit manifest. Cargo was given as: mixed cargo. Port of loading, Saudade. Port of discharge: New Miass, on some rock named Kunene, a hundred lights nearer the Tract. "Here's something odd," she noted. Shipper, consignee and the "notify party" were all the same: one MP Renoko, trading as FUGA-Orthogen, a limited liability operation with all the quantum uncertainty you expected in the Halo—if you knew who ran it, you didn't know what it did, and vice versa. She asked Epstein what he thought of that, and Epstein said he had no opinion. FUGA-Orthogen, it turned out, dealt mainly paper—rights to the images of dead minor celebrities, brands no one bought into any more—but also owned the remaining assets of a once-popular travelling entertainment, Sandra Shen's Observatorium & Native Karma Plant, aka The Circus of Pathet Lao. "Fifty years after he picked them up," the assistant told Epstein, "this man Renoko is moving the assets of a circus around the Halo under the guise of commerce." She read on. One of those assets, it seemed, was an HS-HE cargo hauler, sold as-seen five years ago through a third party to Saudade Bulk Haulage: who renamed it *Nova Swing*.

"Fat Antoyne," the assistant said to herself, "you are a dark horse."

She asked Epstein if he had ever been to Kunene. Epstein said he hadn't, but he thought it wasn't far up the Beach.

Unaware of their desultory exchange, Rig Gaines was on a visit to one of his less demanding projects. This corroded cylinder—about fifty feet long by twenty in diameter, cold enough to chill ham, smelling inside of hydrazine and unwashed feet and known to Gaines as "the Tub"—was heading towards the K-Tract at just over walking pace, piloted by his old friend and ally, Impasse van Sant. Though it rarely produced anything marketable, Gaines liked the Tub. He liked to spend a morning there, drinking Giraffe beer while the pilot brought him up to date.

Keeping in mind EMC's culture of hip self-presentation—not to say its preference for conservatively leveraged joint venture structures with local partners—Gaines kept silent his collaboration with Imps von Sant. Last of the genuinely human beings, Imps passed his day in shower sandals and cargo shorts, often matched with a slogan T-shirt, which might read **SHE's UP YOU, MAN** or **YbAlB4** (pronounce that "yibble before"). In addition he cultivated a range of mid-Twentieth Century conditions from gingivitis to dry skin and had, over the years, grown fat. This old-school viewpoint was what Gaines enjoyed about Imps most: his work being more difficult to fathom. Half the experiment—designed off the shelf a hundred years before to identify strange materials in the big dust clouds and expansion fronts at the edges of the Tract—was broken, while the rest produced data not from outside but from in, giving van Sant a running commentary on its own processes he had begun to describe in his reports as "a cry for help." Needles swung across their dials, redlining jerkily until the Tub's shadow operators woke up murmuring:

"It's not right, dear," and "It's too much to ask."

When Gaines arrived that morning for the weekly performance objectives review, he found van Sant hammering with the heel of his fist on a zinc box about a foot on a side and enamelled green, from which a pair of independent eyepieces dangled on cloth-covered flex.

"I used to be able to see something in here."

"Forget that stuff," Gaines advised him, "and give me a beer."

"It was a view of mountains," van Sant said.

He scratched up a quart of Giraffe, then banged the box again. "Mountains in one eye, and something else in the other, I forget what. No, wait. A lake! That's what it looked like to me."

"Really?"

Gaines had his doubts about the quality of these images—neither did he believe them to be informative in themselves. The instrument, acquired knock-down at the usual Motel Splendido fire sale, was operator-tuned: there would be some way of seeing, something you did with your head, which performed that trick of cross-correlation. Squint though he might, Imps van Sant had never got the knack. He wasn't tailored the right way, though a certain natural shrewdness enabled him to observe:

"It was what they added up to that made the difference."

"You don't want to worry about that," Gaines told him vaguely. "Have we discovered anything this week?"

"Your guess is as good as mine."

They drank beer, then played table tennis in the crew quarters using a new ball Gaines had brought along. The game being a version of his own devising, its rule-like structures and boundary conditions changing visit by visit, Gaines won. Shortly after that, carbon dioxide levels were raised sharply all the way across the Tub environment. Alarms went off. Van Sant had to suit up and go outside—where the ongoing tantrums of probability self-cancel to vacuum—and hit something twice with a wrench; then they had to dump the greenhouse and start again. By then it began to be time for Gaines to leave.

"Biology," he said with a chuckle. "Don't you just wish you could do without it?"

"Very funny."

After his friend had gone, Impasse van Sant sat tiredly in the bottom half of the eva suit and told himself: "I hate going out there. I can feel that thing looking at me." He meant the K-Tract. Gaines felt differently about it, he knew. Like everyone else, Imps had very little idea how he fitted into his friend's schemes: but he sometimes thought that Rig visited the Tub because it was the only place he could relax. Rig loved it out in the dark, away from everything human. Van Sant felt less than comfortable with that. Some time ago—too long ago, perhaps—he had become aware of the Tract hanging up there in front of him, year on year like a huge boiling face—stripped, raw, raddled with Bok globules and dust lanes, flattened and stretched laterally by poorly understood relativistic effects, heaving with emotions you couldn't recognize.

It made him feel routinely anxious. It made him feel alone. So as soon as he was sure Rig Gaines had gone he opened a spread of communications channels and whispered into empty space:

"Hey, babe. Are you out there?"

No answer today.

The assistant booked a ticket to Kunene. Tide-locked with its local sun so that one side froze and the other cooked, this medium-sized venue a few lights into the Bay offered a single habitable time-zone known as "the Magic Hour." Rare earth oxides had kick-started Kunene's first phase of commerce, but it was the Magic Hour's fixed and subtly graded bands of sunset action that brought in the investment partners: badlands, ghost towns and wreck-littered coastal benches seduced tourist and corporate image-maker alike, confirming Kunene as the Halo's primo location for everything from amateur wedding holography through "existence porn" to the edgiest of brand initiatives.

Everyone who enjoys a sunset wishes it would never end; on Kunene, the brochures promised, you could have that wish.

For half a day the assistant stared out the portholes of the shorthauler *Puit Puit Maru*, watching Dynaflow hallucinations stream past like weed life underwater and telling herself, "I don't like to travel. I don't like these cheap seats." No one sat near her. The Kunene Port Authority had never heard of the *Nova Swing*. But the name FUGA-Orthogen seemed familiar to them, and some of the heritage industries still brought machinery in from off-planet: so, because they were overworked and underappreciated, and because after checking her identity not even the police wanted to sit near her, they sent her to the hinterland. There—away from the lightmeter resorts and fuck safaris, towards the unmoving day where landscape began to dissolve in layers of violet and bony grey under the inhospitable glare of late afternoon—the old Kunene Economic Zone had shrunk to a line of semi-derelict processing plants running thirteen thousand miles north to south, coalescing here and there into poverty towns with names like Douglas or Skelton. Fifty years before, at the height of the lanthanides boom, many of these places had featured a rocket field all their own, and it was on one of these the assistant now found herself, the shuttle she came in on a rapidly fading line of ionisation in clear teal skies.

Administration was an eight-acre lot, thick with low-rise accommodation. Blue and white striped awnings creaked in the wind. Heavily blistered signs advertised commodities long past. All seemed deserted: but at Reception in a single storey structure reprising the moderne suburban carport of 1959, the assistant found a short, skinny old man wearing golf cap, box-cut shirt and bronze polyester pleat-front trousers, idly throwing Entreflex dice on the polished wooden counter. A thousand faded bills of lading were pinned upon the wall. A switched-off sign read:

PERDIDOS E ACHADOS

"Hey," he said, "we're closed."

"I came a hundred light years to hear that."

"Things are tough all over," the old man said. He threw the dice, which fell Vegan Snake Eyes, the Levy Flight, the Tower of Cloud. "Closed half a century next Thursday," he reflected. "But you want a drink with me, there's a bar across the way." She laughed.

"That's your dream, buy drinks for a woman from another world?"

"Everyone has to have a dream," he told her, "and it's true you look a lot like mine."

He had run this office, he said, through the whole of the lanthanides boom. "A man called Renoko had it before me. It was as good as owning a mine, but less work. Our lives were different then." He rested his elbows on the counter and arranged the dice in a high-scoring line. The whites of his eyes were curded with age; his hands, big and soft with their crumpled knuckles and nicely kept nails, were never still. "They were mambo days, but I don't need to tell you that."

"I'm looking for a ship," the assistant said.

In reply, he took a green cardboard box off a shelf and emptied it in front of her. Hundreds of dice—some alien, some human, some single, some in pairs—rattled and bounced across the counter. All colours and materials, from bone to ruby plastic, they glittered with buried lights and embedded physics. He passed his hands above them and suddenly it was nothing but win. They were all the same way up. "What we lose is ourselves," he said, sweeping the dice back in the box, then spilling them out again. "I seen luggage and pictures. A parcel of rusty knives. Once a thing that looks like a shoe but I find it's alive. I took delivery of lost kiddies, lost coats, lost antiques including, as you see, these dice of all kinds." He shrugged. "A rocket ship's too big for this office."

The assistant put her hands over his and held them still.

"Don't be afraid of me," she urged. "Black Heart rum is the drink I like, and I take my time over its burnt sugar flavours. That ship I'm after's called the *Nova Swing*?"

The old man looked at her.

"Wait here," he said.

"Lost dice," she called after him: "Unlucky for the finder!"

She waited ten minutes, then twenty.

Behind the counter he kept it neat: just the box on the shelf, the yellowed waybills on the wall. Everything was very clean. There was a locked back room; there was a back door, opening on to fresh views of the Kunene Economic Zone. When he didn't return in half an hour, the assistant went out and walked around calling, "Hello?" Intense afternoon light threw shadows across the empty avenues between the buildings. At the end of one silent perspective the rare earth hills revealed themselves; at the end of another, the cracked cement of the landing field. She was in a maze: silent and static, self-similar in all directions, with the air of temporary habitation made permanent by the forces of commerce and psychic decline. "Hello?" Confused by the sameness of things, her tailoring began to hallucinate objects bigger than the spaces they occupied: she switched it to standby. A few minutes later the old man crossed an intersection fifty or sixty yards in front of her.

He was pushing some long, heavy, tubular object, leaning into its weight as if into a strong wind. She could hear him groaning with the effort.

When he caught sight of her, he gave a little skip of fear.

"I am not Renoko!" he called.

His shirt billowed out behind him. By the time she reached the intersection he had vanished: thereafter she only ever saw him at a remove, dwarfed by the maze, his attempts to run producing comical slow-motion. Eventually, a muted wailing noise rose, as of a painful incident at the most distant edge of the landing field; in the same moment, she rounded a corner to find him hanging eight feet above the ground, revolving in a slow, loose double loop. His white cap was missing. He was smiling. He was dead. Whatever he had been pushing was gone.

Lost and found, the assistant thought.

A voice in her ear whispered, "Hi, my name is Pearlent and—"

Her chops came back up in a rush. The context blurred. The assistant smelled target chemistry, tailored kairomones characteristically sweet and rank. A monster like herself, something fixed up by cutters with an adolescent view of the future, it darted away in front of her in random evasion patterns: stinking of HPA hyperactivity; emitting frequencies she could detect but not produce—27 to 40 gHz, some kind of local surveillance medium; and uploading in an unfocused FTL scream to destinations she couldn't guess. They duelled between the buildings, thirty or forty seconds without coming to terms. When the assistant paused to listen, the creature froze and shut down its systems; otherwise it stayed in the shadows, kept up the momentum, entered one structure even as it seemed to exit from another, smashing down a door whilst bursting out of a sidewall twenty yards away in a suspended explosion of clapboard fragments. It was faster than her. It was angrier. It had made no attempt to identify or engage her. Instead it seemed to be engaged in an argument with itself. Eventually she gave up. Listened to its footfalls thud and rage away into the distance, where the tilted wrecks of space ships—victims as much of commodity prices as of the high-energy astrophysics out in Radio Bay—sank into badland sediments laced with unexposed ore. The creature spurted off between them, churning up plumes of rotten earth until it vanished, two or three kilometres off, into a line of low hills. Not running away, she thought, so much as struggling to contain its own responses. She went back to the corpse.

The sun beat down. Along the avenue, loose asbestos panels banged in the permanent four o'clock wind. The old man lay on the warm air—one arm outstretched, opposite leg bent, as if demonstrating how to swim sidestroke—leaving a faint blissful wake. He was a little higher up now. His smile had secretive qualities, and he seemed to be straining his eyes to look over his shoulder. Two or three dice floated around his head. In addition he'd attracted an advertisement, which, blown fifty miles from some promateur image-safari in the edges of the twilight zone, swooped and fluttered in counterpoint to his lazy, horizontal figure-of-eight. "Amid the perpetual shadows of the terminator," it was informing him when the assistant arrived, "technical challenge abounds for amateur and professional alike: but to those most in harmony with its subtleties, Kunene Golden Hour is first choice for all the haunting, sometimes disturbing moods we most love."

R. I. Gaines remained a mystery to her.

"Skull Radio," he had told her, "brings down most of the major vibes." But when she looked into the device he'd left her, it was like looking in a cheap souvenir. He hadn't told her how to work it. Her shadow operators discovered nothing. "We're happy to help, dear, of course we are," they said: but if Gaines was a name, no one had used it since 2267, the year their kind of records began. "So happy to help," they said. Meanwhile, EMC was a firewall; it was imperturbable. No other agency claimed him. He was a man with the dress sense of another age. He walked through walls. The assistant sat on the bed in her room and held up the radio at eye level. The little baby skull stared back at her, nested in red lace and drifting sequins.

"Hello?" she said.

"Hey!" the radio said excitedly, in R. I. Gaines' voice.

Next, it folded open in some way so that it contained her—though she could still feel it like a solid object in her hands. She heard a kind of music. Sequins floated out of the skull's mouth and through the assistant into her room, where walls and floor absorbed them. It was a process. Gaines swam into view shortly afterwards. He seemed nervous. She couldn't quite see what was going on behind him, but she had the idea it was happening in a very large space. "Hey!" he said again.

He said he was a little busy right then.

"Something happened," the assistant told him. Skull Radio, reaching out along the airwaves, running on all the base inconsistencies of the universe, warmed to flesh heat in her hands. The baby seemed to be looking at her now. More of it was in view at the back of the box. It was less bony than she liked, a fat little baby's body hanging into the box with its legs open. "Do you know about this thing called Pearlant?"

There was a long silence. "Jesus," Gaines said.

She told him about the Toni Reno case, and how the *Nova* crew had lied to her; the things that occurred in the lanthanide badlands of Funene. Gaines looked around and, as if quietly appealing to some other people, said, "You are shitting me." At that point, the field collapsed in on itself, so that Skull Radio became a cheap tin souvenir again: about which the assistant felt relieved. Moments later, in a billow of cold air, Gaines himself entered through the wall of her room. He was wearing Hampton chinos, a classic Guernsey, and over them a high fill-pressure down jacket an oily yellow colour.

"Christ Jesus," he accused the assistant, "is there more to you than meets the eye? Let me ask you: what are you up to here?"

The assistant said she wasn't up to anything.

Gaines sighed. He opened a pipe to the Aleph project. "Get me someone in Containment." There was a pause, during which he considered the assistant as if deciding not to purchase her. "Do you like cake?" he asked her. "I feel like eating cake." Before she could think of an answer, the dial-up caught his attention again.

"I know," he said. He listened intently for thirty-five seconds before interrupting, "Something's got loose and you fuckers don't even know what it is!" To someone else he said, "I think it might have been in touch with her." This brought a prolonged response that failed to calm his evident anxieties. The assistant went to the window so she could watch people in the street below. "Don't go away," Gaines warned her. GlobeTown's small evening rain was already finished. All along the other side of the street, dub joints and crêpe stalls were opening for early business. Later, the port environs would flush themselves into Saudade proper and these streets would be empty. Until then the girls and boys laughed and kissed in the smell of food and perfume. Neon glowed through the soft renewed air; while, up in the room, Gaines presented his back to the assistant. She stared idly at the pictographs marching along her inside forearm. Sometimes they itched. Sometimes they felt like real things moving under her skin. "I don't know," she heard Gaines say. "No one knows anything at this time." He closed the pipe.

When he turned back to her the first thing he said was:

"We should let you go after this, but we agreed we don't want to do that. It wouldn't make sense for us." He smiled. "Hey," he said. "*Do* you like cake? All afternoon, I wanted to eat cake!" He walked her to a well known patisserie stall, Ou Lu Lou's, up on the hill by the New Men warrens off Retiro Street, where the sidewalk was crammed with people eating ambient tart, listening to music and drinking small glasses of espresso or aniseed liqueur while the neon scripts and city lights shimmered across the warm air—love messages from the distant all-night venues along Tupolev and Mirabeau.

"Look at this! Éclair! Cream horn!" Gaines rubbed his hands together. "You look like someone who can eat cake."

"I don't like anything with cream in it," the assistant said.

She laughed. Since the events on Funene, she had felt even more like an impersonation of herself—of any self. Gaines tried to make her dance. She didn't know how to dance. The crowd began to look uneasy, and some of them moved away. "Come on now!" Gaines called after them. "It's only fun." He asked the remainder, didn't they think the assistant was beautiful? "Look at her!" he said. He drank five or six liqueurs, but didn't eat any cake after all. Instead he joked with everyone and made sure the assistant had the things she wanted. Later, back in her room, he sat on the bed with his knees apart and his hands loosely clasped between them, and said without preamble:

"The thing about life is that if you get it wrong you can't go back."

There were two kinds of people, he said: those who lived their lives in the prolonged moment of panic in which they first realized this—"They have no idea where the door is now, let alone how to get it open if they could find it," and who therefore spent their lives thrashing about in what he called "the disorder of hearing it click shut behind them." The other kind, after a single awful pang, "one fast look back," decide to make the best of whatever happens next. "Those people go on," he finished: "They're still hoping for something good."

The assistant did not know how to reply. Nothing he said was in her area of expertise. None of it applied to someone like her. She wasn't sure anyway that he meant her to believe him. In the end she said:

"Surely we can be anything we want in this world."

Gaines dismissed an idea so simple. "When I got in this game," he went on, "I had a little daughter." He said this as if he was just now discovering it; or as if he was discovering it about someone else. "A little girl," he said, after a pause; and after another one, "I was twenty years old." This in itself seemed to be the story: at any rate, there was no more to tell. It was as if, ever since, he had looked at these facts obliquely—as if he couldn't see them but could, with care, make them out as a fairly robust implication of some other data.

He shrugged. "Investigate those mystery deaths if you like," he suggested, "or this *Nova Swing* rocket: but it's a team game now. For all of us. Agreed?" She had no idea who he was talking about. But each liqueur, she noticed, had caused his smile to become a little less intense. "Always bring the results to me," he recommended. "And never, ever say that word to anyone again." The assistant opened her mouth to agree, but before she could speak he walked straight out through the window, vanishing on the other side, and leaving her with the impression that the view from her room was painted on the glass. As if the world fabric was a style of art to which only Gaines and people like him had the secret.

13: Eaten by Dogs

Anna Waterman's bedroom had what she thought of as a suicide bathroom *en suite*—extensive mirrors above sink and bath, everything else black faux-marble cladding. The walls matched the floor, and there was no natural light. Uplighters provided enough of an oily yellowish glow to pee by. But switch on the three hundred watts of fluorescents hidden in the ceiling and you had better keep your eyes closed: otherwise you would see—turning with you when you turned, wincing and holding its palms up to the cruel radiance—whatever pitiful thing you had become over the years. In a bathroom that implacable, even the happiest woman would find it easy to let the Jack Daniel's bottle fall and smash. Display as many bowls of dried rose petals as you like in that kind of bathroom, but after you've changed the peach-coloured bath sheets and broken open a new cake of handcut hemp-oil soap, you'll still find yourself arranging the water glass and Temazepam cartons by the sink, or sitting quietly on the too-low lavatory pan, planning where to make the first cut—and cuts will always seem necessary, whatever the financial or emotional climate.

Some part of Anna sought comfort, or familiarity at least, in the suicide bathroom. That part of her welcomed it as a concept as much as a place, a key theory about the world she had held since she was young, a psychic refuge at the very same time as a site of existential terror, something that would always be there for her: but the part isn't the whole, and by eight o'clock on the morning after her swim the rest of her had begun cheerfully demolishing it.

Marnie found her there just after lunch, crouched under the sink in a cleaning-woman overall, with her hair tied up in a batik scarf.

"What do you think, then?" Anna said.

She had emptied the bathroom of everything that would move and piled it into the bedroom. Patchy success with the marble cladding had encouraged her to lever off one of the larger sections of mirror; this she had dropped from the bedroom window into a flowerbed where it lay, unbroken except for a chip at one corner, amid the childlike planting of lobelia and ox-eye daisy. The pipes and cavities exposed by these operations, she had done in gold or silver, according to mood. "Later," she said, "I'll paint fish on them. Starfish. Seashells. Bubbles. Those kinds of things." The major surfaces had taken their first coat, dark blue emulsion with enough white in it to suggest a kind of Spanish azure, applied fast with a tray and roller. As soon as it was dry she intended to put on more white, in dry combed streaks to give the effect of foam. It covered the walls well enough, but the mirrors would need more. "I'm planning to keep to these pastelly greens and blues," she told Marnie, "for everything but the detail." For the detail she had laid aside three or four of the smallest brushes she could find, beautiful sablehair modelling points. "But also if I can get some light into them, I will."

Marnie stood in the doorway of the suite, stiffly considering the heaps of bath towels and broken fittings; the carrier bags stuffed with leaking Moulton-Brown shower products; the torn black rubbish sack half full of triangular shards of marble, none larger than three inches on a side. On the fitted taupe berber by the bathroom door, Anna had prised open every can of paint in the house, from little unused tins of fancy enamel to five litre drums of professional obliterating emulsion. All of this Marnie observed in disbelief. She picked her way over to the open window and stared down at the mirror in the flowerbed. After a moment she passed one hand over her face and said:

"Anna, for God's sake what are you doing?"

"I'm decorating, dear. What does it look like?" Anna pushed some hair back under the scarf. "You can help if you like."

"Let's have a cup of tea," Marnie said tiredly.

Anna thought that was such a good idea. "Perhaps you could help me get these bags of things down to the dustbins too," she suggested.

Marnie insisted they make lunch—cheese on toast and a salad—and afterwards have a stroll round the garden. They dead-headed some of the sadder-looking roses. They lifted the mirror out of the flowerbed and propped it up by the garage, where Marnie thought it looked almost deliberate, like a mirror designed to extend the space in a corner of some well-known garden off towards Glyndebourne, the name of which she couldn't remember. Down by the summerhouse she said, "I notice you've got rid of the poppies." Anna, who felt unable to admit to her daughter that the poppies had vanished overnight, leaving behind them a strip of earth so packed and dry that nothing could have grown there for years, agreed that she had dug them up. "But I don't see where you've put them," Marnie said. "They're not in the compost."

"Oh, somewhere, darling. I expect I put them somewhere."

Marnie hooked her arm through Anna's. Each time they drew near the house, she steered them away again. "It's such a nice day," she said, or, "Those paint fumes can't be good for you," or, "Oh, Mum, smell all this!"— indicating, with a delighted sweep of her arm and a clear subtext, the roses, the orchard, the August air itself.

It *was* a wonderful day, Anna agreed cautiously, and she had loved lunch; but she must get back to work now.

"I don't know why you're doing this," Marnie accused her.

"These days, I don't know why I'm doing anything," Anna said, trying to make Marnie laugh. "Oh darling, can't you give me a bit of room?"

"If you don't go too far."

It was Anna's turn to be angry.

"How far is that?" she demanded. "This place was always really rather ordinary, Marnie. That was fine for your father. It was fine for you growing up. But now I want something different." Staring across at the summerhouse, she caught a fleeting glimpse of herself thirty years ago in a West London bathroom, two o'clock in the morning. Fishes painted on the wall, amber-coloured soap with a rosebud trapped inside like someone else's past—the past you'll have, once you're in the future. It's the Millennium, or close to it. A dozen scented candles flicker, stuck to the bath surround with their own fat, throwing on the rag-rolled walls the shadows of twigs in vases encrusted with fake verdigris. The bathwater cooling around your nipples but still acceptable as long as you don't move too often. 2 am, and Michael Kearney's footsteps are heard upon the stair; his key is heard in Anna's lock.

"Come with me, Marnie," Anna said. She led Marnie upstairs and made her look at the new bathroom. "I want this. I once had this, and I want it again."

"Mum, I—"

"I was younger than you are now when I last had a bathroom I liked. You have a nice stable life, Marnie, but I didn't. I'm not giving my house to you. I'm not just going to give you my fucking house and live in a shed somewhere."

There was a long, helpless silence. "Anna," Marnie said, "what are you talking about?"

Anna wasn't sure. Every attempt to articulate it left her feeling failed. She was getting the house ready for Michael: as much as common sense, a kind of shyness prevented her from admitting that. Over the next few days she painted. It was hard work. In the end the walls took three coats and the mirrors four. One afternoon, she left the paint to dry and walked along the lanes to a pub called the de Spencer Arms, expecting to be able to sit outside at her favourite table and—a bit windswept and pleasantly sundazzled— watch the retirees from London manoeuvring their Jaguars in and out of the car park. Instead she found the table occupied by a boy and two dogs. The boy had a woollen workshirt on over a loose pullover, and over them a donkey jacket. His jeans were tight, worn a little too long, trodden down by the heels of his black, awkward, lace-up boots. Every item was covered in mud or splattered with paint. He was sitting negligently on the table itself, next to an empty pint glass, kicking his legs and whistling.

"Do you mind if I sit down?" Anna said.

"I'll get off this table, shall I?" the boy said. "It's the cleanest table here, this one. That's why I sat here."

"You're dogs are so beautiful."

"They won't hurt you," the boy said, "these dogs. Some say they're dangerous, but I know they're not." They stood alertly by his legs, identical animals facing away from him into the wind, shaped like greyhounds if a little smaller, with pale blue eyes, patches of long grey, bristly fur and a kind of curled, nervous alertness. Now and then a shiver passed over one or the other of them. Every movement drew their attention. They looked where the boy looked, then looked to him for confirmation of the things they saw. "I'd get another drink," he said to Anna, "but I hate that posh bar in there. You don't need to worry about these dogs, they wouldn't harm a child."

"What kind of dogs are they?"

The boy gave her a sly look. "Working dogs," he said. He lowered his voice confidentially. "I'm out lamping most nights, with that lot in the fields," he said. "They're down the fields every night, with the lights and dogs. They've got some fierce dogs, that lot." Anna said she wasn't sure what lamping was. The boy looked blank at that. It was so much a part of his life, she saw, that there was too much to tell. He was helpless to know where to start. She indicated the pub, with its pleasantly sagging Horsham stone roofs, its wisteria and virginia creeper.

"I could get you a drink," she offered, "if you didn't want to go in."

The boy set his face. "They don't want these dogs in a bar like that," he said. "Fat boys," he said contemptuously. "Pushing their thousand quid mountain bikes up these hills. Pushing them up the hills!"

In fact the bar was full of ex-estate agents and their wives, ignoring the sour smell of the carpets and drinking gin and tonic as fast as they could— withered men in roomy blazers, their shoulders at odd independent angles underneath; women whose gaze seemed unnaturally eager, their cheeks the red you see on pheasants, their hair tightened up chemically to within a nanometre of hair's tolerance, ready to snap. Anna bought the boy a pint of Harveys Mild and a wine-box spritzer for herself. She thought he might like a packet of cheese and onion crisps. She looked forward to talking to him again. Perhaps he would let her stroke the dogs. But when she got out- side with the drinks he was already walking away across the car park, head down, shoulders hunched tensely, hands in his pockets. His long, relaxed stride made it seem as if as if the two halves of his body had nothing to do with each other. The dogs walked one either side of him on their stiff, fragile-looking legs, so attentive that their heads almost touched his knees. He turned round to wave to Anna.

"But your drink—!" she called. He only waved again and went off to- wards Wyndlesham.

Anna ate the cheese and onion crisps, staring out at the curve of the Downs. She drank the wine, then the beer, taking her time. The de Spencer Arms themselves, as represented on the pub sign, featured something for everyone—crosses, chevrons, bars—done in stained-glass colours as rich as the light inside a cathedral; among which was a weirdly modern, penetra- tive, electric blue.

All afternoon the boy's loose stride took him up and down the footpaths and bridleways around Wyndlesham. Patchy woodland fifty yards from back gardens. Dried up ruts in secondary growth already the colour of straw. Sunglare on dusty fields where an inch of soil, parched as early as April, was skimmed on to hectares of raw chalk; then the relief of a wide grassy rake falling away steeply between beeches. Buzzards in the updraughts and a temporary altar of concrete slabs under the tall old- fashioned single-arch railway bridge at Brownlow. He never left the same three or four square miles. He was waiting for it to be dark, so he could go down the low-lying fields between Wyndlesham and Winsthrow and run his dogs along the beam of the lamp. They were a shade heavy, his dogs, but they were good for a long night on the lamp. He loved to see them curl and uncurl in the path of light. He was happy taking rabbit but he liked hares best. "A hare stretches them out, these dogs," he would tell himself. "She gives them a run." It was something to see. It was over in a minute or two. Sometimes he was so excited he saw everything in slow motion as if hare and dogs were swimming ecstatically in the dark air. His heart was so far out to them there! He was seeing faster than they could run. He could feel his heart rocking his body. He could replay every hare his dogs ever caught, like a download in his head. "It's something to see," he would say when people asked him. He didn't know where to begin with them and their mountain bikes, weekend in, weekend out.

That lot in the fields weren't out tonight, so he went on his own. The very first thing, the dogs put up a grey hare, the colour of ash in the light. The boy had never seen that before. The hare seemed to lag, it seemed to wait for him to pay attention. Then the dogs were off and running and the action was so fast he couldn't keep it in the lamplight.

"I never saw anything like this," he told himself.

The dogs were subdued on the way home. They weren't sure what they'd caught. A hare more blue than grey, unmarked by death: though empty, its eyes seemed to focus on him when he took it from them. "Get up," he said to the bitch to cheer her up. "Get on with you." But she stuck so close he felt her head touch his leg. It was cold in the bothy where he lived with the dogs, up there the far side of Ampney. When he got in he thought for a minute he saw a kind of grey mould on everything. Then, later that night, he woke up out of a dream of the woman he had talked to the afternoon before. He didn't remember anything about her and now she was leaning over him in his bed, undressed, whispering something he couldn't catch. Her grey hair was hanging down, her tits thin and white, her eyes the blue of his dogs' eyes. He didn't like the way she tried to catch his attention. It woke him. He was as hard as wood, and it wouldn't go away. He yearned to fuck someone, anyone. "I'd fuck anything," he said to himself. By then, wraiths and dips of mist lay across the fields. He could see all the way to the Arbor barn at Winsthrow, up to its door in mist. Further away, it looked as if something tall had caught fire in that direction, but it was just something in the corner of his eye and when he turned his head it was gone. "She wanted to know all about you," he teased the dogs.

They pressed up close to him then, and all the next day followed him about, quiet and unresourceful. "Get on with you," he said to them. "Get on with the both of you."

Anna Waterman, meanwhile, had passed the rest of the afternoon at the de Spencer Arms, arriving home about five o'clock. By six she had twice rung Marnie, to leave confused messages. "I'm sorry, darling," she began, but then couldn't think of anything else to say. In a sense, she wasn't sorry, she was only in a panic. "Well, anyway, give me a call." Poor Marnie! After that she went round with the vacuum cleaner, and opened all the windows to get rid of the smell of paint. Later, James the cat stalked up and down the arm of the sofa butting his head into her face while she sat in front of the television. "James," she told him, picking uninterestedly at tuna and baked potato, "you're a nuisance." The cat responded with a breathy grinding noise.

Anna retired early; experienced busy dreams, in which her new bathroom, relocated to the station concourse at Waterloo where it drew the late afternoon commute like a football crowd, became filled with water in the azure depths of which flickered real fish; and woke tangled in her damp nightdress in the deep night, convinced that a strange light and heat, coming and going Chinese red and sunflower yellow outside her window, had winked out the instant she opened her eyes. Feeling as if someone might be staring in at her, she struggled up out of bed and went down to look out of the back door. Only the lawn and flowerbeds, suspended in the cool, milky late-summer dark: but in the distance, somewhere the other side of the river, she could hear the long, belling cries of dogs. Cool air flowed around her ankles. Everything out there was very still. James sat in the middle of the lawn like an illustration; turned his head to look at her, then, as she left the house, stretched amiably and walked off. The sound of the dogs became clearer. Musical but inexplicable, detached from anything you might expect to happen on an ordinary night, it was a sound distant and very close at the same time. It wasn't coming from across the river. It was coming from Anna's summerhouse.

Originally stained a colour Tim Waterman had called "Serbian yellow," which faded over the years to the faintest lemon tint in the fibres of the wood, the summerhouse stood as leached and grey as a beach hut, the earth at its base rioting with exotic flowers again—huge foxglove-like bells in pale transparent pastel browns and pinks, round which fluttered hundreds of dusty-white moths. "How beautiful!" Anna thought, though now the sound of dogs was loud and close. Suspended between delight and dread, she approached the summerhouse and pulled at its door, which stuck, then gave. She had time to hallucinate a rolling endless landscape of tall grass, under a lighting effect from the cover of a science fiction novel, and hear a voice say, "Leave here. Leave here, Anna!" Then the dogs were on her. It was hard to count them, jostling and snapping, white teeth and lolling tongues, long hot muscular bodies brindled fawn and violet. It was hard to see what kinds of dogs they were. Before she knew it, the sheer weight and strong smell of them had knocked her off balance, she had stumbled back from the door, she was down on her back on the lawn in the dark, laughing and gasping as they licked her all over. "No!" she said. She laughed. "No, wait!" Too late. The nightdress was up around her waist.

14: Enantiodromic Zones

The Halo is rich with hauntings of one sort or another. They occupy many different kinds of space.

Two of them held a short meeting in the *Nova Swing* main hold. First to arrive was the entity calling itself MP Renoko. Though presently operating himself by FTL transmission from a Faint Dime cashout terminal on the south hemisphere of New Venusport, Renoko self-identified as human; and when he walked through the wall of the hold, he certainly resembled—down to his white stubble, grubby short raincoat and bare ankles—the same individual who had commissioned Fat Antoyne, insulted Irene's sense of business, and argued so fiercely with Ruby Dip about the nature of kitsch. His first act was to inspect the mortsafes, which greeted him with a kind of biddable skittishness.

Renoko patted them like the thoroughbreds they were, whistling in the tuneless but familiar carnie manner. Occasionally he gave a nod of approval. To the smallest of them, he said with a laugh, "I see you've been back at the old game!" Then, opening his arms as if he could embrace all three at once, "It's a real treat to see you together again!"

He busied himself about, using his breath and the sleeve of his raincoat to wipe down a viewport here or buff up a brass detail there. But after a while he sat down suddenly in a corner of the hold. Both his facial expression and his body language collapsed into vacancy. He seemed to be prepared to wait. The mortsafes settled down again. It would be difficult to reproduce Renoko's state of consciousness during this period. He identified as a human being, but he could not be said to be one. Based on a few lines of code last separately aware of itself in the glory days of Sandra Shen's Circus, he was now in all senses an emergent property: not of a single cash register, or indeed a single diner, but of the whole Halo-wide Faint Dime chain (in itself a subsidiary of FUGA-Orthogen), including its wholesaling and accountancy software, its transport and construction departments, its human resources and, especially, their day to day viral loading. The progress of a modified herpes infection through the staff of a given diner did as much to generate, maintain and express MP Renoko as the progress of a restocking order for ketchup or the decision to press forward with a new outlet. These different kinds of events implied, added up to or *gave rise* to him. In a sense he was nothing more than a list of instructions left behind by Madame Shen herself when she abandoned the circus. But you can't accrete fifty years of history without becoming some sort of identity in your own right. That was a guarantee of sorts, Renoko sometimes believed: though of what he wasn't sure.

After perhaps an hour, some activity began in the opposite corner of the hold. A few pale green motes of light floated about near the floor, then vanished. When they reappeared, it was to drift lazily towards one another, whirl together like flies on a hot afternoon, separate, then whirl together again—until over a period of minutes they had assembled themselves into a rough, recognisable shape. This figure hung, slightly over life-size, its shoulders six feet from the deckplates, like a compromise between a man, some strips of meat and a charred coat. It had arms, but was without legs. "Hey," it said softly. At this the mortsafes woke up. They jostled and nudged at one another. LEDs of every colour flashed urgently down their sides. If Renoko had charmed their alien hearts, the newcomer charged them with a strange, immediate, nervous energy. The hold filled up with such a mixture of electromagnetic styles and motives that MP Renoko's hair stood on end. He stirred and sat up. His mind came back from wherever it had been. A private-looking smile passed across his features, so that for a moment he seemed quite human.

"Hey," he said. "Long time no see."

"I remember you, man. You look like shit."

"We both look like shit," said MP Renoko, "but you look dead."

A laugh. "How we doing otherwise?"

Renoko gestured around the hold. "Well enough. As you can see, a little behind schedule."

"You know, I don't think there's a schedule as such."

Renoko seemed to settle in his corner. "I'd like to get it over with anyway," he said. "I've been a little tired lately."

"Fifty years is a long time, man."

"You could say that. I look forward to a holiday."

"Kick back a little," the newcomer agreed. "Sink into the data."

During this dialogue he had been busy opening a panel in the hull of one of the mortsafes. Over this he now bent, his head and shoulders inside, his elbows still visible as he worked at the exposed engine. Field effects rippled across the hold like luminescence in surf. All three mortsafes blurred, fogging the warm air with physics. Various kinds of musical sounds could be heard as they exchanged data. MP Renoko observed alien states of matter crawling across the walls as symbols, hallucinatory lights, scenes from his own past. Much of what was going on made him even more tired than usual. He massaged his left hand with his right. Stood up slowly, suddenly remembering the circus at dawn, some landing field on a forgotten planet. Every morning different, every morning the same. The harsh light on cement, the air full of salt and fried food smells. A tiny Chinese-looking woman with piled up red hair and a tight emerald cheongsam, swaying like a mirage through the heat haze between the carnie booths, every eye's focus, human or alien. "Can code enjoy sex?" the media always ask. MP Renoko remembered something less easy to describe.

"Do you ever see her?" he said softly, one ghost to another.

The newcomer grunted in surprise and shook his head. This simple motion transferred itself to the dangling strips of flesh that comprised his lower half, causing them to whirl like a skirt.

"No one sees her now, man. She's got so much stuff to do. She's working on behalf of others."

"I just wondered."

"We've all got stuff to do now."

Shortly afterwards he left, saying only: "I'll be back for you, Jack," which he seemed to find funny. MP Renoko, whose name had never been Jack or anything like it, laughed dutifully. He waited until the mortsafes had calmed down then he too left the hold, walking out the same wall he had entered by. Unaware of these kinds of events except as a localised cluster of internal surveillance blackouts, the crew of the *Nova Swing* slept, ate, screwed, stared out the portholes at the wonders of space, and drew closer to their next destination: a G-type star, known to the navigational mathematics as an eleven-dimensional mosaic of co-ordinates, but to the generations who lived and died by its light as "Scinde Dawk."

By that time, everyone was in a bad temper with everything: Liv and Antoyne argued over who should clean up the mess in the control room; Irene, bored and with a far-off look in her blue eyes, crafted for herself outfits in increasingly radical expressions of pink, which, to the consternation of the shadow operators, she wore fifteen minutes each before weeping inexplicably and throwing them about. Forty-eight hours later these three found themselves in the parking orbit of the Scinde Dawk system's only inhabitable planet—the tidally locked Funene—searching the twilight zone for an abandoned factory town dubbed by Irene, "some dump called Mambo Rey." Liv Hula hit the retros, ran three cursory aerobrake cycles to save fuel, and was bringing them down on the customary tail of green flame when the ship's instruments picked up surface activity around the Mambo Rey rocket field.

"Fat Antoyne," she said, "something is going on down there."

Why tell him, Antoyne wanted to know.

"Don't sulk! Don't sulk, Antoyne! I fucking have to work in here! My workplace should not smell of someone else's puke!"

Antoyne was of the opinion that nothing could smell as bad as the blanket she kept in there.

"Fuck you, Fat Antoyne."

"The truth often hurts."

"Antoyne, sometimes you are as big a cunt as Toni Reno."

A dry laugh came from the crew quarters.

"No one is as big a cunt as Toni Reno," was Irene's opinion.

"We all can feel the truth of that," Liv Hula admitted. "So Antoyne," she said, in as placatory a voice as she could manage, "help me out here. I don't know what I'm seeing."

Antoyne didn't know either. A rooster-tail of disturbed dust billowed its way between the low hills surrounding the port. At its head could be made out a fierce mote of energy. *Nova Swing*'s arrays were detecting short range RF, broad spectrum FTL transmissions, and some kind of radar: nothing anyone could understand. Neither was there any logic to the object's course. It resembled a spark racing along a carelessly laid fuse, or some weird science particle tangled and looping through invisible fields. Thirty miles into the badlands, it abruptly disappeared. The dust settled slowly. No matter how many times he re-ran the footage, Antoyne couldn't make out what was going on. The object was too small to be a vehicle. It was too fast to be a human being.

"I don't get it," he said.

By then they were on the ground. Irene, who had knowledge of fifty planets before she was fourteen, recognised a dump when she saw one. Mambo

Rey was a place no one wanted, except to hologram themselves getting sex against a collapsing industrial shed in clever light. It was less a world than a lifestyle accessory. "Having a great fuck, wish you were here!" 35 degrees Celsius, humidity nil. A metal taste filled the mouth: rare earth dust, rotting even as it separated out of the ancient strata, blew across the concrete on the wind, silting up the corners of the wooden terminal buildings. As the surrounding mesas eroded, they had exposed the remains of early life in that part of the Halo—huge, bare, cryptic, radioactive forms that looked less like bones than pieces of architecture. Elsewhere in the subtle gradations of Funene's twilight zone, hallucinatory giant insects strode the horizon on long, fragile legs.

"Jesus," Irene said: "Roach planet." And then, bending down suddenly, "Hey! I found a heart-shaped stone!"

After a brief argument with Liv, who claimed it was no more than a tooth washed out of some ancient alluvial deposit, she presented it to Fat Antoyne, and the women set out to find the Snakebite bar. Antoyne watched them trudge off across the hot cement—laughing and arguing arm in arm, an image sharpened and rendered almost unbearable by the glare of the perpetual afternoon—then went back inside the *Nova Swing* and examined the stone. It was pink, translucent, full of small bubbles suspended in a web of hazy fracture planes. It wasn't a tooth. He rubbed it with his thumb, then dialled up MP Renoko.

"We're here," he said.

"Hello?" a voice replied. "Hello?"

The pipe was bad. If it was Renoko, he sounded as if he was already talking to someone else.

"Are you there?" Antoyne said.

"Hello!" the voice shouted. "For a moment I thought you'd gone!"

"Is this Renoko?"

"Who's that? Is that you, Antoyne?"

"We can take delivery of those goods of yours," Antoyne said. At this, he thought he felt Renoko's attention focus suddenly. "Hello?"

"You'll find us in the old lost property office."

"Are you here, then?"

"Well," said Renoko. "That depends what you mean. Do you need me to be there?"

"I'm at Mambo Rey," Antoyne said. "Where are you?"

"Antoyne?" Renoko interrupted. "This is a bad pipe, Antoyne. Hello?" Another pause. "Find the lost property office," he said. "Someone will take care of you."

"I'm here," Antoyne said. "Where are you?"

"PERDIDOS Y ACHADOS!" shouted Renoko.

Directions followed, then the dial-up collapsed. Antoyne looked around the control room, with its homely smells of vomit, fried food and electrical fields. Wondering what Renoko had meant when he described himself as "here," he got up abruptly and searched the ship from top to bottom. It took an hour to check every companionway. Sometimes Antoyne felt the need go back and check the ductwork too. Only when he was sure the *Nova Swing* was empty did he feel safe enough to leave.

Deep in the eight-acres of the Mambo Rey Postindustrial Estate, a curiously self-similar grid of buildings, he found the lost property office. Its door hung open. No one had been there for weeks. Dust had drifted across the floor and gathered as a thin film in the curls and creases of the yellowing waybills pinned to the walls. Antoyne called, "Hello?" and receiving no answer sat down on a chair to wait. He read some of the paper. "Ambo Danse VI, d.i.f. Details at site." Over this someone had written, "Fedy wants to know where this is!" A thousand dice were scattered on the counter, some of them lighting up dimly from inside if you passed your hand above them. Antoyne sat, turning the heart-shaped stone between his fingers and listening to the wind bang about outside as if it had misplaced something. He felt uneasy just sitting there. He found another room: nothing. He poked his head out of the back door, which was off its top hinge, and looked up and down the street. Nothing.

He opened his dial-up and said, "Hi!" but all he could hear in the pipe was a sound like very distant canaries.

"Renoko?"

Halfway through the afternoon, he gave up and went out into the avenues between the buildings. Everything seemed to hang suspended in the late afternoon light, static and fried. Even Antoyne's movements were reluctant. They were the movements of a fatter man. The Mambo Rey Postindustrial State, stripping away his pretensions, had resolved him as an earlier version of himself. It was the story of his life. All the buildings were neglected. In addition some of them were curiously damaged. Splintered wood, deformed aluminium siding. Cracked asbestos panels flung about. In each case it was as if something had burst into the structure from one avenue and out of it into the next. Antoyne could smell the broken wood in the air. He wandered about until he found himself on the edge of the estate where, the other side of a weed-grown strip of cement, the skeletal sheds and rusting hoppers of abandoned lanthanide workings stretched away between empty evaporation ponds and wrecking yards so silted up that the ancient ships seemed to lean at angles out of a milky grey sea. The light was a resin coating on all of it.

Antoyne trudged up one slope of dust, down the next, craned his neck at the stripped hull of an early Creda Starliner, leaned in through a second-floor factory window to find somewhere he could shit. Some people go to the tailor early in life and have themselves cut so they don't need to do that. Antoyne wasn't one of those. A shit was a shit for Antoyne, that's what he always said: it was a sensation he enjoyed. Although sometimes, given the product, you wondered what was going on inside you. He squatted between some items of abandoned machinery for a couple of minutes, groaning, then became aware that something was in there with him. It was very close. Perhaps it was even kneeling right next to him, almost brushing his shoulder, and smelling ranker, whatever it was, than Antoyne's bowel movement. It was amused by him. Full of passive terror, he stared hard away from where he thought it was until it had gone, then pulled up his chinos and fastened his belt. He went into a corner and threw up. Then he left the factory and stared out across the sea of dust, above which, at the horizon, floated mesa after rotting mesa the colour of pigeon's wings. Sex, he thought. It reeked of sex. There were no tracks in the dust but his own. He had neither seen nor heard anything. On his way back through the Mambo Rey Postindustrial Estate he spotted the item they were supposed to pick up, floating motion-lessly at a street intersection in the distance.

It was a bone colour, on the yellow side of white. Closer inspection re-vealed it to be twelve feet long, longitudinally ribbed for about two-thirds of its length, with a blunt sloping point at one end. It seemed to be made of porcelain with the hair-fine brown craqueleur of an ageing urinal. It was very warm to the touch, like anything left standing in the afternoon sun. Antoyne shoved it along, up and down the avenues, looking for the landing field. It wasn't hard work but it wasn't easy either. Soon he came upon Liv Hula, standing in the middle of the street staring up at a corpse which hung in the air about four feet above her head. When Fat Antoyne arrived all she said was, "What do you think of this?"

Antoyne stopped pushing the mortsafe. He wiped his forehead with the back of his hand.

"I never saw anything like it," he said.

"You get dead people," Liv Hula agreed, "but they don't float."

The corpse was of an old guy, snappily dressed in a loose shirt worn outside bronze pleat-front plus fours, with tan loafers, no socks and a white golf cap. He had a quiet smile on his face as if to say, "Being dead means less to me than you'd think," and he was swimming in the air, like an instructor in some new kind of meditational discipline, tracing a slow, graceful butterfly symbol. Two or three dice drifted in loose orbits round his head, and a worn-out advertisement from one of the fuck-resorts further into the twilight zone was trying to draw him into a conversation about photography. A hot wind blew up and down the street. Otherwise things were completely silent. Antoyne said:

"I'm sorry I threw up in your pilot chair."

He offered Liv the heart-shaped stone Irene had given him, which she took absently, still staring up at the corpse.

"Do you want some help with that thing?" she said.

They got round the back of the mortsafe and leaned into it. Pushing was much easier with two. Halfway across the landing field, Liv handed him back the stone.

"This won't work, Antoyne," she said, giving him a very direct look.

15: Random Acts of Downward Causation

Saudade: Autumn when you could tell. Rain, anyway.

At SiteCrime, all the talk was war. The Nastic—allies for a day or two some time in the middle 2400s, but now in possession of new physics and a hybrid cosmology that trumped the rest—were moving out of bases in Delta Carinae. Rumour said that EMC had a new best buy in its arsenal, even now being R&D'd from alien blueprints on a secret research asteroid in the very shadow of the Tract. No one knew what it was. They called it the "field weapon" or the "non-Abelian weapon." Meanwhile, Lens Aschemann's ghost hung in a corner on the fifth floor. I don't pity the dead, the assistant thought, not when they persist like this. Two floors down it was common knowledge: she would be helpless without him. One floor up they said she had no personality. What the assistant thought of these opinions, if she knew, went unrecorded. She did her work. She watched Toni Reno and his loader fade to zero. As Epstein the thin cop put it, there was never a point at which you could safely say, "They're gone," but after ten days only a sketch remained.

Meanwhile, though she had alerted Port Authorities all over the Halo, the *Nova Swing* slipped away, and went curiously unreported.

Forced to await developments on both these cases, and unhindered for once by the mystery that was R. I. Gaines, she investigated the massacre in the basement, working in her office with holograms made at the scene. The vics, viewable from any angle, lay about in louche poses. Even their smell was replicated. Forty-eight hours after the attack, a faint aerosol of lymph had still hung in the air. The evidence team's conclusion: someone had done a job on them. After that, causation itself dribbled away in predictable chains of confusion, each ultimate cause itself shown to be proximate in some other context until everything danced off into metaphysics. Evidently it was a Preter Coeur kill. The room was full of clues to that, the fading signature of hormonal switchgear, the wounds traceable to biomineral weapons—self-sharpening polycrystal mosaics derived from nacre, perhaps expressing as fingernails?

Nanocamera coverage having tanked so completely during the actual crime, it was expected the assistant would go down there in person, if only—as the sixth floor put it—to familiarise herself with the venue. But she never did. She remembered the event on the back stairs. The thought of the basement made her uneasy, and remained with her even in the Cedar Mountain immersion tank on C-Street, where, as Joan the 1950s wife, she dreamed a baby came through the wall in her bright, new, airy, shades-of-primrose kitchen.

First something went wrong with the paintwork. It turned matt olive in the top corners; then in patches on the walls themselves, which spread quickly until everything was covered. Then she noticed that on the kitchen shelves her carefully arranged tins of anchovies and Parma ham had been replaced with stale wrapped sandwiches and bits of half-eaten fruit. These items caused her both disgust and anxiety. Her husband Alan might come in at any moment and see them! But now the kitchen doorway had no door; the kitchen window opened on to a weed-filled lot where it was always raining. Damp had penetrated the cheap formica cabinets, covering them with fibrous ring-shaped blemishes. Looking up at the wall, Joan saw that a slightly more than life-sized vulva had emerged from it like a crop of fungus. It wasn't quite the right colours. The labia had yellow-brown tones, and the rigidity of a wooden model. A body was attached, but less of that had emerged from the wall. It was still emerging, in fact. Joan felt that it might take years to squeeze through. And while the vulva clearly belonged to an adult—she was so embarrassed!—the body was much younger. It still had the fat little belly and undeveloped ribcage of a baby. The vulva presented in the same vertical plane as the wall, but the body and the face were foreshortened and leaning back from it at a wrong angle for the anatomy to work.

At all points it was seamless with the wall. She couldn't see much of the face, but it was smiling.

Saturday morning, Joan had always made cakes. Often her husband found her in the kitchen, still up to her elbows in flour or perhaps setting the "regulator" on her brand new Creda oven. The radio played a little light classical music. Alan loved her cakes. He would put his arms around her, rub a little, bunch up her skirt, then shoot helplessly while he was still trying to slip into her clean underwear from behind. "Oh!" Joan would tell him, "I do love our times together." It was their mid-morning Saturday ritual. He could always surprise her. She was always ready for him, yet never somehow prepared. Today, though, she was only thinking how awful it would be if he came in and saw the vulva in the kitchen wall. And just as she thought that, he did. Once Alan arrived, the walls returned slowly to their original colour. It took all morning but everything was real again. After they held hands the way they did, staring up at the wall together, Joan and Alan felt for a week or two that they had changed. They knew a secret others didn't. Though it was horrible, it made them feel that they had found their way through to some more knowing way of life. Joan said vile things. Alan pulled her skirt up and fucked 'til they were both red and sore. Then they found that all their friends knew the secret too, so it was just a kind of loss everyone went through.

The assistant began to bang her head on the side of the immersion tank and make a sound full of grief. She could hear herself but not stop; the technicians could hear her, but it was too soon to get the lid up. Later, she cancelled her subscription to Cedar Mountain and received a refund; this time no one could explain what had gone wrong.

Panamax IV: "Don't you get sick of the cultural noise?" R. I. Gaines asked Alyssia Fignall. They were sheltering from the noon light in a bony cloister, perhaps a mile from the sea and some miles down the valley from her hilltop site. Its arches were in shade, but full sun fell across the dry central fountain, the pale rhyolite columns, the dry brown vegetation between the cobbles. She had been trying to explain to him how richly decorated the cloister would have been before time stripped off the paint. This had upset his idea of it as bare, quiet, uncommunicative: possessing an almost geological calm. "All I want is the stone, wiped clean." He shrugged. "And perhaps this sense of an unending afternoon."

She smiled. Touched his hand. "You're tired, Rig."

"I'll stay a bit longer," he told her. "The ship won't come until dark. You can tell me all about these sacrificial engines of yours."

"Not mine," she said.

Later, as the air cooled and the sky filled up from the east, local children processed through the town square, dressed as lions, tigers, bears, fairies with wings, the mythical inhabitants of Old Earth.

"What's this?" he asked.

"They're enacting one of the folk-tales of the local river. It's tidal for several miles past here. At each tide, the water leaves a few black lumps of wood on the shore. These, sodden as much with age as water, are the river's gift to the land." None of the children were older than four, but they bore their wands and tinsel garlands—along with a banner reading something like *Los Ninos de Camapasitas*—with considerable gravity, watched by Halo tourists of a certain age, mainly women dressed in a puffy shorts-and-blouse combination which made them resemble, by contrast, someone's baby. "'I brought you these,' the river says to the land. The land declines without having to say anything at all. The river shrugs and tries again later."

"A complex story."

"It loses in translation," Alyssia admitted.

The dark came down soft and warm. They ate in one of the cafés on the edge of the square. Alyssia felt he looked too thin. He should slow down. Rig, she felt, had always seen himself caught between planets, between wars, between conflicting modes of being: a sardonic eye on a world he didn't quite get. "But other people see you differently," she said. "We see how hurt you become. We see so clearly how your personality trapped you in EMC, in the concept of constant war this Aleph of yours is supposed to end. Ask yourself why you called it that, Rig. The Aleph! Honestly, just ask!"

"Other people?" he said, smiling broadly.

She looked down at her plate. "Me," she was forced to admit. "I see you like that."

In his turn, Rig talked about what he called the wanton mystery of things. He couldn't get enough of it, he told her. But Alyssia hated phrases like that, and said: "In the end, maybe it will get enough of you."

Just then something hit the upper atmosphere with a dull thud. Sprays of ionisation flickered like heat lightning in the clouds. Alyssia Fignall sighed. She knew this one too. Everyone did. A warm wind filled the square, and with it the K-ship *Uptown Six*, out of New Venusport on grey ops for EMC's crack Levy Flight. At that time there was no greyer op in the Halo than R. I. Gaines. A mere two hundred feet long yet ten thousand tonnes unloaded, its matt-grey hull profuse with power bulges and ram intakes, *Uptown Six* dipped its blunt nose into the square. Reeking of stealth coatings, strange physics and the exotically dense matter laid in wafers between the poisonous composites of its hull, it hung outside the café door in a nose-down attitude, like a bad dream, full of the intelligence of its captain, a thirteen-year-old self-harmer called Carlo who would live the rest of his life in a tank of fluid somewhere near the stern.

"Here's your boyfriend," Alyssia said.

"Behave yourself," he said. He put his arms round her. "It's just a ride."

"Promise to come back soon, Rig."

He promised. They hugged a long time, then Gaines let her go. Before he had taken three paces he was already part of the darkness. The ship seemed to suck him in without opening any part of itself: though something caused its transformation optics to discharge briefly, distorting Alyssia's perception of the hull into a silvery yet glutinous foetal shape, through patches of which she could see the buildings on the other side of the square.

"You love this," she called after him bitterly, tilting her head to watch the sheet lightning in the clouds.

Ten minutes into the voyage, they were bounced.

"Incoming," Carlo said matter-of-factly. It was less a warning than a courtesy; the action was over before he framed the last syllable. Two middle-weight cruisers, their emissions heavily blocked, had slipped like eels into his ten-dimensional parsec-on-a-side cube of awareness and despatched assets up to and including the substrate disrupter known to K-captains as a "bump." Finding their target absent by a millisecond or more, a long-gone trail of turbulence in the local quantum foam, they had backtracked hastily: only to encounter *Uptown Six*, its mathematics sorting a billion or so tactical and navigational possibilities a nanosecond, already waiting for them.

"Guys," Carlo said, "you thought you could hide. But wherever you go, here I am." He released an asset of his own. "Be sure and have a nice day now."

To Gaines he added: "We seem to be at war." He couldn't say who with; by then he had lost interest anyway.

Projected into the carefully deodorised air of *Uptown Six*'s human quarters, feeds from fifteen planets showed, in quick succession, all the signs of modern conflict: street demonstrations, agitated financial markets, rows of top-shelf EMC hardware hulking around in parking orbits up and down the Beach. Within an hour all sides were broadcasting atrocity-footage as fast as it could be manufactured. Psychodrama raged. Everyone claimed the minority position. Everyone described their grievance as longer-standing and more asymmetric than the enemy's. Iconic buildings fell in towers of smoke. Sleeping genes, inserted into entire populations three or four generations in advance, expressed themselves as plagues of ideological change.

Up and down the Beach, innocent CEOs, brand managers and celebrities found themselves kidnapped, then subjected to sexual assault, at the hands of provocateurs who had no idea why they had begun to act so illiberally. By noon, exhausted attack ads fluttered up and down the streets of every Halo capital. Gaines studied these indicators with a kind of appalled impatience. Away from the media war not a shot had been fired. Except here. After a minute he said absently:

"Leave them alone, Carlo."

"Hey, I didn't start it."

"You know what I mean."

"Yes, OK, *too late*, Rig. Sorry I already killed them. Sorry I did it to keep you safe and all you do is to give me shit feelings about that. And Rig—no, listen to me, listen to me, Rig—this is something that happened two and half minutes ago? Can you hear yourself? Obsessing about something that happened two and half minutes ago? I'm sorry I killed them, because I know they were probably nice people, but excuse me, *they were trying to kill us first.*"

Uptown Six inserted itself into a stationary eddy in the radiation signature of a trio of neutron stars, and, judging itself to be safely hidden for the next thirty-two minutes and forty-eight seconds or so, upped Carlo's dosage of atypical antipsychotics; medicating him, in addition, for a twenty-minute nap. In the ensuing silence Gaines switched off the news channels and concentrated on the images he was receiving from his major project. What he saw, he couldn't believe. He opened an FTL pipe.

"What the fuck is going on here?" he said.

For the boys from Earth their arrival on the Beach was a game-changer. Anything could now happen. In the tidewrack of alien refuse, new universes awaited, furled up like tiny dimensions inside each abandoned technology. Back-engineering became the order of the day. Everyone could find something to work with, from a superconductor experiment the size of a planet to a gravity wave detector assembled from an entire solar system. Everything you found, you could find something bigger. At the other end of the scale: synthesised viruses, new proteins, nanoproducts all the way down to stable neutron-rich isotopes with non-spherical nuclei.

Ten per cent of it was still functioning. Ten per cent of that, you could make a wild guess what it did. Why was it there? All of this effort suggested a five-million-year anxiety spree centred on the enigma of the Tract. Every form of intelligent life that came here had taken one look and lost its nerve.

The boys from Earth didn't care about that, not at the outset: to them, the Beach was an interregnum, a holiday from common sense, an exuberant celebration of the very large and the very small, of the very old and the very new, of the vast, extraordinary, panoramic instant they congratulated themselves on living in: the instant in which everything that went before somehow met and became confected with everything yet to be. It was the point where the known met the unknowable, the mirror of desire.

It was, in short, a chance to make some money.

2410 AD: two Motel Splendido entradistas ran across an alien research tool the size of a brown dwarf, wobbling its way like a dirty balloon along some gravitational instability at the hot edge of the Tract. Their names were Galt & Cole. They made a single pass, looked things over and decided it could be done. Two days later their ride broke up in a Kelvin-Helmholtz eddy a bit further in. Cole, who couldn't think for alarms going off, went down with the ship; Galt, temporarily stripped of ambition by a plume of gas elevated to eleven million degrees Kelvin and observable only in the extreme ultraviolet, made it back to the research tool by escape pod. Five years later, his FTL beacon drew the attention of a Macon 25 long-hauler inbound for Beta Hydrae with ten thousand tonnes of catatonic New Men stacked in the holds like the sacks of harvestable organs they were.

By then Galt was calcium under a weird light. A few shreds of fabric and a polished skull. Who knew where his partner could be said to be? Galt left an autobiography, or maybe a final statement, or maybe only the name they had decided to give the real estate, scrawled on a stone—**PEARLANT**. They died near their fortune, those two, like all losers: but the name stuck. Beneath the pocked and gouged surface, choked with God knew how many million years of dust, lay what came to be called the Pearlant Labyrinth.

Two generations of entradistas hacked their way in. That was a story in itself. Lost expeditions, weird fevers, death. Every side-tunnel full of ancient machinery incubating an acute sense of injustice. They contended with fungus spores, cave-ins, passages flooded by non-Abelian fluids at room temperature. They were driven mad by the feeling of being observed. Worse, the labyrinth, clearly some kind of experiment in itself, had been constructed with such exquisite fractality that the term "centre" could only ever be a distraction. The experimental space, through which temporal anomalies ticked and flared in direct response to events deep inside the Tract ("As if," someone said, "it was built to tell the time in there"), would always contain more distance than its outer surface permitted. Eventually a team of maze-runners from FUGA-Orthogen—an EMC subsidiary specialising in nuclear explosives, capitalised out of New Venusport on the sale of mining machinery somewhat older than the labyrinth itself—hacked its way into the vast, ill-defined chamber which would come to be known as The Old Control Room. Their shadows scattered, jittery and spooked, across its perfectly flat allotropic carbon deck. They gathered at a respectable distance. They cracked their helmets and let fall their thermobaric power tools. They admired the fluttering opalescence of the Aleph where it lay suspended in its cradle of magnetic fields. They knew they had struck it rich.

Fifteen years later, 3D images of this treasure trove filled Gaines' dial-up: they were a little scratchy from distance, not to say the passage through three competing kinds of physics.

Around the time he was in the cloister with Alyssia Fignall, the Aleph had burst—boiling up from the nanoscale like a pocket nova, only to writhe, flicker, and, at the last moment, become something else. Where the containment machinery had been there was only the deck. On it lay an artefact of unknown provenance with the appearance of a woman, just over life-size and wearing a gown of grey metallic fabrics. This woman was barely human. She was neither conscious nor unconscious, dead nor alive. A white paste oozed from the corner of her mouth. There was something wrong with her cheekbones. Gaines stared at her; the woman, her limbs and torso shifting in and out of focus as if viewed through moving water, stared blankly back, her eyes drained of emotion, her face immobile. Whatever she was seeing, it wasn't in the chamber. Whatever effort she was making, it had nothing to do with him, but went on in silence, bitter, determined, undefinable, as if she would never understand what was happening to her yet never give up. She looked, Gaines thought, like someone trying not to die. "I don't think that's a helpful assumption," his site controller, a man called Case, told him. "It assigns values where you might not want them." Case had started out as a serious physicist, then, after a temporal convulsion in the maze aged him sixty years in a day, switched to management. He lived for his work, had written a fictional account of Galt & Cole called "These Dirty Stars," and though unimaginative did well with multidisciplinary teams. "To me she's less like a person than a problem."

"How did this happen?" Gaines said. "How can this have happened?"

No one was willing to make a guess.

"Never mind the Aleph," Case said. "The labyrinth itself is a million years old. We never knew what it was supposed to do; we never even knew which of them we were talking to."

Nanoscale footage presented the field-collapse as a kind of topological suicide. Picoseconds in, the Aleph resembled less a teardrop than a perished rubber ball, first folding to make a comic mouth, then rushing away towards a point beyond representation. "You aren't looking at the event itself," Case warned Gaines. "Only the stuff we could pick up." In the aftermath of the deflation, a full nanosecond later, the containment apparatus itself could be seen softening, flowing—this was visible on cameras run realtime outside the containment facility—and then evaporating into light. Out of the light the artefact emerged, *but could not be observed emerging*: Case thought this important. "No matter what timescale we look at these recordings—no matter how slow we run them—no smooth process can be detected." First the Aleph was there, then the woman was there instead. Her struggle had already begun. "For all we know, she could be an artefact in the other sense," Case said: "An illusion of our data-gathering methods."

"She looks so alive."

"The people in Xenobiology are already calling her Pearl," Case said, to show he could understand that.

"What does this mean for the field weapon?"

"The field weapon?" Case looked at Gaines as if he was mad. "It's fucked. That whole line of research is fucked. I don't think there ever was a field weapon, Rig." He stared around him, into the dark of The Old Control Room. "I think the labyrinth had its own agenda all along."

"Don't let upper management know about this."

16: Carshalton Shangri-La

"I'm having some strange dreams," Anna Waterman said, a few days after her brush with dogs. She had arrived late for Dr Alpert due to a missed connection, but seemed pleased with herself. She sat down immediately and without any indication that she was changing the subject, went on: "Do you know where I'd live, if I had the chance?"

"I don't know. Where?"

"I'd live in the covered bridge that goes over the platforms at Clapham station."

"Mightn't it be a bit draughty?"

"I'd keep it as one big space. Every so often you'd come upon a bit of carpet, some chairs, a bed. My furniture! I'd encourage the trains to keep running," she decided, the way you might say: "I'd encourage birds to visit the garden." She thought for a moment. "Just for the company. But Clapham would no longer be a stop. People would have to understand that." She smiled and sat back expansively in her chair, her body language that of someone who, having made a very fair offer, expects a positive response.

Helen Alpert smiled too. "I thought," she said, "that you were happy with your own house now?"

Anna nodded. "Less unhappy," she agreed.

The doctor made a note. "And Marnie?" she enquired. "How are you getting on with Marnie?"

Around the bathroom issue, and the deeper issues represented by it, Marnie and Anna had developed a kind of considerate wariness. Marnie had phoned the next day, anxious to apologise. In return, Anna sent a card, a kingfisher bursting out of the water with a small silver fish in its beak. Next time she arrived, Marnie brought flowers, a thick bunch of white stocks, blue delphiniums and sunflowers which they made into an arrangement together. One of the sunflowers was left over so Anna put it in a jug in the new bathroom. Every time she went to the loo she felt light and warmth pouring from it, and found herself full of the slow, lazy happiness she had been used to as a child, before things went wrong. The problem with Marnie, Anna had begun to suspect, was that for her nothing had ever really gone wrong.

"I'm not sure Marnie is as grown up as she thinks she is."

The doctor left a pause in case Anna wanted to develop this insight, then when nothing further emerged, enquired:

"And the dreams?"

"The dreams are a nightmare."

In the last few days she had seen everything. Half the time she hadn't even been sure she was asleep. In the dream she could be most certain of—the one in which she was most clearly dreaming—she was up on the Downs again, viewing herself from outside and slightly above: a woman carrying a child's empty coat across her arms as if it were the child itself. This woman was bent forward from the waist, looking into the middle distance at the white chalk paths, then down again at the coat. Her expression was one of neither joy nor musing. Skylarks sang. Hawthorn trees clustered on the hillside below. People appeared and disappeared on long, rising horizons. There were tiny blue flowers in the turf. Quite slowly, she passed out of the picture, vanishing over one of the immense skylines of the Downs.

Carrying a child: perhaps it was a dream about Marnie, perhaps it wasn't. If, in the doctor's consulting room, you acknowledged a dream like that, what might you be admitting to? You couldn't be sure. Anna therefore kept it to herself. But it was always possible to be frank about her standard dream:

The unknown woman lay on the black marble floor in some vast echoing space, dressed in a Givenchy gown; someone very old, unchanging but not yet herself; someone, essentially, waiting to change. Sometimes there was a kind of leaden buzzing noise, less a noise in fact than something that had seeped into you as you dreamed. Or you might hear a kind of high, distant ringing inside the floor, a kind of tinnitus at the heart of things. Sometimes there was the sense of an audience: someone—it might be you, it might be not—had started to clean her teeth, then cut her wrists in a hotel bathroom, only then looking up to find tiers of fully booked seats stretching up into darkness like a university lecture theatre. These were deranged but self-limiting images you could throw all day like sticks for Helen Alpert to chase—both doctor and patient got plenty of exercise out of that. So today Anna began refabricating a version of the dream she had once had while Michael was still alive, in which the first false-colour imagery of the Kefahuchi Tract—a new astronomical discovery for a brand new Millennium—had seemed to detach itself from the television screen and drift up into the dark air of their Boston motel room, where it hung like jewellery in a cheap illusion, then slowly faded away. By that time the room was vast.

"So exciting!" exclaimed Dr Alpert. As a child—eight years old and full of joy—she had loved those pictures so much that she remembered even now the lumbering black cathode-ray TV on which she had first seen them. They were less pictures than promises about the nature of the world, the rewards of study.

Anna—who, to the extent that she could remember the event at all, remembered it differently—could only shrug.

To the postmodern cosmologists of Michael Kearney's generation, entrapped by self-referential mathematical games, habitually mistaking speculation for science, the Tract had presented as the first of a new class of conundrums: the so-called Penfold Object, the singularity without an event horizon. To Kearney himself it was just another artefact of the twenty-four-hour news cycle, data massaged into fantasies for media consumption, less science than the public relations of science. The day NASA/ESA revealed its Tract composites—great hanging towers like black smokers in an ocean trench, luminous rose-coloured fans and pockets of gas, shockfronts with an aluminium sheen, looping through the gaseous medium as sounds 50 or 60 octaves below middle C, all layered-up from a year's observations by half a dozen space-based instruments, not one of them operating in the wavelengths of visible light—he had stiffened like a cat which thinks it sees something through a window; then relaxed equally suddenly and murmured, "Never fall for your own publicity"; later adding with a grin, "They might as well have had it announced by a man in a cloak and a top hat."

A generation later in Dr Alpert's office, Anna asked herself out loud, as if the two ideas were related, "What are dreams anyway?"

What indeed? thought the doctor, after Anna had gone. Sometimes the client beggared belief. Helen Alpert studied her notes; laughed; switched the voice recorder to Play, so that she could listen for a sentence or two which had intrigued her.

The client, meanwhile, her mood still elevated, loitered a moment or two on the consulting-room steps, watching the tide sidle upriver like a long brown dog; then, with the whole afternoon in front of her, made her way by two buses and a train to Carshalton. September, the greenhouse month, wrapped discoloured, vaporous distances around Streatham Vale and Norbury, where silvery showers of rain—falling without warning out of a cloudless blue-brown haze—evaporated from the hot pavements as quickly as they fell. Nothing relieved the humidity. At the other end, Carshalton dreamed supine under its blanket of afternoon heat as Anna made her way cautiously back to the house on The Oaks, approaching this time from the direction of Banstead, crossing the Common on foot—past the prison compounds which lay as innocuous as gated housing in the woods—and entering the maze of long suburban streets at a point halfway between the hospital and the cemetery. 121, The Oaks remained empty, with no sign of the boy who had disturbed her on her previous visit. When she tried the back door it proved to be unfastened as well as unlocked, opening to a push. Inside, economics—as invisible as a poltergeist, a force without apparent agency—was dividing the place up into single rooms. Evidence of its recent activity was easy to come by: stairs and hallways smelling of water-based emulsion and new wood. Bare floors scabbed with spilt filler, power cables lying patiently in the broad fans of dust they had scraped across the parquet, ladders and paint cans that had changed places.

Anna wandered around picking things up and putting them down again, until she came to rest in what had been a large back bedroom, split by means of a plaster partition carefully jigsawed at one end to follow the inner contour of the bay window. In this way, the invisible hand generously accorded its potential tenants half the view of the garden—flowerbeds overgrown with monbretia and ground-ivy, rotting old fruit nets on gooseberry bushes, a burnt lawn across which the damp, caramel-coloured pages of a paperback book had been strewn. Anna blinked in the incoming light, touched the unpainted partition, drew her fingers along the windowsill. Sharp granular dust; builders' dust. Nothing can hurt in these unfinished spaces. Life suspends itself. After a minute or two, an animal—a dog, thin and whippy-looking, brindled grey, with patches of long wiry hair around its muzzle and lower legs—pushed its way through the hedge from the next garden and went sniffing intently along the edge of the lawn, pausing to scrape at the earth suddenly with its front paws. Anna rapped her knuckles on the window. Something about the dog confused her. Rain poured down suddenly through the sunshine, the discarded pages sagged visibly under the onslaught as if made of a paper so cheap it would melt on contact with water. Anna rapped on the window again. At this the dog winced, stared back vaguely over its shoulder into the empty air. It shook itself vigorously—prismatic drops flew up—and ran off. The rain thickened and then tapered away and passed.

Out on the lawn, humidity wrapped about her face like a wet bag, Anna collected up as much of the book as she could and leafed through it. It was the novel the boy had recommended to her, *Lost Horizon*, ripped apart, perhaps, because it had finally failed to deliver on its promises of the world hidden inside our own. None of the pages were consecutive. Anna could assemble only the barest idea of the story. A crashed nuclear bomber pilot, perhaps American, finds himself in a secret country, only to have it—and his heart's desire—snatched away from him at the last; paradoxically, that very loss seems to endorse the reader's hope that such a country might exist. The front cover had been torn down the middle in a kind of careful rage. Anna read: "The classic tale of Shangri-La." A telephone, its ringer set to simulate an old-fashioned electric bell, started up inside the house.

Aluminium foil—as brown and sticky-looking as if it had been used to cook a roast—clung in ragged strips to the inside of the nearest window. Peering anxiously between them, Anna made out the dining room. No improvements were ongoing there; nor was there much furniture or ornament. Two upright chairs. A gate-leg table fifty years old. Green linoleum caught the dim light in ripples. On the table stood a pressed-tin box with a glass front, about eight inches by four, someone's small prize brought back from Mexico during the cheap air-travel decades, in which was displayed the following peculiar diorama: an object the size and shape of a child's skull, nestled on a bed of red lace like offcuts from cheap lingerie and set against a black background (scattered with sequins and meant, perhaps, to represent Night). Otherwise nothing, except the rolled-up carpet propped in the corner opposite the door. Though the telephone seemed close, Anna couldn't see it. It continued to ring for a minute or two. Then came a loud, amplified click succeeded by the impure electronic silence of the open connection, and a clear voice that said:

"My name is Pearlant and I come from the future."

At that the connection broke. A dark figure appeared in the internal doorway, and after two or three quietly bad-tempered attempts a wheelchair was pushed into the room. Its occupant had deteriorated since Anna last saw him getting into a cab in front of Carshalton station. One corner of his mouth was drawn up rigidly; his bald head, exhibiting the deep uniform tan of ten days on some abandoned Almerian beach, shone with ulcers. He entered sitting upright in the chair—ankles crossed and knees apart, one hand performing an unwittingly hieratic gesture at the level of his chest—but fell forward almost immediately against its restraining harness of broad nylon webbing. His head dropped slackly to the right—this brought into sharp relief the tendon at the side of his neck, and offered his left ear to the white cat on his shoulder, which, as if it had been waiting for just such an opportunity, adjusted its balance; purred; licked inside the ear with precise delicate motions. All the time Anna had been in the house, he had been there too, slumped in some other empty room, his liver-coloured underlip drooping and one blue eye open in the heat. The harness, with its central quick-release mechanism, looked too robust for any forces the movement of a wheelchair might produce; while the seat itself had bulky, over-engineered qualities, like something in a now-obsolete experiment. She knew she should have recognised him all along. Perhaps she had. Had he recognised her? Impossible to tell. Underneath her amnesia the memory itself lay swaddled. It was the unthought known, always tucked carefully away, a self-deception under a self-deception. How could he have grown so old? The telephone began to ring again, the white cat jumped on to the table and walked about fiercely. There in the water light of the unreconstructed dining room, the Mexican box glimmered like tarnished silver: the dark figure behind the wheelchair reached over to pick it up.

That was enough to send Anna out of the garden, stumbling down the side passage, hurrying away from 121, The Oaks to the relative sanity of the suburban afternoon, all the rest of which she spent wandering confusedly about, up one long street and down the next, heat ringing around her from cracked paving, until she emerged blinking and puzzled, hard by Carshalton Ponds. The High Street lay uneasily under the sun, full of excavations—shallow, affectless scoops, the product of underpowered machinery and half-hearted plans, fenced off behind a long maze of red and white barriers, which, like the cars in the street, resembled plastic toys pumped up to appeal to some infantile aesthetic.

A room the colour of a headache, she thought. And why had the window once been covered with roasting foil?

Her journey home was slow. The train—as poorly maintained as any public machinery since the serial recessions of the 2010s—failed repeatedly, a minute here, two minutes there; then twenty minutes at a station somewhere near Streatham, during which period, a boy and a girl of college age, who had been kissing energetically since they got on, played a complicated little game at the open carriage door. He stood on the platform, while she leaned out towards him from the train. He kept saying: "Well, tara, I'll see you back there." She would wait for him to go, then—when he remained standing there on the platform five feet away grinning at her—laugh and say, "That's what you think, is it?" Then they would both laugh, the boy would half turn away, and they would start again. "I'll see you back there. We'll decide where to put it then, it'll be fun."

"It won't go in the corner whatever you say."

"I'm off now, anyway."

"I bet you are."

Suddenly the doors began to close. "Tara then," the boy said. "I'll see you back there."

"Tara," the girl said, turning away. At the last minute she squeezed between the doors, struggled off the train and threw her arms round him. They took a few stumbling paces along the platform towards the exit, laughing and bumping hips and wrestling at one another's shoulders. The girl made a fist and scrubbed at the boy's scalp with it. "Hey!" he said.

By the time Anna got back it was almost dark. Craneflies tumbled into the windows, stumbling and crawling stupidly about the glass, pinned there by the papery force of their own wings. The cat was out. Anna filled his bowl with tuna surprise, and put two goat's cheese and spinach tartlets in the oven for herself. Marnie rang while they were heating up. "What a day!" she told Anna. "Work was just appalling." Morning traffic had made her an hour late, she said. "The whole of Clerkenwell was at a standstill."

"Darling," Anna said, "it's been at a standstill for twenty years."

Looking for something equivalent to offer, she told Marnie about the lovers on the train. "After they'd gone," she finished, "I turned to look at the other passengers, and I was the only one smiling."

"How did you feel about that?"

"I felt like a fool," Anna replied, without a moment's thought.

"Still," Marnie said: "Romantic." Then she said that she had a hospital appointment the next morning. "It's just a scan," she said. "But I wondered if you'd come with me."

"Of course I will!" Anna said, astonished.

"It's nothing, I expect," Marnie said. "Absolutely nothing."

One in the morning: unable to sleep, Anna switched on the twenty-four-hour news, hoping, though she would not have admitted it to herself, for some indication that Michael Kearney had come home. Nothing overt, she thought; just something casual buried in the coverage of a scientific conference. A clue. All she received was a sense that there were no longer any real events in the world—that, whatever the "news," nothing was actually happening until the camera turned its eye on each short, jerky scene. Palm trees—enacting "stirred by an evening wind"—would jump suddenly, almost guiltily, into life as the wire service prepared to objectify them. In the satellite lag before the stringer spoke, you heard a faint, repetitive voice which sounded like gak gak gak. Later she stood in the new bathroom, whispering anxiously:

"Are you there?" and, "You do like it, don't you? You did say you liked it!" Her erratic five-year transit of the suburbs and dormitories of South London—launched after the death of Tim Waterman, accelerating when Marnie left home—was over. The events of the afternoon had proved that. Nothing had been solved. She was still unable to remember what happened all those years ago, the night Michael entrusted her with the pocket drive. She stood by the bedroom window, rooting through her handbag. Out in the garden, a faint mist crept across the meadow from the river to melt among the orchard trees. Eventually she found the drive and held it like a titanium shell to her ear, as if it might have verbal instructions for her. "Oh, Michael, I know you're there. Can't you just come back and help?"

No answer: except that in front of her the summerhouse burst grandly and silently into flames, as black against the sky as the woodcut illustration in a book of Tarot cards.

17: Correlation States

When the Kefahuchi Tract expanded, in what came to be known as "the Event," parts of it fell to earth on planets all along the Beach. Event sites appeared everywhere, sometimes in deserts or polar icefields or at the bottom of the sea: but often alongside the cities.

They were assembly-yards of the abnormal—zones where physics seemed to have forgotten its own rules—expanding into the real world via a perimeter of fogs, hallucinations, half-glimpsed movements. From inside could be heard confused laughter, big music, the sound of machinery. Something was being produced in there. Obsolete objects came fountaining out. They were highly energetic and abnormally scaled: rains of enamel badges, cheap rings, windup plastic toys; nuts & bolts, cups & saucers, horses & carts; feathers, doves and black-lacquered boxes, conjuror's props the size of houses. They burst into the air above the roofline, then toppled back and vanished. A blueprint unfolded itself across the sky, then folded itself up again and faded away. No one minded these illusions, if illusions they were. But artefacts and inexplicable new technologies came out of the Event sites too, and sought a foothold on our side of things. Some of them were conscious and looked human. They wandered out into the cities and tried to become part of life. That was when things went wrong. EMC took an interest. Razor wire went up. The observation towers went up. SiteCrime and Quarantine (known popularly as QuaPo) became, for a time, the most powerful police forces in the Halo, second only to Earth Military Contracts itself.

Irene and Liv listened to Fat Antoyne Messner explain these recent history facts they already knew, then said as one voice:

"Antoyne, yadda yadda. What's in it for us?"

"Quarantine orbit work," Fat Antoyne said, and he told them the story of Andy and Martha.

Andy and Martha lived on a planet called Basel Dove. Andy owned a little townhouse, worked human resources for the usual corporate; Martha collected alien ceramics. They had a son they called Bobby, eight that summer, a bright kid if a little needy. Andy found them a young woman, intelligent and ordinary-looking, to tutor Bobby in the afternoons. Her name was Bella. She dressed well but came off a little vague, as if she didn't quite understand how a house or a family worked. Her commonest expression was of a cheerful puzzlement. Bella had her own room, near the top of the house. She worked out well. You'd find her standing in a hallway early evening, staring ahead of herself and wondering what to do next; but she soon settled in, and Bobby no longer followed Martha about all day complaining he was bored. Instead he sat quietly with Bella, listening in awe as she solved problems of classic harmonic analysis in her head. They got on so nicely! It was, as Martha said, a love affair, "Bella and Bobby this, Bella and Bobby that. Always Bella and Bobby." Those two were, really, really inseparable. But soon they were more inseparable than you would hope.

Before Bella arrived, the little boy's mid-afternoon recreation had been to take his clothes off and look at himself in the mirror until he got hard. He rubbed but nothing came out yet. He could feel something coming up but it never arrived. All he got was a sort of shock, a painful little jolt. Bella changed all that. After mathematics she would take him upstairs to her room and style his hair for him. A passive calm came over him at such moments. He loved her smell. With each stroke of the brush, his little cock stuck out harder in his pants. When Bella touched it accidentally with the back of her hand, they looked at one another in wonder. One winter afternoon, Martha found them on the sofa. It was bitterly obvious what had been happening before she came in the room. Bella's tits were bare. The little boy's pants were open. Her hand was on his penis. She leaned over him, he stared up at her, growling and whimpering in his little boy voice as he struggled to come.

It was horrible enough that Martha walked in on her eight-year-old son about to ejaculate in the hand of the hired help. But worse was to be revealed. When she tried to pull them apart, they were stuck together. And when Andy came home he found his wife stuck to them too.

One of Martha's forearms had penetrated Bella's head. Martha was staring angrily at her hand emerging on the other side. Everything was soft. All three of them were covered in a thin, slippery emulsion; they were pulling away from one another, but that only seemed to make things worse. Andy threw up. He called the Quarantine Bureau. By 10 pm the same day, Bobby, Bella and Martha were a fully fledged escape—translucent, infectious, a jelly part human, part virus, part daughter code straight from the local Event site. With Andy's permission, Quarantine sealed this substance into a heavily welded, tapering iron container about seven feet long by three in depth, which they left on the floor of Bella's room. Since Basel Dove was too quiet to have a quarantine orbit of its own, they explained, the sarcophagus would have to be delivered—within a week and by a licensed operator—to the one at New Venusport. They said they were sorry for Andy's loss, and left. Andy, numb with grief and puzzlement and unable to find a local firm willing to handle such a tiny cargo, called Saudade Bulk Haulage.

"He doesn't want to make the trip himself," Antoyne explained. "He's a damaged man. It's very sad."

Liv Hula pursed her lips. "So we're undertakers now?"

"I'm glad to get any kind of work," answered Fat Antoyne. "Besides, we're going there anyway."

So *Nova Swing* became a quarantine dog, and her crew found themselves sharing space with the remains of Martha, Bobby and Bella. They stowed the sarcophagus in a corner of the main hold. By then the contents had settled into a uniform transparent mass weighing slightly less than its original human components. It was liquid, superconductive at room temperature, and retained some memory of its former state: for instance, the little boy could sometimes be seen behind the armoured viewplate, half-formed, curled foetally with his hands between his legs. It made Irene sad. "Oh, his little penis," she said. She was not her usual self. She woke hearing dice rattle in the holds and passageways, soft laughter, voices. If a game was being played, Irene wasn't in it. She opened doors and never found anyone there.

"It wears you down," she complained to Antoyne.

Antoyne, thinner than ever, cultivated a stubble. He feared living hand to mouth. The ordered world being defined for him now by Liv and Irene, he was afraid he would fall out of it and return to his old ways. Irene thought him vague lately, especially since that afternoon at Mambo Rey, and wondered out loud if he was recalling some other lover. "Because that would be all right," she told him. "We all remember the other loves we had." Antoyne looked blank at this and didn't seem to agree. Of course, it was quite a long list for her, Irene admitted, so each one had to work harder to stand out. She had a vision suddenly: men in an endless line, each one awaiting the opportunity to step up and impress her again. One thought he danced well. Another thought his cock was pretty big, but it would never bring tears to her eyes like the cock of that little dead boy. Of course, they weren't really lovers.

"Antoyne," she said in rush, "what if this rocket was haunted?"

He touched her wrist. "All rockets are haunted," he said. "I assumed you knew that."

Liv Hula could only smile at these naive exchanges. Tapped into the pilot systems while everyone else slept, she'd seen the way MP Renoko's mort-safes clustered around the new cargo when they thought they weren't being watched. They sniffed it like dogs, perhaps deciding it wasn't quite their species. On the fifth day out from Basel Dove, *Nova Swing* had sight of New Venusport, a fully Earthlike planet in terms of biome, military presence and fiscal architecture. The Quarantine Bureau hailed on all wavelengths. There were automated warnings. Vast shapes drifted in the void, blinking with dim lights. Antoyne dragged the sarcophagus to an airlock and consigned it to empty space, where it fell into the general hidden turmoil and vanished.

"That poor little thing," Irene whispered.

"Honey, there are two grown women in the casket with him," Liv Hula reminded her. "Ask yourself who put them there."

Life in quarantine: a hundred yards away, someone in an eva suit could be seen welding steel plates over a hatch; further in, pSi engines fired up as two or three hulks worked to phase-lock with the local flow. In the brief strobing flashes, Liv made out the skeleton of a pipeliner, two centuries old, three miles long. She allowed the ship to drift further in, then out again. Renoko's next load awaited them only a few hundred miles beneath. As they departed, a K-ship nosed out from between the hulks and followed them down, at one point fitting itself so closely into the curves of the old freighter's hull that they could feel waste heat radiating from the internal processes it made no attempt to mask. Its signals traffic alone could have cooked a city. It wanted them to know it was there. It wanted them to know that they were a question it could answer if it wanted to; anything it wanted, it could have. It matched them through one and a half cycles of their aerobrake program, then became interested in something else and spun away. Liv, who had felt the K-captain crawling in and out of her brain through the wires in her mouth, shuddered.

"I hate those things," she said.

There was a silence. Then a faint voice, already four lights down the Beach, whispered: "Well I've never said an unkind word about *you*, sweetie."

New Venusport South Hemisphere, 3 am: Madame Shen's old premises, a three-acre strip of cement between the sea and the rocket yards. For a minute or two after the *Nova Swing* came down there was silence. Then the night sounds returned, bustle from the yards, chain-link fences rattling in the offshore breeze. Fat Antoyne Messner stood on the loading platform, looking across a thin layer of marine fog doped with pollution from the yards. It would clear rapidly with the approach of dawn; meanwhile the motors ticked and cooled, and Antoyne relished the damp air in his face. The curve of the bay was lined with clapboard beach motels, blind pigs and empty sex joints—Ivy Mike's, Deleuze Motel, The Palmer Lounge—their cinder lots full of drifted sand. Waves rumbled in from the horizon.

"Look!" Liv Hula said. "No, there!"

A figure was making its way along the line of buildings, silhouetted against the faint luminescence of the waves: female, tall, full of the unresolved tensions of the heavily tailored. Faceless and quiet, she leaned for a moment on the siding of the Deleuze Motel, one arm straight out from the shoulder, palm flat against the wall. The wind smelled of chemicals. She raised her head to it like a dog, looking out to sea, then sat down at the edge of the concrete apron and began pouring sand from one cupped hand to the other: someone who, arriving too late for a meeting, regrets having come at all.

"I know that woman," Liv whispered, "but I can't think where from."

Antoyne was unable to help. He had seen so many people like that, in bars from here to the Core.

After you had yourself rebuilt to such a degree, body language was enough to tell whatever two-dimensional story you had left. You were so wired to yourself you no longer knew what you were. Every response ramped up, every surface tuned to receive rays from space: designed for looks, speed, confidence and security at point of use.

"But who can say what back door access the tailor left?" he concluded.

Liv found this critique unhelpful. "I know her from somewhere," she said. Then: "Look! Antoyne! In the breaks!"

Two hundred yards away, a long cylindrical object was beating up out of the sea, dipping and rolling in the salt spray. In three or four minutes it had found its way on to the beach. It looked like a mine from a forgotten war, rusty, steaming and throwing off curious dark rainbows while it decided where to go next. The woman by the Deleuze Motel was watching it too. She stood up and dusted off her hands. When the mortsafe showed signs of moving away into the dunes, she called out and began running after it at a rate no human being could sustain, becoming in three or four paces a mucoid blur. Almost immediately, she was in collision with an identical blur, which had lunged up at her from a shallow hiding place down in the sand and marram grass. Both of them shrieked loudly. It was as if she had run full tilt into a mirror. Every movement she made, her double matched. Sand flew up around them so it became impossible to tell which was which. Then one of them slowed down suddenly and strode around looking puzzled with her hands to her head. She sat down hard. Fell forward slowly from the waist. Leaving her there motionless, the survivor went fizzing away among the dunes, tearing up the marram grass, startling the shoreline birds.

"They've killed her!" said Liv.

Antoyne put his hand on her arm. "This isn't to do with us."

A third figure, some shadowy little old guy in a shortie raincoat, had watched the encounter from the dunes, clapping his hands, looking round as if appealing to the rest of the audience on a lively evening at the Preter Coeur fights. His face was a white oval. He had the look of an enthusiast. If there had been a way to bet, you thought, he would have set his money down. After a minute or two he approached the dead woman, knelt down near her head and busied himself about there, chuckling. Then he retreated into the dunes a little way and waited, his stillness such that he became difficult to see, until the woman woke up. "Jesus fucking Christ," they heard her complain distinctly. She rolled over, too late to avoid puking an evil pink fluid copiously on herself. She got to her feet and staggered to the side door of the Deleuze Motel, above which blinked a flamingo-coloured neon reading STARLIGHT ROOM with, above that, two stylised palm trees intertwined. Leaning against her own shadow on the blistered wall, she threw up again, more carefully this time, and went inside. The man in the raincoat, meanwhile, had walked off towards the sea without looking back once.

"Fat Antoyne, this is so wrong!"

By now Antoyne had something else to think about. Down at the base of the *Nova Swing*, just outside the harsh glare of the loading lights, the fifth mortsafe awaited him, quiet, unobtrusive, smelling of the sea.

He went down to fetch it and found the usual corroded tin can, leaking its unknown past like a physical substance. This time someone had daubed it with nondrying anti-radar paint, into which a meaningless line of letters and numbers had then been impressed using some kind of stencil. It was warmer than the others. When he had got it stowed away, he found that Irene had left the ship. Liv didn't know where. The two of them went out into the dunes and called around, but Irene didn't answer. "You'd better go and find her," Liv told Antoyne. Then shouted after him, "She's not happy, Antoyne." The wind blew harder and the moon was up. Squalls were headed in across the bay.

Raised on an agricultural planet, Irene had questions from the start, mainly about her ability to empathise. But when you sign for the package they offer you a heart of gold, because it makes you happier in the work. It's free. Really, it's a cheap tweak. No one loses, not you, not your customer. Irene opted in and never regretted it, though maybe her heart was over-tuned now for the quarantine orbit, because here on South Hemisphere NV, made more upset than she could allow herself to understand by the story of the little boy in the sarcophagus, she needed a bar, a bottle of Black Heart, and the company of people she didn't know.

But the other side of the fence things only deteriorated. Seaward in the fog, you could feel distance growing in everything. From Lizard Sex to The Metropole, the shutters were up all along the strip. The old-fashioned signs banged in the wind; rust ran down from blisters in the paintwork. Outside the joint they called 90-Proof & Boys, the air tasted of salt. Ivy Mike's lay silent and unoccupied. The circus wasn't in town, and it was coming on to rain.

Eventually she heard voices. The front doors of the Deleuze Motel, flanked by frosted glass windows and scoured wood panels with tinpot ads, were padlocked shut. She shook them. A wan yellow light could be seen inside. "Hello!" No one answered. They didn't even stop what they were doing. There were distinct rattling sounds and, every so often, outbreaks of a kind of subdued shouting. The yellow light came and went, as if someone was walking jerkily to and fro in front of it. Irene could hear ordinary sounds too: a chair scraped back, ice clattering in a glass. She patted the door as if it was someone's arm. "So hey," she said, "you're having a good time in there." She went round the side and found, under the pink and mint neon STARLIGHT ROOM, another pair of doors, loosely latched and shifting in the wind. Without a thought she put her eye to the gap, where the paint was slick with rain. Whatever she saw in there made her take one startled pace backwards, then run away as fast as a b-girl can.

18: It Takes Place in a Vacuum

Some days the shadow operators vanished the moment daylight fell on them. Others, they fluttered up to meet it, swimming about delightedly in the air above her desk. Their behaviour was as opaque to the assistant as hers was to them. They predated the human. They were a form of life you found everywhere: but what they did before human beings arrived in the Galaxy to make use of them, no one knew, not even the shadow operators themselves. If you asked them they grew shy and thoughtful.

"It's so nice you're interested, dear."

She asked them to list her some names from the files.

They offered Magellan, Radtke and dos Santos. Nevy Furstenberg and John K. Matsuda. They offered the notorious Ephraim Shacklette. They offered MP Renoko.

"Him," the assistant said.

MP Renoko, aka Ronostar Productions, aka Dek Echidna, had begun stripping the assets of Madame Shen's Circus late in 2400, after five consecutive quarters of mixed results. Thereafter you could follow the paper trail across the Halo from South Hemisphere, New Venusport. It led to FUGA-Orthogen—once a thriving EMC subsidiary with interests in mining and recovery, now a single empty Lost & Found office on a badlands planet in the long tail of niche tourism—then trickled away into meaningless local eddies. It was commerce at the edge of viscosity, until Renoko quietly began buying items back. Now he was moving them around under junk certification, using the same ship that had hauled the Halo's favourite travelling entertainment from planet to planet.

131

"So what are we looking at?" she asked the shadow operators.

They were unable to say at this time.

The assistant, who had expected nothing more, took herself off to New Venusport. The travel lounges were rammed with people trying to get home. War had upped the ante on their lives.

South Hemisphere, NV: underlit smoke poured all night from cheap-and-dirty chemical launchers humping payload into secure EMC orbits. Particle jockeys sweated out their radiation meds under the blackened hulls of K-ships. In the breakers' yards, indentured New Men—without benefit of a pair of leather gloves, let alone a lead suit—crawled by the thousand over scrapped Alcubiere warpers the size of small towns. Everywhere you looked, you saw machines which would, if their science was turned off for a second, revert instantly to a slurry of nanotech and a few collapsing magnetic fields. Ionisation flickered through clouds of sulphur dioxide and radioactive steam.

What remained of Sandra Shen's Observatorium & Native Karma Plant—aka The Circus of Pathet Lao—could be found on three acres of fenced-off cement between the rocket pits and the sea. Yard machinery rose up on one side, rippling with bad physics; on the other it was sand dunes steadily absorbing an encrustation of abandoned cabana units, beach bars and hotels—Ivy Mike's, Deleuze Motel, The Palmer Lounge. The fences dripped with condensation, rattling in an offshore wind. Beneath the chemical signature of the yards, the assistant smelled only salt and dust. Her tailoring, attentive to every breeze, picked up particle dogs, scrambled EMC traffic, low-grade electromagnetic haze from unshielded operations. Otherwise, nothing. Then a K-ship ripped towards the marshalling orbit at Mach 40, its line of fusion product lighting everything in the near ultraviolet: a few alien poppies were revealed growing in the earth at the base of a gate, their crumpled metallic flowerheads nodding in the disturbed air. Life at the circus, NV style. Over in a distant corner of the field stood a three-fin short-hauler, stubby and used-looking, its image still rippling with the heat of a recent re-entry. *Nova Swing!*

She listened in to its internal comms for a moment. Well, well, she thought. Now you have some talking to do, you three. She was in no hurry. She smiled to herself and sat down not far from the Deleuze Motel; watched the ocean waves break white on luminous indigo, and let a handful of sand run through her fingers. She wondered if she should call herself Queenie, Aspodoto or Tienes mi Corazon. Roxie. Mexie. Maybe Backstep Cindy.

After a minute or two the acid-clouds parted to reveal stars in subtly different arrangements to the ones she knew.

A minute or two after that, something shot quickly left to right along the front of a breaking wave eighty metres out, then, half-submerged in turbulence, nosed its way up through the swash on to the beach. A corroded bronze pressure tank—tubular, perhaps three metres by one and recently daubed with crude Jaumann absorbers in a resin base—it featured inlaid circuits and a lateral line of deep blue LEDs. A single quartz port glittered at one end. In a universe boiling with algorithms, anything can behave as if it's alive; harder, the assistant thought, to look intelligent, even when you were. The mortsafe, if that's what it was, hunted for some moments through twenty or thirty degrees of arc, as if trying to orient itself; then—hovering three or four feet above the beach, swaying with an oiled resilience in every gust of wind—it slipped inland between the dunes, heading towards the *Nova Swing*.

"Wait!" the assistant called.

Her tailoring redlined, but something much closer than the ship had already begun dismantling it. Whoever it was, they were too quick for her. Structured magnetic fields reached in through the doped protein meshes around her brainstem and squeezed firmly for eight or nine milliseconds. They let her stagger away, choking and dancing. She could feel herself kicking up the sand. Seizure-sites propagated across the cortex in cascades. Proprioception went down. Target acquisition went down. Autonomic functions went down. Everything went down. It wasn't a Preter Coeur kill. It was something EMC. Just before the system folded, IR and active sonar acquired what she thought might be a human figure leaning over her. After that she got: sensation of a door closing: sensation of something frying in the spinothalamic tract: a smell like rendered fat. Just illusions. All she felt as she fell was a kind of shame. Nothing like that had ever happened to her before.

When she woke up it was still night. The tide was a little further out. She was alone. The smell of burnt rocket fuel blew over the dunes and for a moment she interpreted that, too, as synaesthesia from some cortical fuck-up they had done to her. Best to lie in the marram, fitting and retching while the self-repair kits crawled dispassionately over her brain. She felt worse than at any time since she came out of the chopshop tank in Preter Coeur with her new career and her specialised arm. Eventually she got to her feet and staggered into the Deleuze Motel, where she found a ballroom full of drifted sand. Two low-wattage bulbs alive in the chandelier. At the back, by the bar, three old men in white flat caps and polyester trousers, staring at her. They were playing dice. They had a crate of alcopops and two or three bottles of Black Heart barrel proof rum, which they were drinking on its own, no ice.

"For Christ's sake," the assistant said. "If you know what's good for you you'll give me some of that."

Impasse van Sant had come down the Carling Line as just another speck in fifty tonnes of deep-frozen trade gametes. Sperm and egg futures were declining: passed hand to hand for two hundred years, often as a sweetener in some more interesting deal, van Sant was finally thawed out as farmworker potential. After that he couldn't seem to settle. It was a common enough syndrome in the Halo. Dedicated before birth to the gods of irreversible flight and determined-but-unpredictable motion, Imps now stared into empty space and whispered:

"Are you out there?"

No answer. Then a momentary flicker, very quick and faint. In response, the research vessel sorted quantum events. Software injected the system with wide-band noise, pumping it by stochastic resonance into the story of some brief imbalance in the vacuum energy. Data built suddenly, crested, fell away fast. The number of objects in local space had suddenly doubled. Half a parsec towards the Core, something banked like a white wing, caught tilted up against the dark as if on some other errand. He didn't know how many times she had slipped away from him like this before he had time to speak, a huge frail orphan in the substrate of the universe. There were days when he couldn't bear the possibility. Today was one of them. Whatever shit he shot with Rig Gaines over beer and table tennis, Imps knew he was kidding himself when he thought he could get by in outer space on his own. He worked feverishly to reel her in, his expression suddenly soft and desperate in the old-fashioned glow of the control panel.

"Hello?" he called into the dark. "Hello?"

"Hello."

His heart raced. He tried to think of some way to extend their previous conversations; something certain to keep her attention.

"What would you be," he said, "if you could be one other thing?"

"One thing?"

"One other thing."

She turned restlessly in the vacuum. Her shadow fell across him, elegant, high aspect ratio, one thousand metres tip to tip. Sometimes she presented like this, as feathers. Others it would be plasma, superconductors, a tangle of magnetic fields around which raced particles of all energies. Every so often she chose a thick cold slab of flesh instead, it rippled like a manta ray. As if to acknowledge the problems of such diversity, and of the question itself, she answered:

"I never knew what I was anyway."

"You don't know what you were?"

"I was something but I didn't know what, even then."

She thought about it. "Even then I was on a journey back to something. It was a long time ago," she said eventually. "If I knew what I was then, that's what I'd choose to be."

"You've already been something else?"

"I can't explain."

"I was never anything but myself. I was always locked in."

But she wouldn't help him with that, not this time. In the end she whispered bleakly: "We all make bad decisions."

Just then a random pulse of energy shuddered across the face of the K-Tract. A tenuous shell of something—less than gas, more than nothing, dark matter like a kind of ghost velvet—expanded into the local universe. "Oh look!" she called. "Isn't it lovely?" She manoeuvred herself to face it, her hundred-metre tip feathers curling and separating. Meanwhile the wavefront penetrated the hull of van Sant's tub, giving rise to events of such subtlety they couldn't be detected. It touched his face light as lovers' fingers, and left the wiring confused.

"Someone went in there," he heard her whisper.

"So they say."

"It wasn't so long ago. I wondered if I should go too."

Exotic radiation bathed them both, to different ends, for twenty minutes. By the time van Sant emerged from its trailing edge, she had resumed her restless patrol of empty space, and he was alone again.

Don't go! Imps wanted to shout.

He always failed to ask her so many things.

Who are you? What are you? Why are we out here, the two of us? What's the nature of your dialogue with the universe? What happens next? Is it possible for species as different as us to fuck?

All of these questions but one were in fact asked of himself, and might have been rephrased: *Will I ever go home?*

None of them mattered if you were involved with R. I. Gaines. Everything Rig ever did implied that the real action was happening elsewhere. Some other domain of possibilities was being actively explored alongside this one. Gaines' motives were so obscure—his projects went so unreported, even in the hierarchy of EMC—that in the end only your own part in an op could be described (for the same reason, it could hardly be called a "contribution," since you had no idea what it contributed to). Every time Imps' alien visitor appeared, she forced him to query not why Rig Gaines wanted him out here in the middle of nowhere, but what facet of his so-called personality had prompted him to agree to come there in the first place.

Days like that, when she had departed, leaving the lights turned off in van Sant's head, his instruments showed him nothing but his own cast-off past: Levy flight after Levy flight into empty space. He had no consolation but the long slow struggle to understand his own course. That and the Tract. Because the Tract is gaining on us, Imps thought: it's slowly catching up with the real universe. The first place it would wash over was the Beach. Meanwhile, Imps van Sant was closer to it, he believed, than any other living beachcomber: which meant the first one it would wash over was him.

A long way off, in the ballroom of the Deleuze Motel, the assistant sat recovering herself. She drank barrel proof rum from the bottle and watched the old men work the overend on one another at the Ship Game—adjusting their white caps, shooting the cuffs of their formal shirts with sharp economical gestures, whispering, "Well now," or "*Now* you fucked." In their opinion, the night was moving along: every so often one of them would cock his head at the sound of the ocean, lean across, and, black eyes as empty as raisins, assure the assistant that the night was moving right along. Dice rattled and scattered, shedding alien luck as friction brought them to a standstill. The faint smell of vomit coming and going in the cold air, the assistant realised, originated with her. Three am, the tide was fully out. R. I. Gaines walked in through the sea-facing wall.

"Wow!" he said. "The Ship Game! Make room!"

The old men blinked up at him like lizards. They made room. Something he could do with the bone interested them, they were disposed to admit. Soon, they were taking his money, he was taking theirs. "It's a redistributive system," he proposed. Redistribution, they agreed, was the name of that particular game. The assistant watched these events from a distance, then walked over to the door. The breeze was onshore. Dawn wasn't far off. Seeming to notice her for the first time, Gaines jumped to his feet and led her back into the room. He made a gesture that took in the salt-stained walls, the chandelier with its two dim bulbs, the dusty signs behind the bar.

"Sometimes you're quite hard to find," he said.

The assistant shrugged. She offered him the rum. "So," she said, "do you want to go and sit on my bed together?"

He gave her a thoughtful look.

"The Aleph stopped asking for you. We wondered if you knew anything about that."

"I never know what you're talking about."

Gaines grinned. He held up the bottle, studied the label. "'Black Heart,'" he quoted. "'All the sweet lacunae of the Caribbean Sea.'"

The assistant looked down at her arm. Nothing was happening there.

"I wonder if it's time you two met?" Gaines asked himself.

The fact was, he couldn't decide. He had recently come from the Aleph site, where there had been more activity than he expected, reflections of smart displays fluttering across the shiny carbon floor, smells of ionisation and construction. Case's people were devising new containment principles. It was a high risk period for them all. They had no idea what they were dealing with. When Gaines arrived they were arguing if they wanted a bunch of fat cables in here just for the look of it, or do the whole thing tight beam, which, hey, would be the quick and dirty solution. It was a professionally toxic but busy atmosphere. The reason being, Case told Gaines, that early the same morning Pearl had begun to emit pulsed bursts of RF.

"It's not organised, as far as we can tell."

"So what is it?"

Case shrugged. "It's not exactly random noise either," he said.

"I'm impressed. Is there anything you guys don't know?"

"Rig, we're doing what we can here," Case said tiredly.

His imaging team produced a hologram display that rotated the woman smoothly around every axis so that she looked like virtual false-colour shots of a sculpture, spoiled by some sort of faint, in situ interference. Attempts to clean the interference out had only given her the lines of a Deco portrait, freezing the folds of her gown to create strong contentless curves suggestive of power and energy. Her eyes were rendered the same colour as her face, without pupils or lids. "After we took these I had them build a field tomography unit round her," Case said. "Forget it. It was like looking into nacre." As far as X-rays were concerned, she was solid all through. "Positron emission feels the same about her. We decided not to try neutrons, in case she bore some slight resemblance to a human being."

"She looks as if she's falling," Gaines said. "Caught falling."

Her body was strained into such a curve that only the upper left of the ribcage touched the floor. Her right leg was raised at about thirty degrees to the horizontal, the other bent slightly back from the knee; they were as far apart as the skirt of the gown permitted. The feet were bare. The arms, outstretched to either side of the head, curved towards the ceiling of the chamber; the hands were open, palm out, fingers clutching, then relaxing in slow motion. The gown fluttered stiffly, as if caught in strong air currents venting through the floor of the control room. The effect was of someone falling sideways from a great height.

"How close can I get?" Gaines asked.

"Close as you like," Case said.

To Gaines she had that inner focus possessed by the very sick. When he whispered, "Hey, who are you? What is it you don't like about yourself?" she only looked through him, contorting herself slowly, trying to alter her position around the fall-line, her expression full of fear and rage. He stepped in and knelt down until eighteen inches of air separated their faces, but he couldn't force himself any closer—he experienced the sensation of inappropriately invading someone's personal space, but worse. And where he had expected to feel the air moving around her, fluttering her gown, it was just the opposite, very still.

"I can feel heat radiating off her," he told Case.

"Other people think they hear a voice," Case said, "too far away to make out words. Or they smell something, maybe perfume. We think everyone's trying to describe the same sensation, but so far no one's got near enough to find out. You've done better than most."

"Before, there was some kind of paste coming out of her mouth?"

"That's on and off," Case said. As for the RF transmission, he added, it was very low power. It had a very local reach. "If she's hooked up with anything, it's already arrived. It's in the maze."

"Jesus, Case. Do we have any idea at all where she came from?"

Case looked amused.

"No," he said. "One other thing: sometimes there's a convulsion. She dribbles—we can't collect any of it, whatever it is—and there's a lot of shifting and partial fading. Just for a moment she looks like a much older woman. Nothing's finished here."

19: Anyone Can Make a Mistake

"Look at all these women," Anna Waterman said.

Nine in the morning, and the radiography reception area at St Narcissus, Farringdon was full of them, their anxiety expressed as a tendency to text. Their thumbs brushed the keys of their phones at ferocious speeds; they weren't going to look up, in case that meant admitting something about their predicament. The reception area helped. It was less a waiting room than a stylised version of one—a quiet postmodern whimsy about lines of chairs against a wall—featuring upholstery in calm warm shades of blue-grey, uplighters like white porcelain cups, clean little round tables piled with the terrestrial editions of property and gossip magazines which no one read any more. Framed on the walls were silhouettes of a cat, which, when you looked at them in a certain way, proved to resemble two-dimensional slices through the animal, a joke cooked up between the radiologists and St Narcissus' artist-in-residence. But underneath the joke everything it referred to remained, and when you looked up there was a stain on the ceiling tiles, shaped, according to your mood, either like the map of a distant island or a section through someone's tumour.

"That," said Anna, who hated hospitals, "is the giveaway."

Marnie laughed.

"I quite like the uplighters," she said, then: "Mum, I've just got to send a text."

"No one can like uplighters, surely?"

"Mum—"

The receptionist interrupted them. "It's an IUV appointment, isn't it?" he shouted at Anna.

"Excuse me?" Anna said. "I'm not the patient."

"You've had your kidneys done, dear, haven't you? Last week? Now look, why don't you just read this leaflet for me while you wait?"

"Why? Can't you read it yourself?" She glanced at the leaflet, made out the words, "Please attend promptly at the Radiology reception desk," and repeated with ominous clarity, leaving plenty of space between the words: "I'm not the patient."

During the exchange that followed, Marnie's scan was called. "I won't be long," she promised. "Why not sit there, where you can watch the TV?"

"Don't you start."

While she waited, Anna leafed through the magazines. *Homes You Can't Afford* offered high-definition photography of listed buildings in Surrey and Perthshire. Old issues of *Mine* and *Get* brought her the clothes, gadgets and, especially, the elective surgeries of the rich. The eight-year-old male heir to one of the bigger hedge-fund operations of the 2010s had persuaded the family surgeons to fit him with the uterus and womb of "an unknown East Asian donor" for a month; while his mother, upon having her skin genetically modified to produce downy feathers a calculated charcoal-grey colour, announced with satisfaction that she had "achieved the look she had always wanted," as if she'd done the procedures herself at home. She looked a little like a Porsche. Mother and son smiled languidly out of the papagraphs, thoroughly warmed by themselves. September's *Watchtower*, meanwhile, promised Comfort For The Elderly. Anna stared at it with dislike. Then, because she had been awake all night, she fell asleep and dreamed about sex. Marnie woke her not long later, and they went across the road to a branch of Carlucci's to drink cioccolata calda, "nun's revenge," a favourite of Marnie's since she was eight. Anna ordered an almond croissant, but instead of almond paste it turned out to have a kind of thin, rather unpleasant custard in it.

"Well, I'm glad that's over," Marnie said. She put her hand on Anna's. "Thanks for coming with me," she said. "Really."

"Just remind me what kind of scan it was?"

Marnie took her hand away. She looked despondent. "You might at least try and keep up with my life."

"I think you probably told me but I forgot."

"Anna," Marnie said, "I don't feel as if you have any kind of grip on things."

"If you're still upset about the bathroom—"

"It's nothing to do with that."

"Marnie, anyone can make a mistake."

"It isn't the bathroom."

"Well then, what?"

Marnie turned away and looked out of the window. "I'm ill and you pick a quarrel with the receptionist."

"He was patronising me."

"I'm ill," Marnie said stubbornly. "I wouldn't have gone for a scan if I felt well."

"I thought you said it was nothing."

"It is nothing. I'm sure it's nothing. But that's not the point. I tell you not to worry and you just accept that?" Marnie made a dismissive gesture. Suddenly she pushed back her chair. "We don't seem to live in the same world any more, Anna," she said. She got up and walked out.

For some time after she had gone, Anna sat at the table with her hands in her lap. She didn't know what to do or think next. Outside the huge windows of Carlucci's, rain poured down through the sunshine, turning Farringdon — for the first and last time, you imagined—into a romantic film of itself. People hurried by, laughing; Anna watched them until the rain stopped. Across the road, an optician's sign blinked and shifted: her eyes followed that. When the coffee machine hissed, her head turned that way. She listened to the people at the table next to her. Other people went in and out of the doors. For a minute or two a toddler ran about behind her, laughing and shrieking. People never seem to grow up or change, she thought. After about half an hour, Marnie came back and said she was sorry, and went off again to work. Anna took the tube to Waterloo and was home by midday.

She went out into the garden to have lunch and found that in her absence vegetation had filled the beds at the base of the summerhouse again. It was taller this time. Thick bright green rubbery stems wove about in the sunshine, almost as if they were moving, ending in flowers like trumpets or Tiffany lampshades. At the base of the tangle sprouted those unearthly copper poppies; and on the earth between their stems, gelid organs in rose and pastel blue such as the cat brought in nightly. Small birds flew out of the vegetation, all colours but all single-coloured—birds from a child's rag book, they peeped at Anna with their heads on one side. The summerhouse itself seemed to fall away upward in a distorted perspective, the parts of it leaning together as if they had been propped there loosely and abandoned, dilapidated yellow lapboard like a drawing of itself, looming against a sky too blue. She dragged open the door like someone determined to get to the bottom of things, but inside it was just a shed in anyone's garden—dusty, hot, full of slowly bursting boxes, layered spiderwebs and a kind of archeological time. Gardening things. Unused things. Things of Tim's or Marnie's, markers of the fads and bad decisions of long ago: a rolled poster here, too brittle to unroll ever again; there a small clay figure, its limbs arranged to represent a Degas dancer. Suddenly she was bloody sick of it. She could no more manage it than Marnie's mystifying behaviour at Carlucci's. She took her lunch back to the house, binned it and went to the de Spencer Arms instead. There she came across the boy with the dogs, without his dogs. He was sitting at a table as far away from the building itself as he could manage, his arms wrapped round one knee and his donkey jacket bundled up beside him.

"If I buy you something," Anna said, "will you drink it this time?"

Early afternoon at the de Spencer Arms. Warm sunshine. A light wind bringing the scents of gorse and salt over from the other side of the Downs, blowing deflated crisp-bags between the outside tables. The car park was empty. Skylarks hung in the air like clockwork toys, whirring and pouring out notes of music, rising and falling abruptly according to no obvious plan. Inside, it was wall-to-wall weekday afternoon: rank smell of carpet grease, cheese & vegetable fritters, ancient beer fumes; madness of boredom in the blue eyes of the pub collie behind the bar. A couple in matching dark blue double-breasted suits stood by the fake wood fire, posed as if it was October, the woman distinguishable mainly by her stature and the way her bottom stuck out. She sported earrings like little wheels, a piece of ribbon worn as a bow-tie, the air of an American comedienne in a knockabout film of the 1950s. "I told him at Niagara," she was saying as Anna entered, "as I'd told him in Datchet." They looked like tour guides. It was the usual warning, Anna thought, against getting old.

She carried the drinks out carefully.

"This time I got us both Harvey's. I enjoyed the last one. Where are your beautiful dogs? I was looking forward to seeing them again."

"They're dead, those dogs."

"Dead?"

"Wasted away," the boy said. "Some say it's nature, but I'll have none of that."

"You must be heartbroken!"

He seemed to consider this. Then he shrugged. "See over there? Over the Western Brow? Buzzard." He laughed shortly. "He's out for something, that bugger," he said. He drank half his beer in one long swallow. "Them down the fields say it's my fault, but I'm having none of that."

"I don't understand."

The boy shrugged. "Why should you?" he concluded. "But they ran well to the lamp, those dogs."

Though Anna waited for more, that seemed to be the end of it. They sat in the sunshine, half-awkward, half-companionable, then she bought another drink. The Downs were gilded. Something about the slow drift of afternoon to evening, the slow lengthening of shadows under Streat Hill, made objects seem closer than they were. Distant sounds seemed louder, too. Everything seemed more present. Behind them, the car park began to fill with people down from London: single men squeezing their TVRs and Italian motorcycles in between the ill-parked SUVs; single-activity tourists descending from the Downs in their cycling, walking or bird-watching outfits. Half a dozen women, one of whom wore two-tone breeches and brown suede boots with fringes, arrived together on immaculately turned-out horses. Two of them went to get drinks. The boy watched the women. Anna watched the boy.

"Tell me about lamping," she said.

He thought about that. "You want a good dark night," he said eventually.

She could see how hard he found it—how emotionally clouded it was for him. How do you describe something you know so well? His focus was too close. It was a struggle to distinguish sensation from practice, to find sufficient distance without merging all the subtleties; and now his dogs were gone too. "And you want a good lamp, an old Lightforce or like that. You can get that second hand. Another thing, get a battery with a flat discharge curve. Them down the fields know all that, they're always talking about what lamps to get. It's a million candlepower this, a million candlepower that with them." He thought for a moment. "I don't pay much attention to all that," he confessed, as if surprised by himself. "I like it when the dog runs down the light."

"You're hunting the rabbits with your dogs?" Anna said.

He looked at her as if she was mad, as if she had made some statement so simplistic he didn't know how to refute it. At the same time it was a relief to him: it was somewhere to start. "Rabbits, foxes," he said. "Anything." He'd preferred hares until the last time he was out: now he couldn't seem to care about them at all. "You want a good dark night and a bit of a breeze."

"You find the animal with the light?" she said. "Then you encourage the dogs to chase it? That seems cruel."

"I don't know about cruel," he said.

"But it's killed?" Anna said. "They kill the animal?" It seemed cruel to her.

For the boy, though, the light was the thing, the light and the chase: nothing was like slipping a dog, then watching it run down the light. "It's only the most exciting thing in the world!" he said. He wasn't even particular if he caught anything. Any rabbit could make a yard or two on the dog, parley it into an escape. "They're in the hedge before you know it." He could show her if she wanted. "I've took videos of those dogs before they died." He gestured vaguely towards Wyndlesham. "I keep them over there." He kept the videos of his dogs over there, the other side of Ampney, in the bothy where he lived. It wasn't far. "I could show you!" he said.

Both of them were surprised by this. They stared at each other, puzzled by so much contact. The boy turned away.

"If you wanted," he said, in a different voice.

Half past five: in an hour the de Spencer Arms would be rammed again. The sloping back garden would fill with people, shoulder to shoulder in the warm dark. There would be a run on nervous laughter and narcissistic shouting. By closing time the Downs would have bulked up black against the stars. They would absorb it all and provide no echo. Anna raised her glass, considered the inch of beer left at the bottom of it.

"All right," she said.

The bothy, a long single-storey wooden structure which had once housed the unmarried male servants of the local fox hunt (an institution known in its heyday as "the Ampney"), stood in the middle of a field next to a few courses of brick and an overgrown cobbled yard. It was a shed, really, already cold in the afternoon, its untreated cement floors polished by decades of use. There was a kitchen at one end, a storage unit full of rusting bed frames and plastic-wrapped supermarket pallets of dog-food at the other. Between them, five or six empty rooms opened off a narrow windowless passage lighted by a single twenty-watt bulb. To the extent that he had any, the boy had moved his belongings into the kitchen, where it was relatively warm. Two shelves held packets of cereal, tins of baked beans and 8 per cent-proof lager. A single bed was pushed up against the wall in one corner. "I don't need much," he said. "I was never much for things." There was a paraffin heater but no kettle. He made tea using lukewarm water straight from an ancient Creda heater mounted on the wall above the sink and paid his rent directly to "them down the fields," who had acquired the bothy in some cash-free transaction he didn't understand, and who sometimes dragged a bed into one of the other rooms for weekend use.

"It's cheap enough," he said.

The only contemporary thing in the kitchen was a reconditioned laptop from the early 2000s, wired into the overhead light socket through a brownout-protector. "It's all in here," he said, with a kind of shy irony: "My life." He showed as much pride in the machine as in his uploads to YouTube. These unsteady, ill-lit glimpses, caught on a pocket camcorder, didn't even seem cruel, only difficult to interpret. Jittery ellipses and smears of whitish light appeared and disappeared suddenly in a black rectangle. They picked out a hedge, a patch of long grass in a field, a fence post at an odd angle. Something zigzagged into the light and out of it again. Something else turned and turned and vanished suddenly into a hedge. At the end of each clip there was the boy, an ethereal smile on his face, holding up dead rabbits by their ears. Once, the dogs put up a deer, which stared at them, then walked slowly out of camera. He had set some of the videos to contemporary pastoral music, others to thirty-year-old Death Metal. Watching them galvanised him all over again, the way a passing scent had once galvanised his dogs. He sat on the bed next to Anna. There was nowhere else to sit. She could feel him trembling with excitement. "What do you think?" he asked her. "What do you think of that!"

Once she had got over her distaste, Anna felt bored. She was glad when he turned off the computer and with a smile half diffident, half sly, pushed her down. "Let me get these jeans off you," she said. She laughed. "They could do with a wash." And later: "You're hurting me a little bit." He went on without seeming to hear and soon she had forgotten, the way you forget the creak and bang of the bed or the people coming and going in the corridor outside a hotel room. To fuck at all is a blessing. He wasn't Tim Waterman, but he wasn't Michael Kearney either, and he got hard again as quickly as most boys. Anna fell asleep. When she woke the bothy was cold and the boy was standing naked by the window gazing out across the fields towards the village. The light had begun to fade. Wisps of mist were already coming up over the river. He'd had enough for the moment, she could see. His back, whiter and thinner than she had expected, seemed vulnerable, illuminated from within. Anna watched him a minute or two, then gathered her clothes and began to get dressed. When she thought the time was right, she said:

"I've got some work I need doing."

The boy made a movement with one shoulder, a shrug or perhaps a wince. He wasn't looking for work, he said. He had enough work.

"What kind of work is it?" he asked.

It wasn't much, she said. It was just some painting. He had enough of that kind of work, the boy said.

"I need someone to look at my bathroom," Anna said. "I don't live far. If you called later in the week, you could do the work I need."

He moved his shoulder again and kept looking out of the window. "Those dogs of mine were company 'til the grey hare got across them." Anna, receiving this as "grey hair," had no idea what he meant. "That spoiled everything. I could talk to them until then." As she was leaving he turned round and said, "I'll come and see you though? I'll be coming to see you?"

Anna touched his arm and smiled. "Put your clothes on," she said. "It's cold in here."

The lane outside had filled with mist, yet if you looked directly upward you could see the stars. Anna turned towards Wyndlesham, walking as briskly as she could. Once or twice she raised her arms in the air or smiled for no reason. She wondered what had really happened to the dogs. Those lovely, lovely animals. Perhaps he'd sold them. Perhaps he'd just grown tired of them. I can't imagine what Marnie will make of him, she thought: although it's none of her business. She looked for her phone, couldn't find it; stopped suddenly, brought both hands to her mouth and laughed. I can't believe myself, she thought. When she looked back, the bothy seemed to hang without support in the gathering dusk. Everything it represented was history. Since the banking meltdown of 2007, the stable-block itself—built by John Ampney in the late Eighteenth Century from locally sourced brick and pantile and not then intended to house the hunt—had tracked closely the declining economic curve: redevelopment, first as prestige office space, then as a paintball "shoot house"; a decade of squatting and abandonment; finally, annexation by the local authority as Kent and Sussex struggled to contain thousands of Chinese economic refugees washing up in the old Cinque Ports; after which it had been allowed to fall down.

At home there were several messages from Marnie— "Mum, I'm trying to call but your mobile is off again. Mum? Mum, please pick up."—and one from Helen Alpert reminding Anna of her appointment the next morning. Anna, starving, made baked beans on toast. While the beans were heating up, she walked to and fro eating slices of quince cheese with some cold lentils she had found at the back of the fridge. She swept the old cat up in her arms and squeezed him in a way he had never liked. "James, James, oh James," she said: "What *have* you been up to?" She awarded herself half a bottle of Calvet Prestige Rouge, which caused her to fall asleep in front of the TV.

When she woke, it was late. The cat was out again. She drank a glass of water and went to the garden window. The summerhouse seemed quiet. And yet the dreams she had had! She went out and, standing barefoot on the lawn, worked her toes into the damp turf to wake herself up. "James!" she called. A great beam of off-white light struck out from somewhere behind the house—like the sweep of headlights as a car turns in off the road into your drive, but silent, frozen and prolonged. Or like a huge door opened: light squared-off somehow, sharp-edged, looking for something to reveal, in this case the thousands of cats boiling across the water meadow towards Anna's home in an alert, silent rush. Every one of them was either black or white. They poured into the garden, parting around the summerhouse, and up towards Anna, of whom they took no more notice than the garden furniture. On and on they came like a problem in statistical mechanics, without any apparent slackening or falling away of numbers, pouring out of the meadow, pouring away behind the house. Anna, deep in explicatory failure, had no way of placing herself with regard to this event: she did not in any sense know what she felt about it. Now she winced away and tried to climb the garden fence. Now she waded directly into the stream of cats, and stood with tears of pure delight streaming down her face, feeling them flow around her, bringing with them the warmth of their bodies, also a close, dusty but not unpleasant smell—until suddenly the light turned itself off and the garden was empty again. She stood for a moment wiping her eyes and laughing. Then she went back into the house and left a message with Dr Alpert's answering service: "Helen, I don't feel I want to carry on with our conversations. I feel as if I would rather take charge of myself again."

She left a similar message with her daughter. "I'm not sure I can explain. I'm just not such hard work for myself as I used to be." She searched for something else to say. "I saw a lot of cats in the garden this evening!" Since this didn't seem to approach the facts, or give any feeling of the rest of her day, she added: "And, Marnie, I met someone, but I don't know if you'll like him."

She put the phone down and looked for Michael Kearney's computer drive. Excavated from the litter at the bottom of her bag, it lay on the kitchen counter like an enchanted egg, its surface rich with wear, magically transforming ordinary reflected domestic light into year upon year of guilt.

Anna Waterman had no idea if the old man in South London was really Brian Tate. She would have to accept that her memory of the scandals surrounding Michael's death and Tate's downfall would always be clouded; that her struggles with Michael—like her struggles with herself—would grow increasingly meaningless. At a certain age, she now understood, you owe the past nothing except to recognise it as the past. Michael could go to hell, if he wasn't already there. Tomorrow she would take the pocket drive to Carshalton and, one way or another, relinquish responsibility for whatever data it contained; and that would be that.

20: Modern Luminescence

"It came out of nowhere."

"Nothing comes out of nowhere."

"Ha ha. What is it?"

"It says 'biological content.'"

The tank had been through some recent high-temperature event, after which it pitched into empty space a light minute off the *Nova Swing*'s bow, where it hung in a dissipating froth of zero-point energy and junk matter until Fat Antoyne fetched it on board. It was scarred and scraped, losing colour rapidly through a palette of Christmas reds through light plum to the matt grey you would associate with a military asset. Much of the exterior work had vaporised; the remaining fitments made no sense unless it had been an internal component of some other structure. Once it was cool enough to touch Antoyne unbolted the porthole cover.

"Shine the light."

Liv Hula shone the light. "Out of nowhere!" she repeated. "I nearly flew into it." She was excited until she saw what was inside.

Cable trailed from the core-points in the spine. The skin stretched over the skull like the tanned or preserved skin of a bog-burial. No flesh remained between that and the bone beneath. The withered lips drew back over large uneven teeth. The eyes, bloodshot and bugged up past life size, glared from tarry sockets. Something was wrong with the hair. It was hard to make out the rest. The tank proteome—thirty thousand protein species like warm spit—swirled sluggishly about it.

Liv turned away in disgust.

"It's not an alien," she said. "It's a K-captain."

For her, that meant a metaphor for the condition of sky-pilots every-where: dissociation, hallucination, invasive surgery, the surrendering of humanity for a way of life so worthless it made you laugh.

"Throw it back," she advised.

Antoyne didn't want to get into that. He heard it all before. To change the subject he said, "I almost think I recognise this guy."

Liv took another look: shrugged.

"They're all the same. Scoliosis. Pseudo-polio. Half the organs gone, wires everywhere." And when Antoyne wondered what unimaginable forces had blown this one out of his ship: "Don't assume it's male. More than half of them sign up as girls. It's the thinking twelve-year-old's alter-native to anorexia."

Antoyne moved the inspection lamp around. It was like a wreck under water in there. Fine silt fell through the beam.

"Is it dead yet?" Irene the mona called from the crew quarters.

They were thirty lights from anywhere, in the voids by the Tract itself. The big argument they had, which went back and forth while Antoyne screwed the porthole cover back on, was if they had come upon the tank by acci-dent, or whether it was another item on MP Renoko's cargo manifest. It was a measure of how weird their sense of reality had got, Liv Hula insisted, that they couldn't decide. They stood there for a time, arguing back and forth, then left the hold. As soon as the bulkhead door closed behind them, bursts of high-speed code issued from the K-tank—chirps and stutters, odd runs of simple calculus, fragments of ordinary language mysterious yet emphat-ic—as if the occupant was trying to make contact but couldn't remember how. The other items in the hold were inappropriately excited by this, flash-ing and winking in return, humming with subsonics, emitting brief flashes of ionising radiation. After perhaps an hour—its baroque ribs and lumps of melted inlet pipe making it look like a child's coffin decorated with mould-ings of elves, unicorns and dragons—the newcomer seemed to calm down.

"We should dump it in the nearest sun," said Liv.

The day you enlist for the K-ships, you haven't eaten for forty-eight hours. They give you the injections, and within twenty-four hours your blood is teeming with pathogens, artificial parasites, tailored enzymes. You present with the symptoms of MS, lupus and schizophrenia. They strap you down. Over the next three days the shadow operators, running on nanomech, take your sympathetic nervous system to pieces, flushing the waste out continually through the colon. They pump you with a paste of ten-micrometre-range factories, protein farms and metabolic monitors. They core your spine. You remain awake throughout, except for the brief moment when they introduce you to the K-code itself. Many recruits don't make it past that point. If you do, they bolt you into the tank at the front of the ship. By then most of your organs are gone. You're blind and deaf. A kind of nauseous surf is rolling through you. They've cut into your brain so that it will accept the hardware bridge known as 'the Einstein Cross.' You connect with the ship math. You will soon be able to consciously process 15 petabytes of data per second: but you will never walk again. You will never touch someone or be touched, fuck or be fucked. You will never do anything for yourself again. You will never even shit for yourself.

You sign up in a private room at a pleasant temperature: nevertheless, you can't get warm. You say goodbye to your parents. They give you the emetics whether you've eaten or not. Then it's an hour or two to wait before the injections start. Forty years ago—shivering on the edge of a bed, vomiting into a plastic bowl while she tried to hold around her a hospital gown that fell open constantly at the back—it had come to Liv Hula that she would be able to choose the Einstein Cross, but that she would never, ever be able to unchoose it. So she had put the bowl down carefully, and, speaking to no one, got dressed again and gone back to her life.

Everywhere they stopped after that, the talk was war. Provocation was heaped on provocation. Every rhetoric had its counter-rhetoric, every history was self-revised. Riots erupted across Halo cities. Out near Panamax IV, two unidentified cruisers ambushed a helpless K-ship. It was a major flashpoint: the boys from Earth had dropped the ball. Nastic assets roared into known space. Their manoeuvres out near Coahoma and the Red Revenues hadn't been the bumbling, half-hearted adventures presented by EMC: rather they revealed pattern, a cold, technical mind, deft new kinds of hit-and-run, workouts for a major offensive. It was, in a sense, the perfect psychodrama of betrayal. Whole star systems were gas in half a day. Refugees were already on the move. Irene stared at the news and found herself martyred to empathy and nonrecreational mood swings. One moment she would be saying: "I will never get tired of this, all our adventures with these cosmic winds, and tides roaring through space!"; the next it was, "We all got a black heart to our personality, Antoyne."

What had upset her so on New Venusport, she refused to say.

Fat Antoyne had found her a mile from the Deleuze Motel, teetering at the end of a line of footprints on the hard wet sand. It was the hour before dawn. She'd lost her bag, also one of her best shoes. Her face and hands were cold and salty. Overcome in ways he couldn't explain, he tried to put his arms around her. But though Irene had the expression of someone ready to seek help anywhere it could be found, she only stepped away.

"Antoyne, no," she said.

Aboard the *Nova Swing* once more, she kept to herself. Even safe in empty space, she couldn't sleep. On the beach before Antoyne arrived, she had been trying to imagine Madame Shen's Circus in its glory days: music, alien shows, marzipan, white frocks, fresh sunshine on the midway. People laughing and fucking on the very sand where Irene stood! But she couldn't forget that she had wet herself looking into the mysteries of the STARLIGHT ROOM, where the three ghastly white-capped figures of Kokey Food, Mr Freedom and The Saint cast their dice; and when her wonderful, warm man found her, her neck was stiff from staring as hard as she could in the opposite direction to that dispiriting place. "Change your game you change your luck," she told Liv Hula, "that's everything I used to believe in life." The past was gone. Only the present could affect the future, and the future was always open for business: that was how she had always seen it. "But Liv, now I recognise each change of heart is just another scam performed upon yourself!"

Now she could only conclude that the long haul, with its concomitant emptiness and anxiety, had proved as debilitating as the short, which wears you down by insisting you forget everything you knew last week. She was tired, she said. She wanted to go home. Perhaps she would feel better if she saw her old home.

Liv Hula said she could help with that.

Perkins Rent IV, known to its inhabitants as New Midland, supported an agriculture of beet, potatoes and a local variety of squash grown year round under plastic. New Midlanders worked for offworld money. A handful of FTZs in closed compounds—precision assembly plants working from bulk metal glass components—clustered on the major continent, each served by a town of fifty to seventy-five thousand souls where bi-yearly surveys revealed a reassuringly high incidence of obsessive-compulsive traits and, ideologically, a kind of *Janteloven* prevailed. The only other way of earning a living on New Midland was to work the ghost train.

This line of abandoned alien vehicles, all sizes between a kilometre and thirty kilometres long, hung nose to tail in a cometary orbit that reached halfway to the nearest star. Their rindlike hulls presented dusty, lustreless grey. Whoever they belonged to had parked them and walked away before proteins appeared on Planet Earth. They boasted the shapes of asteroids—potato shapes, dumbbell shapes, off-centre shapes with holes in them. By contrast their nautiloid internal spaces were pearly and disorienting, as clean and empty as if nothing had ever lived there. Every so often a short segment of the train fell into the sun, or ploughed ship by ship into the system gas giant. New Midlanders mined them like any other resource. Nobody knew what the ships did, or how they got here, or how to work them: so they cut them up and melted them down, and sold them through sub-contractors to a corporate in the Core. It made an economy. It was the simple, straight line thing to do. They were broken up from inside out. The used-up ones attracted unpredictably shifting clouds of scrap: cinders, meaningless internal structures made of metals no one wanted or even understood, waste product from the automatic smelters. Above the rest bustled the industrial arcologies and futuristic bubble-worlds—factories, refineries, sorting facilities, starship docks busy round the clock.

Liv Hula slipped in from high above the plane of the ecliptic, intending to hide in the debris-belt of her choice. What she found changed her mind.

"Antoyne, look at this."

"What?"

"Someone fought here. Perhaps half a day ago?"

The ghost train had been derailed. Its industries now took the form of a complex metallic vapour through which toppled everything from nuggets of melted aluminium to entire ore-crushers. Shockfronts were still swinging through this medium, here and there compressing it to wispy arcs the colour of mercury. The routers had gone down under the weight of distress traffic—transponder signals from eva suits and escape pods, trickles of RF leaking like the air from punctured living quarters, the papery voices of the already-dead filling the pipes with intimate, matter-of-fact panic. They were saying what the dead always say: "No one's left but me." One moment they were trying to reason with the problem, the next they were begging the guys to pull them out of there. The ghost ships had fared no better: they toppled about, laid open like water-stained illustrations of the Fibonacci spiral. Some of the larger ones, accelerated by hits from high-end ordnance, were wobbling into the distance on interesting new trajectories. Several fragments fifty metres diameter and above had found their way down to the surface of New Midland.

As a result the FTZs were matchwood. Thing Fifty, the little coastal town Irene remembered so well, had begun its day by leaning away from a fifty megaton airburst about two hundred kilometres inland and twelve kilometres high. A hot blue light went across the sky. The heat was so fierce people assumed their hair had caught fire. During this period, fences, trees, houses, low-density warehousing, utility poles and pylons all took on an ordered slant. Half an hour later, a huge ocean surge boiled inland, floated the wreckage and aggregated it in the shallow valleys on the edge of town, piling everything on top of everything else. By the time *Nova Swing* arrived, Thing Fifty was less a place than a list of building materials.

Liv Hula put down in the suburbs, and they wandered about while Irene tried to find her old home. The wreckage resembled a heap of opened-out cardboard boxes. Everything had equal value—dead animals knotted in branches, water gurgling back to the sea along hidden sloughs and creeks, plastic chairs. At your feet a thousand pieces of broken tile; middle distances of uprooted garden shrubs and shattered wooden spars: behind that, in a curious reversal of perspective, the houses tilted and slumped into each other as if they were still floating. Above the high water mark the streets were full of soft toys. Every so often you saw a single figure in the distance; or a dog made its way along the street sniffing everything with enthusiasm, as if any moment it expected to be reunited with what it knew. Everything was entangled. Everything stank of sewage and the sea. There was no ground plan. You didn't know where to assign value. The tarry light didn't seem to come from the sun, diffused by haze, but to leak out of the wreckage itself. Irene sat at the kerb. She looked around at it all. Then she drew up her knees, wrapped her arms about them and wept.

"Come on now, love," Liv said: "I can see everything you've got."

Irene wiped her eyes. She tried to laugh. "Everyone in the Halo's seen it anyway," she whispered.

She took Fat Antoyne's hand and put the back of it next to her cheek, then pushed it away again suddenly. Her skin was wan, her expression indistinct, as if she'd been rinsed out of her own face. The things she missed about this town were gone. They had never been here anyway. They had vanished not into the current disaster, but years ago, into her own. The past wasn't real but it was all she had: that's how you feel when your life has faltered. She stood up and tugged her skirt straight. "I'll just go into this house here," she said.

"Irene!"

It was a building caught in the complex process of kneeling into its own yard. Windows full of broken glass gave on to rooms where the light fell in new and unexpected directions. Irene brightened up after she found an unopened bottle of cocktail mix. She began dragging things into the centre of rooms where she could examine them. "Oh look!" she said, as if Liv and Antoyne were in there with her. "Oh *look*!" They made faces at one another and shrugged, Don't ask me. They heard her feet scraping about. They heard her murmuring to herself as she used the broken toilet. "You guys could help if you liked," she called. "Or don't you want a—" She checked the label of the bottle "—Kyshtym Cream? They're good!" When she emerged at last, her arms were full of clothes, kiddie's toys and household items.

"And look!" she said. "After all these years!"

It was a toddler's My First Experience skirt, in traditional neotony pink.

"I had one just like this."

Liv stared in disbelief, then shook her head. "Irene," she wanted to know, "is this actually your old house?"

"It could be," Irene said. "Yes, it easily could be."

"Because if it isn't—"

"They don't want the stuff, Liv," Irene said. "You should see the condition they're in. Really."

Her mood, which had remained elevated on the way back to the ship, dipped as soon as the Kyshtym Cream wore off. Disposed about her quarters, the repro radio, false-colour hologram of the Kefahuchi Tract and collection of cast iron casserole-ware looked less fun than they had *in situ*. "Disaster chic," she said. "What do you think?" Antoyne didn't think anything. She sighed. "Antoyne, are we bored of each other at last?" Unable to answer that either, he became alert but very still. Irene used her thumb to enlarge a split in the seams of a soft toy shaped like a cockroach, then asked him so suddenly and abjectly if he thought life was worth it that he could only hug her roughly and insist:

"Your life is what you make it in this world."

"I think that's what I mean, Antoyne."

History, the boys from Earth believed, is bunk.

The Angel of History may look backwards, but that pose will make no difference to the storm that blows it into the future. No wonder it has such a surprised expression! This philosophy drove them, in the late decades of the Twenty-first Century, to launch themselves blind into Dynaflow space, with no idea how to navigate it, in craft made of curiously unsophisticated materials. They had no idea where the first jump would take them. By the second jump, they had no idea where they started from. By the third they had no idea what "where" meant.

It was a hard problem, but not insoluble. Within a decade or two they had used the Tet-Kearno equations to derive an eleven-dimensional algorithm from the hunting behaviour of the shark. The Galaxy was theirs. Everywhere they went they found archeological traces of the people who had solved the problem before them—AIs, lobster gods, lizard men from deep time. They learned new science on a steep, fulfilling curve. Everything was waiting to be handled, smelled, eaten. You threw the rind over your shoulder. The eerie beauty of it was that you could be on to the next thing before the previous thing had lost its shine.

But though, as a whole, the human race soon knew how to find its way around, it still had no idea where it was: so that, in Irene the mona's day, the paradigm for individual motion remained a blind if not quite random jump. Before she took the mona package and did so well with it, Irene touched down on fifty worlds.

Thirteen years old, she was already tall and bony. She loved fucking but she had an awkward walk and big feet. She did her hair the way they all did then, in lacquered copper waves so complex they could receive the test tone of Radio Universe. When she smiled her gums showed; when she boarded that rocket she never looked back. Worked her way down through the Swan and out to Stevenson's Reach. Then on to Lila y Flag, L'avventura, McKie, LaFuma RSX, where she hit the wall a little and was forced to rest a year with a sweet alien boy from You're Worth It. There she took the package, opting—from the hundreds of Monroes on offer—for the soft-look Marilyn photographed in black and white by Cecil Beaton at the Ambassador Hotel, 1956. Suddenly she was five foot three, with a kind of receptive liveliness and flossy blond easycare hair that always smelled of peppermint shampoo. After that the journey got easier for her: its inner and outer trajectories seemed to match. She was so happy! Magellan to O'dowd, Pixlet to Oxley; The Discoveries, The Fourth Part, The Thousand Dreams of Stellavista; Massive 49 to Meniere's World; Tregetour, Charo, Entantiodroma, Max Party, Gay Lung and Ambo Danse. American Polaroid, American Diner, American Nosebleed. Oxi, Krokodil, Waitrose Two and Santa Muerte. By then, her suitcase contained: tampons, fourteen pairs of high heel shoes, the dress she left home in, yellow rayon with a faux-Deco feel, which she never wore again. That girl had a sweet way of laughing. Drunk, she'd explain, "I love shoes." She would follow you anywhere for two weeks, then follow someone else, until she'd scattered herself like small change across the Halo and down into Radio Bay. There, where the Beach stars fell away like a cliff over nothing, she fell away too, with a laugh on her face and her arms spread wide to everything.

If you asked Irene to describe her favourite memory, she would bring out a little hologram cube about an inch on a side—

Four am, under a weird grey-blue neon. Raucous laughter. Three and a half minutes of the b-girl life. It had been a long night for whoever captured the pictures. Shadows flickered, the camera looked here and there without purpose. The angles were inventive. Irene began with her back to the camera and her feet planted in the gutter. You could hear her say, "Kinny, take that away! Oh, Kinny, you bugger!" She got her dress part way up and her thong part way down before she started to piss, but after twenty seconds, slowly tipped forward into the road and began to throw up, smoothly and loosely, from the other end. Steam rose in the cold air. After a minute or so of that, she seemed to pass out. Her body tipped forward a little further, arching the lower back and pushing her face into the road, then after a moment or two of equilibrium, subsided sideways and curled up into the foetal position. Her hat fell off and rolled cheerily back and forth. The camera tried to follow it, then there was more laughter and everything went black.

"It's very sentimental I know," she told Fat Antoyne now. "But I loved that hat. And the bolero, with its little satin bows." Clothes like that weren't really clothes at all, she tried to explain: they were semiotics in action. "Party semiotics in action." She sighed and put her hand over his. "It was a lovely world, and sometimes—like now, with you and me in our comfortable little ship, with all these new ornaments—it still is." She had been having such a good time in those pictures that she remembered nothing of it. "Sometimes I'm not even sure it's me!"

He had to laugh, Fat Antoyne said. "Everyone deserves a good time," he added. "Their lives are hard enough."

He smiled and closed her hand over the little cube.

"You keep that safe," he said.

21: Everyone's a VIP to Someone

Between Radia Marelli and Tupolev Avenue, the crime tourism quarter lay under rain and the promise of a short life. There was perpetual graininess in the air and the neon light. Every middle manager on North Hemisphere, New Venusport knew about the donkey parlours on Saudade. The chance to do donkey parlour crime—a near-death experience worth anyone's dollar—drew them off the starliners in numbers second only to Preter Coeur on a warm summer's evening. Their wives came for the sensorium porn. You could tell the wives by their honey-coloured fur coats and ash-blond hair. Sensorium porn was delivered as direct live feed from an alien brain as it tried to understand human sex, or the use of quotidian objects and events from Earth history like a "book group" or a mirror. A mirror was one of the favourites. The EMC wives—puzzled by everything, not so much acting-out as directing the same helpless performance of themselves as they had given all their lives—got off on the cognitive and perceptual gap. The selling point of sensorium porn was that it enabled you, finally, to "see the world from a different point of view." They came down the Creda Line curious and went away users. It was a toxic trade.

The assistant stood with Epstein the thin cop, in the alley off Tupolev where Toni Reno had shucked his mortal coil. They were viewing Toni's corpse. Epstein had called her half an hour ago and said:

"You got a problem."

Since death, Toni Reno's reflective index had dropped eighty-five per cent across most of the electromagnetic spectrum including visible light. As a result he was hard to make out even in good weather. Every day now, Toni drew a crowd composed partly of tourists on their way to the Llubichik Street arcades, and partly of his followers—twelve- and thirteen-year-old boys who received realtime updates on his condition piped directly into their heads. Toni was nationwide. The more he faded, the more they came to view him. They copied his dark blue Sadie Barnham work jacket and bought shoes exactly like Toni Reno's. Arguments sometimes broke out between them and the passing trade. Or the fans themselves got into arguments about what Toni meant to them, what kind of a role-model Toni really, actually, was. So committed to Toni they had committed suicide over the issue, one or two of them now drew small followings of their own. The uniform branch, Epstein told the assistant, took a back seat as far as this activity went, on the grounds that it constituted either commerce or religion, both being a right you had protected in Saudade.

"He's still here then," the assistant said.

"Still here," Epstein said.

"So what's our problem?"

"We don't have a problem."

"Then what?"

"It's you who has the problem."

The assistant adjusted some of her overlays and studied the corpse. In addition to losing visibility it had risen a further sixteen feet in the rainy air. Some thought Toni's rate of rotation had slowed, some thought not: Epstein the thin cop placed himself, with some reservations, in the latter camp. He had money on it. The assistant thought she could detect a faint smell of decay leaking from whatever space Toni now occupied; perhaps thirty molecules in a cubic kilometre of air.

"What problem?" she said.

In lieu of an answer, Epstein ushered her into the building from which they had first viewed the dead broker.

"You remember this place?" he said.

She said she did.

"Well, it's a sensorium parlour, it turns out. Now in this room here—no, in here, this way—they have some bird style of alien, they've drilled his head for access. He's wired the way they are, mainly to look at ordinary stuff, a coat hanger, some needles, those kinds of things. But here's what."

"What?"

"Maybe for an hour a day they got him looking into the street. So our experts play back what's left of his head, and have an operator decode it, and find that the footage covers the period of Toni Reno's death."

Epstein gave the assistant an intent look, then, when she didn't respond, went on to tell her, "This alien was at the window the exact moment Toni arrived in the alley." Reno had come from the direction of the noncorporate spaceport, the retrieved material showed: it showed him running. Then, as he drew level with the house, someone attacked him, straight out of the doorway downstairs. "Toni's looking back over his shoulder. He's so agitated he doesn't present with his usual careful grooming. He's scared of something we can't see. A woman comes up off the ground so fast you can barely see her, and shoots Toni in the armpit with a Chambers gun. From some angles it looks as if she's coming up *through* the ground."

"And?"

He smiled.

"And she's you," he said.

The assistant stared at him without replying. Her nose caught the smell of bird plumage, musty and deep. She recalled how the alien lay on the bed looking up at her helplessly, surrounded by drifts of its own feathers and whispering, "I *am* here. I *am*." They had drilled its skull. What a place, she thought, to end your weird life. As if she was considering evidence the subtlety of which would be lost on Epstein, she walked to the window and stared down into the street. If she ordered up the right combination of overlays, she could examine Toni Reno both in his present condition and as he had been when she was first called to the alley off Tupolev. She consulted her forearm, down which the ideograms flowed Chinese black and chimney red, solid and definite in the grainy crime-tourism air. It was raining again, but now the rain took no account at all of the hanging man. It rained through him. Epstein came and stood at her shoulder so that he could look into the street too.

"I don't want anything to do with this," he said. "The footage goes straight to your office, my people hold off on a report."

When she failed to reply, but only gave him that oblique smile of hers, he knew this was the most difficult part of his day. Even the fifth floor managers at SiteCrime were frightened of her. They said she had no personality, they said she had no empathy: they said she didn't understand people. Epstein knew all these things to be true. What happened to him next would depend on how skilfully he could back away from what he had discovered.

"I'm just a uniform," he emphasised. "This is your issue."

The assistant did not dispute that.

***

All across the Halo, alliances collapsed. Mounting crises in the Pentre De, Uswank and Frand-Portie systems broke into open conflict. Then war was everywhere and it was your war, to be accessed however it fitted best into your busy schedule. Seven-second segments to three-minute documentaries. Focused debate, embedded media. Twenty-four-hour live *mano a mano* between mixed assets in the Lesser Magellanic Cloud, or a catch-up of the entire campaign—including interactive mapping of EMC's feint towards Beta Carinae—from day one. In-depth views included: "How They Took the Pulsed-Gamma War to Cassiotone 9"; "The Ever-Present Threat of Gravity Wave Lasing"; and "We Ask You How You Would Have Done It Differently!" People loved it. The simulacrum of war forced them fully into the present, where they could hone their life-anxieties and interpret them as excitement. Meanwhile, under cover of the coverage, the real war crept across the Halo until it threatened Panamax IV.

Rig Gaines, suddenly uncomfortable with events, not to say his place in them, rode the *Uptown Six* down to Alyssia Fignall's archeological project, hoping he might persuade her to leave the planet with him before things took their inevitable turn for the worse. He didn't imagine she would.

The weather was hot, her house empty. In the cloister he found a note she had left: "Rig, when the rains come, something beautiful happens here." It didn't look like rain. The stones were hot to the touch. Rather than arriving with the sunlight, heat seemed to generate itself between the eight rhyolite pillars around the fountain and spray upwards from there. Gaines sat all afternoon waiting for Alyssia, watching the glare move across the smooth oval cobbles. At four o'clock, the sky clouded over. After a few grand but silent flashes of lightning, it seemed nothing else would happen. But by five it was pouring with rain.

"Jesus, Alyssia," Gaines said. He went out to look for her, and was promptly drenched.

The town square he found empty but for some children, who ran about in front of him laughing and calling "La Cava! La Cava!" in excited voices. He followed them into the covered market. That was deserted too. All over the Halo, people sell each other ordinary things, from empty bottles to leather belts. Here the stalls offered drip trays and shoes, ten-inch holograms of very fat children wearing lace. Then loaves of bread like large, smooth stones on a beach. Then meat. Strips, strings and slivers of meat. Long thin slices of meat hung up like translucent shower-curtains, with a sour iron smell. "Hey kids," called Gaines, temporarily unable to locate them. "La Cava!" they called. The market was a dark, confusing maze. A workman's café offered sesos rebozadas, sautéed brains, eaten standing up. His nostrils were full of that idea until the children led him into the light on the other side, and a different smell took over. Rain poured from the market eaves. The kids beckoned. Gaines stood looking out but suddenly found it impossible either to move or to describe what was happening in the second, smaller square which now revealed itself.

It was under two or three feet of water. The town sewers had backed up. Thigh-deep in putrid water, in which circled all kinds of waste from faecal matter to shattered packing crates, people had gathered to dance. Their clothes, stinking and soaked, clung to them. They were wading and chanting in groups, lifting their legs high, bending down to splash each other with diluted shit, as if this was an afternoon at the beach. Some of them were kneeling in it. Some were neither kneeling nor standing, but were leaning into one another, clasped together, obviously fucking. Gaines had his ideas about the world, but none of them covered this. He saw Alyssia right in there with them, laughing and beckoning to him. The children were tugging at his hands and grinning. Gaines pulled back as hard as he could and eventually broke free. As he ran off through the market, he thought he could hear a low booming sound somewhere deep under his feet.

It rained for eight hours more. Gaines didn't want to sleep. He spent all night in the cloister, piped into an FTL router he had left in orbit; then, when the rain stopped and the sun came up, sat by the fountain until the morning heat began to dry him out. A little after ten, Alyssia Fignall arrived back. She looked tired, but clean and happy. She seemed full of energy. "Rig, you'll burn up out here," she laughed, taking his arm. "Come in and have breakfast. I bought some bread in the market."

Gaines shook his head.

"What's the matter?"

When he didn't answer, she let go of his arm and said: "I knew it. I knew it! Rig, *this is how they celebrate their contract with the world.*" She had been looking forward to seeing him, but he didn't understand anything. The town was another kind of spiritual engine. How could she explain? Under the market lay a chain of limestone caves. It was typical karst country. Run-off from the nearby hills filled the system up within an hour of the rain starting, but as soon as the water reached a certain level some kind of airlock released itself. "The system drains as fast as it fills. The sewage runs away. The rain washes everyone clean, then they hold a wonderful party in the town, with fireworks and food, to celebrate. Everyone clean and fresh and in their best clothes.

They're dirty, then they're clean again, Rig, don't you get it?"

She pulled at his arm again, but he wouldn't move.

"How is that different to what the original inhabitants did, up on the hilltop there, whoever they were, a hundred thousand years ago? How is it different to your fucking war?

Come on, Rig, how different is it?"

Gaines stared at her. A year and a half ago, she had written to him: "The bird cries here grow stranger and stranger. I sit and count the pillars around the fountain, while the tourist rockets lug themselves into the air above me like suitcases full of cheap souvenirs. I love it so. Oh Rig, please come!"

"I just need to deal with this call," he said.

Alyssia gave him a look of death, to which he replied with one of his vague smiles. "I can see that there's a lot of difference between us on this," he said. "I can see you're disappointed." Suddenly the dial-up had his full attention. "What? What do you mean, 'changed again'?" Just as he got rid of whoever it was, the *Uptown Six*, which had been skulking around the Panamax L2 point since it arrived, tapped its fusion drive briefly and dropped out of orbit, coming to a silent halt fifty feet above the house. Alyssia stared uncomprehendingly up at it, then at Gaines.

"Get that foul thing out of here," she said. "I don't want it near me. Not today of all days."

She walked into the house.

Gaines still kept a hologram of Alyssia aged fourteen, wearing the uniform of some EMC youth movement, always laughing at him, always seeking to make contact. Twenty hours after she refused to leave Panamax IV, he stood in the **PEARLANT** control room at a loss. Activity had dropped off sharply. Since his previous visit, Case's team, defeated by ancient labyrinthine physics, had abandoned the containment project: instead they'd pitched a tent of filmy blue halogen light at the centre of the space, around which knots of specialists gathered to stare thoughtfully at the figure which now occupied it.

Pearl had completed her long fall, dawn to dewy eve. She lay on her side on the allotropic carbon deck, one knee raised, the upper part of her body curved at the waist and propped up on her elbow. In the corner of her mouth appeared a humanising trace of what looked like dried toothpaste. Something had happened to her on the way down, as a result of which she now looked partly like a woman in a ruched metallic gown around five hundred years old, and partly like a cat. It was a different part every time Gaines blinked: sometimes the whole of the upper body was wrong, sometimes only one arm or leg. Limbs, skin, armature, nothing fitted together—the cat's long-muzzled facial structure under the woman's flesh, then the other way around. At the same time her eyes—when they were human eyes—had a film of hypnotic calm, even amusement, as if she was asking some unanswerable question, or as if you had caught her in some very sophisticated form of déshabillé you could both enjoy; while the cat's fur collected the light at the edges of the image, leading your gaze out into tenuousness, turbulence and eventual transparency.

It was hard not to see the resulting chimera as a statement—a picture or statue, an out-take from one of the vanished religio-cultural pantheons of Ancient Earth. Though it seemed immobile when you first saw it, the figure was slowly writhing and moving, struggling not to become one thing or the other but to retain both styles of presentation at once. Gaines found himself silenced by the sheer effort of will involved. He felt privy to something no one should be able to see, the hidden mayhem of events prior to the real, the effort to remain complex in the face of the decohering and literalising forces of the universe. Beyond the arena of this struggle—beyond the knots of observers with their insufficiently imaginative physics, their failed intuitions—the light thinned out quickly to grey; a darkness higher up gave the illusion of unlimited space against which events as consistently weird as this might unfold.

Gaines stood there shaking his head and Case asked him, "What do you think now?"

"I don't think anything," Gaines said.

"Things we can tell you," Case offered: "This isn't the Aleph, but the Aleph's still present."

"How do you know?"

"We had an operator go back over the data. What it found was this: fifty minutes before the original convulsion, the Aleph began connecting itself to the maze—" Here, Case brought up hologram schematics supposed to represent the six-and-four-fifths-dimension topology of the maze— "specifically to Sector VF14/2b, a structure of tunnels flooded with highly tuned superconducting liquids."

"I remember VF14," Gaines said, who had come through there with Emil Bonaventure's group in, he thought, 2422 or 23. "Emil believed it was focused on the Tract." Not that they had had time to think anything much. The tunnels were fifty feet in diameter, tiled, dank as a disused subway, curving in directions that made no sense. In some places the stuff was like water. Others it ate into their excursion suits, or floated through them, or slushed around like warm saliva from someone else's mouth. All he remembered was Johnnie Izzet vomiting blood into the headpiece of his suit, and someone else shouting, "Fucking shit!" Johnnie's blood coagulated instantly it touched the visor, as if it had come out in some transition state. Then the whole tube was alive with ionising radiation, along with something that sounded like music but couldn't have been. Every direction was the wrong direction. Things were moving behind them where they couldn't see. Emil and Rig and two other men tried to drag Johnnie away but he was dead before they made a hundred yards. "He thought it might be for measuring time in there."

"Not measuring, it turns out," Case said. "Manipulating. The Aleph sits here for half a million years. It has interesting physics, very different to ours—"

"What's new?"

"—but it does nothing with them until it brings Pearl here. We're not sure if it was waiting for her, or went looking for her, or if it found her by accident." He gestured at the superposition state wrestling with its own deep refusal of identity in front of them. "Did it intend this to happen? We suspect not. What you see now isn't the Aleph. It isn't the woman, either. The two of them are giving rise to some third kind of thing."

Gaines, still seeing Johnnie Izzet's blackened faceplate and hearing the music of non-Abelian states at room temperature, made himself say:

"Where does the cat fit in?"

For a moment, Case looked puzzled.

"Oh, that," he said. "Our best guess is that it isn't really a cat. Any more than she's really a woman. You know?"

"I didn't think physics did metaphors."

"Here's the problem. This thing, whatever it is, has all the hallmarks of an emergent property. It isn't complete, but it's already self-determining. It's already loose. It's in the labyrinth again, operating the VF14/2b anomalies as a machine. It's off on some downward causation adventure, separating itself from what you or I would think of as time."

"Why?" Gaines said.

"Because there's something it doesn't like about its own past."

"Reinvention never looked so hard," was Gaines' opinion. He suspected you would have to have fairly low esteem to put yourself through this. "What if we brought the policewoman here," he suggested.

Case shook his head to indicate disbelief.

"Keep me out of it if you do," he said. Then he laughed.

"You know, the game has changed to such a degree I doubt anything would happen? It hasn't asked for her since before you were last here. It's interested in something else now."

After they had come to an agreement, the assistant left Epstein to it and drove around the city all day in her Cadillac car. Strange forces were at work. She remembered everyone she killed, but she didn't remember killing Toni Reno. Eventually, midnight or gone, she turned up at the Tango du Chat with George the tailor on her arm. George looked under the weather, but he allowed her to buy him several drinks and paid real attention to everything she said. It was quiet at the Tango du Chat. The music was over for the night. Edith Bonaventure, who owned the place, sat behind the bar reading one of her father's diaries. People came in for a late drink, then when they saw the assistant—who was mixing Black Heart rum and bishop's weed, giving everyone those louche amused stares of hers—went out again without having one.

At around two thirty am she asked George:

"Do you think a person like me can forget killing someone?"

She began to tell him all the other things she couldn't remember about herself. For her, she said, talking to George was like talking to a doctor. It was a release. "Someone like you knows everything about someone like me."

George knew nothing, except that in her present form she had come out of a chopshop tank in Preter Coeur. What he didn't get was who else had been involved. SportCrime? EMC? Whatever she had been originally, he thought, the dice were loaded against her from that point in the story. Some bunch of charlatans had reinscribed her as a cruel joke. Fourteen-year-old coders and cut-boys, ripped on growth hormone from a native lemur species. He could imagine the smell of their fried food and *café électrique*. Radio Retro, your Station to the Stars, blaring reconstructed Oort Country tunes across the workshop while they tuned her, laying in a second nervous system on self-organising nanofibres, throttling up her reflexes, deciding whether to put in radar, already placing bets on her in fights she was too illegal to be entered for. She would never remember who she had been.

"At birth," he told her, "this is my guess, you were already thirty, thirty-two years old?"

"Hey," she said. "This is why I like you, George."

Two years later, she said, after a cooling down period to see if she could still be described as human, they had allowed her on stage with all the other walking psychodramas. "In my case, the investigated and the investigators." She struck an attitude. "All those, George, who walk in the shadow. All those who carry a gun. First SportCrime, then SiteCrime. I had a hard time adjusting, but I was soon restoring order. I was expected to do well." She drank some more rum. "George, what's my reward?" She grinned at him. "It is a wank in the twink tank. A once-a-week wank," she said. "It's very upmarket."

"Come out of a tank, you spend your life trying to get back in one."

She didn't know about that, she said. "But you quickly see that every context has another context wrapped around it, and another one round that."

This made her laugh restlessly. A few minutes later, she abandoned the gene tailor to his drink and went out to where the camber of the street tilted her Cadillac into the kerb, its white faux-leather ragtop slicked with fine rain. She got in, moving with the care of all those who are bagged. Started its big, reliable V8 engine and sat looking along Straint. Radio on, she thought. The night was yellow. The narrow perspective of the street phosphoresced away in front of her beneath neon signs—Strait Cuts, New Nueva Cuts, Ambiente Hotel—all the way to the Event site. She would end this night like many others, at the Event site under Kefahuchi stars, staring out across the waste lots and the lonely lovers struggling in the backs of cars just like hers, to where physics outdid even her for strangeness: enabling, for an hour, rest. Liminal zones were her forte, she had boasted to George the tailor. She was a liminal zone herself.

"The moment I understood that, I knew I had to look for a name."

A name, in the Halo, is everything. You are no one without a name. She had tried Fortunata, Ceres, Mad Cyril and Berenice. She'd been Queenie Key, Ms Smith, The Business, Vice, Mildew, Miranda, Calder & Arp and Washburn Guitar. She had tried Mani Pedi, Wellness Lux, Lost Lisa, Fedy Pantera, REX-ISOLDE, Ogou Feray, Restylane and Anicet. She'd been Jet Tone, Justine, Pantopon Rose, The Kleptopastic Fantastic, Lauren Bacall, Avtomat and the little girl who could crack anything. She had tried "Frankie Machine" and Murder Incorporated, The Markov Property, Elise, Ellis and Elissa. She'd been Elissa Mae, Ruby Mae, Lula Mae, Ruby Tuesday, Mae West and May Day. She'd been The One, The Only, The Two Dollar Radio and Flamingo Layne. For a day she had been A Member of the Wedding. Then Spanky. Then Misty. Hanna Reitsch, Jaqueline Auriol, Zhang Yumei, Helen Keller, Christine Keeler, Olga Tovyevski. KM, LM, M3 in Orion. She liked "Sabiha Gokce" but wasn't sure how to pronounce it. A name is no good if people don't know how to pronounce it. She'd been Pauline Gower,

James Newell Osterberg and Celia Renfrew-Marx. Emmeline Pankhurst. Irma X. Colette. Mama Doc. Dot Doc. Did she dare call herself, "The Blister Sisters?" The Best Engine in the World?

Shortly after she drove off thinking these thoughts, George exited the Tango du Chat and, leaning against a wall, threw up. He wiped his mouth, watched the Cadillac's tail-lights grow small. He wondered if she would ever leave him alone.

22: The See-Not Gate

Waking out of a foul dream to gently hectoring telephone calls from her daughter, Anna Waterman allowed herself to be persuaded into one last session with Helen Alpert.

The doctor had spent much of the morning arguing with a Citroën parts supplier in Richmond and was pleasantly surprised when her client arrived carrying take-out lattes and almond croissants for them both. Had Anna lost weight since her previous visit? Perhaps not, Helen Alpert decided; perhaps it was in fact a postural change. "That's very thoughtful of you, Anna," she said, though she never drank coffee after eight in the morning.

On her part, Anna felt ashamed of herself. It was like being the one to break up a relationship. Prior to buying the coffee she had spent half an hour on Hammersmith Bridge, gazing down at the brown water at some people learning to scull, miserably trying to bring herself to face the doctor. After that, the consulting room, with its cut flowers and tranquil light, seemed such a zone of peace, and Helen Alpert so welcoming, that she didn't know where to begin. For years, she explained, she had lived in a kind of suspended animation. That seemed to be over now. During the last few months, life had been waking her out of a sleep she didn't want to relinquish, forcing her to take part again.

"That's what I haven't liked about it."

"No one likes that," the doctor agreed.

"No. But they want it anyway."

"Anna, I'm interested in the way you put it, life 'forcing' you to take part again. What sort of thing do you mean?"

"For example, Marnie's not well."

"I'm sorry to hear that."

"I found that I welcomed it. I know that sounds odd." Having admitted Marnie to the negotiation, Anna became unsure how much space to allow her. "Anyway, it's time someone looked after her for a change."

"You feel she's been the parent for too long?"

"And something else has happened," Anna said, "which I'd rather not talk about."

The doctor smiled. "Your business is your business."

Given their circumstances, Anna considered this the cheapest of jibes. "Actually I just want to live my life," she heard herself say, with somewhat more emphasis than she had intended.

"Everyone wants that. What exactly is wrong with Marnie?"

"She's having tests."

There followed a silence, during which Dr Alpert played with one of her gel pens and made it clear that she was expecting more. Anna considered describing the visit to St Narcissus—the women shackled to their symptoms by the system and to their lives by mobile phone; the fatuous receptionist; the cancer-shaped stain on the ceiling—but preferring to avoid the interpretive bout that would inevitably follow, in which she would feel compelled to take part out of simple courtesy, said instead, "I never wanted to examine my life, I just wanted to be inside it." This had the nature of a bid or gambit, she realised. "Not," she qualified, before Helen Alpert could take it up, "that I never had a point of view on myself. Of course I did. Look," she said. "The fact is, Helen—you'll understand me, I know you will—I've met someone. A man." She laughed. "Well, more of a boy, really. Is that awful? Michael is dead, but I feel alive again, and that's what I want to be. Alive."

This much denial filled the doctor's heart with rueful admiration. "I'm delighted," she said, though it must have been clear that she was not. She wondered why she bothered. She reached across the desk and put her hands over Anna's. "Tell me what you dreamed last night," she said, "and I'll tell you why you mustn't stop coming here. Not yet."

"Do you know, I didn't dream at all last night," Anna said. "Isn't that odd?"

Half an hour later Helen Alpert accompanied her client to the door, where, both eager to admit how they would miss one another, they said goodbye. While Anna walked swiftly up Chiswick Mall towards Hammersmith without looking back, Helen crossed the road and leaned on the river wall. It was a sunny morning, but the air had an edge: September, accepting that the game was up. The Thames ran low, with a sullenness that suggested the tide was on the turn. Two or three mallards, who had looked as if they were going to make a morning of it, honking and squabbling in the mud, suddenly took off and swept west, gaining height until they vanished behind the trees on the far bank.

Back inside, she put the Waterman file away; then changed her mind and, leafing through it angrily, began to make a fresh set of notes. The client, her personality frozen in adolescence, had disguised herself as an adult for the duration of her marriage to Tim Waterman. To what end? She had effectively erased the abjection of her life with her first husband, yet remained bound to it, and through it to the unthought known. Why allow the disguise to fall away now? As to the significance of the repeating dream: other dreams seemed as diagnostically valuable, and moreover came with all the necessary tools for their own decoding. The central problem, of course, was Michael Kearney. Helen Alpert couldn't imagine being unable to forget a man whilst at the same time being unable to remember him. Anna's self-deception seemed to have spread itself, deft and obdurate, into the real world: the very sparseness of Kearney's biography—mathematician, suicide, patch of fog in every life he touched—gave him an unfocused quality.

Today, however, the doctor found herself more interested in Brian Tate, who—casting himself as the assistant, the unassuming experimentalist, workhorse to his friend's conceptual genius—had committed career suicide so as not be left out of the grand finale of Kearney's psychodrama. The great difference between the two men was this: Dr Alpert knew enough about Tate's subsequent life to find him. She even had an address, somewhere deep in gentle Walthamstow, cocoon of the North London academic mafia. The file remained on her desk all morning. She took it with her to her favourite restaurant, Le Vacherin at Acton Green, where she read it again while lunch ran through its rewarding, quietly inevitable cycle—duck egg cocotte to assiette of hare to prune and Armagnac tart—and the tables emptied around her. "Do you know," she told her waitress, looking up in surprise to find it was already two in the afternoon, "I think I'd like the bill."

She was soon on the way to Walthamstow. If he could be found, Brian Tate might perhaps be persuaded to speak—about Kearney, about the events of that time, about the original Anna. It would be unethical to contact him, certainly. She would have to admit, too, that she was uncovering some unsuspected feature of her own personality. Until now she'd made sure to buffer her life from the client's, proud of the fact that in the face of failure she had always been able to find closure without entanglement.

By three in the afternoon, thick moist air had piled itself into Carshalton High Street, the sharpness of the morning having long given way to a sourceless, muggy heat. Anna Waterman wandered fretfully up and down, trying to put off the inevitable encounter.

She leafed through the second hand books in the Oxfam shop; stood for a moment next to the artificial cascade in Grove Park, where the falling water evaporated with a smell like stale bird feathers. Eventually, on the pretext of getting lunch, she went into a pub near the ponds and ordered a pint of beer. The taste of it caused her to remember the boy on top of her, so hard and nervous, his eyes inturned. Her afternoon with him came back less like a memory of events than a single seamless rush of sensation—a shiver everyone knows but no one knows the name of—and she had to walk up and down looking at the posters on the wall by the bar to give herself something to do. Club Chat Noir. The Aviator Club. A traction engine rally in October; in December, the Chinese Circus. After that, she gave up on herself and sat in a corner and let the afternoon fade into evening. People wandered in and out, saying things like, "I can't cope, I was expected not to live." She caught the word "patterning" or perhaps "patenting"; then, decisively, "contracts"; or perhaps it was "contacts." On the TV above the bar, a European football game began. Pulling Anna's third pint of Young's, the barman looked up emptily and then away.

Fake beams, artex ceilings and floral carpet each have a profound—if under-investigated—anxiolytic effect of their own: by seven o'clock, she had managed to forget the discomfort of her encounter with Dr Alpert and gather enough of herself together to face 121, The Oaks.

As she left the pub, the evening rush was under way. "He can't have steak," someone called out, "It'll give him piles!"

Laughter.

Away from the centre the streets were wrapped in foreign-seeming air—air that warmed and yellowed the night without transforming it. You expected to hear cicadas, catch sight of your own shadow on a curved stucco wall behind which growths of palm or jacaranda further enclosed a shuttered domain. But all you found was the usual holly tree and dirty pebbledash, and in the mossy driveway an unreliable British sports car from the 1970s or a short-wheelbase Land Rover bought for a gap-year tour: some late-adolescent project abandoned under its green tarpaulin fifteen years before, as the globalised economies, running out of new services to sell one another, preoccupied themselves with their own decline.

Holding up the pocket drive like a permit, Anna made her way round to the rear of the house. She found the main window dimly lit, as if by a source somewhere else in the house. When she pressed her face against the glass, everything was exactly as she had seen it last: rippled green lino; a roll of carpet propped up in the corner opposite the door; and on the table the little pressed-tin Mexican box containing a downscaled human skull nestled in scarlet lace. An old sofa, loose-covered in what might have been chintz, now faced the table. On it sat two women, short, heavily built and dressed in black clothes, each with an identical Harrods shopping bag resting on her knees. Anna could hear their voices, but not what they were saying. After a few minutes a thin indistinct figure appeared in the doorway, pushing a wheelchair. It was the boy who had offered her *Lost Horizon*.

Brian Tate looked worse than ever. His upper body, no longer able to support itself, sagged forward against the chair's nylon restraints; his skull—bald, ulcered and fragile-looking, as if the bone had thinned year-on-year since Michael Kearney abandoned him to his doomed interpretation of their data—had fallen so far to one side that it rested on his own left shoulder. His mouth was permanently open. One eye was closed, the eyelid drawn down, the cheek beneath sagging; while the other, as blue as a bird's egg, looked brightly at the wall, the window, the Mexican box with its curious contents, whatever he happened to be facing. It was alive and focused, but it was only an eye: it wasn't necessarily connected to anything. In his lap lay a greasy brown paper bag. The boy parked the wheelchair next to the table, facing the sofa. He set the brake carefully, forced a white 1960s motorcycle helmet and ski-goggles on to Tate's head—a process which involved some physical effort—then sat down cross-legged on the floor.

"There," he said, conversationally: "He's here."

The women received this in silence, as listless and bored as patients in a dentist's waiting room. They had left very little space on the sofa, but its third occupant, a small middle-aged man with bright red hair, had managed to squeeze in between them. He wriggled and smiled around, as if it had been a recent, good-natured public struggle. With his dirty fleece, alcohol tan and hoarse, personalised way of breathing, he looked like someone whose lifestyle choices would soon move him outdoors and to the centre of London, where he would limp up and down Shaftsbury Avenue calling, "I'm in bits, me!" and showing the tourists the Krokodil sore on his neck. "Hey, look mate, I'm in bits!"

For two or three minutes these three stared at Brian Tate—they were less acknowledging his presence, Anna thought, than confirming his existence in some way—then, without speaking, and with no sign that they were aware of each other, or had a shared purpose, they busied themselves with their clothes. The women folded back their skirts from their thighs and slid forward so that they could open their legs; the man struggled to unzip the flies of his tight Levis. There was a rustle of cloth, a sigh or two. They all began masturbating. Two or three minutes later, they were still at it, staring ahead with expressions of absolute vacancy on their faces. Anna thought she could smell them through the glass. It was a sharp, yeasty smell, not unpleasant but not very attractive either. At the same time, Brian Tate's liver-spotted hands began to fumble with the brown paper bag in his lap, from which they extracted a half-eaten double bacon cheeseburger. This, Tate broke into pieces, carefully separating the bun from the meat, which he held up, nodding his head and smiling at a point in the air above the Mexican box.

"It's coming up," the boy said suddenly, in a strangled voice. Silence from the others—perhaps a barely perceptible speeding up of their efforts. "It's coming up!"

The women groaned from the couch. The red-haired man yelped and gasped. A telephone rang in the distance. The Mexican box, illuminated suddenly from within, emitted a cloud of fine white ash, which poured up and out into the room. "My name," said a voice from the box. "My name is—" Then: "Is anybody there?" Brian Tate struggled to answer, but nothing would come out of his mouth. He had plunged one hand into the cloud of ash, and seemed to be offering, for the approval of something Anna couldn't see, the remains of the cheeseburger. After a moment, the glass door of the box fell off its hinges and Tate's white oriental cat burst out. Snatching the hamburger, it jumped on to his shoulder and began eating. At this the women redoubled their efforts, moaning, straining, grinding busily at themselves, their activity driving the room towards a state in which it would be both dimensionless and yet full of possibilities. Shimmers distorted the air around the sofa: jumping to his feet, the boy gave the wheelchair a violent shove in a direction without logic—it was parallel, Anna thought, to an axis the room didn't share—and suddenly it had spun away on a curious spiralling trajectory. Tate and his cat went with it, growing smaller and smaller as they accelerated, until they vanished into an upper corner. The figures on the sofa fell silent. Their will dissipated, their clothing disarranged, their shoulders covered with ash like victims of bombardment, they slumped in foetal postures. With a sharp report, the window cracked from side to side and fell into the flowerbed at Anna's feet. The boy poked his head out and said, "Hey, you should have come in!" He was tucking his penis into his jeans like a roll of soft pale chamois. Anna shuddered unhappily. She hurried out on to the street and glared back at the roof of 121. What did she expect to see? She wasn't sure. Brian Tate and his cat, perhaps, spinning upwards into a milky overcast through which could be made out every so often two or three unidentifiable stars, the only evidence anyone has of the infinite space in which we believe we live.

She had remembered everything but it meant nothing.

"I've had enough, Michael," she said, as if Kearney really had come back from the dead and was standing beside her, the way they had stood nearly thirty years ago outside the same house, in the aftermath of events equally strange and destabilising: "I'm up to here with it all."

She caught the nine twenty-seven into town from Carshalton Beeches. Local services were delayed by works. Freight rumbled through Clapham: cement in dry bulk, denser and more real than the place itself or the people passing through with their soft furnishings taped in plastic bags or their cat in a basket. Anna looked around and wished she had never articulated her fantasy of living there: under the mercury lamps it proved to be just another railway station. "I'd encourage the trains to keep running," she remembered saying to Helen Alpert, "if only for the company." Just another poor joke at the therapist's expense, one more bid for attention. A man in a yellow safety vest wandered around, stopping occasionally to peer into the lighted window of the platform café as if the things inside—cups, cakes, cabinets, paper serviettes—weren't perfectly ordinary, perfectly easy to see, perfectly legible *as* things. Otherwise there was hardly anyone around.

Her connection was slow. Its wheels broadcast a mournful ringing noise to the woods and empty pasture. Home at last, thirty-five minutes after midnight, she listened to a message from Marnie, "Mum, please don't just go off like that without telling me. Anyway, how did it go this morning?" Anna sat on the loo with her knickers down; she took off her shoes and scratched the sole of one foot. At school in the late 2000s, Marnie had been so dismayed by the mobile phone that, though it was already the great load-bearing pillar of juvenile culture, she had refused to own one. What had gone wrong since then? "Anyway, I want to hear how it all went!"

Anna could not guess the meaning of the scenes she had witnessed in Carshalton; equally, there seemed to be no way of interpreting her own history. In the end, if you have a certain sort of mind, you can't even separate the mundane from the bizarre. That's why you find yourself face down in the bathroom eighteen years old, studying the reflection of your own pores in the shiny black floor tiles. And if afterwards you choose a dysfunctional person to be your rescuer, how is that your fault? Who could know? More importantly, the past can't be mended—only left behind. People, the dead included, always demand too much. She was sick of being on someone else's errand. "I did my best," she thought, "and now I can't be bothered any more." After making such an indifferent job of it for so long, what she wanted to do was live. As a starter she opened the downstairs doors and windows, then a bottle of red wine. She threw the pocket drive in the recycling bin.

If she called Marnie they would only shout at one another. Preferring to avoid that, she took the bottle to the sofa—

—then almost immediately dragged herself through layers of silent chaos to consciousness, to find James the cat staring into her face, purring coarsely with something between pleasure and possessiveness. She was naked. At some point she had woken without remembering it, closed the house up, taken herself to bed. "Get off, James—" rolling away from him and off the queen size box-spring, desperate for something to drink—"We aren't even the same species." Though she was not directly aware of it, her dream continued.

She lay on her side on a black glass floor in her Versace gown and long black gloves, upper body raised on one elbow. She was not turning from a woman into an animal or from an animal into a woman. If she was not in transit, neither was she in any sense "caught" between those two states: she was busily occupying them both at once. Though to herself she did not seem entirely Anna, she did not seem entirely anything else: she felt smeary and blurred at significant sites of paradox or conflict, in the manner of a Francis Bacon. Waking up never interrupted this hard, thankless work of superposition ("Someone has to do it, darling," she imagined saying to Marnie) or much diminished her sense of it. It was all the worse for being unconscious, implicit, ongoing. It was all the worse because it felt like a commentary on her life, welling up from some internal source she preferred not to acknowledge. Halfway out of the room, she went back and hugged the cat. "I'm sorry, I'm sorry, I'm sorry," she said to him. "James, if you want my advice, never be a failed suicide. You won't hear the bloody last of it, even from yourself."

James allowed her to carry him downstairs. He dashed into the night the moment she opened the kitchen door, only to return excitedly a few minutes later with a neon kidney in his mouth. Perhaps two inches by one and a half, with plump, eye-catching curves, it had a saturated pale blue colour and a transparent rind that seemed both resistant and pliable. James crouched on the worktop and sheared into it with his back teeth, breathing heavily through the same side of his mouth. "Oh for god's sake," Anna said, turning away in case she saw it burst. "I'm closing the door." But a long soft flash of lightning caught her in the doorway, throwing her into silhouette and projecting her shadow against the opposite wall. There was no thunder. A wave of moist heat rolled into the kitchen. It was transformational weather, weather suited to another country: a thick, low cloudbase, smells of static water pocked with rain. The cat looked up, then down again.

"Hello?" Anna whispered. "Hello?" she peeped out into the garden. It stretched away, elongated, too narrow, rippling with heat. Quiet yet catastrophic changes of light revealed, a long way off, the summerhouse.

"On fire again," thought Anna. "How tiresome."

This time it presented as a whole series of buildings: it was a Sixteenth-Century windmill on the Downs, a Dickensian lapboard cottage as tarry as an upturned boat on a beach, a Palladian folly collapsing into the Pagan site on which it stood. These structures slowly replaced one another in a shifting field of view. They loomed and shrank, as if they were approaching or receding. Each arrived not simply with its own architectural style but with its own style of mediation, from hard-edge photographic to St Ives impressionist, from construction-paper silhouette to matchstick hobbyist Gothic. One minute it was a woodcut of a summerhouse, with static flames; the next, impasto rubbed on with someone's thumb.

Pausing only to remove Kearney's computer drive from the recycling bin, Anna went out and stood in the orchard, barefoot, naked, quiet, no longer sure what age she might be.

"Whoever you are," she said reasonably, "I don't know what you want."

As if in response, the summerhouse cycled through a few more versions of itself, becoming in succession a Tarot card (the Tower, always falling, always in flames, index and harbinger of a life in transit); a canonical firework from someone's vanished childhood, a "volcano" wrapped in red and blue paper, pouring out pink-dyed light, smoke, showers of sparks, thick dribbles of lava; and a sagging fairground marquee, with scalloped eaves and pennants in many different colours. Cartoon bottle-rockets fizzed into the air behind it, bursting in showers of objects which toppled back to earth with inappropriate noises—plastic crockery that rang like a bell, an Edwardian railway train pumping out the sinewy sound of pigeon wings in an empty industrial space—folding themselves up and vanishing even as they fell. These objects smelled of leather, frost, lemon meringue pie; they smelled of precursor chemicals. They smelled of Pears Soap.

Anna approached until the heat began to tighten the skin above her eyes. At that distance, the summerhouse steadied itself. It reverted to the familiar. Then a dense spew of smaller items fountained up from the flowerbeds, poured out of the door, blew off the roof, resolving itself into a display of a thousand fireflies, sleet falling through car headlights, showers of jewels and boiled sweets, enamelled lapel badges, shards of stained glass. Strings of coloured fairy lights and fake pearls, glittering Christmas baubles. Little mechanical toys—beetles, novelty swimmers, jumping kangaroos, all powered by rusted-up clockwork from the first great phase of Chinese industrialisation. Particoloured juggling balls. A thousand giveaway pens. A thousand cheap GPS systems that no longer ran. Bells and belts. Birds that really whistled; birds that sang. A million tiny electrical components and bits of ancient circuit boards as if every transistor radio ever made had been buried in the earth, and with them—like a kind of grave-goods!—the faint music and voices of *Workers' Playtime*, *Woman's Hour* or *Journey into Space*, everything they once had played. A fog of small consumer goods. All the rubbish of a life, or someone else's life.

Anna Waterman née Selve stopped a pace or two before the summerhouse door. She tilted her head and listened.

"Hello?" she said.

She said: "Oh, what is it now?"

Everything was very calm and quiet and smelling of the hotel bathroom when she stepped inside and began to fall. She let go of the computer drive in surprise. At the last moment, James the black and white cat darted between her legs. All three of them, the woman, the animal and the data, fell out of this world together. Glare and dark, strobing into sudden silence and things switching off busily, up and down the whole electromagnetic spectrum.

23: Heart Sounds & Bruits

MP Renoko—that mysterious software entity which, people said, was all that remained of Sandra Shen's Circus—had returned lately from an inspection of major Quarantine orbits all over the Halo.

He was tired but happy. With these visits, interesting but necessarily clandestine, his contribution was complete. The cargo in place, the client settled in the hold of the ship they called the *Nova Swing*, his part in things coming to an end, he took a last walk down by the sea, a mile along from the circus ground on South Hemisphere, New Venusport. Away from motel and beach-bar it was all spray and sunshine, the water booming in on a steep shore strewn with rocks the size of white goods, where sunbathing men and women lay like lizards staring blankly at the spray as it exploded up in front of them. The huge waves, MP Renoko said, might have been in a hologram for all the notice they took of them.

"You wonder," he added, to the ghost by his side, "why they have so little common sense."

"But look!" the ghost said. "Look!"

She hacked with her heel at the shingle, then bent down quickly and prised something loose. After the removal of a bit of seaweed it turned out to be an old round coin with a small square hole in the middle, still somehow bright and untarnished. "Down between the rocks," she said, "spiders make their webs. A foot or two from all that surf! They tremble every time a wave comes in, and we can't express the sense of anxiety with which this fills us." A shrug. "Yet every year there are webs and spiders."

The coin, flipped into the air, glittered briefly.

"Heads or tails?" enquired the ghost.

"You were always the best arguer," Renoko acknowledged. "I know it's wrong to say, 'I think.' I should say, 'I am thought.'"

She took his arm, and gave him her faint little oriental smile.

"You should," she said. "I can't stay long. Back to the circus? Or on to the diner?"

"I'm ready to go anywhere."

Beneath the cliffs half a mile distant, the ocean fumed and danced. No one knew why. It wasn't a temperature thing. It was some less mundane kind of physics. Spray hung in thousand-foot prismatic curtains, full of strange colours: filmy pink, lime sherbert, weird metallic blue light through which seagulls could be seen diving and gyring ecstatically. On the very edge of the cliff above, placed to take advantage of the deep pre-human strangeness of the planet's housekeeping, stood a sixty-by-sixteen-foot O'mahony-style diner called Mann Hill Tambourine but known to its habitués—edgy young middle managers from the rocket yards along the coast—simply as "the Tambourine." By day, the gulls dived and gyred above its deco stainless steel and glass tile. Nightly, the Tambourine yearned towards the waves, just as if it ached to fall, and greet the sea with minty greens, deep flickering reds and fractured stainless steel glitters of its own. From seven o'clock on, the tables were deserted. No one came to the Tambourine to eat. Instead they pressed themselves up against the seaward glass, where like called to like in that as-yet-unbettered phase of the universe.

"On your own here," Renoko said, "you can hear voices in the tide."

His weariness amazed him.

Shortly after these events, a strange scene took place on board the *Nova Swing*. The cabin lights flickered. The Dynaflow drivers ran rough, failed briefly, then came back up, inserting a blank space in the crew's experience of their lives roughly equal to the effects of a transient ischemic attack.

Down in the main hold, a wave went through the deck plates, as if matter could experience a stroke too. Light and dark became muddled. The mortsafes bumped together like moored boats. The lid of the K-tank blew off violently and clattered away, revealing the proteome inside, which slopped about like dirty salt water at night. Through its surface burst the occupant of the tank, a wasted Earthman with a partly grown-out Mohican haircut and a couple of snake tattoos, whose body resembled, from the diaphragm down, a charred and tattered coat. His spine was cabled at neurotypical energy sites. Half-drowned, throwing up with the vertigo of aborted interstellar flight, he stared round in panic at the main hold, the gathered mortsafes. Proteome poured off him, smelling of horse glue; rendered fat; the albumen of a bad egg. Whatever he had been dreaming was gone for good. He wasn't used to a non-electronic presence in the universe: it was some time since he had been available in this form. He looked down at himself.

"Jesus, Renoko," he complained to the empty air. "I've got no fucking legs. You didn't tell me that."

He fell to plucking the thick rubber cables out of his spine. He tried and failed to wipe the proteome off himself with his hands.

"Fuck," he said.

The condition of the K-tank seemed to impress him. "Remind me to come the easy way round next time," he said. He addressed the mortsafes. "Anyone got any tissues, or like that?"

What did they think of this performance?

They were content with it. They were aliens. They had, by now, spent a claustrophobic fortnight in the *Nova Swing* main hold with its black and yellow warning stripes, loose tool-cupboard doors, injunctions to work safe with plasma. They understood where they were, and they understood why. It wasn't the first time they'd done this. Working for Sandra Shen had required, at the least, hundreds of years of travel from distant places. They had performed vital functions at the demise of her Observatorium & Native Karma Plant. They had abandoned sane environments, left behind homes and families, to be part of the faux-Chinese woman's engine of change. Like her, they were here to work on behalf of others. They were content with the burnt man because they were content with that.

The *Nova Swing* chewed a long hole between the stars, her doomed crew staring out so that sometimes their faces appeared at the portholes together, sometimes apart. The police were after her on several worlds. The beef: artefact smuggling. Possible Quarantine infringement. Wanted in connection with the death of a Saudade factor going by "Toni Reno." She sneaked from world to world across the Beach. Since she took aboard the crippled K-tank, she had dropped in quietly at Goat's Eye and the Inverted Swan; fallen across the empty spaces between Radio Bay and the Tract itself; drifted seventy-four hours, all systems powered down, at heavily coded co-ordinates in the notorious dXVII-Channing Oort cloud. MP Renoko was a no-show at all those venues. Then, just when they had given up on him, he poked his head through the crew quarters wall and said to Fat Antoyne, as if continuing a conversation they had started in The East Ural Nature Reserve on Vera Rubin's World:

"Everyone their own evolutionary project, Fat Antoyne!"

Antoyne said, "Jesus."

"Who's this little old cunt?" Irene wanted to know. She looked Renoko over, her irises dark with satire. "Oh, it's you," she said. "Antoyne, get off me." It was not Renoko's chinbeard she hated; or even his 1960s paedophile look, which she admitted was chic enough. It was the sense she had that he was always keeping something of himself in reserve. Or not even something: everything. "Come in," she invited, resettling on her hips some items of dress: "We got your cargo of meaningless toys."

"You've done very well," Renoko said.

"That won't work here, Renoko. The only thing that will work here is this—" making the universal sign for money "—then you go, taking the rusty pipework with you." If you were driven by unknown forces, her body language implied, best not be around Irene.

Antoyne put his hand on her arm. "Why kill Toni Reno?" he asked Renoko. "I don't get it."

Renoko looked puzzled.

"We didn't do that," he said.

Irene held out her hand again, palm up. She said, "Well, it wasn't us either."

"Thanks for the information," Renoko said. "I'll make arrangements," he told Antoyne.

He winked, and his face went back through the wall. He didn't mean money, but Antoyne wasn't to know that. Just before his face vanished it added, "You might have some communications problems in the next hour or so. Don't panic." Down in the main hold where he next materialised, he found the charred man working on one of the mortsafes with a pulsed-spray welding set four hundred years old. Sparks flew everywhere. In their heat and light, this shabby enclosed space seemed like the very forge of God. Renoko watched for a minute or two in an impressed way and then said, "Is that Metal Active Gas?"

The charred man pushed back his goggles and shook his head.

"MIG," he said. "You weld?"

"Never," Renoko admitted. "But I love to watch."

The charred man nodded. He heard that all the time, his nod said, but he still appreciated the compliment. Not everyone can weld. After they had allowed a little time to pass around this shared enthusiasm, he said, "Hey, what a shit body you found for me!"

"It's your own," Renoko pointed out.

"I don't remember doing this to it."

"It will serve the purpose," Renoko said. "She says you can begin any time. They're ready for you in the quarantine orbits." .

The charred man scratched his Mohican. "If not now, when?" he asked himself. But he looked as if he had reservations. Then he shrugged and laughed and clapped Renoko's shoulder. "Hey, so she came to say goodbye to you after all, *La Chinoise*?" Renoko smiled. "In the end," he said, "she did."

"You feel good, then?"

"I feel good," Renoko agreed.

"That's good," the charred man said. He reached into Renoko's head with one hand.

"Oh!" said Renoko. He'd seen something very special.

"She tries to do her best for everyone."

Renoko fell back and slipped down the bulkhead with a sigh until he attained a sitting position, after which he began to lose sight of himself. It was an uncanny feeling. In my case, he reminded himself again, it's wrong to say "I think": I should always say, "I'm thought." Then he wasn't. He wasn't thought any more. Although, as long as the boys from Earth ate lunch, a tiny part of Renoko would always live on, a fractal memory in the Faint Dime database—*catch & spread light of all kind wan light thru ripple glass jagged light of pressed chrome reflection film light of pink neon diffused across ceilings formica in fantasy-pastels pressed chrome deco fluting behind the bar a curious cast to chequerboard floors shiny lime sherbert light on each pink faux leather stool all perfect pressed out in perfect sugar colour like candy every item perfect perfectly itself & perfectly the same as everything else these weird blue metallic plastic banquettes*—less glitch than resonance, the remains of a stay-resident program printing itself out as a list of aesthetic possibilities once or twice a year at cash registers across the Halo, with a particular fondness for "the Tambourine" on New Venusport.

Forty seconds later, the main hold filled with light.

Internal comms tanked. Up in the control room, error signals jammed the boards. "Accept!" Liv Hula told the pilot connexion. Nothing. She stuffed the wires into her mouth by hand. "Akphept!" Too late. They were half in, half out when the connect halted. She pushed until she bled, but the system wouldn't receive. Instead, Liv was snatched out of herself and began some long, identityless transit.

When things returned, she was seeing them via an exterior camera-swarm. Autorepair media raced along the brass-coloured hull like dust down a hot street. The stern assembly pulsed in and out of view. Outriggers, fusion pods, the tubby avocado-shaped bulge housing the Dynaflow drive: you could see the stars through them. From a source down there, where the holds and motors had once been, intermittent, washy-looking streams of plasma curved out into the dark, already an AU long and curved like scimitars. Liv felt sick. With the connector a lump of gold wire half-fused into the tissue of her soft palate, she was reduced to flicking switches. "Antoyne? Hello?" No one responded. Inside the ship, engine rooms, holds, companionways, ventilator shafts, stairwells, winked out one by one. Go through the wrong door, who knew what you'd see? Liv was aware but blind. If you could blueprint grey on grey, that's what filled the control room screens—a kind of luminous darkness where her spaceship had been. There was nothing there, but it had a strong sense of order.

"Jesus, Antoyne," she said. "What are you fucking around with now?"

No one heard her.

Antoyne was enjoying a shit. Irene, who trusted Renoko as far as she could throw him, had zipped herself into a lightweight white eva suit, grabbed her favourite Fukushima Hi-Lite Autoloader from the weapons bar and, with a transparent bubble helmet under one arm, was making her way from the crew quarters to the main hold. Latticed stairways leaned at expressionist angles against the moody emergency light; in the rear companionways the ship's gravity had become undependable. Communications were nonexistent. It was hard to tell which way was up. Irene, though, looked good with her close-fit suit, her determined expression and her flossy blond hair. "It's hot as hell down here," she said. "Hello?"

She put her ear to the main hold doors.

"Wow," she said. "Liv? Antoyne? I hear something!" Setting helmet and Hi-Lite on the floor, she opened the door and stepped through.

Just as Liv heard Irene's strange cries, the missing sections of the ship returned. Antoyne never knew any part of it had been gone. He appeared in the control room pulling up his trousers and together he and Liv ran through the *Nova Swing*, throwing themselves down stairwells as they tried to avoid pockets of deteriorating physics. The ship self-reassembled around them. Its hull rang and rang. The door to the main hold slid open on a vertical slice of lemon-yellow light: inside, some unacceptable transition was partially complete. There were oblique shadows, noises like sacred music, sparks on everything, a voice saying, "Fuck!" Antoyne looked determinedly away from it all and at the same time reached in with one arm. It was a stretch, and he had to feel around aimlessly for a time, but eventually he got hold of Irene by one ankle and pulled her out. "Antoyne," she whispered, with a kind of puzzled matter-of-factness, "the universe isn't what we think." She reached out a soft hand to Liv Hula, insisted, "Nothing here was made for us!" Then, writhing about in Antoyne's arms so she could see into his eyes: "Don't look! Don't look!"

"He didn't look," Liv reassured her.

She wasn't sure if he did or not. The backs of her gums were bleeding where she had ripped the pilot connexion out. She could feel a lot of loose tissue up there. Sometimes Liv felt she had died a hundred lights back, on the mystery asteroid. Ever since, her nightmares were of being discovered by retrieval teams, lapped in faint ionising radiation at the junction of two corridors, an unreadable name stencilled above the faceplate of her eva suit. Day after day, plugged straight into the inner life of the hardware, she lay in the acceleration chair, always too cold, reviewing the internal surveillance data. Something had been wrong down there from the very first day of the Renoko contract, but with every new artefact they picked up, ship life had been less easy to observe. She had no idea if the *Nova Swing* could look after itself in its present condition.

"The mortsafes!" Irene screamed. "The mortsafes!"

Liv Hula slammed the main hold door and backed away from it carefully, holding out Irene's Autoloader in both hands.

They dragged Irene back to the crew quarters. She was hanging by a thread the whole way, hallucinating and crying out. When they got there she made Fat Antoyne dress her in her newest clothes and carry her to a porthole. They couldn't find a single mark on her, but she was slipping away so fast you could feel her go past you and out into empty space.

"Those stars! So beautiful!" she said, and closed her eyes. Her skin had a lead-coloured glaze. Antoyne, whose arm had felt weird since he thrust it into the hold, looked down at her and concluded she was already dead. But after a while she smiled and said: "Antoyne, promise me you won't get a cultivar of me. If I have to die I want to die forever, here and now in this utterly for-real place." She seemed to think about it for a moment. Then she clutched his arm and said, "Hey, and I want you to find someone else! Of course I do! We should never be alone in this life, Antoyne, because that is what human beings are for, and you will have many experiences of love yet. But honey, I want you to lose me. Can you understand that?"

Antoyne, dumb with it already, said he could.

"Good," she said.

She sighed and smiled as if that weight was off her mind. "Look out at those stars," she urged Antoyne again. And then, in a change of subject he could not follow: "All the shoes you can eat!" She pulled herself up with her hands on his shoulders to get a look around the crew quarters.

"Oh, Liv," she said. "And our lovely, lovely rocket!"

Antoyne felt himself begin to cry. All three of them were crying after that.

24: Spike Train

Three fifty am, the assistant visited Ou Lu Lou's on Retiro Street, a venue added only recently to her night's round. There she drank a cup of espresso, holding it in both hands and dancing thoughtfully to the sidewalk music the way R. I. Gaines had taught her, watching out for the flash of pre-dawn light above the city. When it came, she drove back over to Straint Street to talk to her friend and confidant, George the gene tailor. It was fine rain like fog. The Cadillac rolled down Straint, its 1000hp engine already turned off, and came quietly to a halt outside Sharp Cuts. The assistant—let's call her the Pantopon Rose—tall, white-blond hair cropped to not much of anything—possessing the kind of height and fuck-off good looks which come naturally from the most radical tailoring—stepped out on to the sidewalk.

"Hey, George!" she called.

No answer. Her expression grew puzzled. The door hung wide open and the rain was blowing in from the street.

She could smell the dockyards. From the factories she could hear the sound of women clocking on for the early shift. The light had a yellow colour: it picked out the ceramic receiver of the reaction gun she now took out quietly, holding it down alongside her thigh. One instant she was outside, the next she was in, silent and motionless, smiling around. The chopshop seemed empty. Nevertheless she didn't feel alone. Something was masking itself in the IR, RF, acoustic and active sonar regimes. It was near. She could hear a rat breathe two rooms away, but it wasn't that. Something was in the room with her. It was impure in the sense it didn't fit. It was the kind of thing that didn't fit in and if you failed to grasp that you had already made a mistake. She couldn't smell it, but she knew it had a smell. She couldn't locate it, but she knew it had a location. Then came the whisper she almost expected, the amused voice from an empty corner:

"My name is Pearlent—"

The assistant put a Chambers round exactly where her systems placed the voice. A soft, coughing thud and the corner of the shop burst into rose and grey flames. Heat splashed back. In the shifting lick of that—the warm flicker of geometry followed by dark—she identified an object moving. It was a decoy. It was all over the room. It was all around her with—

my name　　　　**Pearlent**　*my*

　　　　　name　*is*　　　　　*is Pearle*

　　　　　　　my　　　　　　**Pearl**

—and the low, charismatic laugh of a rebuilt thing.

If it shot back she was dead. It was there, not there: there, not there. Then it was right in her face. Tall, with white-blond hair cropped to nothing much. The fuck-off body language of someone who can run fifty miles an hour and see in sonar. Someone whose very piss is inhuman.

It was herself.

It was gone. It was next to her yet out of range. For an instant everything hung suspended, then fell.

"Christ!" the assistant screamed. She redlined her equipment. She was quick enough to get a round off at the blur in the doorway. The round fizzed away like an angry cat and burst in the street. When the assistant arrived out there she found she had shot her own car. Flames were already reflecting in the window of the Tango du Chat, appearing curiously still, like cut-out flames, or flames in an old book. Spooked drinkers stared out. They hadn't even begun to duck. She could hear running footsteps, but they were unhurried and already three streets away. That was something you might puzzle over later in your room, when you recalled a face just like your own glaring madly into yours from ten inches distance—permitting itself to be seen in five false-colour overlays, teeth bared and laughing with your own perfected fuck-off arrogance—and admitted just how far things had slipped away from you. You would be forced to express it, she thought, in a similar way to this:

But no one is quicker than me!

Back in the chopshop, a few scraps of orange light from the Cadillac fire slipped between the window-boards, barely touching the dusty counter, the shoot-up posters and powered-down proteome tanks. If light could be described as fried, the assistant thought, this was how it would look, this was how it would illuminate a bare resin floor and reveal the open eyes of the corpse. She knelt down. George had bled out an hour ago from a deeply penetrative wound in his right armpit, as if someone had come up from the floor at him—waited there all night, in complete silence in the photon-hungry dark on the dirty floor, then come up at him and driven one of their hands, fingers stiffened to make a cone, deep into his armpit. He looked almost relaxed, as if the worst thing he could imagine—the very thing he was most afraid of—had finally happened, thus relieving him of his anxieties at the same time as it confirmed them.

"George," she whispered. "My poor George."

It was, she imagined, something the Pantopon Rose might have said. If he had been alive, the assistant could have asked George his professional advice: "How can a person like me be shaking like this?"

Forty lights down the Beach, EMC's crack grey ops team was doing a favour for a friend. The Levy Flight comprised a dozen ships, would take on anything. They gave the big No! to the psychopathic conformity of the typical K-pod. Instead they encouraged a shifting membership of ten- to thirteen-year-olds with an interest in Military Collectibilia of Old Earth. Their present mission might seem weird, even unhip, to today's kids: until you realised that a hundred thousand years ago Panamax IV was inhabited by fuck-off telepathic reptile Aztecs from beyond the universe. That was the draw.

Planetary interdiction would normally require one of the Flight to lay off at the L2 point and from there co-ordinate the operations of the others. The mayhem at Panamax IV discouraged this. There being at least four parties to the conflict not counting the pod itself, fighting was going on in several locations at once, from five lights out in the neighbouring system—catalogued as Alpha 5 Flexitone—to the lower reaches of the Panamax parking orbit. EMC heavy assets thugged it out realtime with the Nastic 8th Fleet in a classic exchange of bumps which had already set fire to a nearby gas giant. Two dozen Denebian dipships mined the local sun. Dissident indigenes were arming scramjets and flying them into partial orbits straight off the factory floor; while a gut-shot Alcubiere battleship—the *Daily Deals & Huge Savings*, run by a privateer crew of New Men under the leadership of two Shadow Boys who shared the name "Fermionic Joe"—tried to aerobrake its way down to the surface of the planet. That was how half the Levy pod, including *Whiskey Bravo*, *Pizza Night*, *Fat Mickey from Detroit* and *Uptown Six*, found itself banging about in atmosphere—no one's preferred medium—at Mach

2 and below, negotiating airspace with one another as well as with hostiles. The other half, strung out between Flexitone and the Panamax Oort cloud, ran interference, making all the usual plays through curled-up dimensions at picosecond speeds, flipping in and out of the 3D world as circumstance demanded.

"—incoming, four degrees over the ecliptic, two lights out."

"I have him."

"Steady. In contact. Steady, steady—"

"Right underneath you, *Fat Mickey*."

"All his bases are ours."

Viewing the Flight's efforts—which, in quotidian time, came to him as little more than a coloured dapple of flat-plane lightning across hologram images of empty space, a few quiet voices in an FTL pipe, a historical record of things that had happened a million nanoseconds ago an astronomical unit away—R. I. Gaines was impressed by their calmness and skill. There was so much work for them out there, you got the feeling they were embarrassed. The quiet rhythms and stresses of their exchanges returned language to something reliable. By contrast, the embedded journalism AIs, their commentary piped in by the pilots themselves from commercial routers, were reporting: "There's no let up for the Levy Flight. These boys wouldn't want one. They *want* to work."

"Levy Flight are *here* to work," Peat Teeter told Tanky LaBrom. "Work improves the way they *feel* about themselves."

By any measure they were too late. Alyssia Fignall's hilltop dig had been vaporised before they arrived. Her house, too, was blowing around in the clouds of oily black grit produced by large-scale thermobaric exchanges. The fountain, the stone arches, the long cool spaces and luminous grey shadows of the cloister: all gone and maybe Alyssia with them. Below him now lay his last chance of finding her.

The town had aged since Gaines last saw it, like a photograph of a ruin subsiding into coastline. Somewhere upstream a dam had burst, forcing a million tonnes of water through La Cava in an hour. The karst system had fallen in on itself: the town had fallen into that. He couldn't see how anyone could survive down there. But Carlo the K-captain had manoeuvred *Uptown Six* to within fifty feet of the greyish-brown turbulence, so Gaines gave him the respect of searching every remaining nook of stone. Right and left, other elements of the pod edged nervously about, trying not to run into one another, so low they were dashed with spray. They looked wrong—like a lot of executioners at a birthday party, with an intense interest in people's weight or how muscular their necks were—but they were doing their best to help, a class of behaviour that did not occur naturally to them. Daylight came and went suddenly and without reason. Incoming gamma would light up the local sky, take the top off a hill, dig a trench a kilometre long; then it would get dark again. At moments like that the K-ships shivered and hunted, outlines blurring as their stealth options cut in, weapons extruding with a kind of sluggish ferocity. Incoming gamma was more their kind of environment.

"It's mayhem down there," Carlo remarked. Then he warned one of the other ships, "Tanky, you've still got me off your starboard stern. Ten metres and closing. Keep up."

Gaines watched the floating junk bouncing off buildings and bridges on its way down to the sea. "There's nothing left here," he was forced to admit.

"Jesus, Rig, I'm really sorry," Carlo said. "Hey, we can go lower! How would it be if we went lower?"

"Get us out of here, Carlo."

Carlo switched on the *f*-Ram drivers. All around the *Uptown Six*, the other ships were torching up. The Levy Flight stood on its stern and ascended through the clouds of radioactive ash at Mach 40. They spent a moment or two in the parking orbit, looking down. Someone up there—someone not so far away, with access to top-shelf assets—had lost their temper: Panamax, as Tanky LaBrom put it, was fucked. High-volume X-ray devices quartered the crust, vaporising the first fifty metres on contact, then steadily melting the rest. Surface features higher than a couple of hundred feet were already a kind of geological paste, fairground scarlet at the leading edge and forcing itself across the remains of the landscape like a tongue between your lips. Plate tectonic activity was up. The atmosphere roared and whistled with heated gases. Gaines stared down, wishing he had understood his daughter as well as she had understood him. He remembered her saying, "Rig, these people were so old!" and he wished there could be one single patch of unburnt ground left somewhere down there. As he thought about Alyssia, the Nastic cruiser—on the other side of the planet now, and only 50,000 feet up—switched on its gravity engine and drove itself into the softening crust. Physics ran wild. A huge bulge began to form on the surface beneath *Uptown Six*.

"Fucking shit, guys," Carlo said, "he's coming all the way through."

The Levy Flight weren't going to miss that.

You can originate from a freezer, Impasse van Sant believed, and still make an identity for yourself: but the thing is, you never feel sited. Day after day he hung in empty space, wondering not so much why he had no news from home as where his home had been. He knew there was a war on, but he didn't know who to side with. That made him feel both unreal and nostalgic. How can you be nostalgic for something you never had? Wow, he caught himself thinking: a war at home! It must be something, to have all your certainties knocked over in that way. He caught fragments of media here and there. Wrecked ships slowly tumbling in hard light; long views of planets he never heard of. Children singing something against a black background. A headline that just said—

WAR

It gave him a warm feeling—like "Christmas" or "growing up"—to think that other people were having this most humanising of experiences, losing everything they cared about, everything that made them what they were. The majority of Imps' news came from the K-Tract, as data he couldn't decode, and was only news if you were interested in high-energy magnetic fields. He was thinking about this when the shadow of his friend fell across him. One monitor wasn't enough to display her; she hung there in high-aspect ratio across three of them, allowing the K-Tract to paint her tip feathers mint-blue and rose-pink.

"Hey," Imps breathed.

"What do you want," she said.

"You look beautiful today."

"You broadcast every frequency. You call me up. You stare into the dark until you find me there. What do you want from me?"

Imps thought.

He felt he should tell her, "My day is crap when we don't talk," or "I think you're lonely too," but both of those were too close to the truth. So he decided to say the next thing that came into his head. Sometimes he made lists of the places he might have come from. For instance he liked the sound of Acrux, Adara, Rigil Kentaurus and, particularly, Mogliche Walder. But Motel VI was his favourite. Motel life, as he understood it, wasn't too demanding. It was a lot closer-in than empty space, but still comfortably on the edge of things. It sounded like a good compromise between what he experienced now and some sort of full humanity. He wanted to ease himself into that. He had downloaded a brochure entitled *Mobile Homes of the Galaxy*, which also featured dwellings based on the classic Moderne hamburger joint—all pastel neon, pressed and ribbed aluminium—set against sunsets and mountain dawns. He showed her some of these.

"I want you to help me go back," he said.

"You came here of your own accord."

"Did I?"

She considered this. "Now you want to go back where you came?"

"I came too far," he said.

"You thought this was what you wanted."

"Peer pressure brought me here. It would be too much to suffer the disapprobation of my friends."

Rig and Emil and Fedy von Gang, hacking busily away at the mysteries in Radio Bay; Ed Chianese who, it was rumoured, had himself plugged into a K-ship and fired into the Tract itself, as dumb a thing as anyone had ever done. The entradistas, the sky-pilots like Billy Anker and Liv Hula. People who called their ship *Blind by Light,* or *Hidden Light,* or *500% Light,* or anything with *Light* in it. People who left a note by the bed, a message in the parking orbit: Torched out, catch you later. Who were wired up wrong from the first. Whose engines cooked with hard X-rays. Who went out unassuagable and came back rich or mad, towing a derelict starship from another galaxy. Rocket jockeys the Halo knew by their first names. Imps shrugged. He excused himself and got a beer. When he came back to his seat she was still there, and he said: "Out here thirty years, and I find I was never like them. Whoa! What's this? Imps, you want to go back, find your home? Stop looking in the dark for stuff no one's ever going to understand?"

"You came too far," she mused.

Van Sant didn't know if she was agreeing with him, or what. When he looked up at the monitor again, she had vanished.

She was gone two days, and when she returned it was only so that they could regard one another in a kind of continuing puzzlement—honest on his side, Imps thought, angry on hers.

"What?" he said.

Another screen came to life and began generating images of the war. Naked bodies in vacuum, rows of K-craft so long they vanished in blackness. An entire planet with a hole through it. Chaotic scenes of the displaced. Tourists who had passed this way a week ago, off to make fuck-footage in the twilight zone of Kunene, who now found themselves dirty and sleepless on the concourse of the very terminal which had promised so much. Or were pictured, still dressed in the easy to wear greige stylings of the moment, anxiously disembarking from a chartered shorthaul flight a hundred light years from their point of origin, to be bussed into temporary cities already crammed with refugees, media, aid-agency reps and dysfunctional gap-year adolescents drawn to the inferno for reasons they didn't understand.

"All over the Halo people are losing their way of life," van Sant whispered. He meant: "How lucky is that?"

She took it some other way.

"I remember all these atrocities you're looking at," she said. Then: "I've done worse." And finally: "Is it right to think so much about yourself?"

Imps got the wrong end of this; felt hurt. "Hey, I was careful to ask you things! You claimed you don't remember!" But she was already sailing away again, banking white and narrow against the absolute arc of the vacuum. "Are we having our first quarrel?" Imps called after her. The reply arrived too faint to hear, as if she had slipped out of more than local space.

After she found the dead man, the assistant stayed on at Sharp Cuts for an hour, unsure how to proceed. Once or twice she got up from George's side to look between the window-boards into the street. Eventually she made a call to Epstein the thin cop. She didn't want him too close to the problem, she said, but she could do with some help. Epstein said it was fine with him, but he had heard she would soon run out of favours elsewhere. The uniform branch arrived to disperse the morning drinkers and extinguish the Cadillac fire. A little later, they towed the shell.

"I loved that engine," she said absently.

The fourth floor at Uniment & Poe sent her a new vehicle from the motor pool. She loaded George into the front seat and drove him across the city to her room by the rocket port in GlobeTown. "It's not much of a car, this one," she told him as they passed the Church on the Rock. "Look at the church, George." Each turn they went round, George's upper body sagged to one side or the other. In the end she was driving with one hand and using the other to prop him up. Though moving a corpse about was nothing much for a person like her, it was at least something to do. It was something you could throw yourself into. "George, you're too easy to carry," she laughed. "You should eat more, really. Do less drugs." She bore him up two flights of stairs and laid him on her bed. Then she took his clothes off, washed him with a damp towel, paying attention to the clots round his armpit, and got him under the covers. "There," she said. "You see?" George lay there collapsed-looking and stared at the ceiling.

Down in the street, someone was playing "Ya Skaju Tebe" in a minor key, with pauses a fraction too drawn out. It was sentimental for the people, music for giving things up to, wartime music. Starliners, now converted to troopships, came and went at the port, rays of coloured light pouring off them to wheel across the assistant's walls, leaving small active patches of ruby-red fluorescence which crawled about like living tattoos. Three kinds of psychic blowback lit George's thin face, one after the other, and for a moment it looked as if he might say something despite being dead.

That was how things rested until it got dark. George looked as if he might speak. The assistant sat on the side of the bed waiting to hear. Then R. I. Gaines walked in through the wall, combat pants rolled halfway up his thin, suntanned calves.

Over those he had his signature lightweight shortie raincoat with the sleeves similarly rolled to the elbows. He was carrying a canvas poacher bag with a feature of tan leather fastenings, from which protruded the grip and part of the receiver of a Chambers gun. His feet were bare. He looked tired. "Oh hi," he said to the assistant, as if he hadn't expected to find her there. They stared at one another and he said: "Skull radio." They spent a few minutes searching through her possessions. When she found the radio, he couldn't make it work. He knelt down and banged it on the floor until the glass broke and the baby's lower jaw fell out. A few white motes drifted here and there. "Good enough," he said. He engaged in a conversation his side of which finished, "You know it's almost like we're in a real world out here. Maybe you should think of it like that too." He threw the radio into a corner. "Upper management," he said to the assistant: "What can you do with them?" Next he caught sight of poor dead George, staring at the ceiling with the blankets up to his neck.

"What's this?"

"I killed him," she said. "I don't know how."

"We all make mistakes." Gaines examined the corpse. "Were you trying to have sex with him?"

"It happened across the city."

Suspecting more than a malfunction, Gaines took her hand and encouraged her to stand by the window, where he could examine the data scrolling down her forearm. Still visible: but in that light the Gothic blacks and Chinese reds weakened to faint grey and orange, and her skin was the colour of old ivory. He sniffed the palm of her hand, then let her go. "You've got a Kv12.2 expression problem," he said. "Epilepsy." She stared down at her own hand, then up into Gaines' face—as if, he thought, she was trying to understand the exchange as emotional rather than diagnostic—and after a moment asked:

"Do you want to sit on the bed and talk?"

"You really are someone's project," he said.

Which of them was the cypher? They sat on the bed, with George the tailor behind them, and both of them stared at the wall. Gaines felt tired after Panamax IV, suddenly the only scene he could remember from his whole life was him and Emil Bonaventure in the PEARLANT labyrinth, dragging along some dead entradista whose suit visor was caked an inch thick with the remains of his own lungs. After a moment or two, he put his arm round her shoulders.

"I'm going to need you to do something for me," he said.

25: Lowboy Orbits

They put Irene out into space, so she could drift forever through the incredible refuse of the Beach she loved.

Without her they were soon depressed and rudderless. Life swilled about in the bottom of the trough. Communication failed. Lies returned home. The FTL media brought only war news, and every shift of the light reminded them of some better time in their lives. Neither of them could fly the ship. Liv went to Antoyne and said, "My mouth is damaged, but my mind is worse." Antoyne shrugged: there was no way he could do it. They fucked for comfort, what a mistake that turned out to be. The *Nova Swing* hung there in the middle of nothing. When she fired up her Dynaflows and set a course of her own, back towards Saudade where it had all begun, they were almost relieved to have things taken out of their hands.

They continued to avoid the main hold. Instead, they slept and slept, living separate lives inside their own guilt about Irene. But once the ship got under way, levels of unconscious activity could only rise: Antoyne dreamed he was fat again, fat and hard like an armadillo or half a barrel. He dreamed he was dead. Liv dreamed of ghosts. Sometimes a torn coat seemed to float along the ship's ill-lit companionways and stairwells (in that dream, she admitted wryly, the coat had secured the ontological high ground: it was Liv who felt like the haunting); other times, as if they sought clarity and kindness, her dreams were all of her glory days at the Venice Hotel on France Chance—

Situated between the sea and the city, a stone's throw from the rocket-sport port, the Venice—with its tall, uncurtained windows, tranquil shabby rooms and uncarpeted pale oak floors which always captured the waking light—was, for five years the destination of rocket jockeys all over the Halo. A twenty-four-hour carnival unfolded outside the old hotel: bad paint-jobs, bad haircuts, bad planning. People were building their own starships in sheds at the edge of the field. Inside, you could find the most beautiful pilot, nineteen years old, sleeping in an empty bar at four in the afternoon, and soon go up to his room on the fourth floor back corridor. Next morning you woke alone and smiling, wrapped yourself in a pink cellular blanket, which you later stole and kept it with you your whole life, and went to the window, listening to the illegal sonic booms rolling in from seaward as the returning hyperdips performed low-level aerobrake re-entries.

A few hours before, these cockleshells with alien engines had been toppling through the France Chance chromosphere (filmed in perfect rights-reserved imagery by virtual hydrogen-alpha filter). Now the boys who flew them were determined to be the first human beings to scrub off more than twenty thousand kilometres an hour at less than five hundred feet above sea level. And the frail, utter certainty of it was: you had done that too, and you still couldn't get enough of it, and you would do it again and again until you couldn't do it any more. Later, you found your lovely pilot was the legendary Ed Chianese, and that the two of you were in competition for the Stupidest Achievement of That Year award.

It was from the perspective of this dream that Liv, waking transfixed, understood where she had seen the occupant of the K-tank before. She dialled up Antoyne, who, refusing to leave the crew quarters for three days, played "Ya Skaju Tebe" on infinite repeat and ate raspberry ice cream with his hands.

"Fat Antoyne, listen. We have to go into the hold."

But Antoyne wouldn't budge.

Walls blacked with graffiti flower shapes; armoured bulkheads deformed not by blast, or even melting, but by enforced transition through unnatural physical states; autorepair media busy over everything: someone, Liv thought, had pressed the wrong switch down there.

A section of the hull remained transparent. It was a wall of nothing. Eerie light from a corner of the Tract lengthened out the main hold so that it seemed more like an exterior than an interior. This illusion was increased by the disarray of the mortsafes. They were hard to count now. They lay tumbled on one another into a kind of distance, like corroded boilers in a scrapyard. Repair work was going on among them, but you couldn't quite see where. A sputtering sound filled the air. Sparks flew up and rained back down, cutting gold curves on the watching eye, bouncing off the deck as they cooled to dark cherry. Big shadows danced over the bulkheads.

Everything smelled of mould on bread, and of MP Renoko, who slumped like a traditional wood puppet in the unremitting yet unreliable glare of the welding arc, his clothes blackened, his left arm resting at an odd angle in his lap. One side of his face had dripped into the hollow of his clavicle, where it produced a finish resembling melted plastic; the other side boasted a sceptical grin, an appreciative glint in the eye, as if Renoko had only just died—or as if he was still alive, choosing for some reason to remain incommunicado. In this environment even a dead human being was a comfort. Liv stood next to him and peered into the fountain of sparks.

"You can come out now, Ed," she called.

"*Liv?* Liv Hula?"

For weeks she had watched him drift aimlessly around the ship when he thought everyone was asleep; now he floated towards her with a big smile, his arms wide. Over the years the memory of him had worn down inside her. It was smooth from use and bore little resemblance to the figure he cut at this end of his life. But the Halo is a wall-to-wall freak show: why should Ed Chianese be any different? The ragged flaps and ribbons of his braised organs trailed out behind him.

"Is that you, Liv? Jesus!"

When she didn't respond, Ed looked unhappy; as if, though he had got her name right, he had mistaken her for someone else. For instance a more recent admirer. Focusing slightly to the left of her, he said:

"I'm sorry."

"About what?" she said. "What happened to you, Ed?"

"Just the usual wear and tear."

"I can see." And, when he didn't follow that up: "I called, but you never got in touch." She left a silence but he didn't want to fill that either. "Hey!" she tried. "Someone told me you hijacked a K-ship and flew it into the Tract!"

"That was years ago," Ed said, as though apologising for having once been in the past. "Anyone could do it."

"Fuck off, Ed. No one comes back from there."

"I did," he said, with such a tone of regret that she believed him instantly. "I didn't want to—once you've been in there you'll do anything to stay— but here I am." After some thought he added, as if determined to produce a fair and balanced account: "Actually, the K-ship hijacked me."

"So now you're hijacking the *Nova Swing*."

"Is that what they call her these days?" He looked around vaguely. "Nice name," he said.

"It's cheap, Ed," Liv said. "That's why you like it."

She said: "What do you mean, 'these days'? *Are* you Ed Chianese?"

"Who else could be this fucked up?"

"Fair point, Ed."

Somewhere among the piled mortsafes, the MIG welder was working again. Or perhaps it wasn't that. Sparks, anyway, were fountaining up, so bright the Tract paled into invisibility behind them. There was a sound like a lot of drowsy flies. "Is there someone else in here?" Liv said. Suddenly, Ed had her by the shoulders. His odd, not-unpleasant smell, more ozone than halal, filled the space between them. "Get out!" he said.

His hands hurt. "Fuck, Ed!" Liv said. But though she struggled and kicked, and though he wasn't what you could call all there, he had no difficulty propelling her towards the door. Liv, straining to look back over her shoulder, saw something beautiful and strange beginning to form itself out of the sparks. "What's that? Ed, *what's that?*"

"Don't look!" he said, and pushed her out.

The door slid closed, then open again. Ed's head protruded, lower down than you would expect.

"Let's talk soon," he said.

"Don't let's bother," said Liv, who thought she had heard a woman's voice in the hold behind him. "Just fuck you, Ed," she shouted.

No reply.

"And fuck your stories. Fuck that you know more than us, and our lives are suddenly part of some weird deal of yours. Our friend is dead, also what you did to this ship is a fucking big inconvenience to us."

The worst thing wasn't that so much of him was missing, or that the remainder looked like a display of half-cooked meat in an outdoor market at the end of the day. It wasn't even that he seemed to be only partly aware you were in the room with him. It was that thirty years had passed. Over distances like that, people drive themselves without much deviation towards the simplest expression of what they are. In the meantime you grow out of them. The only feature Ed retained was the weak grin he got when he knew you had found him out. At the Venice Hotel, and for a month or two afterwards, she had interpreted that expression as a measure of how nice he was. Since then, she could see, he had let it become a substitute for raising his game. Why hadn't she expected that?

She went back to the crew quarters and explained the situation. "Listen Antoyne," she said, "we have to get him out of here."

Antoyne, who smelled strongly of Black Heart, would only grunt. As Irene had often predicted, new things are bound to happen to anyone in the end; but Antoyne was bad with any kind of reversal. He had lost weight except over the upper abs, where, in a matter of days, the ice-cream diet had seated itself in a carcinomatic-looking lump. "Ed's not the man we knew," she said. In fact the problem was the reverse of that. Ed—who walked out on Liv because she beat him into the France Chance photosphere; who left Dany LeFebre to die down on Tumblehome; who, when he got as sick of himself as everyone else had, spent fifteen years in the twink tank lapping up some mystery shit the immersion media churn out for kiddies—was exactly the man they knew. "Antoyne, wake up! He's not human any more. He has some plan, it takes no account of us or anyone. Wake up!" Antoyne opened his eyes and considered Liv for a moment with the beginnings of an interest. Then he belched, turned away and began to weep. After that, recent experience told her, no amount of shaking would get his attention.

"Antoyne, you useless fucker," she told him.

From living with himself, Antoyne knew that to be true. Later, when Liv had gone back up to the control room, he rolled over, puked a little, washed up in the corner sink and stared around the cabin at Irene's scattered underwear: party semiotics in action. The little action cube of her was playing on repeat, sounding scratchy and cheap and far away. In his head he heard her real voice say, "It was a lovely world," and then: "Antoyne, you got to lose me." After he cleaned up, he took himself down to the main hold, where he leaned in the doorway and said:

"So."

"Hey," Ed acknowledged. He was wiping his fingers on an oily rag. "It's the pizza guy! What do I owe you?"

Antoyne shrugged. "Very funny."

"It's—" Ed clicked his fingers "—Fat Anthony. Right?"

"That was years ago. They don't call me that any more." He stared at Ed. "What the fuck have you done to yourself this time?" he said.

Ed grinned. "This? I'm not sure. Like it? I picked it up in the Tract."

"I heard you were there."

"Fat Anthony, you should go too, while you can." Ed said he couldn't think of a way to describe it. It was the big achievement. In there it was eleven dimensions of everything. "The entities who run it, they're all charisma." They were over everything, having fun. "Fat Anthony, it's just so fucking different in there. You know?"

"If it's that good," Antoyne pointed out bleakly, "why didn't you stay?"

"Come back with me."

"What?"

"Come back with me now. None of this is real when you've been in the Tract. Come back with me and see."

Ed could sell you his own worst dream, caught with an unsteady camera, lit with a bad light. Juice or jouissance, it was always a plunge into something, with a default to the epic, from which, very often, only Ed returned. For a moment Antoyne wondered what decision he would make. Then he said:

"Why would I do that to myself, Ed?"

The universe went on. *Nova Swing* ploughed across it, creaking under her own internal stresses. Antoyne cleaned up his act, weaning himself off the peppermint ice over a dog day afternoon. He folded Irene's underwear and put it away, and in place of that desperate shrine to her constructed another, using the things she salvaged from Perkins Rent. He burned incense there but within days heard her voice telling him not to be a jerk. "You make your own life in this life, Antoyne."

Ed Chianese, meanwhile, spent his time in the hold, working on the mortsafes. Entities came and went while he was down there. Some looked like angels, some looked like operators. You didn't want to be close enough to tell the difference.

Liv Hula, a passenger in her own ship, dozed in the acceleration chair while, outside, the Halo streamed past, broken into futuristic dazzle patterns by physics and war. The news remained bad. Ed drifted in and out at unpredictable times of day, and hung there staring at the exterior screens. This exasperated her.

"Can't you sit down or something?"

"The day you first came aboard this ship," he said, "you found surplus code in the navigational system. You couldn't work out what it did."

She stared at him. "How do you know that?"

He shrugged.

She remembered the first time she sat in the chair. After all the years away from piloting, she felt so free, even if it was just to swallow the nanofibres and take the ship's inventory:

Electronic infrastructure. Propulsion architecture. Communications schematics, including an ageing FTL uplinker which showed, for reasons unclear, realtime images of selected quarantine orbits from three to a thousand lights along the Beach. Otherwise it was navigation fakebooks, cargo manifests, agency fuel purchases and parking stamps. She remembered advising Fat Antoyne, "You got fifty years of guano in there. Also they used the code to run something my chops don't get."

She looked speculatively at Ed. "I fenced it off," she said. "I didn't want it crawling up someone's rectum at night. Especially mine."

Ed brought up internal views.

"See that junk you collected in the hold?" he said. "It's an engine. The *Nova Swing*'s the only ship in the Galaxy with the software to run it. That was what you found."

She sighed impatiently.

"Just tell me why you're back, Ed. Maybe I can help."

"I came to free the people," Ed said, making a gesture which, perhaps hoping to take in the whole galaxy, explained nothing. "Things are going to get bad out here." This war, he said, was the big one. "They've been working up to it for a hundred and fifty years." It would mean a substantial collapse of EMC infrastructure. It would mean that no one had a right to expect endless progress any more. Quite the reverse. In the long term, that might in itself be good for the boys from Earth. "They can start from the ground up, with a more interesting take on things." Meanwhile it would get worse before it got better.

"Thanks a lot for that prophecy, Ed."

"I *was* a prophet once," he said, "but I left all that behind." For a moment he watched the Dynaflow medium streaming past. "I wish I could talk to Fat Anthony?" he said suddenly. "But he avoids me."

"His name's Antoyne and he's a decent man. Back in the glory days he loved you and admired you, the way we all did. I was just the same. You were crazy and beautiful and that's what we wanted. If you asked us to be heroes, we would have followed you anywhere. But it's France Chance, Ed, win or lose every time you open the throttle. Remember that?" Then, as soon as he began to answer: "And now what? You're the only one who ever came back from the Tract, big achievement. But what have you brought out of there? You might be into something good, you might be deeper in shit than ever." She smiled; her smile said she couldn't help him with that. "You can have the ship. I don't think either of us wants it after what happened, and we can easily get another."

She looked out the porthole one day not long after that, and saw they were back in the Saudade Quarantine orbit.

The planet turned beneath them like some immense flywheel. Deadlights flickered off the bow. All around, it was offworld warehousing of the un-nameable: a million tonnes of a substance half protein, half code, the waste of human interaction with mathematics. She got on the internal comms and said, "Ed, this is the wrong orbit. Park & Ride is further in. Do you want any help?" Silence from the main hold. "Ed?" When she arrived down there, she found the hull back in place and the mortsafes lined up in a neat row.

They didn't look any less disused than usual. "What are you fuckers look-ing at?" she asked them. As if in response they separated suddenly, to re-veal Ed Chianese lying prone on the deckplates while a very small Chinese woman crouched, knees apart, where the small of his back had once been. Ed's face was pressed into the floor, her emerald green cheongsam was hiked up round her waist. Her skin was very white. You couldn't be sure what was happening between them, but white motes the size of clothes moths seemed to be pouring out of her polished little ivory-colored vulva.

"Ed?"

Ed seemed too preoccupied to answer. The woman, if that's what she was, chuckled and looked over at Liv. Liv turned and ran before she could be made to look closer, before she could be made to understand more. From that moment, she felt, everything in her life would depend on not inter-preting what she had seen there. It would depend on remembering no more than a wink, a cigarette, a smile on very red lips. Ed caught up with her in the companionway outside.

"Jesus, Liv. You could at least knock."

"Get us down to Saudade City," Liv said. "And then piss off."

An hour later, the three of them stood on the loading platform, looking out across the damp cement of Carver Field towards the Port Authority buildings and over them to the city itself. It was raining. The new day had a used light all over it; a light which might be described as pre-enjoyed on its passage from Retiro Street to the Church on the Rock. In the crime tour-ism quarter, the hotel neons weren't quite done, but they'd faded to pastels of themselves. Ed Chianese leant on the loading platform rail, his ragged lower half rattling faintly in the wind.

"You're sure you won't come with me?"

Liv found him a smile. "You've walked through one too many walls, Ed. Look at the state of you."

"I've got used to a life," was all Antoyne could think of to say.

When Ed had gone the two of them were left on the cement, craning their necks as the *Nova Swing* groaned her way back to the quarantine orbit on her tail of smoke. They watched until she was a fading green glow in the cloudbase. "Those fucking old engines!" Liv Hula said.

"But she was a boat."

"She was a dog, Antoyne."

They laughed, then they turned towards Saudade City. The streets had a new excitement, they were packed with refugees and military police. Lightning flashed—a K-ship, splitting the sky, trailing thunder! She took his arm, folded it under her own, hugged it against her side, the way she used to walk with Irene.

"Where to next?" she said.

"Some place where Crab Nebula is a main course not a destination."

26: Lizard People from Deep Time

Uptown Six took the Dynaflow highway halfway across the Halo. It was a fast uncluttered trip. Viewed from inside, the dyne fields are just like a human being—a kind of bad-natured origami, accordion-folded to contain more than seems possible or advisable. Is this how the universe dreams of itself? Eels flickering in shoals through some velvet medium? Splashes of coloured light drawn sideways suddenly by the unimaginable stresses of not really being there? The assistant, who felt similar stresses herself, sat uncomfortably by the porthole in the human quarters trying to comprehend these phenomena.

"I don't like to travel like this," she told the shadow operators, "with those fish outside the window." She didn't like the food on the *Uptown Six*. She didn't like the Vicente Fernandez lowrider music Carlo played, with its heavy reliance on traditional ranchera stylings. When he turned it off, she didn't like a noise she thought the air-conditioning made which no one else could hear. Every time the ship changed course she said, "Is it supposed to sound like that?" Her problem wasn't travel itself. It was that she couldn't feel comfortable away from Saudade. The shadow operators—obsessed by anything new and dysfunctional, and thus already deeply invested—took on the grey, slightly translucent appearance of mourning women, rubbed their bony, work-roughened hands together, and begged her:

"Would you prefer something different to eat, dear?"

The cabin was filled briefly with their smell of violets and Vinolia Soap.

"Can we fetch you a blanket?"

An hour or two into the journey R. I. Gaines opened the FTL routers and tried to refamiliarise himself with Galactic events. He fell asleep instead and dreamed he was in a rocket port surrounded by refugees. They resembled people, but they also resembled something like a swarm of bats or locusts too—or even a swarm of shadow operators, with a similar kind of sadness to their voracity and yearning. They were an ongoing process yet they never seemed to change. Gaines sat at a table with his hands in his lap. For a minute or two a toddler ran about behind him, laughing and shrieking. He didn't know what to do or think next. Adverts fluttered overhead like moths: his eyes followed them. People went in and out of the travel terminal doors: his head turned that way. Listening to the chimes of the public address system, he realised that, quite literally, he was not himself. He was someone he knew, but he couldn't remember who. Eventually his number was called and he got to his feet and walked towards the gate.

While Gaines was dealing with these issues, whatever they were, Carlo—whose meds had flattened him off nicely for the day—tried to lure the assistant into the pilot tank with him. Though she seemed interested, even after she had lifted the lid, she would only do sex inside an immersive art experience called *Joan in 1956*, which apparently featured an old car and something she described as "waisted cotton briefs." Carlo wasn't disheartened.

"I'm so fucking in love," he told Gaines when Gaines woke up.

By then they were under the shoulder of the Tract itself, tumbling down a thirty-light-year well between high temperature gas clouds. Soon, Galt & Cole's big score filled the screens, not quite a planet, not quite a machine: a geological madhouse with aspects of both, having the gravitational signature of a low-density rubble pile but eye-watering Mohr-Coloumb figures. It was as porous as sponge yet nothing could pull it apart. The highly cratered surface sported a uniform orange colour, slightly too pale for rust. Across it roiled deep cobalt shadows and strange-looking rivers of dust.

"Home again," Gaines said.

"Keep watching the skies, Carlo," he called as they left the ship.

"These days there's no need to run the maze," he told the assistant. But he took her in anyway. Some part of him still needed to show it off.

Back at the beginning it had been a fracturing, disconnective experience, a space flickering with bad light and worse topology. The tunnels, small-bore and intricately turned one moment, would become huge and simple the next; as full of generated sounds as they were echoes, with no way of telling which was which. "Worse," Gaines told the assistant as he led her along, "they changed their nature." One moment they were tiled with shiny ceramics, next some sort of organic-looking fibre was matted over everything. You could be in a blood vessel or waiting for a train, or feel yourself running like a fluid between glass plates: it was an archeology from which anything could be intuited and of which nothing was true. "It wasn't so much what you might find round the next corner," Gaines said, "as that you were round the next corner before you knew it was there." As a result—at the start, anyway—the maze had seemed more like a condition than a system. Its objects had seemed abstract.

"What's this I'm walking in?" the assistant said.

Gaines stopped. "It's water. It's just water."

He looked down uncertainly.

"These are the safe parts," he said. "Back in the day, entire sections would go missing. They'd be one thing when you lost them, another when you found them again. In circumstances like that, you have to understand that your perception is what's fragmentary, not the space itself. At some level an organising principle exists, but you will never have any confirmation of it. It will always be unavailable to you. Then, just as everyone's stopped trusting themselves, someone finds their way through a trap, the expedition gets a little further in." All expeditions, he told her, failed in some way, but they each had a character of their own: and if, for a while, that character seemed like the reality of the explored space, it was the best you could expect. "You learn to work with it. We were total colonialists. Always on the back foot. Always in the thin slice of the present.

"Who built it?" he said, as if she had asked him. He shrugged. "How would I know? Lizard People from deep time. They were all over the Halo for a while, you find traces of them even on a dump like Panamax IV."

The assistant shivered.

As soon as they left the surface she had felt her tailoring come up. Now she looked back along the passage, which just then was full of brown light and had an old monorail running along it.

"Something's in here with us," she said.

"People often think that." The labyrinth, Gaines said, was a perfect venue for standing acoustic waves: at around nineteen Hertz these would commonly generate feelings of dread, bouts of panic, visual defects and hallucinations. "Down at twelve you just vomit endlessly."

Half a mile along, the architecture changed suddenly and they were in primitive, squared-off passageways driven through basalt. When the boys from Earth arrived, there had been no light here worth speaking of for a hundred millennia. "We call it the PCM," Gaines said. "Pearlant Cultural Minimum. Suddenly you can see the tool marks. These sections may be the oldest of all, tunnelled into the rocky material before it aggregated, when it was part of something else. Or maybe their civilisation just lost traction on things for a while. Or these areas might have had a religious purpose. There's no physics worth speaking of down here, but we get panel art. Look." He stopped in front of what appeared to be a section of bas reliefs, which showed three modified diapsids wearing complex ritual clothing. One of them was strangling a fourth, who lay passively on what looked like a stone bier.

"These people were a million years ahead of us, but they were still trying to work out how to be rational. I don't think they ever quite made it. The Aleph was only one of their projects."

He took her arm again. "Are you ready? It's through that next door."

On Saudade, Epstein the thin cop got a call to go to one of the bonded warehouses at the noncorporate rocket port. It was 4:20 am. Exactly two minutes earlier, the corpse of Enka Mercury had vanished. Edits of the nanocam coverage showed a translucent, fish-coloured image of Enka—through which you could make out the ribbed alloy walls of the warehouse—suddenly replaced by nothing. No matter how many cuts the operator made, there was no transition phase. One minute Enka was clinging on—her expression, when you could see it, as determined as it had been from the start, the expression of someone who had died but had never given up—the next, she was gone.

Epstein stared into the empty air of the warehouse as if his own deep common sense might do better than the technology, then took himself down to the alley off Tupolev, where he arrived in time to see Toni Reno follow his loader into oblivion. It was a cold wet morning, with traffic sparse on Tupolev and light creeping in from the side. As the war re-engaged everyone's libido, Toni's following had dropped off. But a couple of thirteen-year-olds—their calculatedly asymmetric caps of black hair and Fantin & Moretti handcrafted moccasins soaked with rain—still occupied the sidewalk.

"Toni never hurt anyone," one of them complained to Epstein. "Why does this have to happen to him?"

"Beats me, kid," Epstein said.

"You see?" the boy said to his friend, as if Epstein wasn't really there.

"That's exactly what I mean."

He moved them on. He called it in. He tried to get hold of the assistant, but Uniment & Poe were being coy about her whereabouts. Eventually he shrugged and forgot about it. High-grade crime tourism was at a low this month, but in and around the new refugee centres in Placebo Heights and White Train Park, misdemeanours of a puzzlingly old-fashioned nature— simple beatings, direct thefts of food or money—were ensuring the uniform cops a sixteen-hour day. No one had seen anything like it. They were having to develop new theory.

While Epstein made himself busy, the Halo was holding its breath and falling into the mirror. Upper management loved itself at war. In the corporate enclaves—which constructed themselves as little market towns called Saulsignon, Burnham Overy or Brandett Hersham, featuring stone churches and water meadows under blue rain-washed skies, perfect windy weather and ponies on the green—war felt real and grown up, a contingency for which your values and education had prepared you. Although obviously some sacrifices would have to be made.

Other demographics found themselves less convinced. Alyssia Fignall, who had caught the last shuttle off Panamax IV before the war arrived, ended up with three hundred families in a refugee camp on Alum Rock. It was a small camp, three or four acres of tents on a headland under fine blowing rain. From the fence you could see beet fields stretching away inland. In the early afternoons, tired-looking women congregated between the tents to exchange what little information they had. No one in the camp was allowed access to an FTL router, or even a dial-up, so there wasn't much. No one knew when they would be taken off.

"Plenty of rumours," the women told Alyssia, "but no rockets." It was clearly something they said a lot.

On her first day, after the meeting, she lay on her back in her tent, listening to the rain, the sound of a man breaking up wooden pallets with a billhook, the yells of boys as they ran about kicking a ball through other people's living space. She closed her eyes and tried to doze, while the family next door built a wall of straw bales between her and them, working slowly and with care, talking constantly and patiently to their three-year-old daughter who, though she seemed ill, did her best to help.

It was a determined statement—language addressed less, perhaps, to Alyssia than to the situation itself. A response to the unstructuredness of the world in which they now all found themselves.

"I'm cooking now!" the woman called as it got dark.

Alyssia walked about the site, trying to meet people and get news. Then she tried to leave, only to be turned back at the perimeter. A week later she was still there, among the litter, the flapping, badly pegged tents, the acrid fires just after sunset, the sudden savage cries and ugly half-musical noises of the adolescent gangs. By then, her body, or her clothes, or perhaps simply the whole site, had begun to smell of composting toilets. There were rumours that no one was to be repatriated but the whole camp would be moved somewhere else. She pushed a hole in the wall of bales and asked the woman next door if she could help with the child. Over the following months she often thought about Rig and wondered if he was all right. She knew he would be. He was Rig, after all.

Out near the Kefahuchi Tract itself, the news was not the war.

Daily Deals & Huge Savings' encounter with Panamax IV made excellent media. Syndicated to a thousand planets, with a variety of commentaries and factoid enhancements, it enjoyed a well-deserved three minutes in the sun. The initial collision had generated perhaps 200 trillion trillion ergs of energy, equivalent to the explosion of five or six gigatons of conventional explosives. As *Daily Deals & Huge Savings* burst out of the iron core, blowback to the tune of a further five thousand gigatons had cut a channel like a beam of light through the super-heated atmospheric gases and crustal debris. While in no way incalculable, the final release of energy, as the core itself exploded into local space, was in human terms almost meaninglessly large. But meaninglessly large energy events are the daily context of the Tract, where eruptions from the central unshielded singularity—if that is what it is—are so powerful they generate in the surrounding gas clouds pressure waves that manifest themselves as sound.

This gigantic uproar, resonating through million-cubic-parsec cavities in the constituent gas, is the citizen journalism of the Tract; the loops and scribbles left by the shockfronts are its headlines. So for Imps van Sant's instruments the news was not the destruction of Panamax IV. It was a series of discordant and complex groans 60 octaves below middle C.

"Fuck," said Imps, who had never heard anything like it.

Sometimes your situation becomes too plain to you. Strange forces are at work. Imps tore off the headphones and beat them against the instrument panel until the bakelite cracked: the Tract seemed to keep on roaring at him anyway, like a huge face, its expression indescribable in human terms. Rage, elation, despair—even, he thought, some kind of vast weird parental love. It was all of those things and none of them. As for the physics: no one had ever had any idea of that. Some people said it was the physics of the early universe, still running in a leaky envelope, a cyst caught in a very long moment of bursting—the right physics but not in its right time. Imps didn't know. He didn't want to know. To him it was the physics of a face. He leaned back from the console and rubbed his eyes. He thought he might try and have a shower, then a beer. He was just lumbering up out of his chair when he heard a whisper from the broken headset. He grabbed it up.

"Hello?"

George the gene tailor lay where the assistant had left him in her room in GlobeTown, the blankets pulled up lovingly to his chin. George was dead, but not alone in that. Spaceships lit the room's warm air, psychic blowback from their weird science reinscribing on the walls—in layers of swirled colours like graffiti—the thoughts and feelings of everyone who had expired there before he arrived. Did dead George take comfort from these maps, butterflies, and other partially depicted items from alien worlds? Was he aware of the street below, flowering like a glass anemone against the steepening food gradient of the night? Rokit Dub basslines spreading as waves across the city? The bars and nuevo tango joints opening slowly, their facades pulsing and sucking? Even if he was, these things were so much cultural babble. If they want anything, the dead want a rest from all of that.

Though she never had a name, the assistant was used to being someone. People were, for instance, frightened of her, on the fourth floor at Uniment & Poe, on Straint Street or Tupolev, on the sidewalk by the cake stall on Retiro Street. The assistant was used to having a presence in places like that. Here it wasn't the same. Everyone was EMC. They spoke and walked as if they were thinking about something else. She was just someone who had arrived with Rig Gaines. When they came up to talk to him, they ignored her. Her chemistry didn't work on them the way it worked on Epstein or her friend George. For instance a man called Case came up and said:

"Is this her? Jesus."

Case looked as if he had outlived himself. A tall man, with an air of once being heavily built, he walked bent over and bearing down awkwardly on two sticks. Both hips had gone. Like anyone else he could have had himself fixed but he had left it too long, out of carelessness or even some kind of inverted vanity, and now preferred this cooked, hairless look. His hands were ropy with veins, the skin over them shiny and slack. His brown head seemed too big for his neck; his underlip, the texture of braised liver, drooped in exhausted surprise at finding himself still alive. He stood in front of the assistant, staring greedily at her but at the same time with a curious lack of interest, as if he remembered women but his body didn't. He whispered to himself. After a moment or two he leaned forward and tapped her forearm sharply.

"Rig tells me you have some Kv12.2 expression issues," he said.

"Is he talking to me?" she asked Gaines.

"We could help with that," Case said. "It's just a small design flaw. Do you understand Effectively, you have epilepsy." When she didn't answer, he asked Gaines, "Does she understand anything?"

"Honey, you could breathe through your mouth less," the assistant said.

Case blinked at her.

"I never expected any sense out of you, Rig," he said to Gaines, "but this is moronic. You have no idea what will happen if we do this."

Gaines' response was to shrug. One way or another, he supposed, they would get some science out of it. This bland assumption turned into an argument in which Case's team joined. They all talked at once. "Science?" Case shouted at one point. He held both his sticks in one hand so he could make a contemptuous gesture with the other. "Science is off. It's been off ever since you and Emil walked into this fucking place!"

Laughter all round.

"I don't like these people," the assistant said loudly.

Everyone stopped talking.

Gaines took her by the arm. "Hey," he said. "It's OK, really." They stood looking at one another, while Case and his team stared at them. Rig gave her one of his wryest smiles and while he was still smiling at her said to someone nearby:

"We could probably get some coffee here?"

The guy said sure. He could fetch that if they liked. They could get regular with milk or they could get regular without.

"You don't need to stay with us," Gaines told the assistant when the coffee arrived. "Have a look around. Have a look at everything." After that she was left alone with herself to an unfamiliar degree.

The room was as big as a travel terminal, dark but with islands of activity. Vehicles drove about, some quite heavy. Over near the middle of the space they had something isolated under powerful lights. It was moving in a sporadic way, like something natural, but she couldn't see what it was. She found a place to sit, sprawled her legs wide and smiled at some of Case's people until they looked away. She thought of names for herself: Bruna, Kyshtym, Korelev R-7 and "The Angel of the Parking Orbit." She looked down at her forearm: it was registering No Data. Meanwhile, Case's people brought up new equipment, which they organised inside the circle of light. Whatever it was, it meant nothing to the assistant.

Outside the lighted area they had some basic chopshop fitments—a brand new proteome tank enamelled the colour of white goods in 1953, a cutting table and some surgical instruments. She was comfortable with all that. When she had finished her coffee, Gaines led her over there and said, "While we're waiting, why don't we have a look at this seizure activity of yours? Hop up on the table." She hopped up on the table and let him get a couple of probes into her at neurotypical sites. One of them slipped into her chest cavity, high up. She felt it rest momentarily against the collarbone as it pressed past. A sensation difficult to interpret: not painful so much as certain and invasive. Soon she experienced pleasantly warm and lethargic feelings, with everything retreating to a distance as if it had nothing to do with her. "That's great," Gaines told her, "just relax. Fuck," he said, to someone else. "These guys, whoever they were! Look at this. And this." He touched something and colours flew about in her head like small birds. She heard herself laugh. "Oops," Gaines said. "Wrong switch. Did you like that?" She tasted metal, then two or three workshop spaces seemed to open inside her. Gaines began working in one of them. Later Case arrived to have a look.

"I don't want him here," she said.

"It's fine," Gaines said. "It'll be fine."

"I want you to wake me up now," the assistant said.

Gaines bent over her and she saw him smile.

"You'll be fine," he said.

"Are you going to strangle me?"

"You'll be fine."

After that she never seemed to be properly conscious again. She could tell what was happening, but it didn't involve her. "Did you know you've got a 27 to 40 gHz radar option?" Gaines said. His voice came from inside her now, with a clear echo, as if they were back in the tunnels. "Short range local surveillance medium. Not bad. Would you like it switched on?" He switched it on and she saw everything in the control room filmy grey. Case's people rolled the table over into the middle of the space, under the brightest light, where they left it. She lay in a comfortable haze, lighted internally by the 27 to 40 gHz radar, which Gaines had left switched on. She could detect people coming and going but not move her head. Eventually they swung the inspection table on its axis and did something to the probes so that her unforced sensory systems came back on. The assistant saw what was under the lights and why she had been brought here.

Two or three days earlier, after a minor convulsion ripped up the containment area, the object known to Case's team as "Pearl" or "the Pearl" had begun to fall again. This process—less motion than an attempt to express motion in a static medium—seemed as wilful as it was stylised. Her body language, Gaines thought, was that of a sustained struggle against circumstances no one else could be allowed to understand. Case had a different view.

"Fuck that," he said. It would be wise to remember that the falling woman was neither falling nor a woman. It was a monster, heavily misrepresented from the data. It was the nearest guess the instruments could make about what was actually going on. "Much like the universe itself, it's a useless analogy for an unrepresentable state," he said, and laughed. This led to an argument between the two men about the original nature of the Aleph. Case believed they had been wrong about that, too.

"It never contained a fragment of the Tract," he said.

"Then what?"

"It contained the whole of it. It still does."

Once they had the policewoman disabled and in position, the Aleph team brought up their final item of equipment. Shiny one moment, indistinct the next, it was still assembling itself from a nervous slurry of materials— carbon nanofibres, non-Abelian superconductors held at ambient temperatures, fast-evolving AI swarms running on picotech. Next an operator was introduced. It took the form of a young girl, thin and tan, perhaps eight years old, dressed in the dark blue shorts and short-sleeved Aertex shirt of an endless summer holiday in St Steven's Withy or Burnam Agnate, who reminded Gaines of his daughter at that age. The operator was quick to sense this.

"Oh, Rig!" it said, taking his hands and laughing up at him. Its feet were bare. "What have you got for us this time!"

It winked. Raw white light poured out its eyes, mouth and nose. Then it seemed to break up into a shower of sparks and enter the machine. Musical sounds emerged. A single awed voice said: "Strange forces are at work here."

"For fuck's sake, Case," Gaines said. "Let's just get on with it."

Case's people pressed the tit.

For a moment nothing happened. Then the policewoman jumped off the table, swaggered three paces away from it and attempted to switch on her tailoring. Whatever Gaines had done to her switched it off again.

She shouted angrily and tried again, and was switched off again. Visual records showed two or three iterations of this behaviour occurring in a single five-second period, as the assistant's housekeeping systems laid new neural pathways around the blocks put in by Gaines. Learning rates were impressive but capped out quickly: within two minutes she was able to remain overdriven for periods up to twelve seconds, but her repertoire—and her range—of movements became fixed. Anxiety pushed the repertoire through several iterations, during which the subject was observed to:

Jump off the cutting table (once); crouch on the floor and move her head rapidly side to side, emitting active sonar between 200 and 1000 kHz (three times); perform other target-seeking behaviours (twice); become aware of the Pearl in front of her (twice); vomit a white liquid (once); throw up her hands and shout something indistinct (four times); turn left and run three paces (four times); turn left and run four paces (three times); decelerate abruptly (every time); and scream (every time).

Somebody laughed.

"Stop that," said Case.

Overdriven movement registered as the usual mucoid blur. Waste heat systems undervented, raising the subject's body temperature slightly above operating norms at 110 degrees fahrenheit; cortisol, androstenedione and estradiol levels rose sharply. After the fourth iteration, a suite of unplanned arm-movements began to be present. No one was able to explain this.

Throughout, the Pearl remained stable. Viewed as a false-colour display, the folds of its metallic gown fluttered in undetectable drafts. A faint zone of refraction surrounded it, causing the image—now perhaps twice life size—to ripple as if underwater. Its face looked human, then more like a cat's face. After some minutes there came a shift in the index of refraction, like a little step-change in energy states. At the same time the main research tool came to life: elements of the labyrinth began to realign themselves; a grinding vibration could be felt in the floor. Hologram schematics flickered. Seismic arrays were picking up action at the scale of plate tectonics. "VF14/2b is warming up," someone announced, and began to reel off phase-space data. Case's operator said in a calm voice, "There's something massive in the tunnels." The overhead lights dimmed and shifted towards the red. "You may have to extract me," the operator said.

Then it shouted, "Look, look! In the maze! Deep time!" Nothing was heard from it after that.

Meanwhile the Pearl opened and closed its mouth, waving its arms above its head in a kind of boneless, astonished panic. It seemed to be falling faster. Thousands of small objects tumbled along with it, as if the air itself were unloading them, glowing embers or stained-glass fragments, bouncing and rattling as energetically as Entreflex dice where they fell. Waves of perfume—cheap, old-fashioned and bizarrely sexual, something you might smell on Pierpoint Street at four in the morning—billowed through The Old Control Room. As if disheartened by this display, the policewoman tired visibly. She made a last effort to break Gaines' behavioural constraints, then raised her left fist to her mouth and bit at the knuckles. She stared over her shoulder at him.

"Help!" she called (once).

Then she jumped into the Pearl and vanished. After that, the Pearl vanished too, and everything went dark.

"Jesus Christ," said Gaines into the silence.

He was working out how to distance himself from the project and move on when he saw the tall white flower of light slowly beginning to bloom, and heard the voices and sounds which, to him at least, sounded like the voices and sounds of something, as he put it to himself, *arriving*, and began to run like everyone else for the back door of the facility and the debatable safety of the labyrinth beyond, trampling as they did so the ageing Case, who had lost both his sticks.

27: The Medium Is
Not the Message

Aspodoto, Tienes mi Corazon, Backstep Cindy: a name, in the Halo, is every-thing. You are no one without a name. Fortunata, Ceres, Berenice. Queenie Key, Calder & Arp, Washburn Guitar. Mani Pedi, Wellness Lux, Fedy Pantera, REX-ISOLDE, Ogou Feray, Restylane and Anicet...

When Anna Waterman fell through the summerhouse floor and into the Aleph, it was just before dawn on a damp September morning in London. What time it was for the Aleph would be less easy to record.

The space she fell through was a confusing colour, like darkness on a windy night. It was too wide to be a tunnel, too confined to be anything else. Its boundary conditions allowed her to topple; they didn't allow her to touch the sides. The sky quickly contracted to an almost invisible point above her. For a time, the cat was some company. It fell with a comical expression on its face, then seemed to drift in towards her, kneading the air with its front paws and purring loudly, after which they lost sight of one another.

"James, you nuisance," Anna said.

Up above, something settled, as if the summerhouse, properly on fire this time, had begun to collapse. Rattling down towards her came a shower of objects coloured deep wine and amber or fanned by their speed to the fierce yellow of Barbie hair. These hot dolls, burning coals and melted pill-bottles seemed to be falling much faster than Anna; as they passed they matched her velocity for a moment, so that she felt she could have reached out and touched them; then they accelerated away and were quickly lost to sight.

In life, she knew, you might: Fall ill. Fall pregnant. Fall from grace.

God knows she had done all three of those. "Mine was a prolonged fall," she imagined herself explaining, "accompanied by much of the detritus I thought I'd left behind." She addressed the cat: "Name your *jouissance*."

As she fell, she was aware of her arms waving slowly and bonelessly. Her legs pedalled. The sensation of falling was, she thought, much the same as that of treading water: the more you struggled the less control you maintained. Your heart rate increased, all the effort went to waste. You felt closer to drowning. It was a mistake to allow that idea in. The most important distinction of childhood is the one between falling asleep and falling as death. Long before she had fallen into anorexia, or read Milton on the fall from dawn to dewy eve, or fallen victim to Michael Kearney, Anna had been afraid to fall asleep. As soon as she recognised that, she began to struggle. There followed predictable moments of panic, flickering and buzzing on all sides, anguished flashes of light, after which she found herself in an echoing space, the nature of which she would have been hard put to describe.

It was very tall; it was dark and light at the same time. It reminded her of a restaurant she and Marnie used to visit for lunch, built into the shell of an abandoned power station in Wapping. She had a sense of dread. She could see a little, but she didn't know what any of it was. There were people all round her. They gestured and goggled, trying to push their faces close into hers. Their mouths opened and closed, yet it was Anna who felt like the fish in the tank. They were studying her.

"How close can I get?" they asked one another, and: "Do we have any idea where she came from?"

"We don't have an idea about anything."

Laughter.

"She looks as if she's falling. Caught falling."

"I don't think that's a helpful assumption, Gaines."

In fact, Anna felt like someone caught going to the lavatory in the middle of Waterloo station in the rush hour. She had a slightly nauseous sense of James the cat, so close she couldn't quite bring him into focus. It was embarrassing. Though to herself she did not seem entirely Anna, she did not seem entirely anything else. There was something the matter with her cheekbones. She felt smeary and unstable at significant sites, in the manner of a Francis Bacon painting. At the same time she felt as if she had been penetrated by something huge in an inappropriate part of her body; or, worse, that she had penetrated it. What made her condition so impossible was the nature of this object.

It was her own life.

...Sekhet, Sweet Thing. Minnie. Matty. Mutti. Roses, Radtke, Emily-Misere. Girl Heartbreak! & Imogen. L1 Dominette. I pull one way she pulls the other. That woman will never be part of me. I say fall on your own. Fall on your own you bitch. Not near me. There is a third thing in here with us she says & a fourth & a fifth. It stinks of cat in here, some filthy animal. We'll never get where we're going this way. My name is. (Ysabeau, Mirabelle, Rosy Glo. Sweet Thing & Pak 43. Shacklette, Puxie, Temeraire. Stormo!, Te Faaturuma.) I fall into the summerhouse & shout the wrong thing. No one listens...

In Saudade City, the Toni Reno case was duly filed "unsolved."

Not long after, Epstein the thin cop found himself on patrol with a uniform called Grills. It was a mild night. Some rain. The traffic on Tupolev was thinner than usual. For the b-girls, on parade in their candy-coloured mambo pumps at the corner of Johnson & Chrome, business was slow. Over at Preter Coeur, the fights were slow. From Placebo Heights to the Funnel, from Retiro Street to Beasley Street, entire entertainment demographics were staying home.

GlobeTown, 2 am: Epstein and Grills found time to talk about the war. Grills believed it could lead to a permanent change in the social landscape. Crime tourism, she said, had tanked; they also were seeing across-the-board decreases in illegal tailoring, donkey capers, sensorium porn and other personality hacks. But the way Epstein saw it war was only another layer added to a bad cake—these downward trends she outlined being balanced by the growing market in counterfeit identity chips, food stamps and rackrenting. If personality crime was down, smuggling was up, seventeen per cent year on year. After a pause to consider this, Grills opined that a lot more crowd control overtime would be available in the months to come; with that Epstein could only agree, and they left it at that. Suddenly there was a white flash in the sky high up, silent but very sharp, very high-end. Epstein shaded his eyes with one broad hand.

"Is it an attack?"

"I don't think so," Grills said. "I've seen an attack, and there was—" here, she felt around for the right words "—more of it."

Five hundred miles above their heads, K-ships were disappearing from one orbit to reappear almost immediately in another. Empty space was frying with their communications. A minute ago they had been administering their flock of rusted hulks: now they were facing into a void. Ten million metric tonnes of psychophysical gunk, welded into receptacles ranging from the size of a coffin to that of a largish asteroid, had gone missing. The news media were full of it. Some fierce new kind of physics had lit up the sky and in a matter of nanoseconds the entire quarantine orbit of Saudade had drained away like dirty water in front of people's eyes. The Quarantine Police were mystified. Everyone else was excited. All over GlobeTown, they came running out of the bars and nuevo tango joints to stare up into the rain. Epstein and Grills, glad of the action, kept order. "Nothing to see here," they admonished; but they stared up too.

"Who wanted that shit anyway," Grills remarked, voicing the general sense of relief that would set in over the next few hours.

Two or three streets away, in a tenement so close to the corporate port that its geometry shifted a little every time a ship came in, things were holding up well for George the gene tailor.

Perhaps he looked a little bloated. Internal changes had taken place. If you found him, it might not be wise to move him. And he was, of course, dead: so his hold on things had become tenuous. But he still had what might be described as a footprint there, in the assistant's old room. At this scale, anyway. If you were able to see the room as a context fixed across a couple of hundred years, George, like everyone else who had spent time there, would be part of a kind of dark smoke rushing through. However hard they tried to fix an identity for themselves at one scale, it was taken away from them at another. They thought of themselves as people but they were more like ghosts or ads—anything that flocks or swarms.

...Lucky Pantera, Bruna, Kyshtym, Korelev R-7, "The Angel of the Parking Orbit." Janice. Jenny. Geraldine. You blody polse thing. Fucking in me. Get out! & don't come in! October falls into November. West London draws round itself & for one second seems comforting. Then Michael comes in & there's a row. Marnie, seven years old: "It's a dog's poo in a paper bag & he lit it on fire." You aren't a camera, but you are, in everything you do, a description of the present. We fall into the dark street & kill someone. My name! she calls out. We kill someone again...

Meanwhile, a thousand light years from home, the assistant was undergoing transitions of her own. They were quick and dirty. The world, coming apart into pixels, streamed like eels, then reassembled itself around her. She was looking out, as if through tinted glass, or from a very dissociated position, into a room.

Part of her was a million years old and the size of a brown dwarf; other parts were, for the moment at least, describable only as "something else." She was neither conscious nor unconscious, dead nor alive. Sediment oozed from the corner of her mouth. If you had asked how she felt, she would have answered, "Spread thin." There were deep shadows up in the ceiling. There was a noise like tinnitus. People came and went at the wrong speed, in groups and smears like animated statistics. Some of them were people the assistant had talked to earlier. Some of them were pushing racks of equipment about. They were all ignoring her. All she could do was wait for them to notice what had happened, wait for the situation to stabilise, and encourage them to engage with her. She was patient and calm. If she didn't have a name, she could at least identify herself.

"SiteCrime, Saudade City," she repeated at every opportunity. "Junction of Uniment & Poe. Fifth floor investigator."

Someone peered in at her from very close quarters.

"Gaines?" he said, raising his voice and tilting his head almost horizontally into her field of view: "You might be interested in this. It's asking for something."

"There's a data spike in VF14/2b," someone else called.

The assistant was impaled on that spike. It went right through her, and she through it. There was no describing what had happened to either of them.

"It keeps repeating this address."

"Address?"

"It's asking for a detective from some hick police service the other side of the Halo."

...It is like enacting yourself as one sentence over & over again. I redline my equipment & make the moves. That bitch comes up fast but she will never be as fast as me. I call out my warning, they don't want to hear that, so I kill them again. I can't hear the language they talk between themselves. Do you know what it is to be like me, your condition is unnameable. It is relieved of all previous contexts. This freedom! My goodness when you're like me even your piss is inhuman...

Anna Waterman could watch the soap slip off the edge of the bath one night in 1999.

A white figure knelt in the cooling bathwater, while another figure curled round it from behind. Laughter. The water splashed about and the bath made vigorous but mournful sounds.

Unused to skulking around her own life like this, Anna found its details surprising: not so much in themselves but in that they existed at all. It was exciting, in a way, to see your own naked body walking away from you, or hear yourself say with a laugh, "Now, what can we *eat*?" But everything had the false clarity you get with a certain kind of photograph. Every surface proved to be microscopically available to her new vantage point; yet they were without meaning. The facts were often different too. The man in the bath, for instance, who she had always remembered as Michael, turned out to be Tim. How embarrassing. Everything was the same but, in the end, quite different. You could count the varieties of toothpaste in the bathroom, which a memory of sex doesn't normally encourage. She could view every aspect of that event, and of the events surrounding it, and of every other event in her life. A generation later, water poured its yeasty bulk over the Brownlow weir; ponies ran about in a field as if suddenly released; skylarks rose and fell over the South Downs like busy lifts: at exactly the same time, Anna could watch herself, peacefully becalmed in what she had learned to call the Noughties, rapping upon her kitchen window.

"Marnie," she was calling, "you annoying child! Leave the hose alone!"

Marnie at six years old. Anna tidying up for Tim. Anna, alone with her life at last, staring out across the field in the June twilight, drinking her fourth glass of Pinot Noir. She called the cat home, "James, you old fool. What have you found now?" She saw herself undress beneath the willows, hide her shoes, wade into the river in the moonlight. But, as bright and precise as if she was viewing them through optical glass, these scenes only reminded her of her present predicament. As she watched herself go up and down the garden—a neat, doll-like, slightly speeded-up figure seen day after day under mixed lighting conditions, moving inevitably towards its own fall—she began to think how the situation might be retrieved. She could connect with any of those moments. She could have a voice in her own past.

Everything that was wrong stemmed from the summerhouse.

What if Anna didn't fall?

...She is always trying to say her name, how she fell out of love with her parents quite early in life: "They humiliated me in some way before I was five." She was a small, friendly, nervous girl who liked being up early and late. Too anxious on

her own, too anxious in company. I was happiest with one other person. I've seen things here you would not believe: men with cocks two feet long...

All over the Halo, sometimes stealthily, sometimes with an expenditure of energy amounting almost to fanfare, the quarantine orbits had begun to empty themselves out. Reports conflicted. The situation was confused.

Two hundred miles above Mas d'Elies, showers of short-lived exotic vacuum events were detected, nesting inside the usual quantum froth like pearls in a handful of black lace. Such subtle fireworks, originating deep in the graininess of the universe itself, were normally associated with only the most alien of engines—

Twenty-five fuck-tourists from Keks-Varley III claimed to have seen "a wheel of fire" crossing the nightside sky of Funene. Visible to the naked eye for three hours, it broke up into a series of aurora-like pulses, then fell below the horizon. During this period no activity was observed in the quarantine orbit; though shortly afterwards it became invisible to instruments—

Laid out under stark light like dirty ice rings round a methane giant, the vast orbit at Mycenae had been for years a destination in itself, drawing tourists from as far away as Bell Laboratories and Anais Anais. The biggest collection of dead people in the universe, it broke up across a day, only to reassemble not long afterwards just outside the system's heliosheath; flowing away from there into interstellar space, a broad slow river. The K-ships, darting in and out of it like kingfishers, caught nothing: what they saw was not what they got—

In the cold and dark over New Venusport, the hulks blinked out one by one. Last to go: the tiny cockleshell containing Bobby and Martha, along with the outbreak of rogue code known as Bella. The little boy, who didn't remember much, assumed his present condition was a phase everyone went through. Life, enticing and inexplicable by turns, had already demonstrated its weirdness. One thing was certain, Bobby thought: you were out the other side of most things in a year. The women knew better. Since the events in her room Bella had been, in a sense, all three of them. Long before that, she had given up on the idea of knowledge: to her, the sarcophagus was as puzzling as the hallway of a house. Martha, meanwhile, alternating between panic and acceptance, awaited resolution.

...Two feet long and not quite rigid, you had no faith a thing like that could penetrate anyone. It was more of a flag than a cock, something to wave at the world. Jet Tone, Justine, Pantopon Rose, The Kleptopastic Fantastic, Avtomat,

the little girl who could crack anything. Frankie Machine and Murder Incorpo-
rated. The Markov Property. I get fish, the other says. Don't go in the summer-
house! I can do something with my mind but for all things catch fire & flowers
spring up, nothing else happens. You can keep a cock like that I wouldn't want it
near me. I like their legs better. Little boys, they like my stink but they're afraid.
"Is that what you want, hon?"...

As in all bad dreams, there were physical states forbidden to the assistant: in this case anything she had previously understood as movement.

At the same time, generous degrees of freedom opened up in other directions. Through the physics of VF14/2b, her "life"—whatever that had been—now lay open to her at all points and along all axes. She soon found herself looping easily and repeatedly into her own past—

Saudade City on a wet Friday night. In the basement of the old SiteCrime building at the corner of Uniment & Poe, two agents and a wire jockey were servicing a client in the basement. The assistant watched her earlier self leaning in at the basement doorway, attracted by the energy and warmth of the interrogation, experiencing the nearest thing a person like her could feel to a companionable emotion. "Boys," she heard herself tease the interrogation team, "we must do this again!"

She waited for herself to leave and then stepped into the room. "Hi," she said, "my name is Pearlant—" they stared at her puzzledly, their mouths falling open.

South Hemisphere, New Venusport. She tracked herself down to the circus ground, where the empty motels shone with light rain in an offshore wind. There was no hurry, but as soon as she heard her prior self call out that way, the seagull cry of "Wait!," that was the moment. Jump up out of the sand. Reach in through the doped protein meshes around the brainstem. Squeeze. Step away. Let those Kv12.2 expression issues do the work—seizure sites propagating across the cortex in cascades, autonomic functions going down one by one. It was supposed to keep her immobile long enough to talk. "Listen, honey, listen to me: don't jump!" She tried to get her own attention, instead she triggered a built-in EMC shutdown; someone was going to feel some shame over that in the morning.

It was the same wherever she went—

Toni Reno gaped and sweated as she came at him from out of time—Toni thought he was state of the art, but he proved to be wrong about that. Poor George the gene tailor in his little shop, both attracted and terrified by the engineered kairomones in her sweat, overcame his fear at last, clutched gratefully at her tits and dropped dead at her feet in the dark. Only a week or two before that, tissue had burst out of Enka Mercury's armpit like dirty kapok. The assistant just had no luck with these people, and, in a way, even less with herself. She was present in the past: she had a real presence there. But as a communications strategy, communication could never work: not for a person like her. She just wasn't built for it. No one seemed to understand that she was there to speak to them, that she really had something to say. She couldn't control her anger at the people who had built her, she couldn't control her anger at what Gaines had done to her, she couldn't control her anger at herself. Her victims, meanwhile, couldn't control their fear. It was a toxic mixture. To these soft targets—ambushed with a thorough, deft, catlike thoughtlessness, then left dismembered, eviscerated, dangling in the tailored but chaotic space-time eddies of VF14/2b—she brought only the lifetime frustration of the manufactured thing. She was trying to warn everyone in her past about what was coming: but in the end her predictable contribution could only be a corpse and a patch of grainy, dark-bluish air in which the shadows fell at wrong angles because ordinary physics didn't apply. All she achieved was to become the object of her own investigation, the mystery she could never solve.

Those appointments she kept with herself—South Hemisphere NV; the Mambo Rey Postindustrial Estate, Funene; the back stairs at SiteCrime, Uniment & Poe where the light dazzled down the stairwell like the light in a religious painting of Ancient Earth: what had they achieved in the end? Nothing. It turned out she didn't even like herself. They couldn't relate. They were too alike, the two of them. They were too surprised by one another's speed and perfection not to react badly. Too chafed by one another's obduracy to talk. She got the edge over that bitch self at New Venusport. Later, poor George's corpse made her wonder if she'd gone too far.

"Does a person like me kill things too easily?" she remembered asking him in nicer times.

...He opened my head and put in a hand. It was so gentle. I absolutely melted. After that killing yourself is easy, it's the unthought known, toothpaste at the corner of the mouth, reflections on a false marble floor. Though as you abandon your own viewpoint the world so rapidly loses coherence, proves so impossible to understand, that there's nothing to be gained. Sign on a chemist shop: FA Strange. It's FA Strange all right. I don't get it, Michael said. Why should

you? I said. Why should you get it, after all?...

Anna's earlier self was drawn to the summerhouse because the heat she felt in there was her own heat. She was angry in there. She was closer to her own surface. Her attention was easier to attract. But interference proved harder than oversight—

Summer. Night. The feeling of a storm on the way. The Waterman house sits, as unweathered as an architect's drawing, hot and airless in the river valley. It's been a strange, lonely day. Anna Waterman looks at her own hands. She calls the cat. "James, you old fool!" At nine, the phone rings. When she picks it up, expecting to hear her daughter Marnie, there's no one at the other end. But just as she puts down the receiver she hears an electronic scraping noise and a distant voice shouts: "Don't go in there! Don't go in the summerhouse!" Within half an hour, the summerhouse has burst into flames and she sees herself—a woman hard to age, wearing a 1930s-looking floral print—running towards her from the silent conflagration. Consternation is on this woman's face. "Go away!" she calls. "Go away from here!"

A few days later, prone to weep suddenly after a debilitating session in Chiswick with Dr Helen Alpert, Anna wakes to moonlight and Moroccan air, with a feeling that someone has just spoken. She enters the river, and the world is suddenly unknown and unknowable. Everything is so full of mystery as she walks back that magic night, to find the summerhouse on fire again! Beneath the sound of the flames, she's sure she hears a voice. It calls her name, but all she can say in return is:

"Michael? Is this you?"

So it went, every time Anna tried to communicate. "Anna!" she would shout. "Listen to me! Don't go in the summerhouse!" But Anna seemed so dull. She was always so obsessed with herself. You couldn't get her attention, and that was what made you so impatient, the farce of shouting, "Anna! Anna!" until you were hoarse.

In addition, physical limitations seemed to apply. The past was clear enough to see, but you felt as if you were engaging with it from too far away. Sometimes speech failed completely, and Anna could make herself known only in other ways, via the weather, for instance, or showers of emotionally charged objects. It was as if the universe she now inhabited had suffered brain damage, and was experiencing a confusion not between different senses but between different states of energy and matter. She was reduced to a kind of practical synaesthesia. She was reduced to the use of theatre, metaphor, symbols and emotions. She tried eveyything, but remained an epiphenomenon of her own life, a figure distantly semaphoring tragic news from a hill. She made a nightly beacon of the summerhouse, but her earlier self didn't get the message. She made a dozen or so copper-coloured poppies spring up on the Downs in the morning sunshine, but the language of flowers simply didn't work as well as the language of language, and after a while Anna saw that her efforts were only making things worse.

Meanwhile, her body was strained into such a curve that only the upper left side of her ribcage touched the floor. Her right leg was raised about thirty degrees to the horizontal, the other bent slightly back from the knee. Her feet were bare. Her arms, outstretched to either side of her head, curved towards the ceiling; her hands were open, palms out, fingers clutching, then relaxing in slow motion. From this awkward, uncomfortable viewpoint she was forced to stare out into a dazzling nave of light, across a shiny black surface full of reflections. She was toppling into that space and at the same time through it. Everything smelled of electricity. People were pushing strange equipment around. Or they came up close and began talking about her as if she wasn't there. "We're catching it in the Planck time," they told one another. "You can't see it for longer because it's already in its own future, already something different." They said: "Where does the cat fit in?"

Laughter. Then:

"The people in Xenobiology are already calling her Pearl."

It was just like being in the bloody hospital. She hated them, and whatever ghastly world they belonged to. But worse: over a period of time that might have been seconds or years, she became aware that there was someone else trapped in there with her. Sometimes Anna could feel her bones grate together, there was so little room for them both. It wasn't James the cat, though she knew he was inside her too, prowling about and layering his own motives over hers. A growing sense of tension and imprisonment pushed everything else out of her mind, and her attempts to communicate with her earlier self ceased. She could hear a voice, distant-sounding but quite clearly inside her own head. It raged and complained. Whoever it was—whatever it was—they fell and fell together. They were aware of one another. Everything became a dull struggle over the body, or what they thought of as the body...

...I would want to have love if I knew what that was. You can get a patch for it, it's more like an app. It's a mood, very economical, very full of emotion, the love patch down at Uncle Zip for Saturday night. Mary Rose, Moroccan Rose, Mexicali Rose, Rose of Tralee, Rrose Selavi. Immordino, Gianetta, Ona Lukoszaite. There's evidence, Dr Alpert said, of a couple of tiny strokes, nothing to worry about. Did I

lose my memory so I could lose my memories? Put that way it seems not just possible but ordinary...

Alone in the Tub, sucked towards the lee shore of the Kefahuchi Tract by long, gentle gravitational swells, Impasse van Sant lost contact with the management of his little project. Along with Rig Gaines went Imps' last link to what might laughingly be called humanity. In the absence of supervision, he allowed the research to lapse and instead watched war pursue itself across the halo media:

Stars tricked-up as nova bombs. Minds tricked-out with logic bombs. Displaced planetary populations on the move. Duelling gamma jets at 50 million degrees Kelvin. Battleships drifting, holed and untenanted, in clouds of rosy gas. K-ships flickering in and out of it all in time-frames no one could imagine, states of consciousness no one could conceive controlled by mathematics no one understood. In the absence of Gaines' mystery weapon, EMC couldn't dictate the rules of the game, and had already begun to give ground to a loose alliance of aliens whose motives remained unclear and whose names for themselves all ended in x. To this feverish expenditure of energy, van Sant foresaw only the worst of ends: the boys from Earth, driven out of themselves for one perfect moment by psychodramas of blood, risk, terror, and, hey, being the real victim here, would soon be as desperate as children to be fetched back in again. Even that made them human: unlike Imps, who all his life had seen himself not just as dissociated but as protected in some unfair way by his dissociation.

Just then the void behind him opened like a huge door. It was filled with ships. There were hundreds of millions of them, a fleet of lights assembling itself from all over the Beach. They streamed in from as far away as Sector 47, da Silva's Cloud and The Mokite Bench, pooled briefly among the chaotic attractors and gravity-rips of Radio Bay, then poured towards the Kefahuchi Tract. Under magnification they proved to be all sizes and ages, from massy spacetime warpers to last year's one-man escape pod. All they had in common was their condition. They were hulks. They were banged-up, rusty and half-disassembled yet seamed with brand-new welds. They came trailing clouds of smart autorepair media. Out in the lead raced a single three-fin Dynaflow HS-HE cargo hauler, tubby, brass-looking, brought to a dull polish in some places by particle ablation, streaked with bird shit in others as if it had waited out the last forty years in the second-hand lot of some noncorporate field. On its nose someone had stencilled in letters five feet high the legend SAUDADE BULK HAULAGE, then under that, smaller: *Nova Swing*. The space around its stern was fogged with ironising radiation a relentlessly violet colour, through which could be seen—shuttling in tight, complex and only partially visible orbits,

orbits comprising the propulsion topology itself—an unknown number of outboard engines.

"The fuck," Imps asked himself, "is happening here?"

On they came like a problem in statistical mechanics, without any apparent slackening or falling away of numbers, flowing out of the dark and parting around the research vessel, of which they took little more notice than the void itself. SAUDADE BULK HAULAGE, its hull shuddering with the approach of some catastrophic event—the phase change, the leap to the next stable state—aimed itself at the heart of the singularity, which seemed to shift and boil in response with realtime bursts of high-energy photons. The alien engines shuttled faster and faster, producing curious slick pulses that presented to the observer not as light but as a sound, a smell, a taste in the mouth, a vibration in the walls, a perpetual but perpetually decaying echo effect in the context of things. The fleet paused a second, hung in silhouette, then hurled itself in.

For a moment after they had vanished, the vacuum still seemed inhabited. Then it was nothing again. Imps van Sant stared into the eyepieces of his obsolete instruments. Deep in explicatory failure, he had no way of placing himself with regard to what he had witnessed. Man, he thought. Who were those guys? They seemed full of madness and a direct rejection of anything he might have called humanity. It made him lonelier than ever. He was considering this when empty space whispered at him.

"Hello?" it said.

She hung out there, a kilometre long and clean as a herring gull over a windy beach. You looked at her and you could taste salt, ice cream, iodine. Feel for a second fully inside yourself.

"I can be anything I want," she said, "but I don't want that. I want to be the one thing I am."

And when van Sant couldn't think of an answer:

"What do you remember best?"

"I don't remember anything," he said. "I wasn't a regular kid."

He rummaged through the litter of empty beer cans, broken table tennis balls and repro 1970s wank mags around his pilot chair until he found some real estate brochures. "I don't remember anything, but I want to live somewhere like this." Holding up a picture so she could see, a Sandra Shen tableau entitled, *Airstream trailers beside the Salton Sea, 2001.* "Or this," he said: picture of two Japanese-looking people fucking in surf. She's wearing a wedding dress. In the background, mountains. "Or I quite like this." A wooden house with a pier going out into a lake: three brown pelicans diving for fish. Then his favourite, the ice-cream parlour at Roswell, New Mexico, Old Earth. Pastel neon mints and pinks against lightly etched aluminium columns: a holy twilight in the parking lot.

"It's the real McCoy," Imps said.

"I don't recall anything like that," she said. Then, almost immediately: "What would you be if you could be one other thing?"

"One other thing?"

"Yes."

"I'd be gone from here."

"I want to go home too," she said. "Let's start soon."

Just then, off in a corner of the Tub's main display, as in some hallucination accompanying neurological disorder, there bloomed a soft white explosion like a puff of fibres or a cloud of spores. It was low yield, less than a light-day away in the direction of Radio Bay. Not quite as far out as Imps van Sant, but far enough. "Hey!" he said. "What's this?" For a moment he thought the war had caught up with them. On examination, though, it proved to be just some abandoned old research tool which had gone mad after a million years staring into nothing and blown itself up. This close to the Tract, it was always happening. What was the Beach, after all, but a repository of fading memories?

...I said, you made your life a description of the present moment, the warm neon of pizza huts and pubs, blurred by a slight rain and repeating in every shallow puddle; she said she could hear a rat breathe two rooms away, no one believed that. She says: what is time anyway? Don't give me that, I know what time is. Don't, whatever you do, you bitch, give me that. Night's here. It's about being a meme. I light up in RF, radar and batshit 27-40 kHz, immediately get a response from the dunes, come in on the sonar ping & there she is: it's love patch, baby, love patch. In this world we're the remains of our own humanity. Don't jump! I'm calling. I'm calling out to her, The summerhouse! I'm calling, Don't start all this! Don't become part of this! She doesn't hear. Anyway all we can do is kill. Elise, Ellis and Elissa, the Blister Sisters. Elissa Mae. Ruby Mae. Lula Mae. Ruby Tuesday. Mae West and May Day. She's the One, Two Dollar Radio, Flamingo Layne. KM, LM, KLF. A Member of the Wedding. Spanky. Misty. The best little engine in the world. Hanna Reitsch, Jaqueline Auriol, Zhang Yumei, Olga Tovyevski. M3 in Orion. "Sabiha Gokce." Pauline Gower and Celia Renfrew-Marx. Irma X. Colette. Mama Doc. Sfascamenta. My name is Pearlant! My name is Pearlant and I come from the future! Never mind, darling, she tells the other one. Please try to be a bit calmer. At least we're alive. It's not much but it's better than being dea

28: Lay Down Your Weary Tune

The volunteers of the Wyndlesham & District Fire Service, called to a house on Coldmorton Lane when smoke was seen rising just after dawn, attended with a turn-of-the-century pumping unit on a Man chassis and their even older Mercedes turntable (some local enthusiast's "big society" donation, salvaged from the corner of a field in southern France and lovingly restored), to find the occupier, a fifty- or sixty-year-old woman naked and with an inexplicable smile, half in and half out of a small wooden structure at the end of her garden. She was dead. Preparing to damp down, they also discovered that though it had collapsed in on itself in a curiously chaotic way—as if blown about by brief, whirling, highly localised gusts of wind—the structure, a lapboard shed about the same age as their Mercedes, had clearly never been on fire. There was no heat. There was no charring. There was no smell. The banks of glowing embers that had appeared to surround it when they arrived turned out to be only its contents, piles of colourful household stuff which had burst from the damp cardboard boxes inside when the roof fell in.

Police, paramedics and the dead woman's GP all turned up at once. By then, the turntable had returned to its garage in the derelict agricultural college buildings at Plumpton; and the team leader—a raw-looking Yorkshireman called Weatherburn with hacked-off grey hair, thirty years' experience and his own sense of humour—was rocking the Man pump about in front of the house, trying to get it back out into Coldmorton Lane without cutting up the lawn. Weatherburn stuck his head out of the cab's side window and told the doctor: "Whatever the caller spotted, it wasn't a fire."

"You're sure?"

"We can usually recognise one when we see it."

The doctor grinned whitely and, already sick of shouting to be heard over the roar of the diesel, failed to reply.

Not long later he rolled off his powdered nitrile gloves and informed the attending police officers: "A stroke. Massive." Everyone at his practice knew Anna Waterman.

"What's that in her hand?"

When they pried the object loose, it turned out to be an outboard computer drive with a polished titanium shell and a style of connection port no one had seen except in museums. They passed it about, rubbing their fingers over some deep, etched-looking marks at one corner. The paramedics, meanwhile, got the body on to a trolley and pushed it effortfully up the lawn, leaving tracks in the dew. The doctor watched them go. "She was a nice old woman," he said to no one in particular. "A bit mad, like most of that generation." Suddenly depressed, he leant on the orchard fence and looked out across the meadow at some wisps of mist dissipating above the river. He was thirty years old. Anna's age weighed on him. She had seen the world when it was still proud of its future, blown, like its economy, as a stream of bubbles. Behind him, the remains of the summerhouse settled suddenly. Dust puffed up, and from inside came faint scraping noises.

"I think there's an animal in there," one of the police said.

"Hurry and rescue it then," the doctor advised without turning to look. He laughed. "I can't see a health and safety issue." He left them to it and went up to the house to make out the formal notice of death and call the daughter.

When Marnie Waterman arrived she found a note from him. In handwriting precise and careful, it told her how to proceed; he had also left a leaflet entitled *What to do when someone dies*. She folded the note in half, and then in half again. No one seemed to know what had happened to the summerhouse, much less to the cat. She watched the policemen, still waist-high in the wreckage, calling out like people who had never had much to do with pets. Stopping her car to allow the ambulance to pass in the narrow lane between Cottishead and Wyndlesham, she hadn't thought that her mother might be in it.

"Oh Anna," she said, as if Anna had let her down in some way.

She repeated that silently to herself, in one tone of voice or another, all morning—talking to the police, driving to Lewes to identify her mother at the mortuary, filling in forms, making arrangements. "Oh Anna." It was less pejorative than it sounded. It was a murmur of disbelief.

Four hours later, she was back at the end of the garden, where, alone with her thoughts in the sun, she made the same mistake as the firemen—although what she thought she saw at the base of the summerhouse was not a heap of embers but an illustration from an old-fashioned children's book. Kegs and brassbound caskets were depicted spilling their contents—surely "treasure"?—across the floor of a sea-polished cave, in the dimness of which it was difficult to tell salty pebbles from jewels the size of hen's eggs or hanks of weed from fabrics rich and strange.

A washy resolve converted this semiotic boutique to something she could understand: burst removers' boxes, some of them twenty years old, full of stuff she had almost managed to forget. Her father's collection of ancient maps and charts, curtains Anna couldn't be persuaded to throw out. Christmas tree decorations. A Hornby trainset still in its box. A cannon. Coloured plastic crockery too small for a picnic, too large for a toy. Trick items Marnie had collected, age seven, when she determined to be a magician: joke liquorice, "X-Ray Specs," handcuffs you couldn't take off. There was a japanned box in which you placed a billiard ball you would never find again, though you could hear it rattling about in there forever. There was the cup with a reflected face in the bottom that turned out not to be your own; the valentine heart which lit itself up by means of loving diodes within. They were children's things, made of Chinese plastic, cheap rubber, feathers: objects trivial in their day but now of great value to collectors.

"I feel at a loss," Marnie told herself.

While she was in Lewes, the police had given up on James the cat and departed on some other errand. Marnie was relieved. Their energy had been a burden, on a day when she didn't have much energy of her own. Should she have offered them a cup of tea? They hadn't seemed to expect it.

James was an old cat now. She had never much liked him, but her parents had been gently determined that she keep a pet. It was as if they were encouraging her, at the age of thirteen, to accept emotional ties of her own, to love something as much as they loved each other, to take her first steps on the path to becoming them. If she wasn't quite as enthusiastic, Marnie had been willing enough: but James, proving standoffish, stubborn, obsessed even as a kitten, soon relieved her of the effort. She had envied him to start with, then, in a sense, forgotten him. If he had vanished now, it was just another absence in a history of absences. All of this—the cat quietly making a kingdom of its own in the long grass and thistles between the orchard and the river, then Tim dying, now Anna dying—made life seem so sinister for a moment that she sat unable to move. Up in the house the phone rang; but by the time she got there whoever it was had stopped trying. Rather than do nothing, she went through Anna's messages. One was from a decorator whose quote for the bathroom seemed quite high, another the usual failed attempt to connect by an automated cold-calling service; a third was from Marnie herself, left late on the previous evening in a voice so tired she barely recognised it as her own: "Mum, I've got some news about my tests."

The remaining calls, half a dozen of them, were from Anna's psychiatrist. They sounded urgent. About to call her back, Marnie heard a noise in the kitchen, the cat nosing its food bowl about on the tiles.

"James!" she said. "Oh, James!"

Caught in the client's naive but effective web of transference, counter-transference and projective identification—and more rattled than she was willing to admit by Anna's defection—Helen Alpert had made the first of these calls on her way back from Walthamstow the previous evening.

No reply. Quick to associate that with the idea of failing to connect, she had stopped the Citroën at the side of the A406 somewhere on the long arc of planning blight between Brent Cross and Neasden, struggling twenty yards away from it in the roar and swash of the passing traffic to be sure she had a signal. A minicab driver had pulled up and, assuming something was wrong with her car, first opened the bonnet without permission, then kept offering to drive her somewhere. After she had persuaded him to leave her alone she sat exhaustedly in the Citroën's rear seat for half an hour, as if she'd given up after all and allowed herself the luxury of being a passenger. Safe in Richmond, she had begun calling again, three times in a five-minute period. "Anna, I've got news I'm convinced might change your mind. Could we talk just once more? Do call when you get home!" She had leafed through the case notes until late; fallen asleep trying to understand where she had broken her own rules.

Now it was four o'clock in the afternoon. Outside her consulting room the Thames ran backwards; flushed with tidal mud, it spilled across the Mall at the junction with Chiswick Lane. Sunlight, weakened and softened by the riverine air, reflected from the papers spread chaotically across her desk, highlighting the favourite vase, the petals of gladioli. Dr Alpert tried to read. She wrote, "Anna believes that—" but was otherwise unable to commit herself. In the margins of the neurologist's report, she discovered her name written several times in her own hand, as if by someone trying to solve an anagram. It was not the disorganised nature of these responses, she believed, that had made her so anxious.

She picked up the phone.

"Anna!" she greeted Anna's answering service. "Look, I've got some exciting news. I went to see Brian Tate yesterday. He's still alive. Still living in the same house in North London. He's been teaching physics at a school in Walthamstow for thirty years. He's reluctant to talk to me about what happened, of course. That's understandable. But I think he might talk to you. Anna, I think it would do you the world of good to talk to someone else who knew Michael—"

There was a dull clattering sound at the other end of the line, and a half-familiar voice said:

"Hello? Hello? Who's this?"

"Anna," said the doctor. "I'm so relieved! I thought—"

"It's not Anna," said the voice, "it's her daughter." There was a pause. "I'm sorry, but Anna's dead."

Helen Alpert stared at the phone.

"Oh dear," she said. She couldn't think what to add. "Oh dear, I'm sorry about that. Is this Marnie?" She couldn't remember if there was another daughter. All she could remember about Anna's relationship with Marnie was its elegantly unconscious symmetries. Anna, constructing the daughter as a failed adult, had defused Marnie's early sexuality by pressing upon her the role of dowdy, unfulfilled helper; later this had encouraged Marnie to treat her mother as an ageing child whose narcissistic demands were a burden. "I'm very sorry to hear that," she said again.

"It was a stroke," Marnie said. After a pause, she added: "Was there something? I'm quite busy at the moment."

"No, no. It doesn't matter."

"Do send your bill, won't you?" Marnie said.

Helen Alpert said she would.

At the age of six Marnie Waterman wanted to be married. She believed this would happen when she was twenty-one, as the inevitable consequence of reaching that age. She would also have horses and drive a car. Another inevitable consequence was: she would be tall. Though she had no plan for bringing it about, the future seemed already there for her, a dreamy thing with pre-loaded contents. At seven she said to anyone who asked: "I'll *certainly* travel." Ten years old saw her adding an image of herself in blocked pink satin shoes; although this, out of shyness, she kept private.

Around that time the Chinese economy collapsed and everything else went with it. Media dubbed it "the perfect storm." Like most of the other fathers in Wyndlesham, Tim Waterman had put up the hurricane shutters a year or two in advance. They were one of the lucky families, he explained when Marnie was thirteen: nevertheless a lot of things fell out of her future around then. Outside Wyndlesham, stagflation wrote itself over everything like graffiti. Peak oil had come and gone. No one knew how to blow the next bubble. The financial sector, stunned by the discovery that money had been as postmodernised as everything else, passively allowed the state to clip its wings. Bankers seeking explanations read Baudrillard forty years too late. Bonuses tanked. A few footsoldiers got jobs in the remaining heartlands of the industry, where they found competition fierce. Families like Marnie's still drove everywhere, but their Range Rovers and Audis went unreplaced year on year; and though their incomes remained good they felt hard-up. Adults were forced to find new ways of viewing the idea of success; children were having to mature earlier. Some of them felt resentful about that. Sharp divisions appeared at the upper end of the middle class. Suddenly your parents could afford the Wyndlesham cheese shop or they couldn't: Marnie's cohort found itself defined by this. In her mid-to-late teens Marnie revised the contents of the future, but she still expected it to bring itself about. Meanwhile, her father began to look tired, then died without warning of pancreatic cancer. Luckily he'd protected the family from that too. Marnie, nineteen and a half, came home to the funeral by train—a long, grinding journey through a landscape composed of empty industrial estates and abandoned parking structures—to find Anna sad but also frisky. They spoke about how free she felt, but it turned out she hadn't made any plans either. All that time, Marnie had been doing well at a good university, though when her twenty-first birthday arrived she turned out not to be married after all; towards the end of graduation year she accepted a job offer from one of the emerging mutual associations.

Looking back on it all now, she felt that so far her life had been demanding but satisfactory. Women only ten years older than her, encouraged to remain adolescent until they were thirty, had failed to make the transition from the liquid world: they seemed brittle when they had what they wanted, spoiled and bitter when they didn't. The younger ones, struggling to avoid the underclass enclaves of Eastbourne and Hastings, were simply worn down. At twenty-eight, by contrast, Marnie had charge of herself. Though money was no longer a serious career, "the New Economics"—cautious, simplified and heavily shifted to the co-operative—brought her security. A single mother since her last year at uni, she found herself able to rent a small house well away from the chaotic suburbs; her employer financed childcare until Enny Mae was five, then a nice school. Marnie could afford medical insurance. She still saw Enny Mae's father, a man called William. Once or twice a year they had a talk. They were making sure that whatever future the little girl imagined for herself, a plan was put in place for achieving it. Anna, recognising Enny Mae as competition, had never shown much interest; to avoid fractiousness and tantrums, Marnie had learned to keep them apart.

That was how things had rested until this morning.

Marnie put the phone down on Helen Alpert, stared out of the window of the Coldmorton Lane house, which she supposed was now hers, and wondered what would happen next. She had woken eager to share her test results with Anna, suddenly able to feel happy after the inexplicable anxiety-states of the night before (in which relief at being cancer-free was somehow overpowered by the dread of a completely new future—one into which the possibility of cancer had now been firmly embedded): but Anna had somehow evaded her again, deftly remaining the absent parent to the end. Marnie felt weightless. It was too early to collect Enny Mae from school; to obviate further changes in his lifestyle, James the cat had eaten hastily and hidden himself under a wardrobe. Marnie washed Anna's supper things at the sink—there was a dishwasher but she couldn't bring herself to run it—then wandered around the living area. Anna still owned books. In them, the self figured largely: self-help books of thirty years ago, novels about women finding themselves, a book of photographs entitled *Events of the Self,* even books by a man calling himself Self. She turned on the TV—found only news of the Indian reoccupation of Pakistan—turned it off again.

Ten or fifteen minutes later, she caught someone hanging about in the garden. He was a boy of about sixteen, somewhat shorter than Marnie, dressed in tight grey jeans rolled halfway up his calves. His white T-shirt was too small for him, his black lace-up boots were covered in hardened dribbles and spots of yellow and pink enamel paint. With him he had a small dog, a kind of long-legged Border terrier, sand-coloured, with short, bristly hair and scruffy-looking ears. Boy and dog stood in the middle of the lawn. Both of them seemed fascinated by the wreckage of the summerhouse.

Marnie rapped on the window.

"Excuse me," she called. "Excuse me! Can I help you?"

He didn't seem to hear. Marnie went out on to the lawn and marched up behind him. "Excuse me!" she called again, perhaps more loudly than she had intended. "Do you mind if I ask what you're doing here?"

He jumped in surprise. His face had a raw appearance, as if he lived up on the Downs somewhere in the constant blustery wind. His arms were stringy and tough. "I don't know what you think," he said, "but I've come to do some work for a woman who lives here." He stared expectantly, then, when Marnie failed to reply, offered: "She's an older woman. She's lived here years. She does her shopping down in Wyndlesham." He made a movement with one shoulder, a shrug or perhaps a wince. "Some people like her, some don't. She's got some work she needs doing."

"What kind of work?"

It wasn't much, the boy said: it was just some painting.

"I don't live far," he said. "She said if I called, I could do the work she needed."

"There's no work here. No one wants any work done here."

The boy tried to take this in; for him, Marnie could see, the meaning of it lay fully in the words, divorced from body language or tone of voice. "She does her shopping down in Wyndlesham," he said, as if this explained anything. "She likes a pint of Harvey's." He wiped his left forearm across his face. His dog barked suddenly, a small but sharply cut sound that went across the garden like the cry of some less well-known animal. "This new bitch of mine," the boy told Marnie, "I got her from them down the estate. Some say she's dangerous, but I know she's not." Forelegs braced, its little bristly face sniffing the air, the dog appeared too small, too willing, to be a danger to anyone. Every so often it would gaze up at Marnie or the boy, seeking confirmation of the things it saw. Yes, Marnie wanted to explain: this *is* grass. It's a lawn. And that's a tree, with a pigeon in it. And that, which used to be my dad's Russian-looking summerhouse, that's a pile of wood: quite right. This morning my mum died. It was just like her to die without any clothes on, half in and half out of a Russian summerhouse, and be found by firemen. You can tell a lot about her from that. I don't know, she thought suddenly, what Enny Mae's going to say.

"You don't need worry about this bitch," the boy said. "She wouldn't harm a child."

"What kind of dog is it?"

The boy gave her a sly look. "A working dog," he said. "An older woman lives here, her name is Anna. She said she had some work she wanted done."

"There's no work," Marnie said. "I don't know who you are, but whatever you thought you'd get from her it isn't here."

She added: "No one lives here now but me."

The boy blinked. "She's supposed to live round here somewhere," he said; then, accepting the situation suddenly, lunged away across the lawn. His shoulders were hunched, his torso compressed and tense, but his stride had a loose, loping quality; the upper and lower halves of him, it seemed, had little experience of each other. The terrier followed, yapping and gambolling, nibbing at his heels for attention. Up at the house, he stopped and fumbled with the side-gate latch. "If I did the work, I wouldn't have to go to the toilet here," he promised. "I'd go in the village." Marnie, completely unable to interpret this plea, felt that they were misunderstanding one another to a degree that could only be her fault. *She likes a pint of Harvey's.* Where her mother had met the boy, or how, she preferred not to think.

"Wait!" she called. "Wait a moment."

If he wanted work, he might as well deal with the mess Anna had made of the bathroom. He looked strong enough.

The next day, waking in the startled recognition that she had dreamed one of Anna Waterman's dreams, Dr Helen Alpert threw a single worn item of Mulberry soft luggage into the rear seat of the Citroën, cancelled her appointments for the near future and closed the consulting room. By four that afternoon, having used up almost a fortnight's fuel coupons, she was in Studland on the Dorset coast. There, despite the sea wind, the smell of salt, the herring gulls sideslipping in and out of the turbulent air above Great Harry rocks, she found that the dream wouldn't be shaken off.

In it, all her belongings had gone missing from an old-fashioned writing bureau she was using, while, crammed into its hidden drawers and on to its complicated little shelves, she found items the thief had left in return. These stale wrapped sandwiches and bits of half-eaten fruit made her as anxious as she was disgusted. She was afraid he might come back at any moment. The place itself was shabby, half-exterior—the ground floor, possibly the only floor, of a gutted house still in use during some long, slow crisis, some failure of human or political confidence. The doorways had no doors. The windows, though intact, were uncurtained. It was always raining. Damp had got into the furniture—mainly cheap veneered cabinets and shelves from which the varnish had been bleached by sunlight and use—and the walls were covered with fibrous, scaly-looking, ring-shaped blemishes. Looking up at the wall beside a doorway, Helen saw that a slightly more than life-sized vulva had emerged from it like a crop of fungus. It wasn't quite the right colours. The labia had yellow and brown tones, and the startling rigidity of a wooden model. A body was attached, but less of that had emerged from the wall. It was still emerging, in fact, in very slow motion. She felt that it might take years to come through. And while the vulva clearly belonged to an adult, the body was much younger. It still had the fat little belly and undeveloped rib-cage of a child. The vulva presented in the same vertical plane as the wall, but the body and the face were somehow foreshortened and leaning back from it at a wrong angle for the anatomy to work. At all points it was seamless with the wall. She couldn't see much of the face, but it was smiling. In the dream, Helen began to make a shrieking sound, full of the most appalling sense of grief and horror. She could hear herself but she couldn't stop.

It was so clearly all of a piece, she thought: the loss or substitution of her possessions, the decayed building open to the elements but still usable, the body emerging seamlessly from the wall in very slow motion. On waking she had experienced spatial confusion; remained dissociated well into the morn-ing. Even now, staring out across the titanium-coloured water of Studland Bay, where a small white boat was chewing its way towards the grey horizon, she felt as if she hadn't quite re-entered herself. She felt as if, down inside, vital parts of her had separated. She felt that something had broken in her per-sonality—had broken, perhaps, some long time before—but that she would never be able to understand what.

Later, in the hotel restaurant, she listened to a mid-level pharma executive telling his friends about a recent trip to Peru. Really, she thought, he was less entertaining them than issuing a set of instructions. He had chosen a KLM flight, he was careful to emphasise, because it allowed him to do some div-ing en route: they might want to go more directly. When they arrived, there were certain things they should on no account pay for. As for the ruins, well, the visibility had been bad, but "as their apology to us" for not being able to provide the expected view, the natives had cooked him and his girlfriend a special meal. "They didn't charge us for that, obviously." Dr Alpert stared at him in open dislike until he noticed her, then forced him to look away. His name, as far as she could tell, was Dominic. At forty, Dominic still sounded like an MBA undergraduate pretending to be his own father. He seemed like a throwback to another age; so did his friends, with their Boden casual wear and pleasant, affirmative manners. So, she thought, did she. She always kept a pair of boots in the Citroën: she would spend a day or two walking the Downs—to Corfe certainly, perhaps even as far as the Purbeck Hills and Lulworth Cove. She would walk until she felt better. First she would separate Dominic the pharma from his friends, take him upstairs, and fuck him care-fully to a tearful overnight understanding of the life they all led now.

Acknowledgements

Tim Etchells contributed to the list of the assistant's names at the end of Chapter 21. Paragraphs of Chapter 3 appeared in *Locus* as part of an essay. Thanks go, as ever, to Sarah Cunningham for the use of her beautiful house; and to Cath and her family for their support.

MJohn Harrison was born in the UK. He worked briefly as a groom, a teacher and a clerk before his first short story was published in 1966. In 1968, he joined Michael Moorcock's magazine *New Worlds*, for which he wrote fiction & criticism until 1978. His first novel, *The Committed Men,* was published by Hutchinson in 1971. M. John Harrison has reviewed fiction and nonfiction for the *Spectator*, *The Guardian* and *The Times Literary Supplement*, and taught creative writing with a focus on landscape and the autobiographical novel. He lives in London.